THERE GOES SUNDAY SCHOOL

ALEXANDER C. EBERHART

SEVEN SISTERS
PUBLISHING

There Goes Sunday School

E-Book ISBN: 978-1-64255-653-7
Print ISBN: 978-1-64255-654-4

7 Sisters Publishing
P.O. Box 993
Jupiter, Florida 33458

www.alexanderceberhart.com
www.7sisterspublishing.com

FOR EVERYONE WHO QUESTIONS
AND FOR THOSE WHO FIND THEIR OWN ANSWERS.

ONE

"Ow! You're on my foot!" I push the blond away, worried someone will hear us on the other side of the bathroom door.

Lord, it's hot in here.

Sweat drips downy back, and a clump of dark hair sticks to my head. Melancholy music bears down from outside, loud enough it shakes the thin walls around us.

"Sorry," mutters the guy whose name I can't remember. His lips return to my neck, nibbling playfully.

I don't understand his fascination with my Adam's apple, but hey, who am I to judge?

God, I know this is wrong, but I would really appreciate it if you just turned Your omnipotent gaze for, like, five more minutes? That would be awesome, Big Guy.

A nasty smell coming from the urinal in the corner burns my nose.

Maybe this wasn't such a good idea? Then again, it's the last night I'm stuck in this hellhole, and when else am I going to get the chance for an anonymous make-out session?

"All right campers." A charismatic voice echoes through the space over the strumming of a guitar. "We've had a great week here at Pineland, and tomorrow we go back into the world. So, tonight, give it your all!"

"Yeah," I mutter, looking down at the mess of blond hair. "Give it your all."

"Lyrics are up on the screen, so let's praise His name!"

Jeez, Blondie is really getting into it. His hands drop down my stomach, and I jolt.

"Easy!" I slap his hand. "I'm ticklish."

He gives me a grin, flashing pearly whites. He's a little shorter than me, even though he told me he's a senior.

I wonder how he gets his hair to stay up like that? Mine goes flat just walking outside in this muggy weather. I should ask him what product he uses.

His teeth scrape against my throat, and I'm derailed.

"Hey!" I shove him again, legs tangled in mine. "No biting! We talked about this. Nothing that leaves a mark."

"Sorry," the blond boy replies sheepishly, green eyes still lit with excitement. Adorable dimples perfectly frame his snaggletooth smile. "I've never done this before. I'm a little overeager."

The obvious bulge in his jeans rubbing against my thigh is the punctuation that backs up his statement.

"Oh, yeah. Me neither," I lie as he comes at me again.

How many boys have I kissed at this point? I'm sure You're keeping track up there, Big Guy. Want to overlook the blatant lying too? It kinda goes hand in hand with the whole in-the-closet situation.

My hand on his chest stops him. "Just cool it with the bicuspids, okay?"

Blondie nods, closing the space between us as his lips press into mine with enough force to move me back a step. My back hits the wall, and his tongue is practically down my throat.

Jeez. This guy needs to get out more. Then again, judging by the deep drawl, and the fact I saw the church bus he got off earlier this week, I'm guessing there aren't a lot of openly gay guys just floating around Jasper County.

I feel for him. It's easier for me to find someone to lock lips with on the weekend, being so close to Atlanta. Hell, it's the mecca for all gay kids this side of the Mason-Dixon line. It calls to us, promising nights of flashing lights, drug-hazed dancing and—if you're lucky—consensual sex. But that mostly depends on how believable your fake ID is.

"When peace like a river, attendeth me away." The chorus of voices swells from just outside those thin walls, adding to the pressure and heat of the moment.

God, I really love this. Does that make me a bad person?

Blondie presses into me, producing an awesome amount of friction that sends shivers from the base of my spine. For someone so inexperienced, he knows how to turn me on. And on I am turned.

"When sorrows like sea billows roll," the voices sing.

Something rolls down my leg, but it, most assuredly, is not sorrows. If this goes on for much longer, I will have to change pants.

I'm so going to Hell.

"Whatever my lot, thou hast taught me to say."

"Oh, my God." Blondie breaks away, gasping for breath. Saliva clings to his bottom lip and a hunger burns behind his deep green eyes. "This is so much better than I ever imagined it would be. I mean—"

"Yeah, it's incredible. Stop talking," I interrupt before silencing him with another kiss. I pull his shoulder, turning him around so I have him pinned against the wall. My free hand drifts down, running across the front of his jeans. That makes him squirm with delight.

"It is well, it is well, with my soul."

My lips trace his neck, mapping out the spots that cause him to gasp. There is a lot of those.

"Oh, *God*." Blondie jerks, and his words change into unintelligible gasps as a new heat fills the palm of my hand.

I pull away, a fresh stain spreading across his crotch.

"S-Sorry," he mutters, his face flushed and chest heaving.

"Don't be." I laugh, adjusting the discomfort between my legs. "That's kinda the point."

"It is well, it is well, with my soul." The hymn continues through the walls.

"That was so hot." Blondie is still breathing hard, leaning against the wall, eyes half-lidded. "Do you want me to help you get off?"

"Nah." I'm already running my hands under the stream of water in the sink. "I don't want to have to clean up another mess." With a coy smile over my shoulder, I add, "You've already made one."

Blondie blushes again, and I laugh. After my hands are dry, I toss the wad of paper towels in the trash can.

"This was fun." I can already feel the awkwardness growing like a fungus between us. "Great way to end the summer. Thanks, I needed that."

"Can I give you a call sometime?" Blondie is still overeager, despite his emission.

He's cute. But no one is cute enough for me to take that kind of risk.

"Sorry, man." I pat his shoulder. "I can't do phone numbers." I unlock the door and leave my newly moistened friend behind.

Taking a deep breath, I sneak back into the chapel, a little surprised I don't immediately burst into flames. Then again, my parents always say God has a sense of humor. Having me suffer through the rest of this endless song is worse than any circle of Hell.

"It is well, with my soul," I join with the crowd.

"WHERE DID YOU DISAPPEAR TO?" JACKIE ASKS, LIFTING A CURL OF HAIR off her glistening forehead. It's still a million degrees inside, even though the sun went down hours ago. The late-night worship session has just ended. I guess it was naïve of me to think she missed my little detour.

"Had to take a dump," I tell her, clutching my stomach for emphasis. "That cardboard they tried to pass off as pizza today was wreaking havoc." She's bound to believe that one. Camp food is literally the worst.

"Gross." She laughs, swatting at my arm.

Jackie hates it when I talk about normal bodily functions—at least the ones not pertaining to sex. She's classy that way.

"Are you coming to the campfire?" she asks.

"Are you kidding?" I fake offense. "Not even the cardboard pizza shits could keep me away."

"I heard that, Mike!" someone yells from my left.

"Oh, go suck a dick, Bryan!" Jackie comes to my defense.

Jackie and I get sucked into the horde of bodies exiting the chapel. Blondie is coming out of the men's room as we pass, and I can't help winking at him. I'll miss him when we head back to reality in the morning, but probably not as much as he'll miss me.

The gang of sweaty teens moseys on down to the lakeside where I can already see the glow of the bonfire. Every year, our youth group ends the week with fellowship around the warmth of burning pallets, swapping stories about what we've learned through the week's lessons, how we've changed and blah blah blah.

Us heathens use it as an excuse to roast marshmallows while the girls talk shit about each other and the straight bros take bets on who can jump over the flames without singeing their asses. For me, their idiotic exploits are a lesson in exasperation.

The heat smacks me in the face as we clear the trees, and it does nothing to help the swamp-ass situation.

"Jackie!" A brunette girl waves her over to the wooden bench on the outer edge of the space.

I follow Jackie like a puppy, watching Danny Russo take a leap over the fire. Only his sandals are smoking as he lands, and the bros let out a howl into the night air.

The display of testosterone is ridiculous. And kinda hot. I'm wishing I'd let Blondie finish the job he started.

Hey, Big Guy. Quick question. If I'm not supposed to find boys attractive, then why did you make them so fucking irresistible? I don't think that's really fair.

"That was such an amazing experience," the brunette tells Jackie. "I just felt this presence there tonight, you know? Like the Holy Spirit was just with us. Did you feel it too?"

"Oh yeah," Jackie agrees, voice taking on a familiar higher pitch that means she's lying out of her ass. "I totally felt it. Incredible, Sandy."

She turns to mouth, "What the fuck?"

I'm dying.

"What about you, Mike?" Sandy looks at me.

I wipe the remnants of laughter from my face. She's so intense, I can't break away from her stare. "Oh, I completely agree."

She nods as I speak like some possessed bobble-head doll. "It was definitely life-changing. Especially tonight. Sooo good."

"That's exactly how I feel." Sandy's eyes well up. "This whole week has been just such a Godsend for me. I feel like I've grown really close to you guys, and so much closer to God in my walk. You know what I mean?"

Jackie and I just nod as the poor girl rambles. Thankfully, we're saved a few minutes later by another group of loud young ladies who envelop Sandy into their numbers. They keep crying and hugging, and honestly, there are way too many feels for me to even comprehend. Girls are far too emotional for their own good.

Jackie lets out a sigh, leaning her head on my shoulder. "Jesus, I thought she would never shut up."

"I don't think she breathed the whole time she was talking." I laugh. "Like, seriously. Does she have gills on the side of her neck or something?"

Jackie's head shakes against me as she giggles. "Not that I've seen. I had to stand beside her for most of the night," she explains. "She kept crying and grabbing my hand to raise it along with hers. Super awkward. And then, halfway through Amazing Grace, one of the rubber bands from her braces flew off and smacked me in the side of my face. That fucker hurt!"

"I can imagine. But at least you weren't beside Freddie Spitz. Every time his hands went up, I got a mouthful of BO. I think I actually gagged at one point."

We both giggle like school girls. I wonder if it looks like we're a couple. Wouldn't that make things so much easier?

"Where did you really disappear to?" Jackie asks again, turning on me with accusatory eyes. "You were right beside me going in, and then you disappeared. I was minutes away from sending a search party."

That's the thing about Jackie, she's always keeping tabs on me. It's a good thing, I guess. But it sure makes meeting a stranger for random make-outs a challenge.

"You caught me." I shrug, looking away from her. "I was making out with a hot blond in the bathroom."

Her soft giggles balloon into full-blown laughter. "Yeah right," she says through the hilarity, "and I'm the Queen of England. You'd never be skanky enough to take advantage of some girl on a church trip."

"You're right." I marvel at the truth in her words. "No girls for me. But I really *was* in the bathroom. I wouldn't lie to you."

About that.

"I know you wouldn't, Mike. And that's why you're my best friend. Well, that, and the fact I find you slightly less insufferable than the rest of these bastards."

She slugs me on the shoulder, and I smack her back.

"Wanna S'more?" She grabs her pack. "I have a

Hershey bar in my backpack if it hasn't already turned into a puddle. If that's the case, I can just squeeze it right into your mouth."

"That sounds delicious."

The rest of the evening consists of smoky food and conversation as we roast and toast our way into a sugar-induced stupor. After the fire has burned out and the couples have all snuck away for some late-night tonsil hockey in the woods, I say goodnight to Jackie as she heads to the girls' cabins on the other side of camp.

They laid the rules out clearly at the beginning of the week. You gotta have the boys and girls as far away from each other as physically possible after dark. They always like to use that fun little analogy about boys being blue and girls being pink. Don't want anyone making purple on the lawn.

But those rules are fine by me. It means no one even thinks about blues making blue all over the place. That's more my speed anyway.

The hike back is pure torture, and I'm pouring sweat in minutes.

God, is Hell going to be as hot as summer in Georgia? Because I may want to start reconsidering my sexuality if this is what I have to look forward to.

A thousand or so moths flutter around the bright lamppost outside my cabin, and a ruckus to end all ruckuses is going on inside. I open the door, nimbly dodging a Nerf dart as Cameron and Jimmy wage a war of orange foam across the bunk beds. Holding my backpack in front of me, I dash to my corner bunk and dive beneath the safety of the thin sheet because it's far too hot for a blanket.

Jimmy has lost his shirt somehow in the war and is showing off an amazing six pack that sprang up over the summer. That's totally fine with me. Cameron isn't too bad to look at either, which makes concealing my attraction to him that much harder—to the point there's been some awkwardly long stares. Nothing makes Sunday school more uncomfortable than eye contact with hot, straight guys.

The war ends with the two of them wrestling on the floor, and I have to pretend I'm reading to keep myself from gawking. I've never been so hard in my life.

I packed my things already, so I'll be ready when Mom comes to get me in the morning, and now, there's nothing for me to do. Jackie has been giving me shit all day about leaving her to ride the bus on her own, but Mom wants to take me back-to-school shopping, and she likes to go out early enough she doesn't have to fight for a parking spot. That means she'll be here at the crack of dawn to get me. I'll miss the last session in the chapel, but that's a sacrifice I'm willing to make.

This whole week has been a haze of bible studies and sports, and honestly, I'm about sick of the body odor. How can guys smell so terrible and yet amazing at the same time? The slightly queasy feeling I get from the scent is a strange sensation for sure. The only interesting event that's happened to me was Blondie, and that was just dumb luck.

Our story began like all teenage stories do, with prolonged, creeper-level staring. We saw each other across the lawn while playing a game of ultimate Frisbee, and something just clicked.

My youth pastor, Arnold—a dorky name he lives up to beautifully—declared war on a neighboring church group. So, naturally, I was there to help defend our title of undefeated Frisbee champions. Blondie played for the other team, and as a sign the sweet Lord Jesus loves me, it was shirts versus skins. You can probably guess who was who.

There's nothing quite like lust at first sight. He caught me making eyes and couldn't stop smiling at me. He had this goofy grin every time he ran down the field that made my heart flutter to a strange rhythm. That is until I took a Frisbee straight to the face.

I'd like to think I don't give off a super-gay vibe. Not that I really know what that means anymore. My voice finally deepened last summer, and I don't really talk with my hands a lot. I play sports and have never set foot on a stage. So, it's not like I walk down the halls at school draped in a rainbow flag. I *do* secretly love Cher, but that's neither here nor there.

But Blondie somehow knew when he saw me, just like I knew about him, and a week of silent flirting finally built up to ten glorious minutes in Heaven. I'm talking about fictitious gay Heaven, of course. I can't imagine after all the hubbub most churches spout that they would fill the actual place with teenage boys dry humping each other. Then again, I kind of hope they did.

"Get off me, you fag!"

I jump at the word, heart thumping like a thousand volts struck me.

Cameron pushes Jimmy off him, and the other boys continue their raucous laughter. It takes a good ten minutes for my pulse to return to a normal pace. I need a distraction.

Digging through my backpack, I search for a pencil

but stop short of grabbing my sketchbook.

This isn't the place, Mike. Too many prying eyes.

It'll just have to wait until I get home.

Angling myself against the wall, I wrap the sheet around me like a cocoon. Drifting off, the sounds of laughter and wrestling meld, and my dreams fill with flashes of Blondie and his cute dimples.

THREE

"HOW WAS YOUR WEEK, SWEETIE?"

Mom needs to take it down, like, six notches. It's way too early for this shit. We're barreling up I-85, but it's Saturday, so the traffic isn't at its usual glacial pace.

"Hot," I answer. In more ways than one.

A yawn rips through me and rubbing the grit of sleep from my eyes proves to be a challenge. I cradle the overly sweetened Starbucks latte Mom bought me as if it's liquid gold. At least she's thoughtful enough to support my caffeine addiction.

I don't think she's ever been prouder as a mother than the day I started drinking coffee. My dad and Thomas, my older brother, both hate it. But now, she has someone to share her addiction with.

"It's been a scorcher." She smiles as we merge across a few lanes seemingly on a whim.

My knuckles are white, but after sixteen years of riding in the car with her, I think I'm finally getting used to it.

"I hope you kept yourself adequately hydrated out

there."

Mom can't help being overbearing. It's in her genetic makeup.

"Yup." I take another sip of coffee, relishing in the diabetes-laden goodness. "How was the move? Did Thomas get up to school okay?"

"He's up there." Mom's smile fades. "But I don't want to talk about it. Too fresh."

"He'll be fine, Mom." I pat her arm with my non-Starbucks hand. "You don't have to worry. It's not like he's out of the country."

Thomas—AKA, every parent's wet dream of a firstborn—is starting his freshman year at the University of Georgia. Mom and Dad took the day off work yesterday, a huge deal for them, to help him move up to Athens. He's on their swim team, and last I heard, he was third string specialty for the Georgia Bulldogs football team. My parents are over the moon about that. Football is like a religion to them even though they've already got a religion. It's hard to tell which they follow more closely. Someday, someone will start the First Christian Church of the Bulldogs, and my family will line up to be the first members baptized by having Gatorade dumped over their heads.

"I'm fine," Mom tells me, but her eyes are still misty.

Jeez, this is going to be a long day.

We weave through the parking lot for the Mall of Georgia, scoping out the optimal space to house Mom's white Escalade. My high school, Stronghold Christian School, has a strictly enforced dress code that includes a ridiculously priced uniform. I have no idea why we're here. I mean, I don't even have the freedom of choosing my socks. Maybe Mom just wants to spend some quality time with me since I'm the middle child. Or, maybe, she really does have a favorite child despite her claims against the notion, and it's me.

That's hilarious.

You know, I've never really given much thought to the whole middle-child syndrome debate. I guess I don't mind the lack of attention. Thomas has always been the straight-A student and star athlete in the family. Rosy, my younger sister, is the baby, can play three instruments, and does no wrong. I'm somewhere between the two of them. I make decent grades, and I have one of the fastest freestyle lap times at school, but none of that really seems to matter. I'm left to fend for myself in a lot of ways, but I'm totally okay with that.

The less time they spend with me, the less of an opportunity they'll have to see me slip and give something away.

I know the conditions of my parents' love.

"Come on, Mikey!" Mom calls, already out of the car and moving at quite a clip toward the entrance. She is wearing Nikes and yoga pants, so the pace is formidable. I don't know if I'm going to be able to keep up with her.

Hustling to match her stride, I pass through the outer shops toward the food court. The splash pad is deserted, and streams of water shoot through holes in the sidewalk at random intervals. In a few hours, dozens of children will squeal with delight as they get soaked. The sun peeks through the buildings and sweat drips down my neck just from the few minutes of being out of the car. I polish off the last of my sugary beverage with a gulp and toss the empty cardboard into an open trash can as we clear the doors.

That sweet shopping mall smell hits me, along with a burst of cool air.

"Want some breakfast?" Mom asks, already moving toward the counter on our right.

Once she has her sights on Jesus chicken, there's no stopping her. She's like a woman possessed. The siren call of delicate, deep-fried deliciousness is too much for anyone to resist. So, I follow her to the line of people waiting to order from the perky employees who all look suspiciously home-schooled.

As a gay person—albeit only self-admitted—I know I'm not supposed to support these supposed hateful bigots who dress homophobia up in amazingly addictive foodstuffs, but I mean *come on*. How can anyone say no to a piping-hot chicken biscuit smothered in strawberry jelly? No one has that much willpower.

"It's my pleasure!" the lady exclaims, smiling creepily as she hands us our food a few minutes later.

Is it really her pleasure? She says it with such enthusiasm it makes me wonder if there's a sniper hiding in the rafters, waiting to put a bullet in their head the one time an employee doesn't say the signature phrase.

That would certainly explain the strange twitch in the woman's eye.

Mom and I take a seat in the nearly empty dining room, unwrapping our foil lined breakfast and feasting on the innards. The carnage is quick and leaves the table covered in crumbs and sticky patches of jelly.

"Did Rosy not want to join our excursion this

17

morning?" I ask through a mouthful of half-chewed buttermilk biscuit.

"She's got band rehearsal at church," Mom replies before sipping her colossal cup of half-sweet and half-unsweet tea. She would order it by the gallon if it wasn't so hard to carry around. "Did I tell you Rosy got a solo in service tomorrow morning? Be sure you're awake for that part."

I toss my last hash brown into my mouth with practiced dexterity.

"Did you happen to meet any cute girls while you were at camp?"

A sharp inhale sends a chunk of potatoey remains down my windpipe. The resulting coughing fit leaves tears in the corner of my eyes.

"Well?" Mom doesn't drop the subject. I swear the only thing she wants more than me to get into UGA is for me to marry a nice Christian girl and father grandchildren for her. Now that Thomas is at school, I'm the next in line of potential procreators.

Shaking my head, I find it difficult to ignore the sinking feeling in my stomach melding with my breakfast.

"I was too focused on my walk," I lie, feeling sick.

What's one more lie to my mother? My life until this point has been nothing but a series of them.

"That's my boy." Mom smiles, popping the lid off her fruit cup. "Just make sure you don't get so distracted you end up thirty and alone like your Uncle Seth."

Oh, that's a definite possibility. But it won't be due to the reason she thinks, so I just smile and nod.

She'd prefer my being alone to the reality of the truth.

Once we've stuffed our faces and Mom's gotten her second refill from eye-twitch lady, we leave the food court behind. The game is on. Stores roll up their doors, signaling it's time to execute our well-orchestrated plan of attack. My last-minute growth spurt means I've outgrown most of my clothes from last fall, so that means we're on the search for everything from jeans to jackets.

Shopping unlocks this strange notion in Mom's head that she missed her calling as a stylist, right up there with Tim Gunn. Of course, it's completely ridiculous because everything she pulls off a rack for me to try on is terrible and doesn't match in the slightest. Sometimes, I have to wonder if she might be colorblind. I may be in the closet, but that doesn't mean I'm going to look a fool.

She also seems to be laboring under the delusion I want to dress like the other trust fund fueled douchebags named Chad in my class. I'm not kidding. There are three.

I decline her offer of a pink, short-sleeve polo. "No way in Hell."

"Language," she chides, putting the polo back where she found it.

"But Hell's a real place," I say in defense. "I'm just using a proper noun, Mom."

"Michael." Her tone ends the argument.

I wonder what she'd do if she realized my vocabulary is far more colorful when she's absent. Or if she knew I liked to kiss boys. I honestly don't know which one she would disown me for faster.

Actually, I do. My chicken biscuit tosses like a ship on the sea.

After a fruitless three hours, I end up with an armful of thin hoodies, my go-to wardrobe choice on days when the heat index isn't in the triple digits. In other words, I'll be able to wear them around Christmas. Until then, it will be nothing but graphic tees and shorts for me.

"You need to pick out some clothes for church," she tells me as we head to the next stop in the endless cycle of stores.

I let out a groan, digging my way through the rack of dress shirts. The only thing more important than going to church in my family is looking presentable when you do. God, apparently, is pretty judgey when it comes to your wardrobe. Heaven forbid I would attempt to wear a pair of flip-flops. You would think I proposed practicing human sacrifice in the basement.

Formal wear paid for and arms laden with swag, we start back toward the food court entrance. The mall is filling up, and I follow a few steps behind my mother, so I can watch the people passing by. It's one of my favorite pastimes. A guy with a lip ring that really catches my eye passes, but Mom is moving way too fast for me to appreciate the view.

After we pile our spoils into the back seat of the Escalade, I climb into the front, leather searing my flesh in a familiar yet still painful way.

"What do we say?" Mom clambers into the driver's seat, grabbing the rhinestone sunglasses from the visor above.

"Thanks, Mom."

I'm already swiping through the pile of text messages I've missed while distracted by shopping. Jackie's unique perspective and foul mouth make for the most entertaining conversations. I stifle a laugh to keep from having to show my mother.

She flips on the radio, and a really awful Christian song blasts through the speakers. Humming tunelessly, Mom fights our way out of the crowded parking lot. I plug my headphones in a few minutes later, propping a foot on the dashboard as the sweet sound of Fleet Foxes carries me far away from the heat and cliché lyrics.

FOUR

My alarm goes off at seven. I want to throw my phone against the wall. Taking the more rational route, I silence it instead and turn over.

"Let's get a move on!" Dad calls through my door. The distant sound of Mom's hairdryer means I have about ten minutes before she'll be ready to go. Just enough time.

Rosy is putting on makeup in the bathroom mirror when I walk in.

"I suggest you leave unless you want to see me naked," I warn.

"Gross." She rolls her eyes, throwing her mascara into her bag. "Hey, don't jerk off in there. It clogs the drain."

"I'm a grown man." I strip off my shirt. "I'll do what I want."

"I can't wait until you're off to college too." She moves to the door. "Then I can be an only child."

"Keep dreaming." I laugh. "Tommy will have flunked out by then. Or, better yet, he'll knock some poor girl up, and they'll *both* move in. Have fun babysitting."

She flips me the bird, and I moon her as she closes the door. The shower sputters to life with the turn of a handle, steam soon rising to the ceiling. I have to step carefully over the twelve bottles of assorted products lined along the edge of the tub. I don't know how Rosy can possibly use them all, but I'm always one wrong move away from an avalanche of acne scrubs and flowery shit.

Rosy isn't the world's *most* annoying little sister, but she certainly knows how to push my buttons. She is very mature for a fourteen-year-old, but then again, how could you not be with our parents? Mom always jokes we came out of the womb middle-aged, but really, it's the years of high expectations and countless hours of training in social graces that have aged us. We couldn't possibly be anything else.

My shower is quick, and I take my toothbrush with me into the bedroom as I sort through the stack of new clothes. I pick out a nice button-up and a pair of slacks before pulling them on. Throwing a matching tie over my shoulders, I go to spit in the bathroom. With a split second of hesitation, I retrace my steps and retrieve my messenger bag from under my bed. I don't like being away from what's inside.

"Let's go, Mikey!" Dad calls from downstairs. "*Vamos!*"

I hit the stairs, skidding at the bottom as I grab a pair of shoes by the door. Rosy is already waiting in the SUV, her violin case taking up all the legroom.

"What took you so long?" she asks, tapping on her phone.

"I was busy clogging the drain."

The noise she makes is worth the dirty look from Mom.

OUR CHURCH SITS ON THE OUTSKIRTS OF NORTH ATLANTA, IN A TOWN CALLED Sandy Springs. It's mostly rich white people who all drive the same four luxury models and talk about how they miss the good ol' days, which I can only assume is a racist euphemism.

My family is about as controversial as you get at our church. My dad, whose parents moved here from Mexico in the late 1960s, married my mom—the whitest woman *ever*. The two of them joined the church shortly afterward at the behest of Grandma and Grandpa—the non-Hispanic ones. They used to turn a lot of heads, but shortly after Tommy was born, the church welcomed their first African American and Caucasian couple, and the spotlight moved on to the next pariah.

I'm just thankful I inherited Dad's awesome tanned complexion. It takes me literally two days to darken up for summer. No sunburn, just copper skin.

We pull into the parking lot around eight, the huge sanctuary and steeple looming over us. Mom has been tearing up the whole ride because this is the first Sunday Tommy has been away from the family. Rosy and I share the same disgusted expression as we try to put as much distance between us and Mom as possible.

The greeter at the door is at least a thousand years

old, and I always feel like I'm going to break his frail bones when he offers a handshake. The family splits when we hit the lobby, Mom off to the nursery downstairs where she teaches a class of toddlers using the latest in felt board technology. I don't think they've changed the curriculum down there since Mom was a baby. Dad heads up to the choir room to do a vocal warm-up, and Rosy hauls her violin case to the orchestra pit to prepare for her solo.

Being the underachiever I am, I don't have any churchy extracurricular activities at the moment, so I meander to the basement where they confine the rest of the high school squalor.

Maybe I'm early enough to work on a few sketches before Sunday school gets started.

My creative itch spreads across my arm like wildfire.

The walls are a hideous blend of bright colors and vague shapes left over from the nineties. I barely even made it into the nineties, being born just a few months before the turn of the millennium. But I've seen enough of my parents' old shit to know I'm right.

A pair of doors at the end of the hallway lead outside. I push on the heavy metal, knowing Jackie already waits for me, cigarette in hand.

I'm hit with the smell of tobacco and sunshine.

"Look who decided to show up," a deep voice calls.

"Shut up, Tanner," I quip. "Not all of us have the luxury of driving a brand-new Mercedes, asswipe."

Tanner's usual guffaw carries on a little too long. He wears his Sunday best—a torn pair of jeans and a polo shirt. He's cut his golden hair short for the summer, and it makes his head look bigger than usual. He towers over me by at least six inches, and his glasses are a hipster's dream.

"I don't drive a Mercedes," he says, crossing his arms. "*Anymore.* I traded it in for a Honda. Better mileage."

"Can it, you privileged sasquatch." Jackie exhales a stream of pungent smoke. "You're going to get me busted."

Jackie is more paranoid about her mother finding out she smokes cigarettes than she is after we light a joint at Tanner's house. It's probably because her mom used to smoke. She always tries to keep her daughter from turning into her.

"Those names you call me hurt my feelings," Tanner chides.

"You're right." Jackie stomps out the butt of her latest before lighting another one. "I should stop beating around the bush and call you faggot. It's far more accurate."

"Wow." I whistle, lowering into my usual spot on the cracked pavement. "Do you kiss your mother with that mouth?" I lean my back against the wall, digging for my sketchpad and a pencil.

"Yes." Jackie inhales deeply. "But, trust me, it's done a lot worse."

"How was camp?" Tanner asks, leaning his shoulder against the brick building.

"The usual," I offer, flipping through the smudged pages. I can't work on the incomplete sketch in the back of the book I started last night. That one is of Blondie. More specifically, a sketch of Blondie featuring a certain appendage that isn't exactly appropriate for this time or place. I leave that untouched, instead turning to the landscape piece on the sixth page—a river filled with smooth rocks.

That's safe. Jesus can look over my shoulder all he wants.

"Uneventful," Jackie chimes in. "Until the ride home, that is."

Tanner leans forward. "Do tell."

Despite his painfully straight sexual orientation, Tanner is the biggest gossip whore in the entire church. I'm convinced he's actually just a petty, sixty-year-old woman trapped in an eighteen-year-old's body. Secrets are like manna from Heaven to him. On second thought, maybe crack. Manna isn't addictive.

"Well," Jackie starts, voice lowering to just above a whisper, "you know Brad from the praise band?"

Tanner and I nod our heads in unison, but for completely different reasons. Brad is the lead guitar player in the student praise band. Tanner knows him because he's in the same grade. And I know him because he's a total wet dream wrapped in a pair of skin-tight jeans.

God, that freaking beanie he always wears gets me hot and bothered.

"We've been texting for a couple of weeks, but he sat next to me in the back row of the bus," she continues, twirling a strand of dark hair with her free hand. "Well, you know how these things happen. One thing led to another, and long story short, I ended up jerking him off underneath his rain jacket."

"You're kidding me," I breathe, the story already making my heart race.

Jesus, why am I so horny?

I focus on my shading and cross my legs.

Tanner's laughter booms. "In the back of the church

bus, Jackie? That's a new low. Even for you."

"What?" She throws her hands in the air. "It's not like I put it in my mouth or anything. I thought I kept it pretty classy. Plus, I have all these lotions from Bath and Body Works…."

"What would your mother think of your actions?" Tanner questions.

"She would commend me for performing a task that has zero chance of me getting knocked up."

We all laugh, but Jackie is dead serious. Her mom got pregnant when she was only seventeen. Her father, a complete and total jackass of a man, wanted nothing to do with either of them. I think he still lives somewhere around here, running a car dealership.

Why are car salesmen always the worst people?

"I think both my parents would die of a heart attack if they heard I was getting a handy in the back seat of the bus." Tanner jerks his fist back and forth, making a face.

I wonder what my parents would think of me and Blondie in the chapel bathroom. Who cares? No way in Hell will they ever find out.

"Well, they're both ancient." Jackie laughs. "So, it wouldn't surprise me if at least one of them dropped dead. Hey, if they both go, does that mean you get the house?"

Tanner's parents are both in their late sixties, having just retired from the missionary field when they adopted him fifteen years ago. They still travel a lot, but just for fun now. I think they're somewhere in Asia at the moment.

"I sure hope so. Then I can walk around as naked as I please," Tanner muses.

"You're gross." Jackie's face scrunches.

"All right, you guys are keeping the juicy details from me," Tanner says. "I need to update my pregnancy pool. Any chance somebody got knocked up? I mean, you cram a bunch of hormonally stressed out teenagers in the sweltering heat, there's bound to be some scrubbing and rubbing going on. And seeing as no one around here seems keen on the idea of teaching birth control methods, I'm assuming there was a lot of potential baby-making happening. Spill it, people."

"For the record, Tan-tan, I found our abstinence class to be *very* educational." Jackie laughs. "It taught me just how far I can go without being a complete whore in the eyes of the Lord." She drags her hand across her chest, forming the sign of the cross—a habit she picked up from her grandfather. He's Catholic just like my dad's folks.

"The guys in my cabin wouldn't shut up about their supposed sexual conquests," I tell him, the scritching sound of my pencil against the page a steady tempo, "but I don't think any of them were actually true. I mean, what girl in her right mind would want to bang in the middle of the woods? Too many nooks and crannies for bugs to crawl into."

"I saw Timothy Richards and Jenny O. getting it on behind the mess hall," Jackie adds, stomping on a second butt. "But they're always fucking like rabbits. Plus, she's on the pill, so no babies."

"Well, that's a disappointment." Tanner pouts, stroking his non-existent beard. "How am I supposed to update the stats with weak information like this?" He pushes his glasses back into place. "Which class

29

would you bet on having the first pregnancy this year? 'Cause I got a lot of money riding on the freshmen."

"Gross!" Jackie complains.

"What is wrong with you?" I slap the back of Tanner's leg. "They're kids!"

"Horny little kids," he rebuts, "who are too dumb to pull out. I'm telling you, there's going to be at least one by Christmas. If not here, it'll be at school."

"If you say so," I mutter, checking my phone. It's almost time for Sunday school to start. I smudge one more patch on the page with my thumb, blending the lines together.

"You two still coming over after church?" Tanner asks, entranced by his own phone.

"I think that's the plan," I say, flipping the cover of my sketchpad closed. "Jackie?"

"Yeah, yeah." Jackie douses herself with a bottle of Deep Amber from Bath and Body Works. She should probably own stock there. It's almost enough to cover the stale smell of tobacco.

We wait until Jackie airs out a little more before we head back inside. The "Well"—Arnold's most recent renaming of the glorified hovel that is the church basement—is filling up with the usual suspects. I snicker when I see Timothy and Jenny holding hands as they walk in. The three of us discreetly search for signs of a baby bump, but there's nothing.

Tanner heads for the sound booth at the back of the room where he spends his Sunday mornings watching YouTube whilst flipping a few switches on the soundboard. Jackie and I take our seats on the back row of rickety fold out chairs. I toggle my Bible app on my phone, so I can keep up the appearance I actually care about what's going on.

"All right, everyone. Let's settle in!" Arnold's bald head shines from the front of the elevated floor serving as our makeshift stage. The television screens above him flicker to life with a painfully bad stock image of the lesson series title. I've often fantasized about one of the televisions coming loose from the ceiling and crushing him, but sadly, those rusty bolts are surprisingly sturdy.

It's not that I don't like Arnold. I mean the guy tries harder than anyone I've ever seen to reach kids. The only problem is he is so disconnected from everything people my age actually care about, he's never successful. Nothing is more painful than watching him butcher a reference in an attempt to be relevant. Don't even get me started on that time he danced to "Gangnam Style" while dressed as the Apostle Paul. It still haunts my dreams.

This morning, he drones on about something to do with the book of John, but I'm not listening. Jackie has her notebook out, and she doodles along with her pen. She writes a question and then passes the page over to me.

Do you think Brad likes me?

I respond in my chicken scratch.

How the hell should I know?

She snatches it back, scribbling with fury.

Because you're a guy?

What do you do when you like a girl?

I'd call the pope. It's a freaking miracle!

I let her jerk me off in the back seat of a bus.

Arnold talks about living water, and one student shoots him in the face with a Super Soaker. He is really trying today, bless his heart.

You're not helpful.

I snicker as I write.

I do what I can.

"All right, everyone," says a dripping Arnold. "We're going to break up into our Life Groups and really unpack these ideas. Let's get to work!"

The youth group divides, gravitating toward our respective areas of the room. My group always takes the back-left corner where a circle of bean bags lurk, ready to devour unsuspecting students.

Our leader—a silver-haired man with a bushy mustache that looks a little like Tom Selleck if he gained fifty pounds—gathers us around to start the discussion. It's a lesson I've heard at least eighty times before, so I tune out.

Growing up in church has always been a struggle for me. And that doesn't include the multitudes of times someone has brought up homosexuality. Whenever that topic surfaces, I keep my mouth shut and let everyone else debate the damnation reserved for people with my…affliction.

I can't help feeling my silence is betraying my own kind, but the alternative is far too gruesome to compare. I'll march twice as hard in a future Pride Parade to make up for it.

Or just take my secret to the grave. That's a totally viable option.

I pray, one day, this won't be an issue—that I'll be able to love who I love, and no old church lady will look at me funny. But let's face it, this is Georgia, and that's not happening any time soon.

Plus, I'm not totally convinced being gay isn't a sin like everyone says it is. So, throw that complexity in there, and you're looking at a fucked-up layer cake of guilt and self-loathing.

It's not just the gay thing either. I'm finding it hard to believe in anything these days. Apathy is so much easier.

"Mike, what do you think Jesus was talking about when he told the woman who he offers water to that it will quench her thirst forever?"

My name snaps me back from my stupor, and I scramble to make it look like I was listening.

"He's talking about everlasting life," I say without much hesitation. Cycling back to the last time we had this discussion, I repeat an answer. "He's referring to the rebirth through baptism and salvation you find believing in Him."

"That's right," Fat Tom Selleck replies, giving me a smile that makes his bushy mustache twitch. "Jesus was offering this woman…"

And I tune out again. I've heard every Sunday school lesson there is, and I can recite all the popular verses backward and forward. I've spent seventeen years getting the same thing hammered into me time and time again. How can I not zone out?

Man, Trevor looks really cute in his plaid today...

Shit. Stop staring, Mike.

FIVE

"YOU COMING TO BIG CHURCH?" JACKIE ASKS TANNER ONCE WE'RE FREE OF the monotonous clutches of Fat Tom Selleck.

"Yeah," he replies, climbing down from his techy perch. "I wouldn't miss it for the world. I should be able to sit with you guys as long as someone watches Jerry in the sound booth. Whoever convinced him his talents are in soundboard operation needs to be shot. The poor guy keeps switching Myers's mic on at the wrong time. The other week, I kid you not, we heard him taking a piss for a solid minute during the eight o'clock service. It was super awkward."

"Rosy's got her big solo during communion." I sling my messenger bag over my shoulder. "So, if I'm asleep at that point, can you give me a nudge?"

"I'll just pour the blood of Christ up your nose," Jackie offers, her heels clicking against the tile floor as we move down the hallway.

"I knew I could count on you." Without thinking, I wrap an arm through hers.

She stiffens, and I pull away, silently chastising

myself.

Straight boys don't do that, Mike.

But Jackie doesn't linger on the awkwardness as we make our way up to the Sanctuary, which is just a massive gymnasium they've converted with decades-old technology. A weird arrangement of decorations covers the majority of the stage, and I can never tell what exactly they were going for, but it looks like a really cheap wedding. Or my cousin Tina's *quinceañera*. Christmas lights and paper lanterns weave together in a hodgepodge of tacky proportions. All that's missing is a Jesus piñata.

Tanner, Jackie, and I take our seats in the same row we use every week—fourth from the front on the left— and I feel the ever-present stare of my mother like heat from the sun coming from a few rows behind. I will never understand how she watches me like a hawk *and* takes flawlessly detailed notes on the sermon. I mean, they're even color coordinated. She's a fantastic multi-tasker.

Our worship minister takes his place as the music softly drifts in. Dad waves at me from the stage as the choir files in, and I sink a little lower in my chair, trapped between my parents.

The service begins, and I switch to autopilot. My favorite thing about religion is it's so easy to lose myself in the steps. I don't have to be myself when I'm here. I can just give up all the confusion and guilt for a few precious moments of numbing bliss.

To be honest, I like the feeling a little too much.

Then the pastor reaches his pulpit and strips my joy away.

Pastor Myers is about as traditional as people come.

He has been with the church for God only knows how long. His sermons are usually straight from the old testament because he finds the new testament to be a bit too liberal.

In short, the man makes Mike Pence look like RuPaul.

"Good morning congregation," he starts in his deep southern drawl.

The crowd responds in kind, in a creepy cultish kind of way. He has us all well-trained.

"I gotta tell you, congregation, my heart is heavy as I come to bring the gospel this morning." Myers continues, "If you would please turn to Genesis chapter eighteen, we will be diving right on in."

That passage sounds vaguely familiar. Though, I don't know why.

"Brothers and sisters—" He straightens the lapels of his crisp suit. "—my heart weeps for our country this morning. The morals of our great nation are being tested this very day. I speak the truth when I say we are under attack, brothers and sisters. Satan is indeed at work in our lives.

"My beautiful wife, Vanessa and I were walking in the city yesterday, and we bore witness to something that still has me quaking with a righteous fury."

Wow, whatever he saw must have been a doozy. I haven't heard him use the term "righteous fury" since he found out one of the deacons was a closeted Democrat.

"Five bucks says it was a drag queen," Tanner whispers in my ear.

I have to cough to cover the laughter. The elderly woman in front of me cuts her eyes back, and I give her a weak smile.

"Sorry," I whisper, elbowing Tanner in the side.

"When Vanessa and I were making our way down Peachtree after dinner, enjoying the beauty of our fine city," Myers says as he steps around his pulpit, wiping his already sweaty brow with a handkerchief from his pocket, "we passed by a church. And I use that term *very* loosely. It was at this supposed place of worship we observed two men exiting the house of God, having just been bound by what our corrupted government has declared legal marriage."

The murmuring of the congregation is mixed, but all varying shades of discontent. I simply wait for the shocking part. Were the guys dressed in assless leather chaps? Did they have swastikas tattooed on their foreheads? Did they immediately fornicate on the steps of the church? I think I've seen that porno… I recall it being kind of hot.

From his reaction, I half expect there to be an instance of child sacrifice.

I bring up child sacrifice a lot. There's something wrong with me.

"Now, you know our Lord calls on us to have mercy on those who would turn their backs on the sacred vows of marriage but, church, I must be transparent. I'm having a hard time." He props his arm on the pulpit. "For two individuals so twisted in the ways of paganism to display this vulgarity on our very streets and in our places of sanctuary, it was too much for me to handle."

Ah, yes, two people who love each other enough to want to spend the rest of their lives together. How awful. Humanity is doomed. Hide the children.

Okay, Big Guy. You wanna know why You get such a bad rap these days? Just take a look at Your representation. Honestly, he's the worst.

"I pray God grants us the strength as a nation to cast out these sinful lifestyles and turn to Him for forgiveness. I pray, one day, my grandchildren might be saved from the dangers of queers and sodomites stalking the streets under the guise of our neighbors and preying on the young and innocent."

Got it. So, I'm a predator now. Thanks for clearing that up, Pastor. I would never have known. I'll be sure to go out and get a creepy van full of candy after service lets out. Maybe one that plays a fun song to draw the little ones in? Hey, little Timmy, want a lollipop?

My legs are bouncing with nervous energy.

"You gotta pee?" Tanner asks.

I just shake my head.

"Church, we must be ever-mindful in these trying times that we do not let our children be dragged into a world of depravity."

The resounding "Amen" from the congregation makes me squirm in my seat. It's already a little too late for me, I suppose. I'm depraved.

"Let us take a lesson from the heathens of Sodom and Gomorrah," the pastor continues, arms flopping back and forth with what I can only imagine is supposed to be passionate conviction. It looks more like a stroke.

"For God did see it fit to wipe them from the face of the Earth. Lest we forget the sins that condemned them. Most of all, the sin of homosexuality."

Actually, a lot of scholars think it was rape. But, hey, what do they know?

God, I'm not saying the Bible is wrong. But we're

really dumb down here, so I get the feeling we may have misinterpreted a few things….

"Let us begin in verse one…."

I can't bear to listen to anymore, so I tune out, staring at the chair in front of me. The patterned material blurs as I block everything out.

God still loves me. God still loves me. God still loves me.

I repeat that. It helps me retain my sanity in this place.

Before long, Myers wraps up his ranting.

"Keep this in the forefront of your mind as you leave today." He blots his receding hairline once more with his handkerchief. "We must pray for God's mercy on this nation of ours that is speeding toward Sodom and hurtling toward Gomorrah. May those who labor under the yoke of their sinful nature have the strength and courage to denounce their same-sex attraction. And those who turn their back on God in pursuit of sins of the flesh, may they burn in the fires of Hell for all eternity. Amen."

My ears are burning as Rosy takes her place in the center of the stage, bow drawn across strings in preparation.

A serene smile graces her face. How can someone smile after that?

Service continues as if the leader of our congregation hadn't just personally damned me to eternal suffering.

The elders of the church move along the aisles, passing trays of stale, tasteless crackers and watered down grape juice. I take these in my hand like I do every week, mindlessly partaking in the symbolic gesture.

Pastor Myers' words are fluttering around my head,

twisting my insides. Oh man, I'm going to be sick.

This is the hate I've listened to every week for the last sixteen years, and no matter what I do, I can't shake the feeling Pastor Myers is right. There's something wrong with me. Wrong with the way I am. I'm an abomination in the sight of God.

Tears fill my eyes as Rosy ends her song, and the choir takes the stage for the final hymn. I blot my face on my sleeve as the congregation stands and move past Jackie as I walk down the aisle and head for the door. The room is suddenly suffocating.

Hold it together, Mike. It's nothing you haven't heard before.

But, for some reason, those hate-filled words surround me as I walk. With every step, more tears fall. I don't make eye contact with those in the hall. Instead, I keep pressing forward until I can't go any farther. I open the door on my left, diving into the safety of the darkness within.

My nose burns with the scent of chemicals, but that's the last thing on my mind. A dirty bucket sits neglected in the corner. I flip it over, lowering myself onto it. I'm sobbing now, I realize, arms wrapping around my chest. It feels like I'm going to fall apart.

God still loves me. God still loves me. God still loves me.

No amount of prayer can drown out the shame swelling inside me. This certainly isn't the first time I've felt this weight, but I've never had to fight this hard to keep my head above the waves of guilt. Above the noise, one question rises.

How can God love me?

SIX

"CAN HE SAY 'QUEERS'?" JACKIE ASKS, COLLAPSING ONTO THE PLUSH BLACK leather of Tanner's couch.

"He can say whatever he wants," Tanner calls, grabbing a couple of Mountain Dews from the refrigerator in the kitchen.

I remain silent. No way can I talk about it right now. It took almost half an hour to calm down enough so I could leave the custodial closet. My eyes feel puffy, but no one has said anything about them. I hover over Jackie, too worked up to sit down.

This is a problem. I've never had to leave in the middle of service before. I mean, sure, I've had to hold those emotions inside at times and ended up exploding as soon as I closed the bedroom door. But this reaction? I don't like it.

It's dangerous. It'll give me away.

"Are you okay?" Jackie asks, eyebrow cocked. "You look like they just canceled *Once Upon a Time*."

"I'm fine," I snap. She recoils. "And don't joke about that. They'd never cancel OUAT. It's literally the perfect show."

"When you think about it," Tanner continues as he moves into the living room, oblivious to the change in topic. He hands me the cold can, and it opens with a hiss. "A pastor is really just the leader of a cult. He has near ultimate authority inside the walls of the church. He can say whatever he wants."

"Shit," Jackie breathes, letting my reaction slide as she opens her own can. "I've never thought of it like that."

"Scary, isn't it?" Tanner chuckles, plopping on the opposite end of the sofa.

"But why does he have to hate on the gays?" Jackie angles herself toward him. "What did they ever do to him? Oh my God, do you think his uncle molested him? That would explain so much."

"That is terrifying," Tanner muses, "and has a high possibility of being true. I would be comfortable making a sizable wager. Do you think it was an uncle or maybe his dad? I mean, I met the guy once, and he had these eyes—"

"He has a point," I chime in, to my own surprise. "I mean, the scriptures do make it pretty clear it's a sin."

"Yeah," Tanner says slowly, "and so is polyester. And eating shellfish. And sitting somewhere a woman on her period sat. And eating meat with cheese. Plus, the whole masturbation thing. Which I'm pretty sure means all men everywhere are going straight to Hell. Don't pass go and don't collect two hundred dollars."

We all laugh, but his response doesn't ease the knot in my stomach. I have heard endless arguments about homosexuality, whether in support or opposition. So many voices screaming and so little definite truth.

"I trust science more than I do scripture." Tanner leans back, adjusting his thick-rimmed glasses. "I mean there are so many studies out there about how homosexuality is a natural progression of evolution. There's a reason it's been recorded throughout history."

"That argument doesn't mean shit." Jackie slurps her soda. "Most of the members of our church would sooner burn you at the stake than believe in evolution."

"Well, if that doesn't do the trick, I can always tell them I read *Harry Potter*. That'll definitely get a lynch mob up and running."

"Can we change the subject?" I ask abruptly. I'm going to puke if we keep on about this.

"Aw, what's the matter, Mike?" Tanner teases, "Is your parents' homophobia finally rubbing off on you?" He rises from his seat, swatting at my shoulder. "You always look so uncomfortable when we talk about the gays. I think you must—"

"I said drop it!"

Tanner furrows his brow.

"I-I mean," I stammer, in attempts to recover. "It doesn't have anything to do with us, so why talk about it?"

Jackie sets her drink on the coffee table, standing as well. "I don't know about you guys, but I could use a fag."

"A what?" I turn to her, but she's shaking her pack of smokes.

"Don't waste your time," says Tanner, looking back at her. "I have some new shit waiting upstairs."

"Sweet." Jackie stows her vice. "I was hoping you'd say that. I have period cramps like a bitch."

Tanner turns to me. "You up for it, Mike?"

"Y-Yeah. Of course."

"Sweet." He grins.

My defenses are slipping. I can feel it happening, like a dam threatening to burst. Here are my best friends, the two people I love more than anything in the world. Why can't I just tell them? What's the worst that could happen?

But reality quickly sets back in, and I push down all the words I want to say. I'm not ready for them to know. Honestly, I don't know if I'll ever be ready.

We follow Tanner up the winding stairs to his bedroom, which is pristine—as always. His house always makes me feel like such a slob.

"Make yourselves at home," Tanner tells us, heading for the closet. He rummages around the top shelf for the shoebox he hides his stash in.

Jackie sits on the edge of his bed, which, of course, is tucked tighter than a soldier's.

Who the hell makes their bed every day? I thought that only happened on sitcoms.

I settle in on the carpet by her dangling feet.

"Hey, where did you go after communion?" she asks me, knocking a foot against my shoulder.

"Bathroom," I lie. Another lie. I have a story about a clogged toilet ready if she pushes the subject.

She doesn't. "Oh, okay."

"All right, boys and girls." Tanner is back, the slender stick in one hand and a lighter in the other. "Today's selection is called Trainwreck, and I have no idea why. Ready to find out?"

Jackie and I nod as Tanner lights the end of the brown paper, drawing in a deep breath. The strong aroma washes over me, loosening the knot in my stomach by a fraction.

He passes it to me next, exhaling a stream of smoke with a few coughs. "Whoa." He blinks the water from his eyes. "That's...pungent."

I take a drag, holding the smoke in my mouth until it cools before breathing it in. My lungs burn as I pass it on to Jackie. I can't stop the cough, and wisps of smoke escape my nose and lips.

"Amateurs." Jackie laughs, taking a hit. She holds it like a champ, her mouth opening slowly to allow the smoke to drift up into her nose. She doesn't even flinch.

The joint makes its way around a few more times, and soon, the anxious feeling in my stomach is nothing but a memory.

Our afternoon marches on as we relive the best highlights from camp then eat everything in Tanner's refrigerator.

THE FIRST DAY OF SCHOOL IS HERE. I GIVE MYSELF A FINAL ONCE-OVER IN THE mirror, navy blazer buttoned over a dull, striped tie, and ironed to perfection. Running my fingers through my hair, everything looks in place.

Perfect. I'm ready for another day of a flawless facade. Looking my best always helps me remember the role I play on a daily basis.

"Let's get a move on, Mikey!" Dad calls from the stairs.

Mom had to be at the hospital early this morning, so

I guess he's going to drop Rosy and me off.

I grab my bag, slinging it over my shoulder as I traverse the staircase. Dad has his briefcase in hand, and his own suit and tie are in perfect arrangement. Like father like son, except I can't believe Dad has ever had to be anyone other than himself. There's no one more comfortable in their skin than him. He talks on his cell phone as Rosy stands by the door, foot tapping impatiently against the hardwood floor.

"You're going to make me late for my first day of high school." She seethes. Her pleated skirt and face full of makeup make it look like she's headed for a night on the town. She looks much older than she actually is.

"You're not missing much," I tell her, shuffling into the kitchen. I grab an apple from the bowl on the counter, peeling off the sticker before sinking my teeth in with a satisfying crunch. Grabbing my metal tumbler, I fill it halfway with coffee from the pot and then finish it with way more cream than allowed.

"All right, kiddos," Dad calls. "*Vamanos.* Out the door."

I catch the door right before it shuts, locking it behind me. Rosy is already crawling into the back of Dad's Audi coup, and I fold myself into the front seat. Why he drives such a small car, I have no idea.

"You guys got everything you need?" he asks, backing out of the driveway.

"It's a bit late for that," Rosy says, typing away on her phone.

Who is she talking to this early in the morning?

"Right you are, Rosemary." Dad laughs, flipping on the radio.

He listens to the oldies station, but anything's better than Mom's presets. I'll take Eric Clapton over Bill Gaither any day.

Traffic is its usual ridiculousness on the way to school. I'm counting the days until my birthday when I can finally get my driver's license. Stupid Joshua's law has kept me off the road for a year because I failed Driver's Ed.

Parallel parking is a bitch.

We pull into the crowded parking lot, and nerves hit me all a sudden.

God, please let me have a good first day. Or at least give me one attractive teacher. I know You can make that happen.

"Okay, *mi vida*." Dad stops by the curb. "You two have an excellent first day."

"Thanks," I mutter, already climbing out of the car. I don't wait for Rosy, just let my feet carry me along the familiar path. Once I'm sure Dad's pulled away, my course changes, ducking around the building to where the dumpster pad sits.

Jackie's already waiting there, a lit cigarette in one hand and her phone in the other. "About time you showed up," she says without looking at me.

"Where's Tanner?" I ask, stepping around the puddle of grease in front of the putrid-smelling green dumpster.

"He said something about a computer lab project." Jackie's words escape through the cloud of smoke.

"Sounds like something he'd say," I mutter, leaning against the brick wall, surrounding the two slimy containers. "Hey, what happens if someone tells your mom you're out here?"

"She'll probably murder me," Jackie answers, finally

looking up from her phone. "Toss my carcass right in the dumpster I'd imagine."

Jackie's mom, Melissa, is an English teacher here at Stronghold. Her faculty discount is the only reason she can afford to send Jackie. Private, Christian-based education costs a pretty penny, though I can't tell you why. Half of our graduating class got kicked out of public school.

"That or she'd crucify me," Jackie continues. "You know, demonstrate it for her classes. That'll give her the edge she's looking for. Really bring the story to life."

"Can I put the crown of thorns on your head?" I joke.

"Of course, you can, Mike." She drags the butt across the brick wall before tossing it on the ground. Pulling out her trusty bottle of perfume, she takes a whore bath. "I wouldn't want it any other way."

Retreating a few steps back, I cough through the haze of sickeningly sweet air. "I can't tell what smells worse. You or the trash."

"Shut the fuck up." Jackie slugs my shoulder as she passes.

"Get that out of your system," I warn her, walking a few paces ahead to avoid the tailwind of Deep Amber. "I don't want you disgracing your mother with that mouth."

"Too late for that."

I push open the side doors, stepping into the cool hall. Stronghold isn't exactly the world's most advanced school, but you wouldn't think that after seeing the tuition bill. Our principal, Principal Peters—or Double P as we like to call him behind his back—

runs a tight ship. No hemlines are out of place. They hold everyone to a ridiculous standard. Unless your parents are on the board. Then you can do whatever the fuck you want.

Politics ruin everything.

Jackie and I part ways, our class schedule differing for most of the day. I'll see her again at lunch.

I head for New Testament studies, not particularly excited.

Guys pass me left and right, none of them paying me any mind. As terrible as they are for self-expression, at least these uniforms look great on most of the boys here. The trick is to not let my gaze linger too long. Nothing is more awkward than a straight guy catching you staring.

But come on, who doesn't love a tailored suit?

I have to wonder if any of them are like me? If the studies are true, then statistically, there has to be another gay boy here somewhere. Does he wrestle with these same feelings of guilt and loneliness? Maybe they're as good as I am at hiding it. Maybe they don't give into temptation as easily as I do. Maybe they're red-headed with a nice pair of glasses and a cute smile…

Okay, reign it in Mike. You're drooling.

The classroom is almost full as I walk in, and Dr. Redford perches at his desk. He's a stern looking man in his mid-fifties, with salt and pepper hair and a gut that protrudes farther than his toes. Looking down on us it's almost like he's King Solomon himself, full of pomp and God-granted wisdom. His vests stretch so tight across his stomach, I'm always afraid of losing an eye when the buttons give out.

"Mr. Hernandez," he addresses me as I take an empty seat in the second row. He checks off his list of names.

"Good morning, sir," I respond, pulling out my textbook before hanging my bag on the back of my chair.

A few more students file in, and Dr. Redford greets them one at a time, working his way down the clipboard. His frameless glasses blend in so well with his pale face, I almost can't see them.

Dr. Redford is an accurate representation of the teachers here at Stronghold: old, balding men with way too many degrees to be teaching high school students, but enticed by the fat paychecks fueled by our parents' money. There are a few women in the faculty as well, but they're all the same too. Educated pastors' wives, whose children have all grown up and moved out. So, instead of taking up hobbies, they took up teaching.

Jackie's mom is the youngest teacher here by far, and she fought tooth and nail to get where she is. She's actually kind of amazing.

A boy scrambles through the entrance of the classroom just as Dr. Redford goes to lock the door. He gasps for breath, cheeks flushed with color as sweat drips down the side of his face. Shirt untucked and tie hanging loose around his neck, he puts his hands on his knees to help catch his breath.

Where have I seen him before?

"Mr. Myers." Dr. Redford closes the door behind him. "Setting the bar high this year, aren't we?"

Myers. That's right. He's Pastor Myers' son.

That explains why I don't recognize him, and I try

to ignore him as best I can. I just know he shares his father's hatred for the gays. Not worth my time.

"Sorry," the boy says, sprinting to the empty chair to my left.

Shit. Now, I'm stuck beside him for the rest of the semester. Perfect. Maybe I can convince someone to switch with me tomorrow. Dr. Redford won't notice if I don't wait too long.

"Ladies and Gentlemen—" Dr. Redford flips the lock on the door as he speaks. "—let me remind you of my tardiness policy. This door locks at precisely nine o' five. If you wish to be present for my class, you will make sure you are here prior to that time. Do I make myself clear?"

"Yes, sir," the class responds.

"Dickhead," someone mutters to my left.

"Excellent." He moves to the marker board. "Then, if you would please produce your syllabus, we will begin with the Gospel of Matthew."

WITH A BLOW OF THE WHISTLE, I HIT THE COLD WATER LIKE A TORPEDO. THE temperature has long lost its shocking effect on me, and I pulse my arms and legs to propel myself along the lane.

Water fills my ears, muffling the sound from the outside world. Each breath is in perfect rhythm with my stroke, which is only outmatched by my pounding heart.

There aren't many things I enjoy more than swimming. It gives me a sense of purpose, a definitive goal to reach for that doesn't involve anyone but myself. I'm the only factor affecting my performance. I'm the only one I have to depend on. It's just me and the water. It's simple.

Not like the rest of my life.

I burst through the surface, grabbing hold of the edge of the pool. Coach Schmidt is waiting for me as I climb out of the water, his stopwatch suspended in front of him and confusion twisting his bushy brows.

"What was that?" he asks.

"Huh?"

"That time," he clarifies. "You're up to almost a minute. Last year, you could do that blindfolded at forty seconds."

"Oh." That's weird. I felt like I was killing it. "It's just my first run," I say, still catching my breath. "Getting a feel for the pool again."

"That tells me you didn't practice over the summer." Coach resets his watch. "I can't get you into UGA with times like that."

I just nod along, grabbing my towel from the bench. "Sorry, Coach."

"Don't be sorry. Work harder." He pats my shoulder and then moves onto the next lane. "You look like a manatee out there, Davy! And I don't mean that as a compliment!"

UGA. Ugh. Why did he have to bring that up? My parents' dream school for me in the far away land of Athens. It feels worlds away.

Mom and Dad have been dreaming for us kids to attend UGA since before we were born. God, we spend every Saturday during the football season watching games as a family. Now, Thomas is on the team—in the loosest sense of the term—we'll be sure to take more road trips out there to watch them live.

I couldn't care less about football.

Swimming is my ticket in. I mean, maybe there's a chance I'd get in on merit alone, but let's be real. They throw money at athletes. My family may be well off, but that doesn't mean Dad isn't looking for every penny of scholarship money I can apply for.

It would destroy him if he knew the truth. I don't want to go.

UGA is their dream, but it never became mine. My heart beats for only one school—SCAD. Savannah College of Art and Design.

I've always had a talent for sketching and charcoal work. My walls back home are covered from baseboard to ceiling as proof. There's a perpetual graphite stain on my right hand from dragging it across page after page. Then there's the sketchpad in my messenger bag. The one that never leaves my side. That only comes out in private, most of the time late at night when I can't sleep. The sketches in that book are personal. Very personal.

I don't even dare leave it at home, for fear someone will go snooping. Mom's always going through my shit, especially my artwork. So, I carry it with me at all times, tucked safely away from prying eyes. Even if it were to fall into someone else's hands, I made the first few pages a decoy. Just a couple doodles I add to every now and again. You have to travel deep into the pages to get to anything shocking, and I've stuck those pages together with tape, so they don't fall open accidentally. I know it's a dangerous game to play, but I feel like the best hiding place is in plain sight.

I can never explain the feeling I get while drawing. It's this strange sensation down in my gut that makes me think anything is possible, and I can wish something into being just with the stroke of a pencil. Bring anything to life, even the things I only dream of.

Like… Sure, UGA has an art program. And, maybe, I can convince my parents to let me take it, but I'd never hear the end of it.

"That's a hobby, son. Not a career."

"Don't you want a job?"

"Are you going to cut off your ear like that nut job, Picasso?"

Coach's whistle chases away images of severed ears and canvas.

"Back in the water, Mike!" he yells.

I toss my towel aside and do my best to lose myself in the motions.

"DINNER TIME!" DAD'S VOICE ECHOES DOWN THE HALL.

I set my pencil aside, yawning. My drawing is taking shape nicely, smeared lines forming just the right shades. It'll take a few more hours to make it perfect, but then I'll be able to add to it my collection on the wall.

There's hardly any room left up there, the empty spaces covered in old *Kingdom Hearts* posters and dozens of sketches. My favorites hover above the headboard—a portrait of my *Abuela*, a watercolor piece from when I was fourteen, and this really awesome skyline sketch of Atlanta that garnered me the second-place prize at Stronghold's annual art contest. I lost to the blind freshman who finger-painted the crucifixion. But, honestly, how do you compete with something so heavy handed? Jesus wins at everything around here.

The hypnotizing aroma of spices greet me as I jog down the stairs. Dad lays plates out on the table, and Rosy pours everyone a glass of tea. Mom's not home yet, but we usually don't wait for her. She's been working late pretty frequently, and we're lucky if we get the chance to see her before she climbs into bed.

"Smells great, Dad," I say, pulling out a chair.

"I'm glad you think so." He smiles, taking his own seat. "Because you're on dish duty."

Rosy smiles maniacally as she takes her seat across the table. She must have volunteered me.

"Fair enough," I concede, reaching a hand out to her. She takes mine and then Dad's, and I do the same.

"You want to bless the food?" Dad asks.

I groan but nod my head in agreement. "Father," I begin, hands sweating. Despite my countless internal prayers, I hate doing it aloud. I always feel like I'm going to randomly burst into flames or get struck with boils. Maybe both. That would be my luck.

"We are so grateful for this chance to share a meal. We ask You to bless this food to our bodies, and our bodies to Your service. In your Son's holy and precious name, we pray, amen."

And thank you for Blondie. He was a lot of fun. Feel free to send more sexually confused seniors my way.

"Amen," Dad and Rosy echo.

No spontaneous combustion or random pustules, so I have blessings enough to count.

We all dive into our plates. Dad's made his special spaghetti which, in reality, is regular spaghetti sauce he adds some extra garlic and some smoked paprika to. It's one of my favorite meals he cooks. Anything's better than when he makes *lengua*. There's not enough cilantro in the world to cover the taste of cow tongue.

"How was your first day back, Mike?" Dad asks, a stray noodle hanging from the side of his mouth.

"It was pretty uneventful," I reply, twirling my fork until I have a clump of pasta clinging to it. "I didn't get locked out of Dr. Redford's first class this year, so that was good."

"Is he still locking the door?" Dad laughs. "I thought he got in trouble for that last year. What did the board say, he was holding kids hostage?"

I shrug, sopping up sauce with a piece of bread before stuffing it in my face.

"What about you, Rosemary?"

"It was awesome." Rosy beams. She's been waiting for the conversation to shift in her direction. "Dr. Thacker thinks I'll be able to make first chair by my Junior year! I told her I was shooting for sophomore, but we'll see what happens."

"*Estupendo!*" Dad exclaims. "That's so great, honey. How were the rest of your classes?"

Rosy recounts every step she took, and I drift off somewhere around third period. The details of my day play through like a slideshow, but all the faces and conversations end up blending together as I feel the creative itch pulling me back upstairs. It's not to finish the landscape sitting on my desk, but to add the final details to my latest sketch of Blondie. Just thinking about it has my cheeks burning.

The front door opens, and Rosy pauses her story. Mom trudges into the dining room, still dressed in her scrubs and looking like death warmed over.

"Hey, guys." She sinks into the seat across from Dad, her smile faint.

Dad hurries into the kitchen to grab her plate, planting a kiss on her forehead as he returns. "Glad to have you home," he tells her.

"What have I missed?" she asks, pushing her spaghetti around the plate with her fork.

"Oh, you know." I toss my napkin on top of the

remainder of my dinner. "Dr. Redford's locking us up again, Rosy is on her way to becoming the next Vivaldi, and I think someone in Rosy's fourth period called their teacher mom. So, that's pretty embarrassing."

"Sounds like an eventful day." Mom laughs.

Rosy backs the narrative up to the start of her day, and I grab my plate, relishing in an excuse to escape to the kitchen.

The sounds of my family drift away as the door swings closed. My plate clatters in the sink, and I fight the urge to groan at the mountain of pots and pans. Once the leftovers are separated into their respective containers, I fill one side of the sink, squeezing a few drops of soap in.

Next, I reach for the pair of headphones on the kitchen table, plugging them into my phone as I select the perfect dishwashing playlist.

Music makes everything better—even chores. The sweet sound of mandolin strumming starts as I begin my Fleet Foxes playlist. I've been on a folksy kick lately. Soon, I'm moving in rhythm, scrubbing and rinsing to the chorus' ebb and flow.

I don't notice Dad behind me until he dries the stack of dishes to my left. I pull an earbud out. "Thanks, Dad."

"It's a pleasure." He grins.

Sometimes, I forget how much I look like my dad. If it weren't for the ring of green surrounding my pupil, I would be a mirror image of him at my age. Of course, his hair is graying now, streaks of silver mixing into the warm brown. He's getting some serious crow's feet too, but that's the least of his worries. He always says wrinkles are the receipts of life. How else do you know you've lived?

"You okay?" He looks at me, that all-knowing-father gaze seeming to pry into my mind.

"Hm?" I wring out the sponge. "What do you mean?"

"I mean you seem a little distracted tonight. Spacey. Is everything all right?"

Dad has always been super perceptive. I kind of hate that about him. How am I supposed to get through my angsty teenage years of brooding and ignoring my parents if they're so understanding? Then again, I have my share of secrets I never plan to divulge. It's easy to be understanding when your child is well-behaved and straight.

I'm at least one of those things.

"Just had a weird day," I finally conclude, dunking a pot into the suds. "Don't worry about me."

"That's my job," Dad replies, squeezing my shoulder. "I'm not doing it right if I don't worry."

"I'm good," I assure him, plastering on my best smile.

That seems to convince him, so we continue the dishes in silence.

Once everything is clean, I dry my hands. "I'm going to go knock out some homework," I announce.

Dad's cell phone rings, and he doesn't even hear me.

I scale the stairs, heading back to the safety of my room. I can breathe so much easier with at least a wall between me and everyone else. It's the only time I don't have to lie.

The door closes behind me with a click. My parents don't believe in locks, but they're pretty cool about knocking before they come in. There have been some really close calls where that split second of hesitation has saved them from getting an eyeful of things they cannot un-see.

My current project is waiting for me on the drawing table, but I don't return to it. There's something else calling to me now, and I won't be able to focus on anything else until it's done.

The messenger bag is sitting where I left it. I rummage through the main pocket, pulling out my sketchpad. Shoving pillows aside, I climb onto my bed, being sure to angle myself away from the door as I flip through the pages. The one I'm searching for is near the back, and I gingerly pull it away from the tape sticking it to the previous page.

The lines are rough. I didn't have a lot of time when inspiration struck like lightning, but the base is passable. It's almost impossible to glean where the two bodies begin or end, limbs twisted up in each other. Faces meet, locked in a passionate kiss. The expressions are not quite where they need to be yet, but the intention is clear. My heart races.

It's a sketch of me and Blondie.

I set to work, emboldening the lines as I sharpen the two figures.

My cheeks flush as I replay those few glorious minutes in my head. I feel him on me, lips urgently navigating my neck like its uncharted territory. The hunger burning in his eyes that I can only imagine reflected in my own. The sounds escaping from deep in his throat when I touch him….

A quick rap on the door is a bitch slap from reality. I quickly flip the page while crossing my legs. On second thought, I grab a pillow and set it on my lap.

"Come in," I say, voice cracking.

"Hey, sweetheart." Mom's out of her scrubs, but she can't take off the exhaustion she wears on her face. "I'm about to head to bed."

"You're so old," I joke with her.

That makes her smile. "Four thirty comes awful early." She clutches the small of her back, staggering to the foot of my bed in an exaggerated display. "Someday, you'll be my age, and you'll know my pain. And, if you're really lucky, your kid will call you old too."

My kid. As in a child I have with a wife. The woman my parents are expecting me to marry. The thought sinks into my stomach as Mom looks at me, all the hopes and dreams she has for me and a family shining behind those eyes.

It's enough to kill me.

"If I should only be so lucky," I mutter, eyes falling from her gaze. My breath catches in my throat. I focus on moving air around the growing lump.

"Don't worry, Mike." She has obviously misread my melancholy reaction. "You have plenty of time to find the right girl. Who knows, maybe there's one closer than you think?"

I snort. "Me and Jackie are never gonna be a thing, Mom. You can give it a rest."

"I used to say the same thing about your father." She grins. "But I guess time will tell. Try not to stay up too late, sweetheart." She leans forward, pushing back my bangs to plant a kiss on my head. "Goodnight."

"Night, Mom."

My door closes behind her, and I stuff my sketchpad back into my bag, any longing to continue snuffed out.

The weight of her words has extinguished the creative spark once propelling me.

Nothing kills a boner faster than mom guilt.

I'll never be able to give her what she wants. The perfect family, a blushing bride, and grandchildren for her to take to Sunday school. I mean, sure, I can get married and fake it. Maybe even stomach a couple of kids. But that just seems cruel.

There's no easy answer.

A whimper escapes my throat, and a tear falls before I can blink it away. The sorrow is heavy tonight, swelling in my chest and squeezing the air from my lungs. Fingers search along the bed, latching onto the soft plush of a pillow. I draw the cushy square into my chest, wrapping my arms around it as more tears fall.

My lips move with silent words, a prayer I've recited a thousand times before.

But all my prayers go unanswered.

EIGHT

"Let's go, Michael." Dad's voice resonates through the door.

It's another glorious Sunday morning, and the last thing I want to do is leave my bed. But that's not an option, so I mutter a few choice words under my breath as I attempt to detach myself from the tangled sheets.

The first week of school has left me drained, and despite a Saturday of marijuana-fueled Netflix binging with Jackie and Tanner, I haven't really recovered.

I trudge down the hall and into the bathroom. Rosy is in front of the vanity, tracing the outline of her eyelid with a pencil.

It must really suck being a girl. You have to wake up so much earlier if you want to be pretty in the eyes of society.

"Mornin' Rosy," I mutter, flipping the handle of the shower. The head spurts to life with a hiss.

"Keep your pants on," she replies, focused on her work. "I'm almost finished."

Lowering the lid, I pop a squat on the toilet, watching

her move with such precision as she finishes one eye and moves to the other. "Doesn't that hurt?"

"Stabbing myself in the eyeball?" She laughs. "You get used to it after a while."

"Really?"

"No. It still hurts, and I would still rather throw myself down a flight of stairs."

"Then why do you do it?"

"Because Mom always says something if I don't." She winces, pulling the pencil away from her face. "Just be glad you're not a girl."

"I was just thinking that actually."

"All right." Rosy huffs, throwing the eyeliner back into her makeup bag. "Feel free to strip. I'm out of here."

"Hey, Rosy?"

She turns to me. "What?"

I hesitate. "You look great."

Something flickers across her face, but it vanishes under a scowl. "Shut up."

She closes the door behind her, and I peel off my pajamas before hopping under the steaming stream.

THUNDER RUMBLES, VIBRATING THE QUIET HALLWAY AS I MAKE MY WAY down to the Well. A yawn tears out of me like an animal, eyes filling with moisture I lazily wipe away. I stayed up too late last night, finishing the drawing of Blondie and me. Every detail had to be perfect, so I drove myself crazy sweating each stroke of my pencil.

Plus, I had to use my imagination to fill in the blanks

about certain…details. I mean, I copped a feel down there, but I had to go off memory. It's like when they build the dinosaurs at the museum. There's a basic idea, but really, you just fill in the blanks.

I clutch my messenger bag closer to my side. I can't believe I'm carrying around this kind of wondrous smut in the house of God, but what choice do I have? It's safer with me. At least that's what I keep telling myself.

You understand, don't you Big Guy? I mean, it's a drawing of something You created, so it can't be all that bad, right? Your creations are beautiful!

I walk past the door at the end of the hallway, knowing Jackie and Tanner aren't crazy enough to be outside in this weather. There are already a few students milling around the foosball table, but I spy Jackie sitting on a couch in the corner and talking to a guy with dark hair.

Tanner must be running late this morning. I gravitate toward Jackie as another clap of thunder makes the windows shake.

"—t's what I'm saying, I don't understand why people think that way," Jackie says. "People can't help what they feel. Oh…" She looks up at me. "Hey, Mike. You know Chris."

The dark-haired boy looks up as well, and I swallow a scowl.

"What's up, Mike?"

"Not much, Chris." My tone is short. What the hell is Jackie doing hanging out with this dipshit?

"I have to run," Chris says abruptly, rising from his seat. "We'll talk later, Jackie?"

"Sure." Jackie smiles at him as he turns to hurry

away.

"What was that all about?" I ask, flopping beside her. I pull my bag off my shoulder, laying it over the armrest. The farther away Chris Myers gets, the safer I feel.

"We were discussing something that happened in class Friday," Jackie explains, pulling out her phone. "We both have Theology third period, and the teacher's a total tool."

"Aren't they all?" I joke. "Your mother excluded."

"Nah, she's the biggest tool most of the time." Jackie laughs. "Her latest kick is to bug the snot out of me about auditioning for the winter musical. Can you imagine?"

"You have the voice for it."

I always tell her that. She has the kind of singing voice that shuts people up.

"Are you going to do it?"

"Fuck no," she whispers, eyeing Connie Milton as she passes. "I don't want to have to deal with the drama freaks. They're crazy."

"You love drama," I argue.

A flash of lightning fills the room. Jackie jolts, nearly falling out of her seat as the resounding thunder rolls.

"Not that kind." Her voice shrinks back to normal volume. "Besides, that would seriously cut into my free time, and I'm behind on so many shows, Mike. My DVR is just buried."

"At least you have your priorities in order," I say. "Don't you think that—"

A wailing siren cuts me off.

"Shit." Jackie's on her feet in a fraction of a second. "Shit, shit, shit." She flinches as another flash of lightning fills the room.

I stand to comfort her, but Arnold bursts through the doors in a tizzy. "Okay, everyone! We need to take refuge in the stairwell, away from the windows. This is not a drill."

Oh, great. That's not going to help.

"I'm going to die," Jackie whimpers. "Oh my God, we're going to die. Mike, I'm going to die before I've had a threesome!"

"Come on." I grab her trembling arm. Her filter shuts down whenever she freaks out. "How many times have we been through this? It's just a tornado warning. No big deal."

"Tell that to the people in *Twister*," Jackie says, the crack in her voice evidence that she's on the verge of tears.

"I bet I can find two willing participants to make your final wish come true."

She smacks my shoulder. "Ha-ha."

The rest of the students are clearing out, moving down the hallway to the stairwell. Tornadoes are pretty commonplace in the warm months, so nobody is freaking out. Except Jackie, that is.

"We're all going to die," she mutters as she huddles under the metal stairs in the cramped space. Her fingers keep grasping the silver crucifix hanging around her neck.

I crawl in next to her, wrapping an arm around her shoulder. She's kind of causing a scene while the rest of our sardined peers are laughing and joking around. Except for Sandy, who's gathered a couple of her girlfriends into a prayer circle.

Jesus, she's annoying.

"We're not going die," I assure Jackie. "If anything, the roof gets torn off, and we all get to go home. Hey, maybe it'll take Pastor Myers right off the pulpit. Wouldn't that be hilarious?"

She slaps my knee. "You're not helping."

"Wanna join Sandy's prayer circle? It's bound to keep us safe."

"Oh, go fuck a duck, Mike."

"Deep breaths." I suck air through my teeth, hoping she'll follow along. "In and out."

The two of us probably look like we're taking a Lamaze class. That's bound to start rumors.

I'm lightheaded after a few minutes, but then the siren fades, and Jackie slowly releases the death grip on my hand. Arnold ushers us back into the Well, and everyone returns to business as usual. Before long, Tanner shows up in another wave of students.

"You okay, Jackie?" he asks, giving her a hug.

"I'm fine." She sighs, breaking away from him.

"You should have seen it." Tanner's voice drips with excitement. "The sky was totally green outside. The clouds were spinning all over the place, and then this huge tree fell right beside me on the way here. It was awesome!"

"I need to sit down." Jackie moves back to the couch in the corner.

We follow her, Tanner still chattering on about his near-death experience. Something crunches under my foot, and my heart skips a beat when I realize it's a pencil from my bag. It lays haphazardly, contents strewn across the floor. Someone must have knocked it off the armrest in the panic. I stoop down to gather.

"Let me help you." Tanner takes a knee.

"No!" I say a little too loud. "No," I repeat in a semi-calm tone. "It's cool. I got it." I scoop my phone charger, the spilled box of pencils, and the random assortment of papers. Running through the list in my head, I take stock. Wait a second... No sketchbook.

Oh fuck. It's missing.

I check underneath the couch. Nothing. I check each pocket of the bag. Nothing.

This can't be happening. It's gone.

Forget skipping a beat, my heart has completely stopped.

Rationalization kicks in.

Maybe I didn't put it back last night?

No, I clearly remember it being there this morning. This is a disaster. An epic travesty. If someone goes too deep that book will literally ruin my life. And quite possibly the innocence of whoever finds it.

And it has my name and phone number penciled on the back cover. Shit, this is bad!

"You all right, Mike?" Tanner sits beside Jackie, his big blue eyes watching me through thick frames. "You look like they cancelled Once Upon a Time."

"Thank you," mutters Jackie.

"Y-Yeah," I stutter, standing back up. "And, for the last time, that's not funny! I'm just missing my sketchpad is all."

"That's weird." Jackie leans forward. "Are you sure it was in there?"

"No."

Yes, I am.

"I probably left it at home."

I didn't. I'm one hundred percent certain I didn't.

"It's no biggie."

It's a huge McFreakin' deal. God! Why am I so stupid to carry around something that is going to incriminate me? I'm doomed. When that book surfaces, that's it. Game over. It's been nice knowing you, Georgia. Mike, out.

"All right, guys." Arnold's voice booms through the microphone. "That was an exciting way to kick off the morning, huh? Now, let's keep that excitement going with some scripture!"

I sink into the back row, brain spinning out of control as Arnold makes a complete fool of himself in front of everyone. Once he finishes, we split into groups, and it's everything I can do to walk like a zombie to the corner.

Maybe this bean bag will open and swallow me, smothering me in its clutches. That'd be awesome. There's no telling what expression is on my face, but no one seems keen on speaking to me.

All I can picture is the stupid drawing I finished last night. I mean, let's be honest, none of the sketches in the back of that book are family friendly. But the drawing of me and Blondie is by far the most graphic.

Why did I have to draw that? Damn my teenage horniness!

Fat Tom drones on, and I just keep running every possible scenario over and over in my head. What if Arnold finds my sketches? What if he goes straight to my parents with it? I can see it now.

Horror taking over their features as they realize what it is. Hopes and dreams fading from my mother's eyes, replaced by disdain and contempt for her son. Disappointment seeping into the lines on my father's face when he realizes what I am. The look on my face when they kick me out of the house for—

"Mike?"

There's a hand on my knee. Heather Shifflet's, to be specific. She's looking at me with big round eyes. I blink, realizing tears are falling.

"Are you okay?"

"Sorry." I quickly blot them. "Allergies are really acting up," I whisper, trying to smile.

Heather nods, her attention turning back to Fat Tom. I scold myself, wiping my face. Falling apart isn't an option, Mike.

With as much dignity as I can muster, I crawl my way out of my seat, moving to the double doors leading into the hallway.

A splash of cool water, and I'll be good as new. No need to freak out just yet. Maybe no one found the sketchpad? Maybe it fell out in the car? Maybe a wormhole opened up and sucked it into soul-crushing oblivion? There are too many possibilities floating around to resign myself to the gallows.

God, please don't let anyone find it. I'd rather it spontaneously combust than have it fall into the wrong hands. Oh! Could You make that happen? I mean, after Elijah's alter, I figure a sketchbook would be no problem for you.

The men's room is deathly quiet, and my sniffling bounces off the walls. After a quick glance under the stall, I allow myself a moment to gather my wits. A steady drip falls from the sink on the left, and the rhythm is somewhat comforting. I try to match my breathing to it.

"Get ahold of yourself, Mike," I whisper, hoping I can talk myself down from this latest episode of hysteria. I turn the knob on the faucet.

Really, what am I so afraid of here? I mean, what's the worst that could happen? Maybe no one will find it. Or, maybe, it'll get thrown away by the custodian. Or, maybe, Jackie or Tanner picked it up, and they're playing a joke on me. What if it gets passed around the youth group like a plague? Everyone will know I like dick, my life will be over, and I'll have to—

The door of the bathroom opens, and I plunge my face into the stream of water. It's freezing, but at least it won't look like I've been crying. I flush my eyes a few times, and the sound of footsteps echo behind me.

You're okay, Mike. You can keep this up. Just breathe. You're swimming, and you just have to breathe.

The water shuts off with a twist of my wrist, and I grasp to my left for paper towels. My hand meets something warm.

"Um, I don't think that's what you're looking for."

"Sorry," I mutter, squinting through the water in my eyes at the blurry blob I just unintentionally molested. The boy hands me a towel, and I wipe my face.

Chris Myers smirks as I crumple the paper.

Fuck me with a chainsaw. Of all the people to see me in manic mode, why did it have to be *him*?

"What's got you all hot and bothered, Hernandez?"

"N-Nothing," I stammer, heat scalding across my face. "I was just trying to stay awake."

"I see." His eyebrow cocks.

Oh, great. This is exactly what I need, to draw attention from the son of the man who, chances are, will lead my lynch mob. I have to get out of here.

"See you around," I half whisper, eyes trained on the floor. Not waiting for his response, I bolt for the door.

There's no going back to Sunday school now. I can't bear to be around all the people who could know my secret by this point. Plus, there's only twenty minutes before service starts upstairs. Somehow, I have to put my mask back together before my parents see me.

My phone buzzes in my pocket, and a text message from Jackie pops up.

> Where did you disappear to, Houdini? 10:34am

I tap back my response.

> Fat Tom was boring me to tears. I had to bail before I started snoring. I'll see you guys in service. 10:35am

I hardly have time to take another step before it vibrates again.

> You made a wise decision. The only reason I'm not snoozing is because there's this weird purple spot in his moustache. I think he may have some jelly stuck in there. It's fascinating. 10:36 AM

I snicker, picturing Jackie's intense stare that Fat Tom surely suspects to be undivided attention to the lesson. And, for just a second, I almost forget all about the sketchbook.

It's a short-lived second.

NINE

By the end of service, my stomach hurts so badly I think I may have given myself an ulcer. I tell Jackie and Tanner I'm not feeling well, and I must look pretty convincing because they both just nod and abandon the subject. I catch Mom in the hallway as she comes from her week of double duty in the children's wing. She sees my face and jumps right into Supermom mode. She wants to take me to the emergency room, but I convince her to take me home instead.

I spend the rest of the day in bed, a blanket pulled over my head. Only moving to puke my brains out every fifteen minutes.

Mom drops off a bowl of chicken noodle soup around seven that I don't touch. She rests the back of her hand against my forehead then kisses it softly.

I relish in what could possibly be the last time my mother looks at me with sympathy. As soon as the truth shit hits the fan, I don't think she'll even be able to look at me again.

Monday morning comes with the promise of certain

doom streaming through the window along with the sunlight. My body moves as if I'm on autopilot, knotting my tie and pulling on my blazer. Dad gives me a strange look as I clear the landing, pulling his cell phone away from his ear.

"You sure you want to go to school, Mike? I heard you ralphing all night, so I'm all for you staying home."

"I'm fine," I say, voice puny.

"If you say so." He puts the phone back to his ear. "Sorry about that…."

Rosy steps away from me, holding her index fingers in the shape of a cross. "Stay away, patient zero."

I roll my eyes as she climbs into the backseat.

Once we're on the road, I press my head against the cool window in an attempt to quell the nausea.

"I can still run you home, *hijito*," Dad offers as we pull up to the sidewalk. "I'll just cancel my first meeting—"

"I'll be fine, Dad," I interrupt while opening the car door. "Love you."

He gives me another strange look. "Love you too, son."

I distance myself from Rosy. I want to be far away from her when the bomb hits. No need for her to be collateral damage. Resting my hands against the handle of the door, I hesitate. This could very well be the last time I set foot in this school. If that book fell into the wrong hands, my secret is all over Stronghold by now.

I've stashed all my savings in my bag, so if things head south, I can just leave from here. Disappear into the chaotic streets of Atlanta, never to be seen again. A plan I developed between trips to the toilet last night. Honestly, it's a shitty plan, but a plan nonetheless.

With a final breath of resolve, I push the door in. My pace is frantic as I hit the hallway, head down and refusing to make eye contact with anyone as I go. There are people laughing on the left.

Are they laughing at me?

I don't stop to find out. Someone's waiting beside my locker, and I mutter a curse when I realize it's Jackie.

"Hey, Lazarus," she greets me, leaning against the row of metal doors. "Glad to see you're back from the dead."

"Hi, Jackie," I say, turning my lock until it opens with a click. It's a struggle to keep my voice level. "What's up?"

"Oh, nothing," she says, brushing off the front of her skirt. "Just wondering when you were planning to tell me your little secret."

Shit. So much for hoping. This is it, the beginning of the end. Prepare for impact!

"What secret?" I play dumb, intent on enjoying every last moment of normalcy before my life crumbles.

She stares me down, and a bead of sweat rolls down the side of my head.

"Tanner told me all about it yesterday."

Tanner? What the fuck does he know? I swear to God, if he picked up my book, I'm going to kill the bastard!

"He said you were thinking about abandoning me for SCAD? Come on! We had a plan, dude!"

The balloon in my chest deflates. She's talking about college, not Mike's homo-extravaganza, starring yours truly. I definitely think I'm getting an ulcer.

"You caught me." I grab a text book from my locker, stashing it in my bag.

"You should know by now you can't keep things from me." Jackie grins, pleased with herself. "I know you better than anyone else."

"You sure do." I let out a nervous laugh.

Has she ever really known me?

"Hey, Jackie."

A new voice makes me spin. Chris Myers is standing next to Jackie, tie hanging loose around his neck.

"You finish your quiz for theology?"

Oh God, he's the last person I want to see.

Our awkward encounter in the bathroom is on action replay in my head, and it summons heat to my face.

"Actually," Jackie says as she kicks off the locker, "that reminds me, I need to go finish it. I'll just have to go visit the little ladies'...."

Jackie slinks away, and I contemplate just bolting now. But that might look bad, and the last thing I need is to draw more attention from Chris.

"How's it going, Mike?"

Fucking horrible, dickhead.

"Fine," I reply, busying myself with the contents of my locker. There's never been a better time to alphabetize my textbooks.

"Cool, cool." His arms fold over his chest. "Hey, you're an artist, right?"

"W-Why do you ask?" I don't look at him, just keep rearranging.

"I have this project I'm working on." Chris leans against the locker beside me, tossing a strand of dark hair out of his face. "Maybe you could help me with a part of it? I suck when it comes to drawing. Like, not even stick figures come out right."

"Oh. Um, yeah, sure. Whatever."

"Awesome. We can talk about it this afternoon."

"This afternoon?"

"Yeah." He kicks off the locker, swinging his backpack over his shoulder. "Jackie invited me over to Tanner's after school. I assumed you'd be there."

"Right." My locker closes with a click. "Tanner's."

"Sweet." Chris looks down at his watch. "We'd better hurry if we don't want to get locked out."

I nod, trying to shake the weird vibe he's giving.

He's almost...nice.

TEN

CHRIS AND JACKIE ARE WAITING BY MY LOCKER AFTER THE LAST BELL. They're locked in a deep conversation, but my arrival ends it.

"Hey, guys." I stow my Algebra book, the pages stained with sweat from my hands.

"Mike!" Jackie smiles. "I was starting to think you'd ditched us."

"Ms. Abernathy held me after class," I lie. "She wanted to talk about the pop quiz from last Friday."

In reality, I was dry heaving into a trashcan outside the teacher's lounge, but that detail isn't important.

"Hey, Jackie," Chris interjects, "I can give you guys a ride if you want."

"Oh, thank God." Jackie laughs. "I'm convinced Tanner's driving has shaved years off my life. I found my first gray hair the other day, and I just know he's the reason."

"You sure it's not your pack-a-day habit?" I tease, resulting in a slap to my nipple. "Ow!"

"Well, it's settled then. I will be your chauffeur."

Chris grins at Jackie, and I wonder if maybe that's why he's being so nice to me. He wouldn't be the first boy who wanted to get in her pants.

The tension in my stomach eases up, ever so slightly, as the day goes on. I even keep a couple bites of lunch down for a few minutes. So, that's an improvement. But something about being around Chris amplifies the feeling.

"All right," Jackie announces. "Let's find the sasquatch and blow this joint!"

CHRIS DRIVES A PRETTY NICE CAR. IT'S AN OLDER BMW, BUT IT'S WELL TAKEN care of and has leather seats, so that's cool. We're fighting our way northbound on the 400, which is kind of terrible. Thankfully, his taste in music doesn't suck, so at least there's that to keep us entertained.

Jackie sits in the front seat, and I'm exiled to the back, which is totally fine. I swipe through my Facebook feed, fully expecting someone to have posted a hateful message by now, but there's nothing.

Maybe this sketchbook thing won't be a problem after all. I mean, it's been a full twenty-four hours. If it hasn't ruined my life by now, then who knows?

Chris and Jackie are going on about something in Theology class again, and honestly, I'm tuning them out. I took the class last year, and it triggered my first existential crisis, so I'm not looking to re-open that can of worms.

It's probably right up Chris's alley. Being the pastor's son, he must have no trouble following blindly. His beliefs are crystal clear, I'm sure.

My beliefs are murky at best. I mean, yes, I've been a card-carrying Christian my entire life, but that doesn't mean I don't have my doubts. Lately, more so than usual.

It's not that I don't believe in You, Big Guy. It's more to the fact I find it hard to believe in anything. Like, at all. Apathy and ignorance are just so much easier.

We pull into Tanner's driveway before I can get too lost in the deep end of the theologian's swimming pool.

"Wait, go back," Jackie says, opening her door. "What do you mean it's like gaslighting?"

"Think about it," Chris replies as we climb the steps to the front door.

I'm a few feet ahead, trying to outrun the conversation.

"They start when we're young, telling us all about how God is this enormous thing we can't even wrap our head around, and we're all doomed to suffer forever in a horrifying place if we don't do exactly what God says, which really means what *they* say. And then, somewhere along the way, they switch it on you! Now, God is this loving and benevolent force who takes you as you are. So, you end up thinking you're this terrible person who can't do anything right. And this God has condemned you to an eternity of suffering, but He's also just and merciful, so obviously—"

I open the door, not bothering to knock. Tanner's sound system echoes through the house. He's probably already up to his neck in zombies.

"—even thought about it that way."

The noise drowns out Jackie's voice, and I start up

the stairs to Tanner's room.

He's hunched over in his gaming chair, transfixed on the avatar who's currently being munched on by a pus-oozing, maggot-covered corpse.

God, I love zombies.

"I'm tagging in," I tell him, picking up the spare controller from his desk.

He doesn't even look over. "About fucking time. Come get this bitch off me."

Jackie and Chris enter the room, still locked in their discussion.

"What are they talking about?" asks Tanner, grabbing a fistful of Doritos from the bag in his lap.

"Something from Theology class," I reply, hacking a zombie in half with a cleaver.

"Gross." Crumbs spew from his mouth. "Hey, losers. How about we leave school at school, and you guys help me stop a zombie invasion here?"

"I suck at that game." Jackie plops down on the bed. "Besides, you always yell at me when I play."

"That's because you always kill us instead of the zombies."

"You two are a lot easier to kill. Let's play Kart Racer. I always win at that one."

"What about you, Chris?" Tanner looks over his shoulder. "Does the heart of a zombie hunter beat inside you?"

"Uh, not so much." Chris shakes his head. "I don't like anything gory."

"Fuck!" My character's head gets separated from his body, blood spewing onto the screen.

"Spoken like a true P.K." Tanner laughs.

"P.K.?" Chris echoes.

"Preacher's Kid," Tanner answers, pausing the game. "Wait, you've never heard that before?"

Chris gives him a puzzled look. "Guess not."

"Lame." Tanner frowns. "That means we've failed to emotionally scar you. No worries, Chris. I'll personally see to it that you get the tormenting you deserve!"

"Oh, please." Jackie leans forward, smacking Tanner's shoulder. "You couldn't torment someone even if you tried. You don't have the attention span."

"True," he agrees, controller now smeared in orange dust. For someone whose bedroom is always immaculate, he sure doesn't mind cheesy residue.

"Maybe we can just watch a movie," Jackie suggests, "and get blazed?"

"On a school night, Jackie?" Tanner laughs. "You're incorrigible."

"Yeah, yeah. Now, move your ass."

He pauses the game, and I set my controller down. I can't help watching Chris and Jackie. They sit on the bed, Chris angled toward her as if she's some kind of magnet. Every time she moves, he counters her. I was stupid not to see it sooner. Of course, he's into her. The entire junior class is into Jackie. Though, she won't give them the time of day.

"When you say get blazed…" Chris leans into Jackie.

"It's exactly what you think." She laughs. "Do you not partake, P.K.?"

"Not really." He smiles, cheeks burning scarlet. "Guess I am kind of lame."

"Nonsense." Jackie places her hand over his. "You're just not a horrible person like the rest of us. Don't worry, we won't judge. Much."

"I might," Tanner says from his closet. "But I'm only

going to call you a pussy behind your back."

"Ugh!" Jackie's face twists in disgust. "What did I tell you about using that word, Tanner Mitchell?"

"Uh oh." I laugh. "She broke out the middle name, Tan. I'd run if I were you."

"Fuck that." He snickers, carrying in his shoebox. "This is my house, and I'll use whatever language I want. If you don't like it, you can go lick a pu—"

"That's it!" Jackie flings herself at him, wrapping around his legs to pull him to the ground. They roll over each other in a playful tousle.

"Ow! Jackie, that was my eye!"

"Cry me a river!"

I rescue the shoebox from the scuffle, carrying it to the safety of the bed. Chris watches the two of them wrestle, hands tangled in a nervous clump. I grind a nugget and ignore them.

"Do they do this often?"

"You'll get used to it," I tease, portioning out a couple pinches of strong-smelling greenery. Then, my smile fades when I remember who I'm talking to.

He isn't someone to get chummy with, Mike. Remember that.

Jackie's got Tanner in a headlock at this point. "Who's your president?"

"I'm...not...saying it!" he manages through her hold.

"You're looking a little blue, Tan," I point out.

"Who's your president?"

"...you are."

"Damn right!" She releases him.

Tanner's glasses hang off the side of his face as he comes up for air.

Jackie rises to her feet. "Now, then." She brushes off the edges of her uniform skirt. "Where were we before I was so rudely interrupted?"

"I think you bruised my windpipe." Tanner rubs his throat and winces.

"That was intense," Chris says.

"Sorry you had to see that." Jackie pats Chris on the head. "But, sometimes, I just have to put a man in his place."

"Amen." I raise the freshly rolled joint. "Now, let's get this show on the road."

"Do I need to leave?" Chris asks, rising from his seat.

"Only if you want to." Jackie moves to open the window. "Like I said, horrible influences."

"Feel free to hang out," Tanner says, clambering to his feet. "This stuff isn't strong enough to give you a contact high."

"All right, cool." He retakes his place, still looking like a cat in a room full of rocking chairs.

Jackie lights the end, taking a long drag before leaning her head out the window. "That's just what I needed to end my shitty Monday."

"No kidding," I agree, taking the next toke. My lungs burn, but I don't choke like normal. I aspire to be as adept a stoner as Jackie one day.

"Sure you don't want some, P.K.?" Tanner offers.

"I'm good." Chris waves his hand. "With my luck, my dad will catch me the minute I walk in the door. Better not risk it."

"Oh, yeah." Jackie looks back at him. "I keep forgetting your dad is Pastor Myers. What's that like?"

"I'm sure it's not as bad as you imagine."

"I have a pretty vivid imagination," Jackie replies.

"He's like any other parent, I guess."

"So, can you, like, date?" Tanner exhales a noxious cloud.

"Haven't really had anyone interested," Chris admits. "So, I guess I don't really know."

"I find that hard to believe," Jackie chimes in, sitting next to him on the bed. "A handsome guy like you must beat girls off with a stick."

"I'm afraid not." He laughs.

Jackie grabs the sides of Chris's face, adjusting him to stare into her eyes. He gulps, the quickest flash of fear changing his features.

After a few seconds, Jackie releases him with a shrug. "Meh, I don't get it. You're adorable."

"T-Thanks," Chris mutters, edging away from Jackie.

Why would he do that?

Tanner offers me the joint before I can dissect Chris's behavior any further. Another hit, and I forget all about Chris, the tension in my stomach finally easing.

"Well, we need to solve this conundrum," Jackie continues. "Tanner, you're the resident gossip whore. What's the rumor mill churning out these days regarding our friend, Chris?"

"I haven't really heard of anyone pining after him," Tanner answers, taking a seat at his computer. "But give me five minutes, and I'll cast a few lines out there to see who's biting."

"Don't you worry, Chris." Jackie leans on his shoulder. "By the end of the night, we'll have you bumping uglies. I mean, erm, *courting* with the best."

"Uh, thanks." Chris smiles, shrugging Jackie off as he stands. "But I have to hit the road. Dad will expect me home for dinner."

"You sure you don't want to stick around to see who I have?" Tanner asks.

"I'm already going to be late." He trips over his feet stepping toward the door. "But I'll see you guys at school tomorrow."

"Sure thing." Jackie rises to give him a hug.

He breaks away, giving a nod to Tanner before leaving the room.

"Kid's way too uptight," Tanner says after Chris leaves.

"Totally," Jackie agrees, taking the joint from me.

I'm flying pretty high at this point, so I just nod along with what they're saying.

"I just think he needs a little pussy." Tanner laughs, typing away.

"Seriously?" Jackie's livid. "Mike, hold this." She returns the joint.

"Sorry." Tanner smirks like a smart-ass. "It slipped."

Jackie tackles him, chair and all falling to the floor.

I take another hit, watching Chris pull out of the driveway.

"Who's your president?"

ELEVEN

> Hey, it's Chris. I got your number from Jackie. Do you think you could come over and help me with that project for school today? 2:21 AM

THE TEXT COMES IN THE MIDDLE OF THE NIGHT, SO NATURALLY, I DON'T READ it until the next morning. I squint at the message for a solid thirty seconds and still can't comprehend it, so I just respond with a thumbs-up emoji. An hour later, what I just agreed to clicks in my head.

I'm going into deep enemy territory—the home of Pastor Myers. The thought makes the back of my neck itch.

Tension builds through the rest of my morning, knotting my stomach. Rosy and I climb out of Dad's car, and I head straight for the dumpster pad. I have to do something about this Myers situation.

"Morning," Jackie puffs.

"Hey." I pat the side of my messenger bag—a nervous habit. It's lighter than usual without my sketchbook, but I have to remind myself it still hasn't resurfaced. "What are you doing after school?"

"I'm going to go hang out with Brad and his friends," she says, typing on her phone with her free hand. "Why?"

"No reason."

Shit. There has to be a buffer between me and Chris. I don't know if I can make it through an afternoon alone at *Casa de Myers*.

"You've been kinda jumpy lately." Jackie flicks the end of her cigarette. "What's going on?"

"N-Nothing," I lie. I'm getting really sick of everyone asking that question. Can't I have my emotional breakdown in peace? "Just haven't been sleeping very well, I guess."

Jackie pauses, watching me, and then shrugs. "It's probably all that coffee you drink. I'm surprised your heart hasn't burst out of your chest. It's not good for you, ya know."

"Seriously?" I snap. "Look who's talking. You'll be lucky to make it to forty at this rate. Your lungs must look like a coal miner's!"

"Jesus, Mike." Jackie raises her hands in defense. "I was only teasing."

"Right. Sorry."

This whole book situation has me seriously on edge.

"You sure you're okay?"

Maybe I should just tell her. I mean, of all people, Jackie will be understanding. Hell, she'll probably be thrilled for me. She'll want to talk about which boys I think are cute and plan my dream gay wedding—

which would definitely involve us riding in on a unicorn.

But secrets never stay between two people. And, although I love Jackie to pieces, I don't trust her to keep this under wraps.

I can't tell her. Not right now.

I nod my head. "Yeah, of course."

"Well, all right then." She snuffs the cherry on the wall.

"So, how are things going?" I ask, desperate to change the subject. "With Brad, I mean."

"They're going, I guess." Jackie pulls out her phone again, tucking a strand of her tawny hair behind her ear. "Why? Are you jealous?"

"Gross." I laugh. "No thanks. I know where those hands have been."

"I'm way out of your league, anyway." Jackie grins.

"Something like that."

"Come on, Mike. Let's get inside. It's Tuesday, and the lunch ladies will be by any second to dump the spoiled milk." She grabs her purse. "I, for one, would rather not be here to watch."

TWELVE

THE LAST PERIOD BELL RANG FIVE MINUTES AGO, AND I CAN'T THINK OF AN excuse, *any* excuse, to delay the inevitable.

Maybe I can smash a hand in my locker? A trip to the hospital would be better than what's ahead of me.

But alas, I'm a wuss and can't bring myself to follow through. Damn my low pain tolerance. That's what I get for not playing a contact sport.

"Hey, Mike!" Chris catches me outside the school. His shirt already haphazardly untucked, jacket hanging off one shoulder. "You ready to head out?"

"Yeah." I nod, looking back toward the school. Maybe Jackie changed her plans, and she'll swoop in to save me. But that's a fat chance. "Let's get this over with."

"What was that?"

"I said, 'Can't wait to get started!'"

"That's the spirit!" Chris smiles, clapping me on the shoulder.

The weather is still steamy enough I'm sweating by the time we get to Chris's car. He cracks the windows and starts the AC as soon as the engine turns over. The leather is roasting my ass like a rotisserie chicken.

"So, what exactly is this project of yours?" I ask. The more information I gather now, the less time I have to spend in the house of Myers. For some reason, I've been picturing a portrait of Hitler hanging above their fireplace, right next to Jesus. But that's a bit of a stretch. Donald Trump portrait? That's a definite possibility.

"It's for my mom, actually," Chris says, pulling out of the parking lot. "Sorry for the lie. Her birthday is next week, and I was hoping I could commission you to sketch something for me."

"Commission?" That's not what I expected.

"Yeah, I saw that portrait you did of your grandmother last year for the art midterm. It was crazy good. So, I want you to do one for my mom. If that's okay."

"Oh." I lean back in my chair. "Why didn't you just say that to begin with?"

"Because it may have sounded creepy for me to walk up to you and say, 'Hey, can I pay you to draw my mother?'"

I snort, and Chris laughs.

"I definitely would have been creeped out."

"See? It sounds better if you just say it's a project."

"Well, just to warn you, I haven't done a portrait in a while. So, I can't promise the quality." That's a lie, too. Honestly, I haven't been able to bring myself to lift a pencil since my sketchbook went missing. So that's a thing.

"I'm sure you'll do fine." Chris waves off my warning. "Besides, if it's junk, I'll just spatter it with paint and call it an abstract piece."

"Hey!" I fake offense. "That's my theoretically terrible artwork you're talking about!"

We share another laugh. Maybe this won't be so bad. At least, that's what I think until we pull up to his house, and I see his mom's station wagon in the driveway. The fish symbol prominently displayed beside the 'I support traditional marriage' bumper sticker is a nice touch. All that's missing is a confederate flag, and they'd have the complete bigot set.

I follow Chris up the stairs of the front porch, and we step into the foyer.

"Take your shoes off," He bends down to untie his before adding, "please."

Following suit, I add my loafers to the stack of shoes already by the door. The carpet is plush shag under my feet. The house smells...old. But not unpleasant.

"Chris? Is that you, sweetheart?"

"Hey, Mom!" he calls down the hall.

"I need to talk to you," Ms. Myers replies. "Come here, please."

Chris sighs. "Hey, I'll just be a second. Make yourself at home."

I nod, and suddenly, I'm left alone in the alien surroundings of my pastor's home. Which means it's time to snoop.

I step into the living room, simultaneously disappointed and relieved at the lack of Nazi paraphernalia. Even more shocking is that everything feels...*normal*. The furniture is older, but well-maintained. There are family photos hung in clusters on the wall, and a mantle full of knickknacks above the fireplace.

Several ribbons with Chris's name on them rest on a

bookshelf. I get close enough to read them, but Chris catches me.

"Ready to head upstairs?" he asks.

I try to look innocent. "Y-Yeah. Of course."

We climb the creaky staircase, and Chris opens the door when we reach the top of the stairs. His bedroom is tidy, the ceiling slanting down on either side of the room. Three bookshelves, stuffed to the gills, cover the wall to the far end, the rows of book covers creating a spectrum of colors. To the right, sits a modest laptop on an old desk and a rickety-looking computer chair with duct tape covering several holes in the upholstery. Across from that, under the octagonal window, sits his bed. Posters cover the rest of the walls, mostly bands I've never heard of.

"Come on in," Chris invites, moving to the closet in the corner. He opens the door and digs through a pile of boxes. "I have a photo I wanted you to use for reference." He sets a plastic tub on the desk. With a snap, the lid comes off, and he sorts through the pictures.

"When's her birthday?" I ask, wringing my hands together to keep them busy. My stomach is in knots even though I haven't seen Pastor Myers yet.

"Not 'til next week," Chris answers, extracting a photo from the stack. He hands me the print. "I think that one's the best."

I hold the photo up to eye level. Wow, his mother was striking in her youth. She can't be more than twenty in this photo, dark hair pulled back off her face and wearing a beautiful blue sundress.

"She's stunning," I tell him.

"If you say so." Chris laughs. He looks back to the

closet then stomps his foot. "Damn! I bought a big sketchpad for you to use. I must have left it in the trunk. Be right back!"

He scurries down the stairs, leaving me alone again.

My nerves propel me to pace.

You can really learn a lot from looking at someone's bedroom. If you were looking at mine, you would know, first off, I am an artist. The second thing you would know is I don't keep up with my laundry, and there are socks under the bed you should never touch.

Chris's room feels familiar, though I can't quite place the reason why. The bookshelves are neat and organized, but when I get close, most of the books look beaten to Hell and back. He must reread them often. Cups, pens, and textbooks clutter the desk. A small stand by his bed holds a stack of paperbacks, the one on top dog-eared to hold his place. It's a poetry book, but I don't catch the title before I hear his footsteps on the stairs.

"Sorry about that," he huffs, carrying the large pad. "Is this size okay? I kinda just let the lady at the shop pick it out for me. I'm clueless when it comes to this kind of thing."

"That'll be fine," I tell him, grabbing the photo from the desk. "Did you want me to go ahead and start on it now?"

"If you wouldn't mind, that would be awesome. Is fifty dollars enough?"

"It's plenty." I take the pad from him, digging in my bag for a pencil set.

"I can clear off the desk if you need me to," Chris offers.

"It's fine," I assure him, setting my bag on the

ground and crouching down. "I do my best work on the floor anyway."

"Cool." Chris sits down on the edge of his bed, grabbing a small remote control. "Um, do you mind if I put on some music? I have to work on the rest of her present, and it always helps me think."

"Sure." I drag my 4H pencil—perfect for outlining— across the blank page. "It doesn't bother me."

Chris presses a button, and a familiar strumming plays from the set of speakers on top of the bookshelf.

I stop, my ears perking up like a dog. "Is this Fleet Foxes?"

"You know them?" Chris asks.

"Hell yeah." I can't help bobbing my head to the infectious tones. "They're my favorite."

"Excellent." He picks up a notebook from the floor by his bed. "I always listen to them when I'm writing. They just put me in the mood, you know?"

"Writing?" I pause. "What do you write?"

"Just poems and stuff." Chris blushes, looking down at his socks. "It's a hobby. Nothing serious."

Poetry? He doesn't exactly strike me as the poetic type. Then again, before this week, he really didn't strike me as any type other than a guilty-by-association bigot.

That's pretty small-minded of me.

"Is that the rest of your mom's gift?"

Chris nods, cheeks still flushed. "It's lame, I know. But I've been doing it since I was six, so I figure why mess with a good thing?"

"I think it's nice." I lower my gaze back to the photo. The sparkle in her eyes got passed onto Chris. They look very similar. "My mom gets a bag of M&Ms

and a gift card for Starbucks. Your gift is actually thoughtful."

"Thanks." Chris crosses his legs, pen pressing to paper.

We work in silence, mellow tunes spurring us along.

I've lost track of everything by the time Chris's mom calls up the stairs.

"Boys! It's dinnertime!"

"Shit." I look down at my phone. I've missed two texts from my Dad. "I didn't realize it was so late."

"You're more than welcome to stay for dinner," Chris offers, setting aside his notebook. He shed his uniform jacket at some point and pushed the sleeves of his button-up past his elbows.

"Sure," I say before I realize that means we'll be eating with his parents. More importantly, his father. I try to back-peddle. "Um, I mean, I should probably call my dad and make sure it's okay."

"Whoa," Chris breathes.

I didn't hear him move. He looks over my shoulder at the sketch. I haven't added any details to her hair, but I've almost finished the outline of the face.

"That's ridiculous, Mike."

"Thanks." I shake the cramp out of my hand, noticing the shining silvery stain. It's the proof of my work.

"I'm going to go wash up." He moves to the door. "Let me know what your dad says. I can just run you home if I need to."

I nod as he leaves, dialing Dad's number.

"Hey, kiddo," he answers. "Where are you?"

"Hey, Dad. Sorry I didn't see your text. I'm at Chris Myers' place. He needed help with a project."

There's a pause on the other end.

"Chris Myers?" Dad repeats. "As in Roger's boy?"

"Sure?" I shrug. "I don't know Pastor Myers' first name."

"That answers my question." He laughs. "Well, all right then. I didn't know the two of you were friends."

I bite my tongue to keep from denying that claim.

"How long are you staying out?"

"They invited me for dinner," I say, "but I should be home by nine."

"Sounds good, *hijito*. Say hello to Chris's folks for me."

"Right, will do."

"Love you, son."

"Love-you-bye," I say with a sigh.

I end the call, weighing my options. I can always lie and say Dad wants me home now, sparing myself from what's bound to be an incredibly awkward dinner. The only problem is I already told him they've invited me, so I can't just show up at home. Plus, Dad might talk to Chris's father on Sunday and ask about it.

Shit. That means I'm stuck.

"What did he say?" Chris calls from downstairs.

"We're all good," I answer, pushing myself off the floor.

The stairs whine as I descend to the main level. Chris waves for me to follow him into the kitchen, and a garlicky, delicious smell slaps me in the face as he pushes the door open.

His mom, Vanessa, pulls a pan out of the oven, setting it on the stove top. It feels strange to see her in motion. I've been staring at her photo for the better part of two hours.

The photograph leaves out so many details.

"Michael." She greets me with a smile. "It's so good to see you. I trust you boys have been working hard on that Social Studies project."

"Huh?"

"Of course, we have!" Chris interjects, covering my slip up. "I feel an A+ coming on."

Oh, duh. Of course, he wouldn't tell her what we're doing.

"That's what I like to hear." Vanessa hands me a plate filled to the brim and gives a second one to Chris. "Well, dig in, boys. Your father is working late again, Chris. So, he told us to get started without him."

My relief is immediate and incredibly satisfying. I don't have to share a table with my nemesis. It's like a huge weight lifts off my shoulders. If I'm not careful, I just might float up to the ceiling.

The three of us take a seat. The utensils and napkins are already in place. A beautiful arrangement stands in the center of the table, containing shades of fall oranges and browns. They must host a lot of guests.

"Chris," Vanessa says with a nod, "would you bless it?"

He clears his throat, bowing his head. I follow suit. If he's anything like his father, this could take a while. I hope I don't nod off.

"Oh God," Chris starts, "thanks for this food. And stuff. Yeah. Amen."

Wait, what?

"Amen," Vanessa echoes, tucking the cloth napkin into her lap, unfazed by her son's blatantly irreverent prayer. "How are your parents, Michael?"

"They're...great." I'm still trying to process Chris's behavior.

"That's good to hear." She smiles, and it holds the warmth of an embrace.

I'll never understand how Pastor Myers came to marry such a kind and compassionate woman. For as long as I can remember, Vanessa has been a pillar both in the church and the community. While her husband teaches hellfire and brimstone, you'll never hear her so much as raise her voice. She always displays kindness, no matter who walks in those doors every Sunday.

Without people like her, I would have lost my faith long ago.

Why can't everyone be like that, Big Guy? Then You'd have no worries getting everyone onboard with the whole religion thing. You'd have a line around the block.

"Is everything okay?" Vanessa stares at me. "You haven't touched your plate."

"Y-Yeah." I grab my fork, stabbing into the cheese-stuffed tube. It's love at first bite. "It's delicious."

"I'm glad." She wipes the edges of her mouth. "There's plenty, so please have as much as you like."

I nod, mouth full of ooey gooey wonder.

"How are your classes going, Michael?" Vanessa asks.

"Really well, actually," I answer through a hunk of garlic bread. I swallow hard. "At least I haven't failed anything so far."

"How wonderful. That makes one of you...." Vanessa replies, cutting her eyes to Chris.

"That's not fair." He raises his hands in defense. "Pop quizzes don't count. How can I prepare for something I have no idea is coming?"

"It's called studying, sweetheart."

"I *do* study! You know, it's just, sometimes, I don't study the right thing."

"Let's not argue in front of company." Vanessa smiles apologetically toward me. "I'm sorry, Michael."

"No worries." I take another bite of cheesy pasta.

Vanessa refills my sweet tea from the pitcher. "I really enjoyed watching your sister perform last Sunday, Michael," she tells me. "How long has she played?"

"Depends on which instrument," I reply. "She plays three. The violin is her favorite though. She picked that up when she was five."

"That's crazy," Chris contributes.

"She's blessed with many talents." Vanessa folds her hands in her lap. "I'm sure it runs in the family."

"You've never heard my mom sing." I chuckle.

"Actually…" She makes a face.

I choke on my bread.

"Nancy is a wonderful woman." Vanessa scrambles to explain herself. "It's just—"

"It's okay," I say, cutting her off. "Oh God." I wipe a tear. "That was the funniest thing I've heard in a long time."

"Maybe keep that little joke between us?"

"Your secret is safe with me," I assure her.

The conversation continues effortlessly, and before long, Vanessa grabs some ice cream from the freezer for dessert.

It's kind of nice knowing the Myers talk about the same dumb shit my family does. Here I was thinking the topics of discussion would be theology and scriptures, but it's been homework and whose turn it

102

is to wash the dishes.

Once we've had our sweets, Chris offers to drive me home.

"It was lovely having you, Michael." Vanessa gives me a polite one-armed hug over my shoulder. "Be sure to tell your parents I said hello."

"Sure," I reply. Why do adults always seem so keen on telling each other hello through their offspring? We all know they have Facebook. Just poke each other and leave me out of it. "Thank you for dinner, it was so good."

"You're welcome anytime. Chris, please drive safely."

"Yes, ma'am." He nods, jingling his keys.

The two of us make it to the car just as his dad pulls into the driveway. I climb into the car, head ducking instinctively. Chris hesitates.

"I'll be just a second," he tells me, leaning over the steering wheel to start the engine. He walks across to his father's car, speaking to him through the driver's window.

I can't hear what they're saying, but I watch Pastor Myers's face in the side mirror. He doesn't look happy. Then again, he doesn't really ever look happy unless he's talking about Revelations or, maybe, the annual church picnic. The man loves his picnics.

After another minute, Chris trudges back to his car, plopping down in the driver's seat.

"Everything all right?" I ask.

"Yeah, yeah." He waves the question off. "Sorry about that." He flicks on the radio without further explanation, cranking the volume.

Thankfully, traffic has died down from rush hour,

and it doesn't take us long to reach my house. Chris pulls into the driveway, lowering the music back to a reasonable level.

"Thanks again," he says, "for helping me out. I should have cash for you tomorrow. Do you think you could come over again and finish it up?"

"Yeah." I retrieve my messenger bag from the floorboard. "Maybe I can invite Jackie to come hang out while I work?"

"Nah." Chris shakes his head. "She'd be too much of a distraction. We'd never be able to get any work done."

He laughs, and I'm more than a little confused. I would have thought he'd jump at the chance to hang out with her. Doesn't he want to get in her pants?

But then again, what do I know about straight guys? They're an enigma.

"Cool." I climb out of the car. "See you tomorrow then?"

"See ya." He waits for me to shut the door before backing out a little faster than he should.

I suck in a breath as he clears the mailbox by a fraction of an inch.

Once he's out of sight, I head inside. The living room is dark, meaning Dad's working in his home office. Mom must be asleep by this time, and Rosy is probably in her room, like always. We're all creatures of habit.

Climbing the stairs, I flex my hand, knuckles cracking. It felt good to sketch today. Or should I say to have the urge to draw? I haven't been able to bring myself to so much as lift a pencil since my sketchbook went missing.

But this was easy. Maybe that's because it was for someone else? It's always easier to do something for someone else. It's the people pleaser in me.

I shed my jacket, hanging it on the back of my computer chair.

The day has kept me so busy, I haven't really had a moment to worry about the whole missing book situation. But now I'm slowing down, the deferred anxiety builds in my stomach once more. Suddenly, I'm regretting that second helping of pasta.

Big Guy? Just checking in on that request for a sketchbook incineration. We still on schedule for that?

I let out a sigh. These one-sided conversations are getting old. Maybe a good night's sleep will help things look better in the morning.

THIRTEEN

"How was the bro-date with Chris?" Jackie stomps out the end of a cigarette while lighting a new one. Are all women good multi-taskers?

"All we did was sit in his room, working on his mom's gift. I don't think that classifies as a bro-date," I reply, attempting to rub the sleep from my eyes. I fell into a Tumblr trap last night when I got home, ruining my plans for a full night's sleep. Three hours later, I was wide awake, scrolling through an endless feed of puppies and pornography.

"Anything can be a bro-date if you believe, Mike."

"Then it was fine."

"You're no fun to tease." She pouts. "Where's Tanner when I need him?"

"The computer lab, doing something incredibly boring, I'm sure."

"That boy and technology. I'm surprised he hasn't built himself a girlfriend by now."

"Why waste time and resources? God gave you hands for a reason...."

Jackie snorts, checking her phone. "Hey, did you ever find your sketchbook?"

My pulse quickens. "Why do you ask?"

"Just wondering." She types with her free hand. "I haven't seen you doodling in a couple of days. I figure you have creative blue balls by now."

"That's a lovely way to put it."

"I thought so too."

"But the answer is no. I haven't found it yet."

"Fuck. That's a bummer. Might be time to just let it go. Maybe go get a new one?"

If only letting go was that simple. If only any of this were that simple.

"Yeah, you may be right."

"Don't worry, Mike." She pats my shoulder, showering my collar with ashes. "It'll turn up. Or it won't. Either way, you'll keep on living."

And with that piece of wisdom, she snuffs her vice, and we head for class.

"WE'VE BURNED THROUGH HELPLESSNESS BLUES," CHRIS ANNOUNCES, laying his pen and paper down as he scrolls through the music on his phone. "What do you want to listen to next?"

"It doesn't matter," I tell him. I'm too wrapped up in shaping stands of hair to care what's playing. I've almost finished the portrait. Just a few final touches left before I turn it over to Chris.

"Sylvan Esso it is," he concludes, starting a song with a synth-heavy beat.

The afternoon has flown by, and I can't believe I'm so close to finishing. It must be a record for me. Chris hit a writer's block an hour ago and has devolved into spinning around in his chair, mumbling incoherent phrases.

With more music selected, he continues on with this strange behavior.

"Chris!" a deep voice booms from downstairs. "I need you!"

"Shit," Chris mutters and then realizes what he said. "Sorry."

"You don't have to apologize." I laugh. "Shit is one of my favorite words."

"I'll be right back." He stands from his chair, kicking it back a little harder than I think he anticipated. It collides with a bookshelf as he clears the door.

The clatter and things scattering across the floor ruin my concentration. I glance over at a mess of papers and books strewn from the bookshelf. A box sits overturned on top of the chair. It must have fallen from the top shelf.

I set my pencil down, flexing my wrist. Gathering the loose scraps, I notice they're lined with what appear to be poems. It's difficult, but I try not to look at Chris's private words. Once I've returned them to the box, I strain to return it back to the shelf, but I'm not quite tall enough. Using the chair, I balance carefully, placing the box back where it belongs.

Awesome. Now, I can get back to…

I stop.

Pushed against the wall on the top shelf, beside a random trophy and some old baseball cards, sits a sketchbook with a brown cover.

My heart hammers in my ears as I reach for it, pushing everything out of the way haphazardly. I seize the book, almost face planting as I step off the chair. My fingers tremble as I flip open the back cover to see my name and phone number scrawled in a familiar script.

I don't feel relieved, especially given my surroundings. My jaw clenches so tight I don't even think I can form words. Anger like a flash fire courses through me.

Why would Chris take this? More importantly, why would he hide it?

I don't have long to question his motives before he comes back up the stairs.

"Sorry about that." He steps back into the room. "Dad needed me to— Oh, shit."

"What is this?" I hold the book out.

He freezes like a deer in headlights.

"What the *fuck*, Chris?"

"Shh!"

He shuts the door behind him, and suddenly, I feel very trapped. I need to get out of here.

"I can explain," he whispers. "Let me—"

"Don't take another fucking step!"

"Mike." Chris holds his hands up in surrender. "I'm not doing anything."

"Is this some kind of joke?" I spit my words. "A game you like to play with that bigot of a father? Let's torture the fag!"

"Please, Mike, this is all just a misunderstanding." He takes a step toward me.

I pull the chair in front of me like a shield. "Bullshit!" I shout. "This is all some kind of trick. You kept it, so you could humiliate me with it!"

"Why would I do that?"

"I don't know!"

I push the chair at him, and he knocks it aside.

"Maybe, to you, this is just some joke, but it's not funny. You and your sadistic father can both just burn in He—"

Chris catches my arm, pulling me toward him. In a split second, lips find mine, and he presses into me.

I'm paralyzed with shock. My brain shuts down. Hot tears roll down my cheeks.

Chris breaks away, and it only takes a second to regain my senses. His head jerks to the side as my palm connects with his face. I dash by him, pulling the door open and taking the steps two at a time.

"Mike!"

"Michael?" Vanessa calls as I hit the front door, bursting through it and down to the driveway.

I don't stop. I keep running until my lungs are bursting and a stitch burns in my side.

Thankfully, when my body can't go any farther, my brain kicks in. I pull out my phone and signal an Uber to take me home.

FOURTEEN

I'VE BEEN IN BED FOR THREE HOURS, STARING AT THE CEILING. EVERY TIME I think I have an explanation, an answer to my situation, three more questions pop up.

Just what was Chris planning to do with my sketches, anyway?

And what was that kiss? Just another way for him to humiliate me? That has to be the reason. No way he would have done that if it wasn't to degrade me.

I flip through the book again, taking stock. The sketches are all here, unharmed and just as I left them. The knots in my stomach twist as I picture Chris going through them. He must think I'm some sick, demented freak.

And, *Jesus Christ*, why the hell do I care what he thinks about me?

He's nothing but a liar. A hateful piece of shit just like his dad.

I stow the book in my bag, clutching it against my chest and reveling in the familiar weight. It's back where it belongs, but I have a feeling my troubles are far from over.

CHRIS IS WAITING FOR ME THE NEXT MORNING, LEANING AGAINST MY locker and fidgeting with his hands. I want to knock his teeth in, but Jackie is with me, and that might raise some suspicions.

"Hey, Chris," Jackie greets him, oblivious to the fact he is the scum of the fucking Earth.

"Hey, Jackie." Chris doesn't move from his perch, just stares at me.

I open my locker, not giving him the satisfaction of eye contact.

"Did you guys finish the thing for your mom?" she asks.

"For the most part," he answers. He looks like he wants to say more but stops himself.

What, Chris? Don't you want to out me right here in the hallway? Don't you want to lead the mob of angry villagers to crucify me?

"Oh cool." Jackie types away on her phone.

Chris looks at me again, and I hate that my heart is hammering in my ears. Any second, he's going to spill my secret. He's going to ruin my life in an instant, and nothing will ever be the same. It's killing me that he has so much power.

He inhales but chokes on the words.

I grab my New Testament book from my locker, slamming it shut with excess force.

"Jeez, Mike." Jackie looks up from her phone. "Been juicing up?"

"Something like that," I say flatly.

"How was your night, Jackie?" Chris asks through clenched teeth.

"It was all right. I stayed up way too late working on that stupid history— Shit!" Jackie hisses, pulling her backpack off to dig through. "I left it in the car! I have to go find Mom before the bell. See you guys at lunch!"

She hurries off, leaving me to stare daggers at Chris and imagine all the wonderful ways in which he could die a slow and painful death.

"We need to talk," he says in a hushed tone.

I laugh in his face. "You got to be fucking kidding me." I turn to leave, but he catches my arm.

"*Please*," he insists, tears shining in the corners of his eyes. "Please, I just need to explain myself."

My anger flickers. I wasn't expecting tears. With an exasperated sigh, I nod.

"Not here." He throws a glance over his shoulder. "Someplace private."

"Fine." I shake his hand off. "Come on."

My face is still flushed when we exit the school, heading for the back of the building. I lead him into the brick-walled sanctuary that is the dumpster pad.

"Jesus." Chris covers his nose. "It smells like something died."

"Just wait 'til Tuesday." I snort. It makes me feel a little better that I'm forcing him to endure the stench. "Now, what the fuck do you want, Myers?"

Chris recoils from his last name like an obscenity.

"I wanted to explain about the sketchbook," he starts. "And to apologize."

Apologize? Once again, not exactly what I had in

mind.

"Okay?"

"I'm sorry I didn't tell you I found it." He drops his head, so I can't see his face. "That was really shitty of me, but you have to understand I had my reasons."

He doesn't keep going.

"And they are?" I prod.

"The thing is..." Chris's hands fidget with his backpack straps.

"What?" I can't keep the frustration out of my voice. "What reason could you possibly have to take my book other than to hold it against me?"

"You don't understand," he replies.

"Try me." The stench of the garbage is getting worse by the minute. I blame the sun that's making its way over the brick wall. "Why did you keep it?"

"I don't know."

"Bullshit." I sneer, stepping past him. "See you around, Myers."

He catches my shoulder.

"Fine!" he shouts, spinning me around. "Fine, okay? I kept the dumb thing because I liked the drawings."

I blink.

Chris pulls on his straps, eyes trained downward.

"You *like* my sketches?"

He nods his head.

"Okay, I'll bite. Which ones?"

"The...the ones in the back," he says, face flushing a deep scarlet.

Oh. *Oh.* Oh, holy shit.

"I swear to God, if you are messing with me, Myers—"

"Stop calling me that!" he snaps, eyes lifting to me.

114

"And why would I lie about something like this?"

"Because this doesn't make any sense!" I'm beyond dumbfounded.

"Look…" Chris takes a shuddered breath. "I kept that book because I was building up the courage to give it back to you. I knew I couldn't just walk up and say I found it. So, I had this plan to get you to do that portrait just as an excuse to be alone with you. So, maybe I could bring it up. I didn't—"

"Wait." I stop him. "So, it's not your mom's birthday next Saturday?"

"No, it's in November."

"So, not only did you steal my sketchbook, but you lied and abused my art. Here I was thinking you asked me to help because I'm a good artist. Thanks a lot."

"You are. That's not the point!" Chris grunts. "Look, I'm sorry I took it. But you have to believe me when I say I never intended to do anything with it. I saw it lying on the ground in the Well, and I just couldn't help myself. And then, when I saw what was on those pages, I…" He trails off, scarlet-faced.

"Are you saying what I think you're saying?"

He has to say it. I won't believe it until he does. The whole thing is just too bizarre.

"I'm…gay," he whispers, throwing a worried glance over his shoulder.

There it is. The word. But it's not exactly in the context I thought it would come. I take a second to process.

Seriously, Big Guy? I mean, I know You had to have something special in store for Myers, but giving him a gay son? That's just cruel.

"Mike?"

Chris's eyes are dinner plates. His hands have passed fidgeting into full-on tremble mode. The poor kid is falling apart.

"You have to promise me you won't tell anyone," he whispers, throwing another paranoid glance over his shoulder.

I burst out laughing. I can't help it.

"You don't have to be a dick about it," Chris huffs, crossing his arms. "You know I did all this because I thought, of all people, you'd understand."

"W-Wait." I regain my composure. "I'm sorry. It's just... I've been freaking out for the past three days, thinking my secret will come out one way or the other. Then, I was sure you would ruin my life. And, now, here you are asking me to keep the very same secret I thought you'd expose. You can see the irony."

Chris doesn't smile. "And why exactly did you think I'd do something like that?"

"Um, your last name may have a little something to do with that."

"Jesus," he hisses. "My fucking last name dictates *everything* I do."

"Whoa, there." I grin. "I don't think that's appropriate language for a P.K. to be using."

"Oh, go fuck yourself." A hint of a smile hangs on his lips, and it's enough to lighten the mood.

"Dude," I say as I place a hand on his shoulder, "your secret is safe with me. What kind of person would I be to take advantage of that?"

He nods slowly. "Thanks, Mike."

"Plus, you still owe me fifty bucks."

That gets a smile.

FIFTEEN

By lunchtime, I'm as light as a feather. I practically dance my way through the line and back to the table where Jackie and Tanner are waiting.

"What's up with you?" Tanner asks, looking up from his laptop. "Did you get a hummer in the bathroom or something?"

"That's not appropriate meal-time discussion," Jackie scolds him. "Besides, if that were the case, he would have already told me."

"Don't be so sure." Tanner elbows her side. "He doesn't want to make you jealous."

"Knock it off you two." I kick both their shins under the table. "No one is getting a hummer. Well, unless you're talking about an actual Hummer, because I think Allen Coleman got one of those for his birthday last week."

"Fucking rich white people." Jackie scoffs, stabbing a tater tot with her fork.

"I hate to break it to you, Jackie," I say with a laugh, "but you're the most basic of white people."

117

"That is not true!" she rebuts. "I'm woke. I listen to NPR."

"Uh-huh."

"Well, I'm certainly not rich!"

"Just privileged," chimes Tanner.

"Um, mind if I sit with y'all?"

Chris stands at the head of the table, doing an awkward shuffle with his feet.

What's he doing here?

"Duh," Jackie replies. "Scoot over, Sasquatch."

Tanner slides down, moving his laptop with him.

"And to what do we owe the pleasure of your presence today, Mr. Myers?" Jackie asks, brandishing her potato-loaded utensil.

"I invited him," I jump in before Chris can answer.

"So, this is super-secret project business then." She narrows her eyes. "Well, fine. You two just whisper in each other's ears, and I'll pretend I'm not eavesdropping."

Chris makes eye contact, and I hope my smile is reassuring. Now I know he isn't out to ruin my life, he might actually be fun to hang around.

"Okay, I lied. I'm not going to be able to keep myself quiet." Jackie leans back toward us. "Can we talk about theology class for a second?"

Chris and Jackie become engrossed in their conversation while I zone out. Even though I'm no longer burdened, I keep thinking about Chris. How awful it must be to have *that* for a father? I mean, Mom and Dad aren't the most progressive parents in the world, but they don't go around openly bashing gay people. They just make snide passing comments every now and again. Those sting but not anywhere near what Chris must feel on the daily.

"Mike, are you even listening?"

"Huh?"

"I said Mom wants to know what the game plan is for next Saturday."

"Oh, right." I press my palm to my forehead. They've switched topics on me. "Your party."

"Not just any party," Jackie replies for Chris's sake. "My not-quite-as-sweet-as-sixteen-but-still-pretty-sweet-like-maybe-some-kind-of-artificial-sweetener seventeenth birthday party."

"Actually," interjects Tanner, "most artificial sweeteners are thousands of times sweeter than cane sugar. So, that's not an accurate example for—"

"Did I fucking ask you, Tanner?" Jackie smacks him on the shoulder. "I need you to work with me here."

"What did you want to do?" I ask.

"Nothing special." She leans forward on her elbows. "I told her we'd probably just order pizza and binge Bill Nye on Netflix."

"That's what we do every weekend," Tanner points out.

"But this time it will be with a larger circle of friends, so I can get lots of presents."

"Fair enough."

"You're totally invited, Chris." Jackie puts her arm around his shoulder. "The more the merrier."

"Sure." He smiles. "That'd be great."

"It'll be a blast," I tell him.

God knows he could use a little fun.

SIXTEEN

"HEY, MIKE?"

I close my locker, slinging my messenger bag back on my shoulder. Chris makes his way over from the other side of the hall.

"What's up?"

It feels weird to not immediately fill with dread when he says my name.

"I was wondering if you were busy this afternoon?"

"I'm not actually," I answer. "Swim practice was canceled. Something about coach Schmidt's hemorrhoids flaring up. Honestly, I wasn't listening that carefully."

"Wow." Chris laughs. "That was way more information than I ever needed."

"You're welcome." I lean against the locker. "What exactly did you have in mind?"

"I was going to head into the city and wanted to see if you'd like to tag along?"

"Oh, sure." I pull out my phone. "Just let me clear it with the parental units."

"Yeah, of course. I have to go check-in with Dr. Redford about that stupid pop quiz anyway. Meet you at the car?"

"Yeah." I nod, holding my phone to my ear.

Dad's phone goes to voicemail, so I try Rosy next.

"What?" she answers.

"Why are you like that?" I ask.

"It's my job. Now, stop beating around the bush."

"I'm going into the city with Chris," I tell her. "Would you let Dad know when he picks you up?"

"You got it, fam."

She hangs up before I can say anything else.

I stow my phone, heading for the parking lot.

WE DON'T SAY MUCH AS WE DRIVE SOUTH ON I-75.

"Have you listened to Ben Howard?" Chris asks as we come to a halt just short of the Grady curve.

"Yeah," I reply, turning the volume up a tad. "I think he came up on Spotify for me a few months ago. I like him."

"Me too." Chris selects the track while edging his way onto the exit ramp.

"Where did you say we're going?" I ask, peering out the window. I don't recognize any of my surroundings, but we're moving away from the heinous traffic, so that's a plus.

Everyone who's been to Atlanta knows what I'm talking about. It's a special kind of hell, being trapped on the highway with a million of your closest friends in standstill traffic and wondering if you'll ever see the end of the monotonous stop and go or if you'll eventually just blow your brains out.

I heard on the radio, a few weeks ago, Atlanta has somewhere close to three million commuters a day. Now the film industry is here, it will only get worse. If you can hear this message, get out while you still can.

The tall buildings distort by the shimmer of heat coming from the asphalt and cars. It transforms the city into a mirage—a place where nothing is solid, and everything changes by the way you look at it.

That familiar creative itch works its way up my arm.

I don't usually come this far downtown. My family spends a lot of time in Buckhead and Lenox on the north side. Mom avoids what she thinks are the sketchy parts of town. Which, apparently, is most of the city.

"It's a surprise," Chris finally replies. "Guess you'll just have to wait and see."

He leaves me to ponder as we keep moving east of the city. Passing outside the window are an interesting blend of new buildings and ones that are practically crumbling. Then again, you could say that about most of Atlanta. Something old beside something new.

"I've never seen this part of the city." I raise my voice over the music. The juxtaposition on the streets creates a strange beauty. A subtle harmony of vitality and history, the majority falling somewhere between the two.

I really want to sketch right now.

"Dude, you need to get out more." Chris laughs.

A new song starts, and I'm pulled away from the hustle and bustle of the street.

"I love this song," I say.

"I know," Chris replies. "You said it the other night in my room."

"Oh, yeah," I reply, soaking up every beat of the hypnotic rhythm.

"I have one rule for this song." He presses the buttons on the armrest, windows lowering as warm wind whips the hair off my forehead. "All windows must be down."

"Perfect." I reach my arm out the side of the car, a buffeting breeze coaxing it back and forth.

Freedom hangs in the air.

After they get their fill of the city, my eyes wander to Chris. I've never really given him a second glance before. I guess I always assumed he was off limits, given his parental situation. So, I just skipped over him in my discreet ogling. Now, I feel like I'm almost required to check him out.

His hair is darker than mine—jet black and cut short on the sides—but his bangs fall down to his eyebrows. I'm jealous of how straight it lays. I have so many curls I have to keep my hair short if I want any chance at styling it. Chris sits rigidly in his seat, posture immaculate. It must come with the rigor of a strict upbringing. He's rolled his shirt to the elbow, patterned tie hanging loose around his neck. A faded line of freckles runs along his cheekbones, just under his eyes. It's kind of adorable.

He's kind of adorable.

Ugh. What am I thinking? This guy almost ruined my life. But, then again…he didn't.

We pulled off the highway almost half an hour ago and are now carving our way through a sketchy section of Moreland Avenue. A big sign welcomes us to the East Atlanta Village. It's funny, I've never heard of it before.

When we reach a particularly colorful part of the village, Chris pulls over, rolling the windows up and parking on the side of the road.

"Where are we?" I ask, in no hurry to open my door.

"Little Five Points," Chris answers, already climbing out of the driver's seat. "I'm guessing you've never been here either?"

"Never," I confess, opening my door. I step out on the sidewalk, feeling incredibly out of place. Two men walk past us, hand in hand, laughing together. That's *definitely* something I don't see every day.

"Then you haven't lived." Chris slaps me on the back with a playful grin. "Come on, we gotta walk a little way."

Once we're out in the heat, my eyes have more than their fair share of things to devour. The cracked and withered sidewalk doesn't seem to bother those passing by. They move in tandem, each step like the beating of a heart. I guess people are like blood in that way, carrying life to every inch of the neighborhood. It's beautiful to watch.

This village houses an eclectic mix of people, each of them more vibrant than the last. Couples walk in stride, businessmen talk on cell phones as they traverse the pavement, and everywhere I look, there's something new to see.

Chris acts as my guide, pointing out shops as we pass. "That is Junkman's Daughter," he says, motioning to the blue building covered in graffiti. "A great place to waste an afternoon. That place over there serves the best burgers in town, but you gotta be twenty-one to get in. They have this huge wooden dick right when you walk in. It's great. Oh! If you've ever wondered what your parents wore when they were our age, check out that shop. It's terrifying. And next door is this amazing record store. My dad loves spending hours there; it drives my mom crazy."

Pastor Myers spends time in this neighborhood? I try to picture him walking under the plethora of rainbow flags fluttering in the breeze, but it just doesn't feel right. It's like those terrible magazines you see at the grocery store—blurry Photoshop pictures of famous people in places they've never been.

"This way." Chris leads me.

We turn the corner, and houses line either side now as we head down McLendon Avenue. There are even more flags here. One house, in particular, displays a beautiful collection of colored glass, and it's stunning when the sun hits it. I've never seen so much pride in one place before.

"How often does your family come here?" I ask, curiosity getting the better of me.

"Not so much anymore," he replies, eyes locked directly ahead as we stroll down the sidewalk. "But we used to visit a lot when I was younger. Sometimes, Mom and I will come down on the weekend, but it's complicated now."

I don't press the subject. I can't imagine being here with my parents. They'd take one look at me, eyes wide with awe, and know exactly what I am. My face must scream, "Take me, Atlanta, into your gay bosom!"

"I'm guessing your family doesn't spend much time in the city?" He looks to me now.

"Definitely not." I knock a pebble along with my foot. "The last time we even went downtown was for the College Football Hall of Fame. That's four hours of my life I can never get back. To be honest, I can't imagine them stopping anywhere like this."

"Well, it's their loss." He stops in front of a rust-colored building with a big red door. There are a few metal tables and chairs out front, and the wooden sign hanging above displays a large painted mustache.

"What is this place?" I peer through the huge window. A weird assortment of furniture spreads across the room, covering a massive red patterned rug.

"This is our destination. Welcome to Dr. Bombay's Underwater Tea Party." He holds the door open expectantly.

"Excuse me?"

"Just go in." Chris smiles.

Heat rises to my cheeks.

That's…weird.

I pass over the threshold, the sweet smell of coffee blending with the musty scent of old books. More dusty carpet sprawls under my feet, patterned red. Chris steps behind me, making his way to the counter.

I've never seen so much crammed into a tiny space. To be honest, a bit of claustrophobia sets in. Bookshelves line the mustard tinted walls on my left and right, an assortment of colored covers and bindings splashed against the dark wooden shelves. A wooden birdcage hangs above my head, surrounded by dozens of folded paper cranes—frozen in flight. The mismatched tables and chairs fill all possible space, people draped around them in various stages of engagement.

Some huddle over laptops, their faces illuminated by the glow of their screens. Others are sipping tea from beautiful china, three-tiered trays piled with cookies and sandwiches resting on the tables. And still more sit quietly, a book held in their hands as they turn page after page, oblivious to onlookers.

I meander to the counter where Chris is speaking with a young woman with several lip piercings. Her hair is a strange shade of teal, and it makes her russet skin look warmer. Chalkboards hanging from simple black chains cover the walls beside us. They're riddled with lists I quickly realize must be different teas—more than I would have imagined possible.

An icebox sits beside the pickup counter, displaying a spectrum of delicious looking ice cream. Beside that is a glass display full of cakes and pastries. My stomach rumbles just looking at them. My sweet tooth is insatiable.

"Thank you very much." Chris turns back to me, excitement bubbling under his usually reserved demeanor. "We have a table in the other room. Come on!"

We step through the doorframe to our left, Chris half-dragging me into the other side of the shop. More bookshelves line the walls, rows of paper lanterns, parasols, lampshades, and various other peculiar things suspended above us by fishing line. They cast pockets of light down on the floor from above. An old piano sits in the corner by the window, the stool seated in front of it covered in a knit slipcover with a floral print. Two long tables run the length of the room, parallel to each other. Laughter bubbles from the cluster of friends at the end of the table closest to us.

"That's ours." Chris points to the small table by the window and ushers me toward it.

"This place is ridiculous." I marvel, senses overwhelmed. Chris moves to the table. Behind him, a cluster of paintings catches my attention—a vase of flowers, antique style portraits, a sailing ship on deep blue waves, and a lush meadow landscape piece. "It looks like it jumped off the page of a book."

"You'd be surprised what you can find if you look hard enough." Chris pulls out his chair, the wooden legs scraping against the concrete floor. "Have a seat. It's a better vantage point."

Taking the spot across from him, I sink into the chair. The cacophony of bright colors and vivacious chatter from the other side of the room make it difficult for me to focus.

"We're just in time for high tea," Chris tells me, leaning his elbows on the table.

"You're kidding." Images of *Pride and Prejudice* era waistcoats and gloves fill my head. "We're having a tea party?"

"In a sense, yeah, I guess we are. Are you a coffee drinker?"

I nod my head. "Avid."

"Then you're in for a treat."

He smiles at me again, and his eyes are alight with even more excitement. Just what exactly is going on here?

"Here we go." The lip-ringed goddess with teal hair sets our own tiered tray down on the table, the golden plates piled with more sweets than I can dream of. Next, comes a porcelain teapot and two cups on saucers. Last, she sets down a plate with a cup of what looks like whipped cream and plastic containers of jam. "Enjoy, fellas."

"Whoa." The floral scent coming from the steaming pot is strong enough to make my eyes water. "What is that?"

"It's dandelion tea," Chris explains, grabbing one of the triangular scones and popping the lid off the orange-hued jelly. "You have to let it steep for a few minutes before you pour it or else it's gross. But, when it's done, it tastes a lot like coffee."

"It smells…interesting," I say, stealing a mini cupcake from the tray and pulling the wax paper from the bottom. I take a bite. It's strawberry and delicious.

"My mom and I used to come here once a week," Chris mumbles through the crumbs of his pastry. "She loves this tea, so I kinda got attached to it. Now, I can't get anything else."

Wiping the frosting from my fingers on the white cloth napkin, I'm drawn to the massive white and blue striped oil paper umbrella above us. It's tattered, and bits of the beautiful design hang from the frame.

"So, you must wonder why I wanted to bring you here?" Chris pulls me away from the absurdity of the scenery.

"Mildly curious would be the best description."

He squirms in his seat, pulling at the ends of the tablecloth. "I was hoping, if we came someplace like this, it would be easier to talk."

For some reason, my heart leaps into my throat. I have to clear it before I can speak.

"And what is it you want to talk about, exactly?"

"I think you already know."

So, that's his play. This has all been an elaborate trap set to ensnare me into discussing details about myself I don't ever care to disclose.

"Maybe now is not the best time."

"Why not?" He leans forward, dark eyes watching my every move.

"Because it's not something I want to talk about." I inject as much finality into my tone as possible.

"Oh." His back hits the chair, shoulders slumping as he lets out a breath. "I'm sorry. I didn't mean to make you uncomfortable."

"You didn't make me uncomfortable, it's just..."

No excuse comes to mind. I look around. No one is paying us the tiniest bit of attention. Why *can't* I talk about this? A switch flips and suddenly, I'm the one leaning forward.

"Actually," I say and set an elbow on the table, "I *am* uncomfortable. I've been uncomfortable in my own skin for the last sixteen years. So, it may take me a minute to get used to it, but...why shouldn't we talk about it?"

Chris smiles, reaching for the teapot. "I was hoping you'd say that."

He pours a cup of the dark liquid, and floral aromas waft toward me. I take the delicate porcelain from him, filling my own cup before setting the pot back down on the plate.

"Fair warning." Chris sips his own tea. "It's really strong. If the taste doesn't appeal to you, just try adding cream and sugar."

Water wells in my eyes after a sniff. Downing a horrible sip, I reach for the sugar. Chris chuckles while I pour almost half the container in.

"I told you." He passes a dish of what I think is whipped cream. "It's clotted cream," he explains, "just like they use in Britain. Authentic, huh? It'll help take some of the edge off."

I stir a huge dollop in before taking another sip of the newly sweetened drink. A bitter aftertaste still lingers, but it's not so unpleasant.

"It tastes like licorice," I realize after another sip. The more I drink, the better it tastes.

Chris lifts his own cup, taking a sip of the straight stuff. He doesn't even make a face.

A minute of silence feels like an eternity.

Questions buzz around my head in a swarm, stinging the edges of my brain until one forces its way out.

"When did you know?"

His eyebrows rise, cup clinking back onto the saucer.

"You're going to need to be more specific."

I lean forward, my voice involuntarily lowering. "When did you realize you were... You know?"

"Alarmingly attractive?" Chris leans back in his chair. "From a young age. I've always suspected my dashing good looks would be the downfall of countless men and women alike."

I roll my eyes. "You know what I'm saying."

"Do I?" He folds his arms.

"Jesus, *fine!*" I blurt out. "When did you know you were *gay*?"

"If we're going to talk about it, there's no point in tip-toeing around the subject." Chris drinks from his mug.

"Fine, whatever. Answer the question." You could fry an egg on my forehead.

"Honestly, I couldn't tell you when the thought first popped in my head," Chris says, eyes drifting from me and out the window to the right. "All I remember is that one day I woke up, and suddenly, it was like I was seeing boys for the first time.

"I had a best friend when I was nine. His name was Russell, and we used to spend every minute together. That was until the day I decided we should paint our fingernails with watercolor paint. Well, after we showed my little art project to our parents, suddenly Russell didn't come around anymore. I remember Mom and Dad talking about it one night when they thought I was asleep, but it wasn't until two years later I understood what they'd been saying. And it's been one cautious step after another to keep my secret."

The story sounds familiar even though I've never heard it.

"Was it the same for you?" Chris asks.

"I guess." I reach for another cupcake, peeling the wax paper slowly. "For the most part. Except, I can remember the first time I realized I might be different. My brother's friend actually made me think about it."

Blond curls and tanned skin flash through my mind, and I take a second to let the details resurface.

"His name was… I mean *is* Phillip. He's not dead or anything." A nervous laugh escapes, and I feel like an idiot. "I just haven't seen him in years. Anyway…he was spending the night with Tommy one week, and the two of them were jumping on the old trampoline in the backyard. And I just kept staring at Phillip. The way his shirt would ride up, or how his muscles would contract each time he landed. And there was this feeling in my gut I couldn't figure out. Did I want to be like Phillip, or did I want to be *with* Phillip?

"It was a very long, hot summer." More nervous chuckles overtake me, and my cheeks fill with searing heat. "After that point, I just kind of knew. I'd heard of gay before, but it was never discussed in my family. Just swept under the rug like the majority of serious issues, I suppose."

Taking a bite of the cake, I chew slowly, glad to have something other than awkward topics to keep my mouth busy.

"Crushes are the worst," Chris says, filling the silence before sipping his horrifyingly unsweetened tea. "Especially for us. I mean, straight guys can walk into any place, flirt it up with a girl, and not worry about being punched in the face. At least, the majority of the time. I wouldn't be surprised if Jackie has slugged a douchebag or two."

I snort, lips spreading with a smile. "She much prefers a swift kick to the dick. It sends a clearer message."

"Jesus." Chris cups his crotch. "Remind me not to piss her off."

We both chuckle before our eyes drift to the window. The sun begins to set behind the buildings across the street and golden beams of light stream in through cracks and gaps. It's kind of beautiful here. I would never have guessed we were so close to the city.

Another question threatens its way out of my head. One I've been dying to ask the entire afternoon but haven't been able to think of the words to say. Then again, tact has never been my strong suit. So, I ask anyway.

"So, not to be rude," I start, which universally means

I'm about to say something incredibly rude. "But how can you stand to live with that hateful piece of shit you call a dad?"

Fuck, Mike. That wasn't even close to chill.

Chris blinks a few times, his head giving a little twitch as if trying to shake off what I said. "Excuse me?"

"S-Sorry." I attempt to save face. "That didn't come out right. I mean, I just wanted to know—"

His laughter stops me.

"It's fine." His shoulders still shake. "Honestly, there's nothing you can really say about him that I haven't already thought. I just wasn't expecting you to come right out with it, I guess."

"Yeah, sorry again."

"Don't be," Chris says. "As you can imagine, my relationship with him is strained at best. And, to answer your question, it's very difficult. I would love nothing more than to tell him to go fuck himself and then bounce. But that would mean leaving my mother alone with him, which is not exactly something I'd want to do." His eyes drop to the table, fingers circling the edge of his mug. "She means too much to me. I know she'd choose me over him in a heartbeat. But, when it comes down to it, I don't think she has the strength to leave him."

"Well, shit."

That sums things up nicely. His situation is all kinds of fucked up.

"My sentiments exactly." Chris nods. "But what's even more annoying is it's not just my sexuality I have to keep hidden from him. These days, it's almost everything about me. My writing, my college plans, my faith issues—"

"Faith issues?" I pluck that one from the list.

"Yeah," he replies. "Don't you have them too? They kind of go hand in hand with our situations."

"I mean, sure, there are days I don't know what to believe. But I didn't think you'd struggle with that too. You *are* a P.K. for Christ's sake."

"And that means I automatically have a bulletproof faith?"

"Well, yeah. I guess."

"That's ridiculous." He scoffs. "I have more reasons than anyone to struggle with this stuff. I've seen it all from the inside for so long I'm not even sure I believe in *anything* anymore."

"What do you mean?"

Chris doesn't respond right away, just traces a pattern into the white tablecloth with his index finger. When he does speak, it's hushed. "I just can't believe. Not right now, at least."

Is he serious? Here I hoped he'd be able to quell the raging thoughts in my head. Guess that was wishful thinking.

"Well, fuck!"

He jumps as I bang my hand on the table, nearly tipping my cup over.

"Some preacher's kid you are. You're just as fucked up as the rest of us!"

He gives a small smile, and he looks like his mother. Her face is still fresh in my mind.

"So, not to change the subject," I say, even though that's exactly what I'm doing, "but do you think you could bring me that portrait of your mom tomorrow? I want to finish the details."

"I didn't think you'd want to finish it." His eyes widen.

"What, and leave Vanessa hanging for her fake birthday? What kind of friend do you think I am?"

"Friend," Chris repeats. "I think I'm even more surprised you'd want to be that, all things considered."

"Well, I'm just full of surprises," I tell him before taking another sip of my tea. "And, as your friend, can I be completely honest? This stuff still tastes like shit. I'm gonna grab a cup of coffee."

"Sure." Chris refills his cup. "More for me."

Getting up from the table, I find a way back to the counter where the teal-tinted lady waits for me.

"Not a fan of the dandelion?" She grins as I make a face.

"There's not enough sugar in the world," I reply, looking back to the chalkboards hanging from the wall. "Can I get a latte, please? Extra sugar?"

"Coming right up, sweetie." She winks at me then sets to work on my beverage.

I lean against the counter, surveying my surroundings as I wait. The rest of the tables are filling up. Apparently, afternoon tea is very popular around here.

At the table in the corner, there are two boys that look to be about my age sitting across from each other, one with blond hair, and the other with red hair cropped short. They lean in close, talking just low enough I can only hear a murmur. The blond one reaches across the table and twists his fingers around the other boy's with a smile.

The gesture is so innocent, and yet, I feel my cheeks flare with unexplained heat.

Why am I like this, Big Guy? They're just holding hands, but I feel like I'm watching them go at it on top of the table. We both know I've watched far raunchier things happen between two guys.

Maybe that's the reason. This isn't something I'm seeing under my blanket at midnight. This is the real world. And these are real people, just drinking tea and holding hands.

So, calm down, Mike.

"Here you go." The barista slides my drink over the counter.

"Thank you," I say, balancing the saucer as I retrace my steps back to our table.

"I've officially used all the orange jam," Chris announces, staring sadly at the empty plastic container. "Hope you didn't want any."

"That's okay," I tell him before sipping foam from my latte. "I won't hold it against you."

"You're a saint," he quips, eyes drifting back to the window.

And, just like that, I don't know what to say next. So, I sip my coffee and grab a cookie from the tray.

I'm going to have the worst breakout of my life after all these sweets. I'll have to wash my face three times a day.

"Can I ask you something?" Chris looks at me.

"Sure," I answer.

He hesitates, fingers tracing the tablecloth again. "Never mind. Forget I said anything…"

"Are you asking if I'm a virgin?" I joke, breaking the tension.

Chris's pale cheeks turn scarlet as his head drops.

"Oh, shit." I laugh. "You were really going to ask me

that, weren't you?"

"N-Not if you were a virgin," he stammers. "Jesus. I'm not that bold. Just…you know, if you'd done anything with a guy before."

My heart does this weird fluttering thing, and I look over my shoulder to make sure no one is within earshot. "I mean, yeah. Duh. Haven't you?"

Chris shakes his head, looking like he's about to die from embarrassment. "How could I? Almost every spare moment of my time leading up to this point has been spent at the church with my parents. Not exactly a ton of opportunities for…*that.*"

We share another awkward laugh, and a thought hits me like a truck. My stomach tightens. "Hey, the other night… That wasn't your first kiss, was it?"

He looks away from me, and I have my answer.

"Whoa." I sigh. "That's pretty shitty. I would say I was sorry for hitting you, but you really deserved it."

Chris nods. "What was it like for you? Your first kiss, I mean."

"Ugh, I'd rather forget it."

Neon braces and zits. Not the best combination.

"It couldn't have been that bad."

"You didn't have to kiss him," I retort as vivid details of that day race back in. I start reluctantly. "I was thirteen, and it was a game of truth or dare at Jackie's birthday party. His name was Freddie, and he had a mouthful of braces. It was my turn, and I picked dare, so Taylor Shay made us kiss. It was terrible on so many levels. Yet, I found the idea of kissing Freddie more exciting than kissing any of the girls at the party. Poor guy was mortified, and I had to pretend to be just as opposing."

"Okay." Chris is trying not to laugh. "I take it back. That sounds awful."

"Thank you." I take another swig of my latte.

"Well, at least he didn't slap you because you were being a dick."

"That's true."

"I imagine thirteen-year-old Jackie must have laughed her ass off."

"She was pissed actually." I grin. "She had a thing for Freddie."

Jeez, I haven't thought about that in forever. An age of my life I'd rather forget.

"What drama." Chris leans on an elbow. "I'm glad to see your friendship didn't suffer."

"She didn't talk to me for a month."

"That doesn't surprise me." He chuckles. "She's ridiculous."

And I thought you wanted to get in her pants. Boy, was I wrong?

"I have a confession to make," I tell him, taking another sip of my coffee.

"That's not terrifying at all."

"It's actually pretty funny," I say.

Chris exhales his tension.

"But, until yesterday, I thought you had a thing for Jackie."

Chris blinks. "Really?"

I nod, draining the last of my latte. "I know right? Ironic I have a faulty gaydar."

Chris explodes with laughter, and the group of people from the other side of the room crane their heads to see the ruckus. It goes on for a little too long in my opinion.

"Oh, my gosh." He wipes a tear. "I'm sorry. But that's the funniest thing I've heard in a really long time."

"You don't get out a lot, do you?"

"Well, I don't know about you," Chris says as he claps, giving me a start, "but I've had enough tea. Let's get out of here." He rises to his feet, dusting crumbs off the front of his shirt.

"Oh." I stand too, my knee knocking into the table. "Sure, I guess it is getting late."

"Don't worry, the night's just getting started," Chris says, a glimmer of mischief in his eye.

"Uh, what are you talking about?" I ask, but he's already moving for the door. "T-Thanks!" I call to the teal-haired woman behind the counter as I follow him out to the sidewalk. The deep orange sun is hot against my skin, and the heat shimmers up from the ground with such intensity I swear I've stepped into an oven.

"Where are we going?" I call after Chris.

"Somewhere." He smiles, crossing the street without a care.

I hurry after him, passing colorful shops at a breakneck pace. A steady flow of people fills the sidewalk now the heat of the day has passed. They walk dogs, jog by, or move in tandem with fingers linked while laughing.

This neighborhood is teeming with life, and it's infectious.

Chris comes to a halt in front of the storefront, and I almost run into him. A metal sign above the door reads Piercing Experience.

"You can't be serious." My eyes widen.

"Come on, you big baby." He laughs, pulling the

glass door open. He disappears inside, leaving me alone.

Hesitating, I glance down the sidewalk. If he thinks I'm letting anyone near me with a fucking piercing gun, he has another thing coming. But, after a deep breath, I push the door open and step into the cool air of the shop.

The wooden floor creaks underneath me, and a long glass counter runs along the wall to my right. A plethora of rings are on display, everything from gauges to tiny eyebrow loops in gold, silver, and black materials. Chris leans over the display cabinet, pointing something out to the terrifyingly large man with a long, red beard.

"That one right there," he says. "That's the one I want."

"What are you doing?" I move beside him.

"I'm getting my ear pierced," he replies, tucking his hair away to tap his left lobe. "It's something I've always wanted to do it, so I figured why not today?"

"Don't you think your parents might have something to say about that?"

"Who cares?" He smiles at me. "I'm already going to Hell, so what are a few piercings gonna do?"

I don't like the way he says that with such certainty.

"All right, man," Big Red says, retrieving the small, black spike from the glass cabinet. "You can follow me back to the piercing room."

"I'll be right back," Chris says. "Unless, of course, you want to join me?"

"I'd rather not." I shake my head vigorously. "I don't do well with pain."

"There won't be a lot," Big Red assures us.

I let out a nervous laugh. "That's what they all say."

"All right then." Chris grabs my hand, giving it a squeeze. "Wish me luck."

My pulse quickens, like his touch jolts my heart.

"Hope you don't die."

Chris laughs again, releasing me and turning the corner with his new ginger-bearded friend.

A tightness winds around my stomach like a snake. Any tighter and I'll shit out an organ.

This is not good at all. Pastor Myers is going to hit the ceiling when he sees Chris's ear. What is he thinking? I spend most days trying to blend in, so I honestly can't see the appeal of sticking out like a sore thumb.

A giggle comes from behind me, and I turn to see two women standing by the entrance. One of them focuses on a terrifying septum rod, but the other is smiling at me. She looks older than I am. A ring dangles from her nose, and a row of studs run up both earlobes. Her hair is short, bangs spiked out in front of her forehead.

"You two are adorable," she says.

I take a second to realize what she means.

"Oh!" My cheeks fill with heat. "T-Thanks."

"Don't you want to be back there with him?" the woman asks. "You know, hold his hand?"

"I don't do well with blood," I lie.

"Be glad you're dating a boy then, sweetheart." She laughs.

I cringe. Gross.

A yelp comes from the back of the store, and we both jump.

"Well, shit." The second woman steps over. She's shorter than the first, with a similar haircut and tattoo sleeves covering both arms. "Is he getting a Prince

Albert in there?"

"Excuse me?" I have no idea what that is.

"Shut the fuck up, Cindy." Nose-ring lady slaps the shorter woman's shoulder. "You're going to scare him off."

"Look it up, kid," Cindy whispers, smiling.

Why do I feel like I'm going to need to delete my browser history after doing so?

The ladies move to the display case, discussing spacers. Whatever the hell those are.

I drift away from them and lower myself onto the leather seat in the corner by the window. As I do in all uncomfortable situations, I pull out my phone. A missed call icon flashes. I've missed a call from my dad. I'll get back with him later. I just hope he doesn't pull up his phone tracking app and see me in some sketchy neighborhood. He'll think I'm dead in a ditch.

Chris comes back in with Big Red before long, face paler than before but a smile tugging at his lips. The large man hands him a tube of something from behind the register.

"Be sure to clean it three times a day for the next two weeks." He punches a few keys. "And that stud needs to stay in constantly for six to eight weeks."

"You got it, boss." Chris hands him a debit card and turns to me, giving a thumbs-up.

"There you are." Big Red passes him a receipt. "Take care, guys."

I rise from my chair, giving a small wave to Cindy and the taller lady whose name I don't know. Chris is beside me, his left hand raised to his ear as he fiddles with the new piercing.

We exit the parlor, the sweltering heat still holding

on by a death grip. As we start back toward the car, the promise of air conditioning calls to me like a siren song.

"Hey, Chris," I ask as we round the corner of McLendon and Moreland, "do you know what a Prince Albert is?"

"Huh?" He lowers his phone, pausing a selfie-taking montage featuring his new piercing. "What are you talking about?"

"Those two women asked me if you were getting a Prince Albert," I explain, "but I have no clue what that is."

"Well," Chris says as he raises his phone once more, "we have the magic of Google at our fingertips."

We're both silent as he types his question in.

That strange tightness in my gut from when he touched me has faded, but I don't like that I'm clueless as to what caused it.

"Holy fuck!" Chris exclaims, shoving the phone away from him. "Holy fucking fuck!"

"What?" I grab the phone from him. My face burns with a new heat when I realize what I'm looking at. Google Images shows picture after picture of dicks, each of them pierced through the head with various metal rings and rods. My stomach sinks to the ground, a strange aching radiating from between my legs. I hand the phone back, feeling queasy.

"Why would you ever do that?"

"No idea." Chris stows the phone back in his pocket. "But no way that would ever happen. Like ever."

"I have so many questions." I laugh. "What happens if it gets caught on something?"

"How do you pee?" Chris poses his own question.

"Can you pass through a metal detector?"

"Do people think it's attractive?"

"Are there clip-on versions?"

I'm almost in tears from laughing when we reach Chris's car. The interior is a sauna as we climb in. But, soon, the air is blasting, and the windows are down. The last rays of sunlight sink below the horizon as we merge onto the interstate headed north.

Today definitely did not go as planned. But I can't stop smiling as we drive. It's nice to have someone in on my secret. Someone who has the same vested interest as I do to keep it that way. I haven't felt this relaxed in forever.

"Hey, Chris?"

"What's up?" He turns down the music.

"I'm glad we did this," I say, rolling up my window so he can hear me.

He glances over, a smile playing across his lips. "Yeah, me too."

He cranks the music back up, and I turn to stare out the window. The lights of the city glow bright against a dark sky.

SEVENTEEN

We PULL INTO MY DRIVEWAY A LITTLE PAST NINE.

"Thanks for the tea party," I tell Chris. "I had a lot of fun. Despite the more traumatic discovery of our dear Prince Albert. Expect a bill from my therapist."

Chris snorts, his eyes black in the darkness. "It was a blast." He angles himself toward me. "I guess I'll see you at school tomorrow?"

"Definitely." I open my door. "Jackie and I usually hang out by the dumpster before first period if you want to join us."

"Sounds disgusting." He grins. "I'll be there."

"Okay." Silence blooms between us. My head tips forward, ever so slightly, but I catch myself.

What are you doing, Mike?

"Goodnight, Mike."

"Goodnight," I repeat, grabbing my bag from the floorboard as I climb out of the car. He backs out, slowly this time, still dangerously close to our mailbox. The headlights blind me momentarily before he disappears down the road.

146

With the turn of a key, I open the door and step into the foyer. It's quiet, and I wonder if everyone has already turned in for the night. Dad's bound to still be answering emails.

"Mike?"

I jump as my mother's voice calls from the dining room. I follow it, finding her and Dad sitting at the table, both looking very stern.

Uh oh.

"Hey." I greet them with a smile. "Sorry I missed your call, Dad. I totally spaced and forgot to call you back."

"Where've you been, Michael? I tried to call you."

Shit. I'd forgotten all about it. "Y-Yeah," I stammer. "I'm sorry. I missed it. Didn't Rosy tell you I was helping a friend with their project for English?"

"Who?" Mom interjects.

My eyes drift to her. "What?"

"Who were you helping?" she inquires.

I'm fucking toast. They'll figure everything out. I might as well tell them part of the truth.

"Chris Myers." I release his name with a sigh, still staring down at my shoes.

"Oh." Relief fills my mother's expression. "Pastor Myers's son?"

I nod in response.

"Thought you two finished that project a couple days ago?" Dad scratches his goatee. "Why didn't you just say so? See, Nancy." His gaze turns to Mom. "I told you there was a perfectly reasonable explanation."

"Next time, answer your phone when we call you." Mom's voice still has an edge, but I can tell Chris's name has defused the situation. "And try to be home by nine, sweetheart. It's a school night."

"Got it," I say, fighting the grin tugging at the corner of my mouth. "Sorry to worry you guys."

"We're used to it." Dad smiles. "One day, you'll have to adult and worry about everything too. Now, head up to bed."

Are they for real? All I have to do was mention Chris's name and they believe whatever I tell them?

"S-Sure." I move to the table, hugging Mom over her shoulder. "Night."

"Sleep tight." Mom wraps her arm around my waist.

"*Dulces sueños.*" Dad gives me a lame fist bump across the table.

Counting my blessings, I untangle myself from my mother and head up the stairs. Once I'm safe inside the four walls of my bedroom, I decompress. This week has been a rollercoaster of emotional exhaustion.

I retrace the day's events as I get ready to sleep.

Driving the freeway with the windows down…

I hang up my uniform jacket.

Walking through Little Fives…

I fold tomorrow's clothes and set them on top of my dresser.

The tightness in my stomach when Chris grabbed my hand…

I'm too wound up to even think of sleep, so I fish through my bag, retrieving my sketchpad and a pencil.

I scroll through a playlist on my phone, selecting one before I stick it on the sound dock sitting on the bedside table. The soft and sweet tones play as I drag my hand against the page to create the first outlines.

I've never been able to adequately describe the feeling I get when I draw. I suppose the closest thing I can equate it to is the love a parent has for their child. At least, that's how I imagine it. No matter how they end up, my creations are my children. I love them all equally, no matter what. They make me feel like I'm doing what I was put in this world to do.

And, sometimes, they frustrate the hell out of me. But I always come back, picking them up and cradling them once more as I help them become the best they can be.

I don't feel the passage of time while I work.

The woman on the page looks back at me. She holds a tray in her hand, filled with a teapot and a three-tiered arrangement of pastries. Paper cranes hang around her in a swarm.

I let out a yawn, grabbing my phone off the dock. Oh God, it's three in the morning. I flip my book closed, inserting the pencil into the spiral binding as I shove it back into my bag. I set my alarm app then notice the icon above my text messages.

How did I miss that? I check the time stamp. It came in an hour ago. Who is texting me at two AM?

> Sometimes I just want everything to stop. 2:03am

I read Chris's text a second time before typing back a response.

> Are you okay? 3:05am

I press send, my eyes heavy.
Staring at my phone, I wait for his reply.
I don't know when I fall asleep, but paper cranes

and scones smeared with orange jelly fill my dreams.

EIGHTEEN

"Jesus." Smoke trails from Jackie's lips. "You look like shit."

"Thank you." I yawn loudly, rubbing my eyes. "That's what I was going for."

The air is thick this morning, humidity making my hair stick to my forehead. It will probably rain at some point, but that's not my concern at the moment. Chris never responded to my text, and I'm getting worried. I keep looking over my shoulder, thinking he'll show up with that stupid grin on his face.

"Who are you waiting for?" Jackie asks, snuffing her cigarette on the brick wall beside the dumpster. "Tanner is tied up with his stupid coding project."

"No one," I blurt. "Just stretching my neck."

"Uh huh." Her eyes narrow, but she doesn't press the subject.

I check my phone for the ten thousandth time this morning. Nothing.

"I told Mom about the party next Saturday." Jackie tosses her lighter, which looks like a tube of lipstick to the unsuspecting eye, into the outside pocket of her backpack and slings the strap over her shoulder.

Where could Chris be? He said he was going to be here.

"Mike!"

Jackie snaps her fingers in front of my face, making me jump.

"Seriously, what is going on with you today?"

"S-Sorry." I shake my head. "I'm still half-asleep." I let out another yawn to emphasize the point.

"Well, come on, Sleeping Beauty." She punches me on the shoulder. "We're going to be late to class."

Rain falls as we duck under the awning, a rumble of thunder sounding in the distance.

The weather matches my mood today.

"You better hurry if you don't want to be locked out," Jackie tells me before sprinting in the opposite direction.

I move as quickly as my sleep-deprived body will allow, making it to Dr. Redford's room with just minutes to spare. The chair beside mine is empty. Still no Chris. I sink into my seat, burying my face in the fold of my arms. I have to focus on not falling asleep right here and now.

"At least you are consistent, Mr. Myers." Dr. Redford's voice rumbles.

My head shoots up so fast I'm sure I've given myself whiplash. Chris shuffles to his seat beside me, and I wince. He has a long cut across his lower lip, a swollen cheek, and a blue and black patch just below his left eye.

"What happened to you?" I whisper.

He doesn't respond, only looks straight ahead.

"Chris?"

"Mr. Hernandez," Dr. Redford says as he looks right at me, "Jesus said he who has ears, let him hear. Not he who has a mouth, let him speak."

"Yes, sir," I say.

"Good. Now then, let's discuss the sociological factors that played a role in Jesus's parables during the Gospel of Luke."

I hear a sniffle beside me and turn to see Chris wipe his face.

CHRIS ABRUPTLY STANDS AS DR. REDFORD DISMISSES THE CLASS, BOLTING FOR the door before I can even stow my textbook. I rush after him, but he's already gone when I hit the hallway.

What's his deal?

I can't focus during the next two periods. My brain is completely fixated on solving the mystery surrounding Chris's busted face. By the time lunch rolls around, my head is throbbing.

A quick scan of the cafeteria shows he's nowhere.

Jackie waves me over to a table. Tanner sits beside her, typing away on his laptop.

"Hey, Mike." Tanner doesn't look up. He shovels a handful of tater tots into his mouth and continues working, greasy fingers smearing a layer of shine across the keyboard.

"You look a little better," Jackie tells me, picking at her own plate. She hasn't been eating much since her grandmother told her she was looking chunky. "Did you get a nap in during English class?"

"Of course not." I scoff. "Your mom would have

crucified me."

"Nah." Jackie laughs. "She just would have drawn on your face with a Sharpie. That's what she did to Jamie Tutts last year. Almost got fired for that one."

"I love your mom." I smile before biting into my apple. Worry has my stomach tied in knots, so I chew slowly.

"Oh, hey." Tanner looks up from his screen. "Did you guys hear about Jenny O. yet?"

"The singer?" asks Jackie. "I didn't think you listened to anything but dub-step trash."

"Hardy-ha-ha." He wipes the side of his ketchup-stained chin. "Jenny O'Conner from church."

I look at Jackie, and we both shake our heads.

"Totally preggers." He grins, popping another tot into his mouth.

"No way!" Jackie leans closer, keeping her voice low. "I thought she was on the pill?"

"She was," Tanner continues, "*and* he used a condom. They're calling it the immaculate contraceptive-conception."

"Jesus Christ." Jackie leans back in her chair. "That makes me never want to have sex. Well, maybe just anal. Right, Mike?"

I suck in a piece of apple peel, coughing until my eyes water.

"How do you know about her?" Jackie ignores my convulsions. "She doesn't even go to school here."

"I have my sources." He grins again. "I see all. I know all. There's no secret I won't find out!"

Except one. Right, Big Guy? I mean, obviously nobody knows, or else they would have run me out of town on a rail. That one's just between You and me. And Chris.

154

"Have you heard anything about Chris Myers?"

Jackie's head turns to me.

I quickly add, "I saw him this morning in New Testament, and it looks like he got in some kind of fight."

Tanner's brow furrows. "Seriously? No, I haven't heard about that. But let me see what I can come up with." He resumes typing. "We still on for this afternoon?"

"Do you even have to ask?" Jackie piles her napkin on top of her barely touched lunch.

"Sweet," Tanner replies. "I'll be sure to have a full report by then."

"Cool." I take another bite of my apple.

"My money is on a secret, underground fight club," Jackie jokes.

NINETEEN

TANNER DRIVES US BACK TO HIS PLACE AFTER SCHOOL IN HIS SUV. HE AND Jackie spend the entire trip arguing about what movie we're going to watch. I just stare out the window, trying to repress my building anxiety over the Chris situation.

I didn't see him again after first period, and I've checked my phone so often the battery is almost shot. I can't explain why I'm so desperate for answers. It's not like the situation affects me. Chris isn't even really my friend. At least, he wasn't. After yesterday, I really don't know where we stand.

"If I watch that fucking movie one more time," Jackie seethes, "I'm going to gouge my own eyes out. I don't care if Keanu Reeves is at peak hotness. It's dumb."

"It's a modern-day masterpiece," Tanner argues as we turn into his neighborhood. "Mike, we need you to be the tiebreaker."

"What are the options again?" I ask.

"Are you serious?" Tanner eyes me through the rearview mirror. "Where are you today, man?"

"Don't mind Mike," Jackie tells him. "He's been a zombie all day."

"Your choices are a no-brainer. The incredible piece of art that is *The Matrix*," he says, "or the two-and-a-half-hour snooze fest, *The Great Gatsby*."

"Tough choice." I drum my fingers together in a pensive gesture. "But seeing as we've watched *The Matrix* three times this month, I'm going to have to side with Jackie."

"Yes!" Jackie pumps her fist. "In your face, you *Neo*-phyte. See what I did there?"

"Solid pun."

"Shut up, traitor," Tanner mutters. The car bounces as we pull into the driveway, garage doors opening with a touch of a button to welcome us.

After a quick raid of the refrigerator for soda and snacks, the three of us climb the stairs to Tanner's bedroom. We don't have to worry about spilling something on the super-expensive furniture in here, and his TV is just as big as the one in the living room.

Tanner reluctantly selects the movie on his DVR, plopping down in his computer chair.

The opening song plays, and I can't contain myself anymore. "Did you hear anything from the rumor pool about Chris?"

"Oh, yeah." Tanner spins toward his desktop, waking it up with a click of the space bar. He types for a minute then lets out a low whistle. "It ain't pretty."

"What?" I'm beside him before I realize it, looking over his shoulder.

"Tammy Richardson says she heard it was his dad," Tanner says, scrolling through his Facebook messages.

They're full of everyone's secrets.

I wonder if they say anything about me?

"Pastor Myers?" Jackie asks from the floor, munching on a handful of popcorn. "Did he hit him?"

"There aren't a lot of details," Tanner says, skimming over the message. "But, apparently, it was a disagreement that went south."

My fists clench at my side, I'm straining to hear over the ringing in my ears. His father did that to him? Just when I thought I couldn't think lesser of the man. What kind of fucked up person would do that to their kid?

"Whoa, Mike. You're freaking me out, man." Tanner looks up through his thick frames, eyes wide.

I try to wipe off whatever expression is on my face. "Sorry." I look away from him, sinking back down to the floor beside Jackie while her fingers dance across the screen of her phone. "That's just really awful. What sick fuck would do that to their son?"

Jackie lets out a girlish giggle, and both of our heads turn to her.

"Huh?" She looks up at us. "What?"

"Who are you texting?" Tanner asks. The fact he doesn't already know is miraculous.

"Brad." She resumes texting.

"Wait," I interject, thoughts of Chris fading for the moment. "Praise band Brad?"

"Back-of-the-bus-handjob Brad?" Tanner joins in.

"Yes, and yes." Jackie smiles, tucking a loose strand of hair behind her ear. "I don't know why this is a shock to you two. We've been talking for a while now. He's taking me to dinner tomorrow night."

"Isn't he like, thirty?" Tanner lowers himself to our level from his chair, all three of us ignoring the movie playing. They mostly serve as background noise, anyway.

"So, what if he is?" Jackie scoffs. "I always wanted a sugar daddy."

"Tell that to the judge presiding over your statutory rape case." Tanner grabs the popcorn bowl.

"He's the same age as you, dipshit." Jackie smacks his shoulder.

"What does your mom think about you dating?" I ask, knowing there's no way she's okay with this.

"What she doesn't know won't hurt her."

"And Jackie enters the pregnancy race," Tanner announces in his best sportscaster voice. "All right, Mike, what month do you want in the pool?"

"Put me down for December," I joke, pulling out my wallet.

"Fuck you guys," Jackie curses, but she smiles too.

TWENTY

CHRIS HAS AVOIDED ME LIKE THE PLAGUE FOR OVER A WEEK NOW. EVERY TIME I get close to him, he bolts like he's afraid I'm going to murder him or something. He even got Randall Josep to trade seats with him in Dr. Redford's class. He is three rows behind me now, which means I can't look at him without drawing attention to myself. So, I'm stuck smelling Randall's disgusting mixture of BO and aftershave.

I give up even trying by Friday, resigning myself to pouting into my plate at lunch. The usual suspects are here, and I really am trying not to be a Debbie-downer.

"Guess who I saw smoking in the second-floor bathrooms?" Tabby Freeman taunts Tanner from across the table.

Tabby's practically a walking cesspool of gossip. I'm shocked she and Tanner aren't married yet. They would be the nosiest neighbors on the fucking planet.

"Who?" He looks up from his laptop, a certain excitement in his eyes that only comes from secrets and source code.

"Chris Myers," Tabby replies, tossing a strand of greasy, tawny hair out of her eyes.

My head snaps up at the mention of his name. I angle myself to hear them better.

"Huh." Tanner grabs another tater tot from his tray, dragging it through a puddle of ketchup. "I didn't even know he smoked. You hear that, Jackie? You two are practically soul mates. At least you'll both die of lung cancer."

"Shut your face," quips Jackie, not even bothering to glance away from her phone. She's more than likely sexting Brad.

"What were you doing in the boy's restroom?" I ask Tabby, looking for a way to insert myself into the conversation.

"None of your business, Hernandez." She snarls through yellowed teeth.

I wonder if she has actually cooked meth before, or if she just *looks* like she has.

"Well, you obviously weren't observing any kind of dental hygiene."

A few of the others around the table snicker, and Tabby cuts daggers at me with her eyes. I couldn't care less. Even if I wasn't Kinsey-6 gay, I wouldn't touch her with a ten-foot pole.

"Watch it, queerbait." Tabby seethes.

My blood runs cold even though I know she doesn't actually mean it. I would know if someone was spreading rumors about me. It's the unspoken agreement I have with Tanner.

I roll my eyes, rising to my feet. Hopefully, my terrible poker face hasn't given me away.

"Swhere hue goin'?" Tanner asks through his half-chewed potatoes.

"I have to finish up a quiz for Geometry," I lie, slinging my bag over my shoulder. "I'll see you guys this afternoon."

Time to flee Tabby's putrid breath and the mention of my queerness as quickly as I can. I dump my tray in the trash, almost crashing through the door.

That wasn't funny, Big Guy. I swear, if I get outed by Tabby fucking Freeman, I'm going to just end it all right here and now.

My body is on autopilot as I move into the hallways. I don't realize where I'm heading until I'm almost there.

The second floor is quiet since most of the students are in the cafeteria right now. I push open the men's room door, the stale smell of tobacco hitting me like a wall. There are three stalls, but only one of them has the door closed. I knock on it, waiting for a response.

"Chris?"

No answer.

"I know it's you in there," I say. "Tabby ratted you out. Hey, you didn't let her blow you, did you? Because I would definitely go get that checked out. I mean there has to be at least four STD's rolling around that disgusting mouth of hers."

Still nothing verbal, but I hear the sharp intake of air from his laugh.

"Look, I just want to talk." My head is getting light from all the smoke. "Can you come out of there?"

A pair of feet hit the ground, shuffling coming next. The door swings open.

"You're persistent." Chris's voice is gruff.

"It's one of my better qualities," I joke, but the smile

fades when I get a good look at him. It's the first time I've really been able to since he isn't running away from me.

His eyes are bloodshot, the dark bruise under his eye shining purple. His lip has scabbed over, and a cigarette hangs off it.

"What do you want, Mike?" he demands, pulling the filter away from his mouth as he exhales a cloud of white in my face.

I wave it away with my hand. "Why are you avoiding me?"

"I'm not," he says.

I can't look away from the shiner. It fills me with rage.

"Bullshit," I snap. "Look, if you don't want me here, then just tell me. I don't care, but I deserve more than a cold shoulder."

The edges of Chris's lips curl into a smile. "Are you breaking up with me?"

"Fuck you." I punch his shoulder, but I can't keep my own smile from escaping. "Seriously, Chris, what the hell is going on? You stressed me out with that text, and then you show up to school like you've been in fight club. There's a pool going around about that actually. And then you just drop off the radar?"

"Right." Chris scoffs. "Like I don't know what people are saying about me. Everyone thinks my dad beat the shit out of me because of one thing or another."

Wait, his dad didn't do this to him?

"Then what did happen?" I press. "Set the record straight."

Chris drops the cigarette to the floor, stepping on it

to snuff the fire. "It's my own stupid fault," he says, staring at the smear of ash on the tile. "I was just so pissed at him. He didn't do anything wrong." His voice wavers, bottom lip trembling.

My anger melts faster than a snow cone in Phoenix. "H-Hey." I grab his shoulder, giving a comforting squeeze. "It's okay, man. You don't have to tell me."

He shakes his head, wiping the tears from his eyes with a half-hearted laugh. "If he saw me now, he'd have a few choice words for me. 'Suck it up,' or maybe, 'I didn't raise a pussy.' Those are classics."

And the anger is back in a flash. It radiates through me, setting my blood on fire. "I hate him."

"You don't even know him," Chris says, brushing my hand off.

"I know enough." I spit the words. "He's a homophobic piece of sh—" Pain explodes in my cheek as Chris's palm slaps me across the face.

"Shut up." He seethes.

"Why are you defending him?" Heat radiates from my face, whether from the impact or my own emotions, I can't tell. "He *hit* you, Chris. He thinks you and I are abominations who should be rounded up and stuck in a cage. Or did you forget that little gem from his sermon last month? Because I sure haven't!"

Chris recoils as if I've returned his blow.

"That one really stuck with me," I continue, anger-fueled words spewing. "I took a lot of really good notes. My parents *loved* it. They wouldn't stop talking about it at lunch. I just sat there quietly, wishing I was anything other than gay. And don't even get me started on a few weeks ago when your dad enlightened me to the fact that, apparently, I'm a pedophile. I had no idea but, thank God, he was there to set me straight."

"Stop," Chris whimpers. "Please, just stop."

"Why? I'm just telling the truth." I keep on, turning away from him. "This isn't something I'm making up. Although, I wish it was. He said these horrible things. So, why are you defending him?"

"Because he's my dad," Chris whispers.

And, once again, the flames of my anger smother. I watch him blot away the tears from his cheeks. He's a mess, and I'm being a jackass.

"I'm sorry," I say quietly. "I didn't mean to make you upset."

"It's not like I don't know he's terrible," he replies, sniffling. "I sit through the same services you do. I live with the man. Can you imagine how much I hear from him? He's my father, and I know, deep down, how much he hates me. Maybe he doesn't know it yet, but he hates me, Mike. His only child."

I don't know what to say, so I just stand here, arms crossed and silent.

Is this funny to You up there, Big Guy? Because we aren't laughing.

"I...I took a swing at him that night. The night I sent you that text. I mean, I was on cloud nine. We'd had such a great time, and I'd finally gotten up the courage to get my ear pierced. Then, I get home, and he's ranting about a story he saw on the news. Apparently, a friend of his from seminary is getting threatened with legal action because he refused to perform a wedding ceremony for a same-sex couple in Nashville."

Dad mentioned something about it at dinner last week. He called the guy courageous. I just smiled and stuffed my mouth with potato salad.

"He just kept going on about how gays were destroying the foundation of the country and nothing was sacred anymore. Naturally, I played the Devil's advocate and tried to defend some couple I'd never even met before, and things got out of hand pretty quick."

He leans over, propping himself on the wall of the stall. "I don't even remember what he said that set me off. I flaunted my earring, and he lost his shit and started shouting. It was so bad my mom tried to step in, but Dad told her to leave the room. She was in tears the whole time.

"And after our shouting match, I took a swing at him. He caught me by the wrist and pushed me back. That's when I hit the bookcase, and his stupid wrought-iron globe fell from the top shelf." He pulls up the sleeve of his jacket, showing the long purple spot on his forearm. "My arm took most of the hit, but not all of it." He raises his arm in front of his face, so I can see the outline of the bar that hit him.

So, his dad didn't do it. At least not on purpose. That doesn't mean I don't still hate his fucking guts.

"As you can imagine, that kind of killed the argument." Chris pulls his sleeve back in place. "He was so mortified, he just kept asking if I was all right. I kicked him off me and locked myself in my room. I couldn't even think straight. So, I took out a bottle of whiskey I stole from my uncle's liquor cabinet over the summer and drank the whole thing. Ugh, just thinking about it makes me queasy. That was not a fun night."

That's when he texted me.

"Did you…?" I can't bring myself to say it.

"No," Chris says quietly. "But I can't say I didn't think about it. Look, I'm sorry I sent you that message. I wasn't exactly doing so hot, and it was fueled by far too much alcohol."

"I didn't know what to think," I reply, "and when I saw you at school, I got so worried."

"Yeah?" Chris lifts his head, the ghost of a smile playing across his face. "You were worried about me?"

"Of course, I was." I shuffle my feet. "You're my friend, and you were obviously in pain."

"So, we're friends?"

"Dude, seriously?" I unfold my arms. "Yes, you are my friend. Maybe more so than anyone. You know the most about me at least."

This makes him smile. Not a half-hearted one, but a genuine, lets-see-those-pearly-whites smile. My heart feels lighter just seeing it.

"Good," he says, tossing his bangs out of his eyes.

"So, can you please stop avoiding me?" I step closer to him. "Because it's getting really fucking annoying."

He nods, sniffling one last time.

"Look, I have swim practice after school today. But do you want to hang when I'm done? I'm totally free."

"Sure." Chris clears his throat. "Thanks, Mike."

"Don't mention it."

TWENTY ONE

WITH THE BLOW OF A WHISTLE, I DIVE INTO THE POOL. BURSTING THROUGH the surface, my arms and legs move in unison to propel me toward the other end.

Stroke, stroke, breathe. Stroke, stroke, breathe.

I let myself fall into a familiar rhythm, pausing only once I reach the wall of the pool. I somersault and push off the rough cement.

When I haul myself out of the water, Coach Schmidt is waiting for me.

"Still running behind," he tells me, writing my time on his red clipboard. "Are you focusing?"

"As much as I can," I admit, lifting the goggles from my eyes and grabbing a towel.

"We might be in trouble then," Coach mutters. "Look, Michael, you'll never place if you keep this pace. I can't keep babysitting you here. You have to want it for yourself."

I nod. My current concerns are far from lap times and trophies.

"Go ahead and hit the showers," he says, running a

hand through his patchy black hair. "I don't think it's gonna get any better for you today."

"Yes, sir." It's tough to hide my excitement, so I wrap my towel around my neck and dash for the locker room. Fresh towel in hand from the stack in the corner, I head for the showers.

The novelty of being in a place where I get to see a bunch of mostly naked boys walk around has worn off somewhat in the past few months. Maybe it's because I've grown more comfortable in my skin, or more likely, it's because I've found a porn site I actually enjoy. By now, I've seen it all, and the monotony of topless guys in towels has lost its effect on me.

However, there's something to be said about these private school showers. Everyone gets their own stall, and it offers far more privacy than traditional ones, at least so I hear. They're perfect for concealing the boner of a closeted sixteen-year-old.

I pull the curtain back, stepping into the warm spray of water. Someone hums in the stall next to mine, and it sounds like a Coldplay song I like. I fight the urge to join in.

Once the chlorine is out of my hair, the shower shuts off with a twist of the knob. I reach for my towel on the other side of the curtain but come up empty. My heart races. I pull back the curtain, squinting into the steamy tiled room. My gym bag sits across the room, mocking me. My towel is beside it.

Fuck.

My cheeks burn as I weigh my options.

God, please don't let anyone walk in.

I can't stay in here forever, so I gather my courage. After I carefully cup my goodies, I step gingerly from the shower and into the cold air. I throw another glance left and right, making sure no one is walking around the corner. The coast is clear, so I make a mad dash for the towel.

"Whoa!"

I spin toward the voice, pulling the white cloth in front of me. "What the fuck?"

Chris stands by the entrance of the showers, a hand covering his face as he sputters.

"S-Sorry!"

I quickly wrap the fluffy towel around me. "What are you doing here?" I whisper, head whipping back and forth. The other shower is still going, so hopefully, no one can hear us.

"Figured I would come watch you practice." He brushes a piece of hair out of his face, his other hand still concealing his eyes. "But the coach said you were in here. I didn't think— I'm just gonna go now."

"I'll be dressed in a few," I offer, trying to recover from the horribly awkward exchange.

"R-Right. I'll just wait in the car."

Good grief. What a day.

I run a hand through my hair as Chris leaves, and then I pull my cell phone out of my gym bag. I need to avoid another parental freak out, so I send Dad a text message.

> Hey, I'm helping Chris Myers with his project again. I'll be home before 9. Love you. 4:36pm

He probably won't reply, but at least I'll have evidence I attempted communication.

The room falls quiet, and I realize the humming has stopped. I grab my stuff, making for the exit, but a voice catches me.

"Hey, Mike."

Davy steps out of the shower, his own towel wrapped snugly around his waist.

Davy is one of my teammates, Master of the Butterfly. He's a year younger than me, but you'd never know it by looking at him. I have to remind myself not to stare at his body as he comes closer, blond hair slicked back.

"What's up, Davy?" I say, cringing as my voice cracks. "How was your time today?"

"Eh." He shrugs his shoulder, tanned skin pulling taut as his muscles move.

They're hypnotic.

"Schmidt-head isn't happy, but I shaved a second off today. Hopefully, it'll get me to state this year."

"That would be awesome." I tear my eyes from his perfect pectorals. "I totally think you'll get there."

"Thanks, man."

He smiles, and my knees go a little weak.

"Was that Chris Myers I heard you talking to?"

"Huh?"

"I thought I recognized his voice," Davy continues, sauntering over to the bench. "He's in my literature class. I got advanced placement for some reason, but he's wicked smart. We got paired up for a writing project, and I couldn't be more glad. I suck at that kind of stuff, but he's insanely good."

"Oh, yeah." I breathe my relief. "That was him. He's going to help me with an essay."

"You two sound pretty chummy."

Something behind his voice makes my stomach

squirm. What does he know?

"Y-Yeah," I stammer, "we know each other from church. So, you could say that."

Without warning, Davy loosens his towel and pulls it off. He throws it over his head, tousling it back and forth.

Don't look. Don't look. Don't look.

"Gotcha," he says, removing the hood. "Well, you guys have fun with that." He tosses his towel aside, and I swear he winks at me.

Wait. Did that just happen, or did I imagine it?

"T-Thanks." I take a few steps back. "Well, he's waiting on me."

"Tell him I said not to work too hard." Davy smiles again.

I have to leave right now before I consider doing something I regret.

After I dress, I practically run out of the locker room. Before long, I'm at Chris's car.

"What's got you so worked up?" he asks as I hurl myself into the passenger seat.

"Don't ask."

TWENTY TWO

"DOES THIS MAKE ME LOOK FAT?"

Chris pulls back the curtain separating us, the sparkling spandex suit looking like a twinkling nightmare. He's pushed his dark hair back with a matching sequin headband.

"I don't think fat is the word I would use." I laugh as he strikes a pose in the mirror.

My phone buzzes in my pocket, and I drag myself away from Chris's fashion show. It's a text from Tanner.

> I thought you were coming over after practice? Jackie is making me watch a terrible Hillary Duff movie, and no one was here to vote her down. 5:43pm

Shit. I forgot to call him. I blame it on my conversation with naked Davy. That practically left my brain melted. I type back a response.

"Are you going to try yours on?"

Chris holds up an identical jumpsuit, sequins and all.

"No way in Hell that will ever be on my body."

"Fine, crush my dreams why don't you?" Chris laughs, sliding the curtain closed. "Hey," he calls through the divide, "I'm glad we could do this."

"Me too," I reply as I eye the wall of colorful belts hanging to my right. He dragged me to this weird clothing shop in Little Fives. A place packed with rack after rack of dated clothes. Mom would have a field day here. She would never leave.

"Do you want to grab a cup of coffee?" Chris asks.

"What, no dandelion tea?"

"Not today." He laughs. The curtain draws open, and he hangs the jumpsuit on the rack outside the dressing room. "There's this great place just a few doors down."

"Sounds awesome," I agree, following him to the counter.

"You getting anything?" he asks, handing his own purchases over to the cashier. The guy is really cute, but he's wearing a fedora which is an immediate no thank you.

"Nah," I reply. "I'm more a hoodie and jeans kind of guy."

"Yeah, I can tell." Chris laughs.

After he pays for his three bracelets and a bright

174

orange belt, we leave the cramped store. I take a breath of fresh air, shaking the musty smell of old clothes from my head.

"This way." Chris moves down the sidewalk, swinging his new purchases over his shoulder. He stops after a second, digging for the change from his pocket. He stoops down to the man I didn't even notice before. "Thought that was you. You doing okay, Sal?"

"Christian, my main man." The dark-skinned guy smiles a toothless grin. "How you doin'?"

Christian? Why did I always assume Chris was short for Christopher?

"Can't complain." Chris returns the smile, giving the obviously homeless man a fist bump. "Where are you staying nowadays?"

"The mission up on Ivan Allen," Sal replies. "They're giving me a job next week in one of the shops."

"That's great!" Chris exclaims. "I hope it works out for you, Sal."

"Thanking ya."

"Hey, Sal, this is my friend Mike." Chris gestures to me.

I shuffle forward awkwardly to shake the man's hand.

"Nice to meet you," I say as Sal's potent body odor hits my nose. I attempt to keep my face from wrinkling.

"Likewise," Sal responds, looking back to Chris. "You been scrapping?"

Chris chuckles. "Something like that. You should see the other guy."

"That's what I'm talking about." Sal raises his fists to eye level. "Gotta keep that pretty mug protected."

"I'll try to remember that." Chris laughs, straightening. "We gotta get going, but you take it easy, Sal."

"Sure thing." He chuckles. "Tell your pops I said thanks for his help a couple weeks ago."

"You got it," Chris says.

We keep moving down the sidewalk, and I wave back to Sal.

The more time I spend with Chris, the more he surprises me.

We pass Junkman's Daughter and enter the last shop on the strip, Aurora Coffee. The wonderful aroma wipes away all my cares.

I need coffee like I need air.

We step up to the counter, and I peruse the chalkboard menus. The menu is smack full of options, and I don't know what half of them mean. I fucking love coffee shops.

"How's it going, guys?" the barista asks. He's young, tattooed, and beautiful. Why is everyone around here so fucking hot?

"Great," Chris says. "I'll have a Brown Bear, please."

"What's that?" I ask.

"It's iced coffee with chocolate milk," Chris replies.

"Ditto for me," I tell the barista, digging for my wallet.

"I got it." Chris pulls out his debit card, swiping it on the terminal.

"Thanks."

We take a seat as our drinks are being made. Snow-capped mountains and clouds decorate the wall behind Chris. There's some kind of bird painted there too, but a television screen covers where its head should be. It's a metaphor for something, I'm sure.

"I love all the art around here," I say, marveling at the blending colors of the feathers. "They're unlike anything I've ever seen."

"That's for sure." Chris chuckles, scooting out of his seat to go grab our glasses from the bar. He returns a second later, setting them down on the table. They're a rich chocolaty color with a layer of white bubbles on top.

I take a sip, and it's pure heaven.

"How do you know that guy outside?" I ask, leaning back in my chair.

"Sal?" Chris sips his own drink, pausing before he speaks again. "My dad used to help out a shelter downtown. We'd come down every Saturday to serve meals or whatever they needed us to do. Dad met Sal before that though. He's been here for decades."

"That's really cool of you guys." I guess it shouldn't surprise me to hear about Pastor Myers doing charitable work. I mean the guy is a *pastor* for crying out loud. But it doesn't change my picture of him.

"I used to hate it." Chris shrugs. "But I guess, as I got older, I started to gain some perspective. There were kids around my age, and one day, it just finally clicked. I thought, 'This could be me. I'm no different from any of them.' And after that, it was different. I just want to help them with what I can."

Whoa. That wasn't what I expected at all.

"Sorry." Chris looks down at his hands. "I'm not trying to brag or anything." He swirls his cup. "Let's change the subject."

"I didn't think you were," I assure him.

His face flushes with color, and he won't meet my

gaze.

"Do you know Davy from school?"

That grabs his attention. "Davy Daniels?"

I nod, trying not to dwell on flashes of his naked body from earlier.

"Yeah." He leans his elbows on the wooden tabletop. "He's in my lit class. Why do you ask?"

"I ran into him in the shower after you left," I tell him. "I think he suspects something is going on between us."

"Is there something going on between us?" Chris's signature smirk is back.

I roll my eyes. "He insinuated there was." I laugh. "And then he dropped his towel and gave me a wink."

"No shit!" Chris leans forward even more. "What did you do?"

"I covered my eyes and ran away," I confess. "No way I was going to stand there and have a conversation with him with his dick out."

"Aw…" Chris sits back in his seat. "I was hoping for something a little steamier."

"Jeez, P.K." I tease. "So scandalous. Sorry to be such a disappointment."

"He's been giving off some pretty strong vibes in class." He slides his cup across the table, passing it back and forth between hands. "But I was almost certain it was wishful thinking on my part."

"It was shocking, to say the least." I laugh.

"Then are the rumors about him true?" Chris raises an eyebrow.

Heat radiates from my face as I nod. "I can verify it is indeed true. No padding. Just au naturel."

"Jesus," breathes Chris. "And he's my partner for

Stephens's joint essay assignment. Now, I'm going to be too distracted to work."

We both laugh, and it feels natural.

It's strange. I've spent a collective two afternoons with Chris, and it feels like we've known each other forever. Could it be I have nothing to hide? Nothing I'm afraid will give me away. There's only Chris, me, and the freedom to say what I'm thinking.

I could get used to this.

"Hey, Chris." I wipe a laughter-fueled tear from my eye. "Are you coming to Jackie's birthday party Sunday?"

"I wasn't planning on it." He sips his drink.

"You should," I continue. "I need a ride, anyway."

"Okay." He nods, "Sure. That sounds like fun."

"Sweet. It's a date."

IT'S A DATE.

I lay awake in my bed, those stupid words playing over and over in my head.

Why did I say that? It's not like I really meant it. It doesn't change the fact neither Chris nor I will behave any differently at the party. We'll be the same closet cases we've always been. So why did I ask?

I reach for my bag from the drawing desk, pulling out my sketchpad. I'm never going to fall asleep, so I might as well do something. Flipping to a blank page, I make lines as my mind continues to wander. The constant motion helps me think.

Chris smiled ever so slightly when I asked him. Did

that mean something? Did he want it to be a date? Does he like me that way? Do I like him that way? And why the fuck does this even matter? It's not like I'm able to have a boyfriend. The same goes for him.

I don't think I have the mental fortitude to keep a relationship secret. I would be a nervous wreck, like, all the time. More so than usual, that is.

Maybe I should tell Jackie. She would totally help me keep it a secret if Chris and I saw each other in a more intimate way. At least, I think she would. But I've already been over this. That involves her knowing everything, and eventually, the truth would get out.

I look down at the page, smeared lines forming the shape of a figure seated at a table, a large painted bird on the wall behind him. Shaggy hair and smirk.

Fuck.

I flip the book closed, taking a steadying breath as I face the hard truth. I can't stop thinking about Chris.

TWENTY THREE

"So, how's this going to go?" Chris asks as we pull into Jackie's driveway. Her grandparents own a couple of acres west of Roswell, near the Clary lakes. Their driveway takes a good two minutes to drive down to get to the house. I used to think these woods went on for miles when Jackie and I would play in them.

She and her mom, Melissa, live here with her grandparents. They have her entire life. Melissa is the youngest of her siblings, and she had Jackie when she was sixteen. Mr. and Mrs. Stephenson are awesome, and I consider them to be like my own grandparents.

"What do you mean?" I ask as we wind down the curvy path, thick woods on either side of the car.

"I mean, like, do you want me to talk to you while we're here? Or should I like, avoid you."

"Why would you avoid me?" I ask. "That's stupid. Talk to me like a normal person. Just keep it straight. No bent comments."

"Roger that," Chris replies, his knuckles white as he grips the steering wheel.

"Dude," I say as I place my hand on his knee, "you need to calm down. Just relax and have a good time."

"Kind of hard to think about relaxing with your hand there."

"That's your last gay comment for the night," I tell him, and he laughs as we pull into the grass beside Tanner's SUV. "All right, let's do this."

I grab Jackie's gift from the backseat. Mom's wrapping job is flawless as always. I swear, she's the only person I've ever seen use a protractor to make sure her folds are at just the right angle. It takes a special kind of woman to be that anal-retentive.

We walk to the front door, and I let myself in.

Laughter comes from the living room to our left, and I quickly drop my gift on the dining room table. Nana Stephenson sees me from the kitchen and hustles to greet me. She wraps me up in a bone-crushing hug.

"It's been too long, Michael!"

"It's good to see you, Nana," I croak through her grip. She's a large woman with silver hair and a pair of half-moon glasses usually hanging from her neck. She wears one of her signature outfits which always include some kind of bedazzled design on the front. Today she wears brightly colored balloons. They dig into my skin as she squeezes me.

"You need to stop growin'," she says as she releases me, holding me at arm's length. "It seems like just yesterday you and Jackie were this tall."

"I don't even remember those days," I kid.

She laughs her throaty laugh.

"Who do we have here?" she asks, looking to where Chris stands awkwardly in the foyer.

"You know Chris Myers from church?"

"That you, little Christian?" She waddles over to him and crushes him next.

His eyes are wide as he looks to me, and it's all I can do to keep from laughing.

"Good to see you," he tells her.

"You look just like your mama," Nana Stephenson says, pinching his cheek.

"Thanks." Chris smiles at her.

"Good Lord, what happened to your face?"

"It's a long story." He laughs nervously.

"Well, the rest of the young'uns are in the livin' room. You two go join 'em, and supper will be ready in just a little bit."

"Yes, ma'am," we say in unison.

I lead Chris down the hallway.

"I think my ribs are cracked," he whispers.

I can't hold in the laugh this time. I'm still smiling when we enter the living room.

"There you are." Jackie looks up from the couch. "I was starting to think you died."

"Nah, you'll be the first to know when that happens," I joke. "I think you're listed as my emergency contact."

"Perfect," she murmurs, turning her attention back to the card game being played on the coffee table.

Entering the Stephenson's living room is like taking a step back in time. The wooden paneling on the walls is dark and absorbs all the light in the room. A mismatched assortment of furniture spreads across the floor, and Papa Stephenson's collection of antique coo-coo clocks covers one wall. Every hour is a symphony of bells and chimes. The television, which is one of those old-school, huge monsters that predates anything plasma or flat screen, flickers pretty bad. But Jackie hooked up an Apple TV, so we can stream Netflix.

I relish the familiar, musty smell.

It's one of my favorite places in the world.

"Hey, Tanner," I call over.

He sits in one of the cracked leather chairs, laptop balanced on his legs as he types furiously. He waves without looking up.

Tabby Freeman perches on the armrest, looking over his shoulder as he types. She's actually kind of pretty when not wearing her school uniform. And as long as she keeps her mouth closed.

The rest of our rotating lunch table is here too—Mark Routon, Taylor Shay, Larry Fletcher, and Katie Reese. They're not exactly my friends, but Jackie attracts a variety of people, so I know them all by association. I don't think a single one of them has ever invited me to do anything outside of school unless I'm Jackie's plus one. And, to be honest, I'm okay with that. The fewer people I spend time with, the less likely someone will figure out my secret.

"All right, make room!" I step over Katie and flop onto the floor next to Jackie as I wrap her neck in a hug. "Happy birthday, slut face."

"Thanks, ass hat," she replies, tickling my ribs.

I yelp, and laughter spreads through the group. Chris sinks down at the coffee table across from me, looking very uncomfortable. I give him a smile.

"What are we playing?" I ask, looking at the strange black and white cards.

"Cards Against Humanity," says Mark, holding his own hand of the white cards. "It's hilarious."

"Is that so?" I peek over at Jackie's hand, heat rising

184

to my cheeks.

"Don't be so bashful, Mike," teases Larry, flipping over a black card and reading it aloud. "All right, everyone. Why am I sticky?"

Katie leans over to Chris, whispering, "Now, we pick the best card that goes with that question," she explains.

She's always making sure everyone is included. Katie might be the nicest person I know.

Each player lays down a card in a stack. Larry shuffles them together then reads them aloud.

"Why am I sticky? We have, flying sex snakes. Classic."

Giggles spread like rippling water through the group.

"Next, we have Michelle Obama's arms. That's not right. She's like my second mom."

"Don't ever say that around my parents," says Taylor, clutching his shoulder.

They're a new couple, and I can't imagine her parents are keen on the idea of her dating a black guy who's also a Democrat. He can be one or the other, but heaven forbid both.

"Third, we have incest. You guys just ain't right."

Another round of laughter.

"And last, but not least, anal orgasms. Wow."

"You'd know all about those, wouldn't you, Larry?" Mark laughs.

"At least I have a girlfriend, Marky Mark."

The friendly argument quickly devolves into the two of them wrestling each other on the floor, laughing and tumbling over one another. I roll my eyes in exasperation.

"Hey! If you break something, you're going to have to explain yourselves to my nana!" Jackie warns.

The two of them separate, still laughing.

"Who won, Larry?" Taylor asks, batting her eyelashes.

"The award goes to Anal Orgasms," he says, raising it high in the air like a champion celebrating victory.

"Yes!" Jackie snatches the black card from the table. "And the birthday girl retains her title!"

A collective groan resounds as everyone tosses their cards into a pile.

"Why am I not surprised you own at this game?" I tug on Jackie's sleeve.

"Because I win at everything?" she replies, giving me a coy smile. "Well, everything that doesn't include killing zombies."

"All right, kids!" Nana Stephenson's voice echoes from down the hall. "Come and get it!"

The room devolves into chaos before we fall into a single file herd toward the kitchen.

"I didn't think Chris was going to show," Jackie whispers to me.

We're close to the back of the line.

"Did he give you a ride?"

"Yeah." I keep my voice nonchalant. There's nothing weird about sharing a car with another guy, especially when she knows I can't drive. "I was helping him with some homework, and he asked if I wanted to carpool."

"You two seem to be spending a considerable amount of time together."

"So, what?" My heart hammers.

Jackie shrugs. "Hey, the more the merrier. Just means more presents for me."

That's Jackie. She's okay with anything as long as she profits.

The kitchen devolves into chaos as we cram nine hungry teenagers into one place. A feast of all Jackie's favorite foods awaits us. A tray of Chick-fil-A chicken nuggets, Nana Stephenson's famous mac and cheese, a massive bowl of buttery mashed potatoes, and a loaf of garlic bread. Jackie is a carb girl. On the corner of the counter is an untouched plate of asparagus Nana Stephenson made in case anyone wanted something a little healthier. Needless to say, it remains untouched.

"Lord, Jackie," Taylor says, scooping potatoes onto her plate. "Are you trying to kill us?"

"Shut up, matchstick girl." Jackie laughs, squeezing ketchup on top of her mac and cheese.

Chris watches in horror as the tomatoey stream continues.

"Not everyone can live off carrots and diet Coke like you can. Us big girls like to eat real food."

I'll never understand girls. Jackie isn't by any means a big girl though she calls herself one at least twice a day. And she teases Taylor for being a matchstick, but honestly, they probably weigh the same. Maybe it's just because Taylor's a little taller, but I'm still at a loss.

I give Chris a pat on the shoulder. "You get used to her after a while," I whisper.

After everyone has their carbohydrate-loaded plates, we all crowd around Nana Stephenson's dining table, shoving the small mountain of gifts into the middle. The laughter and chatter continue as we eat.

"Where's your mom?" I lean over to Jackie as Tanner entertains everyone with a funny video on his laptop.

"She said she had to go run an errand a few hours

ago." Jackie stabs another pile of red-soaked noodles. "If you ask me, it's really fishy. She's probably picking up my present."

"Maybe she got you a car?" I say, but we both laugh.

"Yeah right." Jackie giggles. "Maybe it's a Maserati! We can go cruising!"

"It's nice to dream." I chew a hunk of garlic bread.

"Keep dreaming."

I look over to Chris, who's nestled between Tanner and Tabby. I have no idea how that happened, but I feel for the poor guy. Knowing those two, they're probably trying to play footsie under the table, and that makes Chris's feet collateral damage.

As if on cue, a look of surprise registers on Chris's face, and he peers under the table.

I join in everyone's laughter, but for my own reasons.

Once we've had our fill of starch and bread, Nana Stephenson comes back with the cake. It's homemade and slathered in Jackie's favorite strawberry frosting—another thing we have in common.

In the words of one of my favorite movies, "It looks like a pink nightmare."

"Where's Mom?" Jackie asks as her grandmother lights the candles.

"She called just a few minutes ago, Bug," Nana Stephenson replies. "She got held up in traffic but is on her way. Told me to go ahead and keep things rolling."

Jackie rolls her eyes but doesn't push the subject.

We all join in a chorus of "Happy Birthday," and not a single person sings on pitch. Jackie is the only one who can sing here, and she is cringing. Nana Stephenson hits a note at the end I'm sure is sending dogs across the neighborhood howling.

Cheers and jeers explode as Jackie blows out her candles, and Nana Stephenson sets to work carving it with practiced hands.

"Is this Pepto Bismol flavored?" jokes Mark. "How'd you know that was my favorite flavor?"

"Just lucky, I guess." Jackie digs a finger into her slice, popping the pink smothered tip into her mouth.

"Are you going to get your license tomorrow?" Katie asks, gently raising her fork as she takes a delicate bite of cake. She told us earlier that her parents made her take cotillion classes when she was in middle school. That explains the table manners.

"That's the plan," Jackie replies. "Mom got someone to cover her last class of the day, so we can hurry over before the DDS closes."

"Good luck," Taylor calls from the other end of the table. "I failed that thing three times before they gave me a license. They're super strict."

"I don't think it's strict of them to deny you a license when you hit someone during your test." Tanner points a cake-covered fork at her.

"That could have happened to anyone!" Taylor defends herself.

"I think they finally just gave it to you to save them from the liability charges," says Mark. "How many innocent people had to die?"

"No one died!" Taylor yells. "Besides, the lady was fine after a few weeks in the ICU."

Chris and I make eye contact and bust out laughing.

"Well, it certainly sounds like you guys are having a blast," a new voice says. Jackie's mom, Melissa, wraps her arms around her daughter's shoulders, resting her chin on the crown of her head.

"Hey, Mom." She pats her mother's arm. "'Bout time you showed up."

"Is that how you talk to the woman who gave you life?"

"Yeah, yeah." Jackie laughs. "And who never lets me forget it?"

"Good to see everyone." Melissa waves at the rest of the table. "I hope you all finished your homework for Monday. I don't give extensions for late night partying."

The table grumbles, and Melissa smiles.

"Where were you, Mom?" Jackie takes another bite of her cake.

"I was getting your present," she responds, digging through her pocket. "Are you ready for it?"

"As ready as I'll ever be." Jackie gets up from her seat, facing her mother.

"Here you go." Melissa hands over a small black oval.

"No way," Jackie breathes. "No way!"

"What, what is it?" I ask.

Everyone at the table cranes their necks to see the gift.

"It's a car key!" Jackie bolts, moving like a flash.

A chorus of, "What?" resounds from the rest of the table.

In a flurry of motion, we all abandon our half-eaten cake and chase Jackie out the front door.

She lies on the hood of the sedan sitting beside the garage with a huge red bow planted on the roof. Patches of paint are faded in some places, and the windshield looks cracked, but I don't think she cares. She cries and bounces up and down like she just won the lottery.

"Thank you, thank you, thank you!" she yells at her mom, who holds her phone at eye level—more than likely recording every moment of her daughter's freak out.

Jackie may regret her exuberance when this hits Facebook later tonight, but for now, she's living in the moment.

"Don't dent the hood!" Melissa calls over her daughter's shrieks of excitement.

"This is the best day of my life!" Jackie slides off the front of the car, opening the driver's door. The engine comes to life with a stutter.

Taylor, Tabby, and Katie pile into the backseat. Mark pops the hood to take a look at the engine while Tanner and Larry stand behind him, pretending they know the first thing about cars.

"Some party."

Chris's voice makes me jump.

"You can say that again." I laugh, suddenly aware of how close he's standing to me. I take a half step away. "Sorry if you're not having a good time."

"Are you kidding?" Chris folds his arms over his chest. "This is way more entertaining than a night sitting at home with my parents. I'd be stuck watching the Falcon's game with my dad as he works on next week's sermon notes."

"Gross." I can't keep the smile from my lips. "I thank God every day my family is just into college football. I think I would have killed myself if they watched it on Sunday too."

Chris's posture stiffens beside me.

"Are you okay?"

"I'm fine," he says, but his gaze is distant.

Shit. What did I say?

"All right, all right," yells Melissa. "You don't actually have your license yet, so everybody out of the car."

The girls chatter excitedly as they climb out. Jackie knocks her mother over with a hug, and Mark has the other guys wrapped in a conversation about the benefits of performing your own oil changes.

Then there's Chris and me. The two closet cases who don't really fit into either conversation, so we watch from the outside.

Is there really a difference between us and them, Big Guy? Why is this such an alienating feeling? Even though Chris is here with me, I'm feeling more alone than ever.

"Isn't this great?"

Jackie's voice pulls me back from my thoughts.

"Y-Yeah, I'm so excited for you."

"Now, I can give you rides!"

She beams at me, and a weight forms in my chest.

I'm feeling it again—the urge to tell her. To reveal the reason behind all the weird things I've been doing. To not be alone in this. It will change our relationship. Though, I don't know how. The only thing I do know is it'll never be the same between us.

Everything will change.

And I'm not ready for that.

"You okay?"

I blink away the threat of tears. "Of course."

I feel Chris's gaze on me as we move back into the house.

TWENTY FOUR

The road underneath the car is a steady noise helping to drown out my thoughts. Headlights pass on the opposite side of the road, flooding us in light for a split second before they're gone.

The rest of Jackie's party had involved her opening a huge stack of gifts, watching four reruns of *Big Bang Theory,* and a really raunchy round of Cards Against Humanity that—to everyone's surprise—Chris won.

Jackie's hodgepodge group of friends finally warmed up to him by the end of the evening, and Mark even invited Chris to hang out with him and Tanner in the computer lab after school. If I didn't know any better, I'd say they liked him more than me. I should probably take some offense to that, but honestly, I couldn't care less.

"Thank you." A soft voice comes from the dark.

"Huh?"

"I said thank you," Chris repeats, louder. "You know, for inviting me to come along tonight. It was nice to be able to hang out."

"I'm pretty sure Jackie invited you first," I reply, watching another pair of yellowed lights roll by.

"You know what I mean."

I shrug. "You kinda turned out to be the life of the party." I fiddle with the flip door on the cigarette lighter. "I don't think I've ever seen that much soda shoot out of Jackie's nose before. She was dying."

"It just kept going." Chris chuckles. "It was like Niagara Falls."

Once the laughter fades, silence resumes between us. His hand lays open on the armrest, palm facing up.

Is he trying to hold my hand?

The idea comes a little too easy for my taste. I'll admit, Chris has been on my mind a lot lately, but that doesn't mean I'm anywhere close to considering the possibility of something happening between us.

"I had somewhat of an epiphany yesterday after I got home."

"Really?" I angle myself toward him, thankful for the interruption. "And what's that?"

He hesitates. "Never mind. It's kind of a long story." Chris's eyes reflect the headlights as they pass, flecks of starlight in each pupil.

"Hey." My hand finds his shoulder. "You can tell me if you want."

"All right." He silences the music. "Um…here goes. Well, for the past couple years, I have felt the space between what I believe and what I feel growing. The divide gets wider every day. I'm sure you know exactly where I'm coming from here."

I nod, encouraging him to go on.

"Faith commands one thing from me, but my heart… Jesus, that sounds corny. Sorry. It's really my whole self. I'm not satisfied. I can't tell you how many times I've cried out to God, begging him to make me straight. To make me normal." He snorts a laugh. "Just hoping, one day, I'd wake up and realize this is all some cosmic mistake, or I'd meet the one woman that would change things for me."

That sounds familiar. His story makes my heart race.

"But, surprise, surprise, that day never came. It felt like God was laughing at me and just ignoring the persistent whining of a lost gay boy. The longer this went on, the angrier I got. Furious God wouldn't take these thoughts away from me.

"They consumed my life, every waking moment. It was all I could think about. My reaction was to dive deeper into the doctrine, to immerse myself in scripture. I would fill my head so full of righteousness it would squeeze all the impure things out. And to match a busy mind, I needed a busy body.

"There were youth group functions and school activities. Hell, I even became the vice president of our local garden club. Anything to distract. Still, no matter how hard I worked, no matter how busy I stayed, the thoughts were there. Like a black hole, they continued to consume and consume until I felt nothing. A void."

He pauses, whole body tense. He squeezes words out like they're causing him pain.

"Nothing I did filled that space, Mike. Nothing. I was completely empty."

Silence swallows us. I release a breath I didn't know I was holding.

"Then last summer—" He starts, then stalls, voice thick. "Something cracked. A splinter, digging deep into me. And that's when I decided…I had this all wrong."

When he doesn't continue, I find my voice. "Had what wrong?"

"Everything. And that's exactly what I decided to let go of. All the guilt, all the shame, it fled like a bird from a cage just as soon as I opened the door."

Chills spread down my spine, the hair on my arms standing.

"That expanding space, the hollowness, it halted. I can't begin to explain how amazing it was, Mike. To look myself in the eye and not be overwhelmed with hate."

The back of my neck is hot and itchy. I squirm in my seat.

"And last night?"

"Right." Chris nods. "I couldn't sleep. This tugging sensation in my stomach kept me awake. It was like someone pulling a thread. I lay there for an hour, just wracking my mind for answers. Even spent an embarrassing amount of time on WebMD. And then I realized what it was, this alien feeling. Something I'd never allowed myself to experience before."

My stomach flutters. Is he saying what I think he's saying?

"And what was it?"

"I think…I have a crush on you, Michael."

He says it so quietly I almost miss it.

"Oh." I look ahead, stomach sinking.

The car stops at a red light, and his eyes are on me. I don't turn though. I wish I was anywhere but here.

"Obviously, you don't feel the same." His voice is thick with disappointment.

It makes my chest ache.

"But I thought you should know."

"What do you want me to say, Chris?" I still can't bring myself to look at him. "Even if I did, what good will that do either of us? It's not like we'd be able to do anything about it."

"Why not?"

The innocence in his voice grates on my nerves. How can he be so naïve?

"Because this is the real world!" I shout, frustration boiling over. "Come on, Chris. What would our parents do if we just walked into church tomorrow morning, hand in hand? Let's be honest."

The light changes, but the car doesn't move.

"I'm not saying I want to go home and rub it in their faces," Chris says. "I'm just asking a simple question. Don't we deserve the chance to *feel* normal? To be happy?"

"Chris, the light is green."

"That's not an answer."

"Just fucking drive!"

"Answer the question!"

A horn blares behind us.

"I don't know!"

Chris latches onto my hand. "Tell me this doesn't feel right to you."

I can't breathe. The air inside the car is stifling, and the roof is caving in above me. With a bit of effort, I pull away from Chris, fiddling with my seatbelt.

"I can't do this." I gasp, my free hand opening the door behind me. I nearly fall out of the car before scrambling to my feet.

Headlights follow me onto the shoulder as I run away from Chris, his impossible questions, and that suffocating car. My insides are vibrating, organs bouncing off each other until I wrap my arms around my abdomen, attempting to hold myself together. At this rate, I'm going to burst.

"Mike! Wait!"

Footsteps sound against the pavement, but I keep moving. If I stop, then I have to face all these things ricocheting around in my head, and that's not something I want to do.

Chris tails me until I can't go any farther. I stop, leaning against the metal railing running parallel to the road. It's dark on this stretch, the only light coming from the headlights and the moon above.

He rests against the rail beside me, arms folded against his chest.

I let out a staggered breath, raking my hand through sweat-dampened hair. Stupid Georgia humidity.

We stare at the ground, neither one of us speaking.

"I fucked this up," Chris says finally.

That's an understatement.

"Yeah," I agree. "You kinda did."

"What was I supposed to do, Mike?" he asks. "This is all new to me here."

"You ask me as if I'm some expert." Another car passes, and I wonder if they think we're just hooligans up to no good. "I can barely make it through a day without having a panic attack as it is, Chris. And you want to throw another secret on top of that stress? It'll kill me."

He's quiet for a while.

"I guess it's too late to ask you to forget I said anything." He gives me a nudge with his shoulder.

My laugh is pained. "What and deprive you of this

delightfully awkward experience? You wanted to be normal. Well, here you go. Crushes suck."

He lets out a sigh, arms falling to his side.

Big Guy, this is not how I saw this evening going. Lots of sugar? Sure. Crude humor? A given. A fun party? Eh, it was all right. But this? This is a curve ball if ever— Oh God! I'm making a baseball reference? Jesus, take me now!

"Can I ask a question?"

Chris perks up slightly. "Yeah?"

"Why me?" I watch another car go by. "Is this just because I'm the only other gay guy you know?"

"I thought about that," he says, "but this is different from anything I've felt before. There's been attraction to other guys. I mean, come on. I may be a P.K., but I *am* a guy. This time isn't the same."

"Then what makes it different?"

"Who knows? I don't think I could explain it even if I wanted to."

"That's not super frustrating."

"Tell me about it."

"So, what are we doing here?" I shove off the railing.

"I'm making an ass of myself," says Chris, "and you're freaking out. And I'm pretty sure both of our pancreases are attempting to produce enough insulin to keep us from going into shock."

I'm laughing again, though I don't know how. He looks at me with eyes that hold the stars hostage.

I have to admit to myself, even with a swollen cheek, Chris is handsome. Even more so by moonlight. How easy would it be for me to just wrap my arms around him?

But I can't let myself feel these things he asks of me. No way I can keep up the charade if I do. Dad tells me I wear my emotions on my sleeve for a reason. No matter how hard I try, they come out. If I end up loving this boy, there will be no way for me to hide it.

I can't take that risk.

"Can you take me home now?"

He nods, stepping past me. I follow, allowing a few feet of buffer. Man, I didn't realize just how far I went. I'm wiping sweat off my forehead by the time we make it back to the car.

Lowering myself into the seat, I fasten my belt. He does the same, face expressionless as he pulls back onto the road. Thank God, we aren't far from my house. That means I'll only have to endure this awkward torture for a few minutes.

The silence is oppressive. It's heavy, weighing on my shoulders and pressing against my ears. I would kill for some music—even a Christian radio station at this point. Anything would be better than being forced to process how my night went from totally awesome to the screaming train wreck of fuckery it is now.

Chris has feelings for me. Crush feelings, but feelings nonetheless. And it's something new and strange, being the object of someone's crush. I mean, I'm sure at least a couple of girls over the years have developed an affection for me. Lord knows I didn't pay them any mind, but this is different. This is someone I can actually picture having a relationship with, not just a onetime fling of heavy petting in a small, dark, undisclosed place.

Oh God, is this what straight people feel like? This constant anxiety about people liking them?

No wonder they're all so miserable on MTV.

Then again, what if this is it? What if this is my chance

to find the happiness I've only ever seen on sitcoms? Me and Chris getting married, raising a family, and going through life in front of a live studio audience with *real* laughter, none of that canned garbage.

The thought makes me smile.

And then a familiar crushing sense of guilt takes over, shredding my fantasy into tiny little confetti bits and throwing them back into my face like a deranged birthday clown. It's wrong, what I want. There are no happy endings for me, not with Chris, not with anyone. Abominations don't get those, do they?

The lump in my throat sticks, and I can't swallow around it. This is all too much, too quick. Too many variables spinning in my head. Heat burns behind my cheeks as anger bubbles to the surface. I blink the stinging tears from my eyes, nails digging into my palms as I clench my fists.

I have to do something before I explode.

"Fuck." The word escapes my lips with a hiss. "Fuck, fuck, fuck!" My first slams into the dashboard with every expletive. Pain barely registers, but I pull away bloodied knuckles.

"Hey!" Chris grabs my wrist, halting my assault. "What's your damage?"

"Nothing." Everything.

"Look." He holds firm. "I know I upset you, but that's no reason to go ballistic and take it out on my car! Jesus."

I pull my arm free. "Just drive."

Chris lets out a breath, hitting the accelerator. The car rolls forward, but with a jerk of the wheel, we're on the shoulder again.

"What are you doing?"

"What's wrong?" Chris shuts the engine off, lights above us flickering to life.

He stares at me, like *really* stares at me.

"What are you talking about?"

He motions to the crimson smear on his dashboard. "I may be new to this whole crush thing, but I think there's something you're not telling me, Mike."

"That's none of your business. I don't have to tell you shit."

"I suppose that's true." He crosses his arms. "But it's also kind of childish, don't you think?"

"Fuck you."

"Ha!" Chris laughs. "That's even better! Come on, just tell me what's wrong and maybe I can help."

"I don't want your— I don't *need* help."

Another lie. Pile them up until they bury me, and I don't have to think about who I am.

"Everyone needs help," Chris says, voice soft. "But some people are too stubborn to ask for it. Most people, however, don't randomly decide to Mike Tyson my dashboard unless there's something pretty serious going on."

I don't want anything from him. There are so many things I want from him. "I'm fine," I tell him. "Now, can you please drive? My parents will freak the fuck out if I'm not home in the next fifteen minutes."

"That leaves us ten minutes to talk."

"*Jesus*," I hiss, "will you just give it a rest? I'm perfectly fine, okay? End of story. I just had to blow off a little steam."

"Steam?" Chris echoes. "Is that what you want to call that?"

"Chris, please. Just go."

He's quiet for a moment, and I watch him wrestle with his decision. His eyes tell me as much. I don't like how easy it is to look into them. With a turn of his wrist, the car comes back to life, and he pulls out onto the road.

I'm crying, of course, because tonight just isn't embarrassing enough. I crank down the window, warm air helping them to dry. Fuck, my hand hurts. I hope there's nothing broken. That's not something I want to deal with right now.

"You can just let me out here," I say as we pull in front of the house.

"Mike—" Chris starts.

I cut him off. "Chris, don't make this any worse." I open the car door with my unbattered hand. "I'll see you around," I call over my shoulder.

The wet grass soaks my ankles, and I don't turn to watch him leave. The house is quiet, Mom and Dad long asleep by this point. That's for the best, seeing as I will probably burst into tears if anyone tries to talk to me right now.

The stairs creak their usual dirge as I retreat into my room.

I don't undress, just fall onto my comforter, careful to avoid getting blood on the cloth. I should have grabbed some ibuprofen, but hindsight is twenty-twenty, I guess. And, at this point, not even God himself could get me out of this bed.

My dumb brain plays the last fifteen minutes on a loop, and I just want to shove an icepick into my eye. That's how they used to do lobotomies, right? I should probably Google that.

Like it or not, it's processing time.

Why did Chris have to do this? We had a good thing going. I was even getting used to the fact someone knew my secret. Then, he had to go ruin it by catching the feels. Feelings ruin everything.

His stupid face flashes into focus. *"Don't we deserve the chance to be normal, to be happy?"*

That's just the thing, Big Guy. I don't know *if I deserve that. I can't know for certain if anything I feel is right. And there's this nagging in the back of my mind, gnawing at me like a rabid weasel. Maybe I'm miserable because this is* wrong. *I'm* wrong.

And I can ask and ask until I'm blue in the face, but I don't ever get an answer from You. That's not super frustrating. What is it? Did I piss You off from the womb or something? Did I draw the short straw at conception, so You just cursed me with these stupid ass feelings? Cause that's a really shitty thing to do, Buddy.

What? No come back? No hellfire and brimstone? No smiting? No, of course not. Because it's me, and those things would require You actually acknowledging my existence.

Okay, Mike. Let's bring it down a notch. There's no need to silently yell into the void. We're going to focus on the real world and your very real problems.

Maybe, if I write them all down, that will help me sort through them. Organization at least gives me the illusion of control. I grab a notebook and pencil from my bedside table, flipping to an empty page.

Now, what are my problems?

Number one: Chris

There's not really much more I can say about this one. I have absolutely no clue what to do about it, other than ignore him completely. Which is easier said than done. Then again, how can I possibly face him after tonight? I feel like such an idiot. Plus, he has to clean my blood off his dashboard. God, my fucking hand hurts.

Number two: Global Warming

That's a great problem to distract me from my other, less world-ruining problems. You know, despite what the insane newscasters my parents listen to say, I believe in global warming. I really think someone should do something. Maybe I can start a club or whatever at school. Then again, half my class doesn't believe climate change is a thing, so maybe not. Let's circle back to this one.

Number three: The essay due tomorrow for Dr. Redford

Fuck. I forgot all about that until just now. I crumple my useless list and toss it into the pile of paper underneath my drafting table. Letting out a yawn, I fish my laptop from its bag on the floor, booting it up with the push of a button.

Time to half-ass something and make it seem pretentious by including a bunch of words no one's heard of while silently counting up to my word-count requirement.

At least I have cake frosting coursing through my veins.

TWENTY FIVE

My alarm goes off, and I wish I was never born. The sugar high ran out somewhere around 1 AM, so I had to resort to slapping myself in the face to stay awake long enough to finish my paper. Surprisingly, it isn't the worst thing I've ever written. Plus, it actually almost makes sense, so that's a plus.

Dad hums to the radio on the way to school, and I really want to nap, but I can't without getting carsick. So, there's no relief in sight as we pull into the parking lot, and I begin my obligatory trajectory toward the smelly dumpsters.

"There you are!" Jackie flicks the end of her cig, scattering the ashes in the breeze. "Hey, Mom let me drive Winnie in this morning, so I can get used to her before the driving test later today."

"Winnie?" Is she driving a yellow stuffed bear to school? I'm way too tired to deal with this bullshit.

"Yep! I decided on the name last night." Another puff of smoke twirls in the garbage breeze. "I was going back and forth between Winifred and Gertrude, but eventually Winifred won out. Isn't it perfect?"

"If you say so." I cross my arms, leaning up against the least greasy looking spot on the wall. Leave it to Jackie to pick the ugliest, hipster name for her inanimate objects. Just another item to add to the growing list of dumb shit white girls do.

"You okay?" Jackie leans closer, tossing her spent cigarette aside. "You don't look too good."

"Peachy," I say, giving a weak smile. My life is just falling apart. Don't worry about me.

"Well, keep your distance." She retreats a few steps. "No way I'm getting sick right before I have my first taste of freedom."

"I'm not sick," I tell her.

"Yeah, yeah." Jackie scoffs. "That's exactly what the sick guy always says before all hell breaks loose. If you turn me into a zombie, I'll never forgive you."

The muffled sound of the bell reaches our trashy outskirts.

"Come on." I'm just not in the mood for our usual repartee. "We're gonna be late for class."

This whole Chris situation has got me all turned around. The worst part? I can't stop thinking about how sad he looked last night. After seeing him change over the couple of weeks we've been hanging out, it's kinda soul-crushing to see that fade. In like a second.

That's what happens when you catch feels, I guess.

Jackie and I join the stream of half-awake teens, moving obliviously through their morning. It baffles me how so many people can go about their normal lives while mine is constantly on the verge of falling apart. Just doesn't seem fair.

"I'm glad Chris joined us last night," Jackie says.

My stomach tightens with the mention of his name. Stupid fucker. "He was so much fun!"

"Yup." Until he ruins your life.

"Katie was macking pretty hard on him," she continues.

"Really?" My whole body tenses. "What do you mean?"

Why are you asking that, Mike?

"Oh, come on, Mike. I know you're pretty dense, but you had to see the thirst in that poor girl's eyes." We stop by her locker, and she riffles through a stack of textbooks before closing it. "When he was sitting next to me after dinner, she was hardcore staring. She'd blush like crazy every time I caught her. She's a precious bee-bee."

"I guess I didn't notice," I reply.

"So naïve." She pats my shoulder.

I can only shrug. I don't care who stares at Chris. Wait… Shit. I *do* care about it.

"I'll see you at lunch!" she calls, leaving me to sort through these horribly conflicting feelings. Some friend.

Why should I care if a girl stares at the boy I don't like? That just doesn't make sense. Like at all. Where's an adult?

I hang a left into Dr. Redford's classroom. He perches behind his desk, a stack of papers in front of him and glasses pulled as far down his nose as they can go. Today's vest of choice is a shade of maroon that makes him look like he's been swimming in wine.

Shuffling through my bag, I hand over my paper with as much of a smile as I can muster. Best of luck, Redford. That one's going to be rough.

"Thank you, Mr. Hernandez," Dr. Redford says without looking up.

I turn to take my seat, greeted with a surprise I never asked for.

Chris is already at his desk, leg bouncing up and down. He looks like a caged puppy, all trembles and shaking and excitement.

It's kind of cute.

No. No, no, no. We aren't doing this today, Mike. Operation Ignore Chris is a go.

"Hey, Mike," he whispers as I take my seat.

I pull out my textbook, flipping aimlessly through the pages.

"I was hoping we could talk today," he continues. "About last night."

"What about it?" I ask casually. That's it. Stay strong, you got this. You're suave AF.

Chris lets out an annoyed huff. "You can't act like nothing happened."

"Actually," I say as I toss a glance his way, "that's exactly what I can do."

"Mike, please—"

"Mr. Myers," Dr. Redford says as he flips the lock on the door, "just because you arrived earlier than usual doesn't mean you get the privilege of speaking in my classroom, is that understood?"

"Yes, sir." Chris falls silent, leg starting up again. He's gonna lose a shoe at this point.

Okay, so we're off to a good start. Eventually, he'll give up. I just need to hold out until then. I can totally do this.

"Ladies and gentlemen," Dr. Redford says as he leans against his desk, speaking in his usual bored tone, "it has been brought to the attention of the administration that some of the school policies need reviewing. Principal Peters has asked me to reiterate these here in the classroom, so I must advise you to please pay attention as I will not be repeating myself. Failure to adhere to these policies may lead to expulsion. Do I make myself clear?"

Half-hearted murmurs of agreement pass in a wave.

Oh, great. Who decided to graffiti the bathroom wall again? I hope it was another flattering caricature of Double P where his chin is a pair of balls. That was epic. I think I still have a snap of that on my phone.

"There have been several reports of inappropriate behavior between students on school property," he continues. "More specifically, between students of the same sex."

"Gaaaay," someone calls from the back of the room.

My cheeks burn, and I drop my eyes to the floor. I can't show a reaction. Don't give yourself away, Mike.

"Even though the administration realizes these incidents are most likely ill-natured jokes." Dr. Redford drones on as if he heard nothing, reading his notes like a bad teleprompter. "We would like to remind you any inappropriate contact between two parties of the same sex is in direct violation to school policy and may lead to disciplinary actions including, but not limited to, suspension, expulsion, and mandatory counseling."

I lift my head to the side, pretending to check the clock hanging on the wall. Chris looks like he's about to throw up.

Good. He needs to know just what he's asking me to risk here. Maybe this little reminder will solve my Chris problem. Now, I can focus on getting through the next two years without getting myself expelled.

"Excuse me?"

"Yes, Mr. Myers?" Dr. Redford sighs.

Chris lowers his hand. "May I ask a question?"

Dr. Redford nods his bald head, a sheen of light reflecting off it.

"I believe the policy forbids inappropriate contact between *any* two parties," Chris starts. "And, speaking from experience, I've seen plenty of contact between a boy and a girl on school grounds."

"Yeah, Tabby," a guy calls from the back. "Keep it in your pants."

"Shut up, Reed!" Tabby Freeman hisses from the back row.

I can smell her breath from up here. Does she know that toothpaste is a thing?

"What's your point, Mr. Myers?" Dr. Redford sounds about as interested as a sloth with ADD.

"My point is," Chris adds, "the administration doesn't bat an eye when someone violates this policy as long as it's a boy and a girl. But if, let's say, two boys share a friendly hug, then alarms go off like someone's been shot. I think it's kind of a double standard."

My heart is a jackhammer. What the fuck is he doing? You might as well just lie under a huge fucking magnifying glass, Chris!

Dr. Redford lowers his glasses even farther down his crooked nose to look at Chris. "One could conclude, Mr. Myers, that your argument calls for the condoning of homosexual behavior. Is that your intention?"

Muttering ripples through the classroom.

This can't be happening. Please, stop.

"I-It's not that," he stammers. "It's just I think there

should be the same awareness and punishment for the same violation of policy."

The class goes dead silent. All eyes focus on Chris and Redford. I want to crawl under my desk and die.

"This is an interesting topic," Dr. Redford replies finally, though he doesn't actually sound interested at all. "I would like to open this up for discussion. Just so everyone understands," he addresses the class, "Mr. Myers believes the punishment for engaging in inappropriate behavior with someone of the same sex and someone of the opposite sex should be treated in the same manner. I would like to hear some of your thoughts."

Surprisingly, a few hands shoot up.

"Yes, Miss Freeman."

"You can't possibly compare the two," Tabby answers. "Love between a man and a woman is from God. They're just acting on their natural inclinations. But same-sex attraction is unnatural. God despises it, so we should too."

Yeah, well, I despise your putrid breath, you cow.

"Is that why you spread your love so freely, Tabby?" Chris fires back.

"That's enough Mr. Myers. And caution, Miss Freeman," Dr. Redford responds. "Our natural inclination is sin. We must hold ourselves to a higher standard."

"I would like to point out," Chris interrupts, "we aren't talking about what's right or wrong in God's eyes. We're discussing an issue of school policy."

"Which should mirror," Dr. Redford replies, pointedly. "Yes, Mr. Durham?"

"I have to side with Myers on this one," Hunter

212

Durham says from the back row. "If it's wrong, it's wrong. I don't think it should matter who does it."

More mixed murmurs resound.

"You make a valid point, as does Mr. Myers." Dr. Redford removes his glasses, making his eyes small and beady. "However, your understanding of the subject is a bit narrow, so let me help you see it from another perspective." He moves along the rows of desks. "Let's try to explain this the way Jesus would, through an allegory."

The class responds with a resounding groan.

Tim Green kicks the back of Chris's chair. "Thanks a lot, Myers."

Redford goes on. "A man hosts a gathering of friends. A party, rave, shindig, or whatever it is you call it these days."

We call it a party. What the hell is a shindig?

"After the party concludes, the man notices one of his valuable possessions has gone missing. Let's say his Walkman."

"His what?" someone calls from the row behind me.

"Not important." Redford clears his throat. "The man confronts his friends one at a time and discovers one of them has stolen from him. The friend apologizes, showing repentance for their actions, and the man forgives him.

"The next night, the man wakes to the sound of someone breaking into his home. Upon inspection, he finds the thief has taken his Walkman."

"I still don't know what that is."

"It's not— Listen. Bear with me. The authorities apprehend the thief and bring him before the man for judgment."

213

"That's not how the legal system works."

"Allegory, Miss Taft," Redford responds. "Now, hush. The thief is brought before the man from who he stole, and the man condemns this man to be imprisoned for the rest of his days." Redford pauses, replacing his glasses to stare right at me.

My heart is a hummingbird in my ear.

"Now, let me pose this question. Why do you think the man's reaction was so different between the two thieves though their initial crime was identical?"

The class remains silent. Though, to be honest, I think half of them are Googling what a Walkman is.

"Yes, Miss Taft."

"He reacted differently because the other one was his friend."

"Not necessarily," Redford replies. "The main difference between the thieves was far simpler. The first was invited into the man's home. Their presence was expected. It was right they were there. Now, let's consider the second thief. Was he invited into the man's home?"

"No." Samantha Taft shakes her head.

"That's correct. So, inherently, the second thief was wrong from the moment he set foot in the house. In the eyes of the man, the second thief had committed a greater injustice, even though it was the same."

"I don't get it," Sam says.

God bless her. She's pretty.

Dr. Redford lets out a sigh that most likely is the side effect of his dreams slowly dying. "The point is this," he says as he reaches the front of the classroom, turning to us. "Even though both parties were in the wrong, the second was condemned because of the intent in their heart. To better compare our two situations, Mr. Myers, these instances you mention between boys and girls, are they against the school's policy? Absolutely. But, as Miss Freeman pointed out, they are not inherently evil at their root. Therefore, they are forgiven far easier in the eyes of the school.

"However, the other situation I am referring to is represented by the second thief in our story. Their perversions are wrong from the moment they act on them. And so, in that regard, they are to be condemned more harshly because their intent isn't pure. They go against God's very nature."

I'm pretty sure everyone can hear my heartbeat at this point. The room is that quiet.

"Does everyone understand?"

More muttering.

"Someone who gives into their sinful nature is wrong from the moment they decide to act. Now, then, Mr. Myers," Dr. Redford says once he is back at his desk. "I believe that settles your question, does it not?"

"Yes, sir," Chris's answer is almost a whisper.

"Good. Now, then, shall we move into the Gospel of John?"

TWENTY SIX

"MIKE," CHRIS CALLS AFTER ME.

I keep moving down the hall. That was such a shit show, I don't know how I even made it through. I want to go cry in the bathroom. Instead, I'm running away from Chris.

"Mike!"

Jesus, is he *trying* to stick out like a sore thumb?

My locker opens with a click, and I cycle the books in my bag.

"Can we talk for a second?" he asks, coming up beside me.

"What is there to talk about, Chris? You were sitting in the same classroom I was. You heard what's at stake here."

"I heard this school doesn't treat everyone equally, and that's not fair."

"Well, no shit, Sherlock," I hiss. The fact I have to tell him that is ridiculous. He's the same age as I am. Why doesn't he know this? "Life isn't fair. It baffles me you haven't realized that yet."

"Is that supposed to be a joke?" Chris says a little too loud. "Because I know just as much as anyone."

"Then why is everything such a big shock to you, huh?" I slam my locker shut. "We got the short end of the stick, Chris. Deal with it."

"This *is* me dealing with it." He doesn't seem keen on lowering his volume anytime soon. "I'm trying to make sense of everything, but I can't. Not when I'm surrounded from all sides with people screaming ignorance. Not by myself."

If I don't get out of here soon, someone will see how he is looking at me.

"I have to go."

"Wait."

His fingers wrap around my forearm. His eyes find mine, and that funny squeezing feeling rears its ugly head, wrapping around my chest.

"*Please.*"

A guy across the hall watches us. He whispers to the girl beside him.

This has gone on long enough.

I pull away from Chris, shaking my head. "I'm sorry."

It's a conscious effort to stop myself from running as I move away from him, dodging glances left and right. I catch a glimpse of the girl across the hall. It's Tabby.

Great. That's just who I need watching me.

THE LUNCH TABLE IS AS NOISY AS EVER, BUT THE WORDS JUST MELT TOGETHER as I try not to look as guilty as I feel.

Now I'm no stranger to the churnings of guilt twisting inside me, but today's batch is especially powerful. Or maybe it's the horrendous smell of Tabby's breath coming from across the table. She leans over to whisper in Tanner's ear. I'm surprised his flesh doesn't peel off the bone. I swear, her insides are rotting.

Chris's stupid face pops back in my head. His hurt expression as I walked away from him is engraved in my memory.

"Wait, what?" Tanner says, loud enough to catch my attention.

She cuts her eyes at him, then leans in again, red-stained lips moving silently.

What is she saying?

Tanner makes eye contact with me and my blood runs cold. Oh shit, this is it. I'm a dead man.

"Hey, Mike." He closes his laptop—an indicator I'm not going to like what he says next. "You have Dr. Red-turd for first period, right?"

"Uhh…" I can't seem to form coherent words, so I settle for nodding my head.

"Did he really say they caught two girls making out behind the gym?"

"Huh?"

He turns back to Tabby. "See? This is why I never believe you."

"I didn't say Redford *confirmed* the rumor," Tabby defends herself. "But what he *did* say should be evidence enough."

"Well, what did he actually say?"

"It was some policy mumbo-jumbo." She twists a strand of hair around her finger. "But he was talking

218

about inappropriate same-sex behavior, so I figured it had to be the lezzies the softball team keeps talking about."

"Why am I never around for the hot stuff?" Tanner asks, opening his laptop once more. "I mean, next you're going to tell me they wrestled in a pool full of pudding."

"Pudding?" Jackie calls from the other end of the table. She and Larry have been locked in an intense round of tot-toss, which fortunately isn't about lobbing small children into the air.

A tater tot flies into the opening of her blouse.

"Yes!" Larry leaps to his feet. "Undefeated champ!"

The rest of the table half-heartedly applauds his triumph, except Taylor, who shows her undying support.

"Rematch!" Jackie yells over the noise, digging through her cleavage. "I was seduced by a pudding daydream."

"Hey, Mike." Katie's soft voice barely registers, even though she's sitting right beside me. "Where's Chris? I haven't seen him all day."

"How should I know?" It comes out harsher than I intend.

Katie lowers her head and I'm officially the shittiest person.

"I saw him this morning in Theology," I offer.

She nods but doesn't say anything else.

Jesus, how could this day get any worse?

TWENTY SEVEN

"HERNANDEZ!"

I pull myself out of the water, hair dripping into my eyes.

"Now you're just starting to p— *tick* me off." Coach Schmidt waddles his way over to me. "That's the worst lap time you've ever had. What's going on?"

"I-I pulled a muscle," I lie. I should probably worry. I'm getting so good at it.

Coach grunts in my direction, marking something on his clipboard that makes me feel self-conscious. Maybe I've already peaked at sixteen, and the rest of my athletic career is just a sad downhill slope, ending with a botched deal to get my face on a box of cereal.

"Is everything okay, Mike?" he asks without looking away from his work.

"Yes, sir."

"Nothing going on at home?"

"No, sir."

"Girl problems?"

I actually have to keep myself from laughing.

"Definitely not, sir."

"Well, whatever's going on here, you need to solve it and get your head outta the sky and into the pool. Do I make myself clear?"

"Yes, sir."

"Good." He gives me a slap on the shoulder and moves on to the next lane.

I stare at the water, watching small waves lap against the walls. Swimming has always been easy for me. It's simple. No thought required. I can lose myself in the motions and coast.

So, what changed?

"Hey, Mike!"

Davy jogs up to me, blond hair slicked down with water. A towel hangs around his neck, and his lips are spread in a smile.

It's a struggle to keep my eyes above the waist.

"H-Hey." I take a step back because he feels too close.

"How's it going?"

"It's fine." I grab my own towel from the bench, wrapping it around my exposed body. I just feel like I need a barrier between us.

"I heard Schmidt-head laying into you pretty hard," Davy says.

"Yeah." I shuffle my feet in the puddle of water beneath me. "Guess I'm not all here today."

"He can be a real dick sometimes." Davy throws a glance over his shoulder. "And I for one would like to know just what exactly qualified him to coach. I doubt that man has ever swam a lap without needing an oxygen tank waiting on the side of the pool."

The image of Coach Schmidt floundering around

the pool like some deranged sea cow pops into my head. I can't help giggling.

"You're picturing it right now, aren't you?" Davy chuckles along with me. "I mean, the guy looks like Danny DeVito fucked a midget and he popped out nine months later, holding that same clipboard."

The giggles are full-blown laughter now.

"There," he says, giving me a pat on the shoulder, "I like this look on you a lot more. You aren't one for sullen expressions."

A whistle blows from behind us, and Davy sheds his towel.

"The midget spawn beckons." He gives me one last smile, then dives into the pool.

I watch him for just a moment, memorizing how his body slices through the water.

OPERATION IGNORE CHRIS HAS BEEN GOING BEAUTIFULLY ALL WEEK, AND I'M starting to think he gets the idea. By Friday, he doesn't even look at me as we pass in the hallway, just keeps his head down and keeps moving like the rest of us.

Good. He'll be much safer that way.

And bonus, that guilty feeling I've been dealing with gets a little more bearable every day. So that's good.

I think.

"What's the movie choice tonight?" Tanner asks as we step into the blazing sun outside the school.

"I don't care," Jackie whines. "After that fucking Algebra quiz, I'll watch anything as long as I'm stoned out of my mind."

"All right, Mike," Tanner leans over and wraps his arm around my shoulder. "We both heard her. She has forfeited her right to complain about our movie choice."

"I swear to God, Tanner," Jackie says. She swings at his shoulder but misses, "if you make me watch the Matrix one more time, I'm going to just unplug myself."

"What a perk. I'll get it queued."

"Fine then." Jackie pulls me away from him. "Mike is riding with me, so he can't be influenced by your sadist tendencies." She strokes the back of my hand. "Someone has to make sure he stays pure and unchaste in the eyes of the Lord."

She probably thinks I'm laughing at her absurdity, but it's really because I'm wondering if she knows where that hand has been.

"And you think you're a better influence than me?" Tanner lowers his glasses to look down at her. "Are you going to teach him how to jerk off under a raincoat in the back of the church bus?"

"Touché." Jackie releases her hold on me.

"Mom, Dad, stop fighting," I tell them, batting my eyelashes. "It only hurts the children."

"Jesus." Jackie laughs, opening her driver's door. "What a fucked-up family we'd make."

"Is it any worse than the real ones?" Tanner asks, leaning against the trunk.

We take a moment before shaking our heads.

"I'd be okay being related to you two," I tell them.

"Speak for yourself," Tanner says in all seriousness. "I enjoy being an only child, thank you."

"Same here," Jackie chimes in. "Then again,

sometimes I do feel the urge to annoy the shit out of someone, and I guess that's what family's really for. Just don't come looking if you need a kidney. Now, Gweny here and I will see you at *tu casa*."

"What, who's Gweny?" I ask.

"And what's that about two croissants?" Tanner joins.

I reel on him. "You're joking, right? How many times have you been to my house, Tan? You haven't picked up any Spanglish from Dad's blathering?"

He just shrugs. "I thought she was talking about flaky pastries. Now, I'm hungry."

I can only blink at him.

"Anyway…" Jackie leans into the car to crank it. "I changed my mind. Winnie is out, and Gweny is in. Gwendolyn just rolls off the tongue…."

"Funny," Tanner says as he squints his eyes, "she doesn't look like a car from the nineteen-twenties."

"Hardy-har-har." She climbs in, lowering the window. "Don't spend too much time making out, you two. I have a long week to forget."

"We'll keep it short." Tanner bangs on the top of the car. "Try not to run over any little old ladies."

"Do I look like Taylor?"

I'm still laughing as she drives away, blaring some old-timey Broadway number about a modern major general. Whatever that is.

Tanner's SUV isn't far, but I feel like I've been baked by the time we climb in.

"You're not actually going to make us watch that movie again, are you?"

"*Et tu, Michael?*" Tanner cranks the car, hot air blasting through the vents.

224

"Oh, I see." I draw the belt across my lap, fastening it. "You know Latin, but no Spanish."

"That's what a private education affords me. I can learn a dead language for only forty thousand a year." He plugs his phone into the aux cord and starts one of his infamous dub-step playlists. I'm sure to have a headache by the time we reach his house.

We ride for a few minutes before he speaks, raising his voice over the music.

"So, I heard an interesting rumor today." Tanner pushes his glasses up his nose.

"And what's that?" I inquire, adjusting the vent closest to me. There's not enough air conditioning in the world.

"It's about Chris," he says.

At this point, you'd think my heart would have burst out of my chest. But it holds tight, ricocheting off my ribs.

"Oh really?"

"Yeah." We turn onto Roswell road, traffic coming to a halt. "I was gonna say something earlier, but Jackie seems to be a taking a shining to him, so I didn't want to invoke her wrath."

"Smart choice," I reply, stomach tighter than a pair of skinny jeans.

"Now, keep in mind, I heard this little bit of gossip from Tabby, so there's a fifty-fifty chance it's true."

Of course, it was that trash mouth. She is quickly becoming my least favorite person.

"So, what did she say?"

"Well, you know the story about how he got the black eye," he starts, "but rumor has it that it really *was* a fight with his old man. And the topic of their

225

quarrel? Apparently, Chris is gay."

My pulse hits light speed. The edges of my vision are blurring. Isn't that what happens right before you faint? A metallic taste in my mouth makes me want to gag.

"And what makes her say that?"

"Tabby was in his class when he and Redford went toe to toe over the school policy," he continues, oblivious to the fact I can't fucking breathe. "She says things got pretty heated."

"I wouldn't say that." I try to play down the situation. "I was there too. Chris just seemed to be pointing out facts. Totally neutral."

Except, he wasn't. He was enraged and doing a poor job of trying to keep it under the surface. And Tabby might be an idiot, but she's an idiot with observational skills and a knack for spilling secrets. She'll be a great politician one day.

"Like I said," Tanner says as we turn onto a side street. "Tabby's info isn't always the most reliable. I just found this bit to be especially interesting, given Chris's situation with his dad."

"I wouldn't read too much into it," I mutter, finding it increasingly difficult to speak around the lump lodged in my throat.

"Surprisingly, I'm hoping this one isn't true." Tanner lowers the volume of the screeching music. "I can't imagine Mr. Myers would tolerate his son doing that kind of thing."

That kind of thing.

Those words hurt more than the time I broke my wrist riding Tanner's mountain bike when I was nine. He picked me up and carried me all the way back to the house, never once complaining.

Tanner's always been that way. Sure, he's nosy and gossips a bit too much, but that's because he cares, and he's my brother. Maybe even more so than Tommy. He and Jackie are the family I got to choose. We tell each other everything.

Well, *mostly* everything.

Tanner readjusts the volume and I stare out the window, trying to blink away the threat of tears. When we pull into his driveway, Jackie's waiting on us, perched on the trunk of her car.

"What took so long?" she complains. "Did you two strangle a drifter together?"

"You must be psychic," Tanner calls, bounding up the stoop. "What am I thinking now?"

"You're imagining a threesome with Trinity and Neo from the Matrix." She chases him, flinging the door wide open.

"Bingo!" he shouts from inside.

They already act like brother and sister, despite their hesitation to draw the similarities. They're my best friends, and that makes them family. My best friends, and I can't even tell them I'm hurting.

I could tell them. I could tell them right here, right now. Just throw myself over that boundary, never to look back again. No turning back.

But there's a chance I could lose them. I could lose everything. And I'm not ready for that. I don't know if I'll ever be ready for it.

"Come on, Mike!" Jackie calls. "You're going to miss me breaking Tan-Tan's fingers if he even thinks about playing this fucking movie!"

TWENTY EIGHT

SATURDAY COMES, AND I FIND MYSELF ALONE IN THE HOUSE.

Mom and Dad had a wedding up in Blue Ridge, and they couldn't talk me into tagging along. Rosy is staying over at a friend's for the night. So, it's just me, myself and I.

After I've done what every warm-blooded teenage boy would do in a house to himself, I clear my internet history then settle in on the couch, desperately bored. A stack of homework I'm putting off until tomorrow waits upstairs along with half a dozen sketches just begging me to finish them, but I lack the motivation to focus on any of it.

Tanner and Jackie are busy today, too. How am the only person who doesn't have someplace to be?

So, here I am, flipping through endless channels of shows I don't care about on a beautiful Saturday afternoon.

A half hour of Food Network later, my phone buzzes. I dig it out, swiping through the message to open it.

> Hey, lazy bones. Wanna grab a cup of coffee? 2:35pm

I smile at Jackie's text. Maybe my friends haven't completely forgotten about me.

> Thank God. I was seriously contemplating blowing my brains out from boredom. 2:35pm

The television shuts off with the click of a button, and I look for a pair of shoes.

> I thought so. I'm already on the way. Don't tell my mother I'm texting and driving she'll have a 2:36pm

The message ends abruptly. I have a small anxiety attack before my phone buzzes again.

> Cow. Sorry, speed bump. I'll be there in five. 2:37pm

I exhale, bending down to grab a pair of sneakers. Locking the door behind me, I sit on the front steps, waiting for my best friend/distracted chauffeur.

THE COFFEE SHOP BUZZES WITH LIFE AS JACKIE AND I STEP INSIDE, ESCAPING the beating Georgia sun.

"What's so special about this place?" I ask, looking around. "We passed like a hundred Starbucks on the way here."

"I dunno," Jackie replies, brushing cigarette ash off her jeans. "Chris wanted to meet here."

"Wait." I stop in my tracks. "We're meeting Chris? I thought you said Tanner was going to be here."

"No." Jackie keeps moving toward the barista at the counter. "I said I *wish* Tanner could be here. He always buys my drink for me. Now, I have to spend birthday money. Chris asked me to meet him here. Though I'm not really sure why. Oh my God!" She turns back to me. "What if he's going to confess his undying love for me?" She makes a swooning motion.

My eyes roll involuntarily. "Why do you just assume everyone is in love with you?"

"Because they are," she replies, giving me a quick wink before resuming her path to caffeine.

"Not quite," I mutter under my breath. This is just great. How am I going to ignore him properly without Jackie getting suspicious and asking questions I'd rather she didn't?

I step up to the counter beside her, snickering as she orders a hot chocolate. She's a twelve-year-old.

"Extra whipped cream, please." She hands the barista her debit card. "Hey, Mike. I'm going to go grab that table in the corner. Grab my drink, would ya?"

I nod, and she practically runs across the shop, swooping in to snipe the table from a little old lady. She's the best.

"Hey, Mike." Davy stands behind the counter, an apron tied around his waist and a cap covering his blond curls.

"H-Hey." What is he doing here? God, he's even cuter with clothes on. "What's up?"

"Just working," he replies, flashing a row of his pearly whites. "My uncle owns the shop, so I get put to work pretty regularly. Especially on poetry nights."

"Poetry nights?"

"Oh, yeah." Davy leans against the counter. "We do poetry readings every other Tuesday."

"Oh, okay. Cool." Thank goodness, it's not today. I don't love Jackie that much.

Davy leans toward me, and I instinctively take a step back.

"…Did you want to order something?"

"R-Right!" I glance up at the menu. "A latte, please."

I pass him my card.

"Coming right up,"

Our hands brush as he gives me the receipt. He gives me a wink. Or am I imagining that again? Maybe he just has a tick.

"T-Thanks," I stammer, moving down the counter to the 'pick up' sign.

Jeez, what a cluster this day is turning into. Why couldn't I be content with a night of vegging out on the couch?

"Mike?"

I turn to see Chris looking at me like he's seen a ghost.

"What are you doing here?" he questions.

"Last I checked, this was still a free country," I answer. "Plus, Jackie invited me. And believe me, I would have declined if I'd known you'd be here."

"Well isn't that nice of you to say," he sneers.

"Look," I say as I inch closer, so I can lower my voice. "Let's just get through this with as little awkwardness as possible, okay?"

"I don't see how that's going to be an option…."

"What?"

"Nothing," Chris cranes his head. "It's… I'm going to sit down."

He stalks away, and heat rises into my cheeks. Why does he make me so upset?

"Mike."

The woman behind the counter slides two mugs toward me.

I grab the saucers, performing a balancing act as I navigate to the table in the corner.

"—hoping that it would be the two of us." Chris looks up as I approach. "But it's not a big deal."

"What's so important, Chris?" Jackie asks, taking her mug. The hot chocolate has a mountain of white fluff on top like some cocoa dusted mountain.

"We'll get to it," he says, wiping a bead of sweat from his forehead. "I'm going to grab a drink." He leaves the table but heads for the restrooms, not the counter.

"What's his deal?" I play dumb.

"Who knows?" Jackie swipes a finger through her whipped cream. "He seems worried you're here."

"I can see that."

"You don't really think he's in love with me, do you?"

I suppress a laugh. "Could be."

"Oh, I hope not." Jackie fidgets in her chair. "Damn my classic beauty!"

My latte is still scalding as I raise it to my lips. "Fuck,

that hurt!"

The little old lady that lost out on our table cuts me a nasty look from across the room.

"Jesus, Mike." Jackie elbows me. "You can't just shout 'fuck' in a public place."

"Fucking watch me," I fire back, running my burnt tongue over the inside of my cheek.

"You okay?" Jackie raises an eyebrow. "You seem a little more bitter than usual, not that I don't fucking love it."

"Fuck you."

Chris emerges from his hiding place, walking back to the table with a seemingly new confidence.

"Sorry about that," he says, sitting down.

"Didn't you say you were getting a drink?" Jackie asks.

"That's not important." Chris leans forward to rest his elbows on the table. "Jackie, I have something I want to tell you. And Mike, since you're here, I guess you can listen too."

"Oh, boy." Jackie folds her hands in her lap. "Chris, I'm flattered, really. But I don't think this is going to work out."

Chris blinks. "What?"

"I mean, I know we've been hanging out a lot lately," Jackie continues. "And I'm a lot of fun, but that doesn't mean we're compatible."

"What are you talking—"

"Chris, *please*." Jackie places her hand on his arm. "Just stop this before it gets awkward. I mean, Mike is sitting right here. Let's just promise to stay friends, then we can go about like none of this ever happen—"

"*Jackie*," Chris says as he slaps his palms against the

table, "stop it!"

She recoils.

"That's not what I wanted to tell you," he says.

"Oh." She almost looks disappointed. "What then?"

Chris lets out a breath, throwing a glance over his shoulders.

Oh God, please don't let him say what I think he's about to say.

"Jackie," he whispers. "I'm…gay."

Jackie's expression mirrors my own—eyes wide and mouth hanging slightly open.

Come on, Big Guy! What the fuck is he doing?

"Um…" Jackie pulls herself together, eyes fluttering as she tries to process. "Okay. *Okay.* That was… Yeah. Okay."

"You're one of the first people I've told," Chris says, cutting his eyes to me. I sink in my chair, away from his gaze. "But I wanted you to know."

"Wow…" She looks over at me.

I honestly don't even know what emotion I'm displaying at this point.

"I'm honored, Chris. Really. What made you want to tell people? If that's okay for me to ask. I mean you don't have to answer anything you don't want to. It's totally okay if—"

"It's fine." Chris cuts her off. Jackie rambles when she's nervous. "I just feel like it's time, ya know?"

He looks at me, and an idea explodes to life. A horrible idea. A heinous idea. One that makes me want to jump across this table and throttle him.

Is he trying to force me out? Is that what all this has been? He's trying to get me to tell Jackie too.

"Have you told your parents yet?" Jackie asks.

"No," Chris answers. "For pretty obvious reasons."

"That's understandable." She wrings her hands together. "Shit, what about school? They can't find out."

"I was hoping you'd help me keep it under wraps." Chris runs his fingers through his hair. "For now, at least."

"Of course," she agrees. "Jesus, I'm so embarrassed. Here I was thinking you were going to confess your love for me. How much further off could I have been?"

They share an awkward laugh, and I'm still swimming in conspiracy theories.

"So…" Jackie leans over her hot chocolate. "Do you, like, have a secret boyfriend?"

"Not even." Chris laughs.

"That's a shame…" She pouts. "Are you at least interested in anyone?"

"There is this one guy," he replies. "But it was just a crush, and it didn't work out."

I shoot him a look that says, 'Shut the fuck up.'

"Who was it?" Jackie inquires.

"Nobody." Chris waves her off. "Just some jerk."

Oh no, he didn't.

"He must have been," Jackie agrees.

Is that any way to talk about your best friend, Jackie?

"Anyway…" Chris changes the subject. "Now that's over with, did you finish that paper for Ms. Reed?"

"Fuuuck." Jackie groans. "Yes. And I hate that evil bitch."

Chris laughs, and I try to pretend I'm someplace far away.

TWENTY NINE

"CAN YOU BELIEVE IT?" JACKIE ASKS AS SOON AS WE GET IN THE CAR. "I mean, looking back, I guess there were a few signs, but…"

"It's crazy," I mutter, fastening my seatbelt.

"Poor guy." She cranks the ignition, backing out. "Being gay must be hard enough, but being a gay P.K.? Jesus."

"Uh-huh."

"What's your deal, Mike?" Jackie questions. "You hardly said a word. Would it have killed you to be supportive?"

I don't respond.

"Don't tell me you're weirded out by Chris now. What, you don't want to be his friend because he's gay?"

"That's not it," I tell her.

"Then enlighten me."

"It's nothing."

"Whatever." She huffs, switching the radio on.

I wish I could tell her, but like always, the words

catch in my throat and it's all I can do to keep from choking on them.

THE LAST THING I WANT TO DO IS WALK INTO SUNDAY SCHOOL WHERE I'LL have to suffer from Jackie and Chris's combined looks of disappointment. However, my alternative is to stay in the car and roast. So, I suppose the decision is easy to make.

After I lumber down to the basement level, I step through the side door, expecting the lung-burning scent of cigarette smoke to greet me. Instead, I find only fresh air and a fat squirrel.

Where is everyone?

I shut the door, resuming my path to The Well. It doesn't take long to spot Jackie, seated on the couch in the corner and talking in a low voice. Chris sits beside her, and just seeing him makes my blood boil.

Fine. If that's the game he wants to play, I can't help that. But he won't force me to do something I don't want to do.

"Good morning, Mike," Katie calls from where she's observing a round of foosball.

"Hey, Katie." I tear my eyes from Jackie and Chris, moving toward the table. "How are you?"

"I'm alright, thank you," she replies, throwing a glance to the corner. "They've been over there all morning," she tells me. "I didn't know they were so close."

"Me neither," I respond. Poor Katie. Now, not only does she think Chris is into Jackie, she doesn't know she literally has no chance with him.

We both watch the game for a moment until I see Tanner walk in.

I've been going back and forth all night, thinking about whether I want to do this. Another glance at the happy friend-couple on the couch steels my resolve.

"See you," I tell Katie, walking back to the sound booth where Tanner is stowing his backpack.

"What's with those two?" he asks me, digging for his laptop.

"Turns out Tabby was right," I tell him.

"Right about what?" Tanner lowers himself onto the stool as he adjusts a few knobs on the board.

"Chris. He told me and Jackie yesterday he's gay."

"Holy shit," Tanner breathes, ceasing his tuning. "Wait, why would he tell you guys that?"

"I have no idea," I lie.

"Still...that's pretty crazy. Oh God, that poor guy. What's his dad gonna do when he finds out?"

"Who knows?"

"Okay, everyone!" Arnold calls from the stage. "Today, we have a great lesson in store. So, let's gather!"

"I want more details," Tanner tells me, "after Sunday school."

I nod, climbing out of the booth and making my way to my usual chair in the back row. Jackie never comes to join me.

Arnold rants for a few minutes then grabs this ridiculous cardboard cutout of a jail cell. He holds onto the bars, making some cliché metaphor.

"All right, guys and gals," he concludes, "let's split into life groups and discuss these ideas from the

Gospel of John."

The crowd scatters around the room, and I sink into my beanbag. Fat Tom Selleck must be sick today, which means Arnold is leading our group. What a treat.

"All right, all right, all right," he plops down on one of the bags, struggling to sit up enough to see us. "Was there a particular verse that stood out for you guys?"

Chris raises his hand.

"Yes, Chris?"

"Verse thirty-two really spoke to me this morning," he says, locking eyes with me.

"Excellent." Arnold flips through his bible. "Hang on, let's refresh everyone's memory. Verse thirty-two reads, 'Then you will know the truth, and the truth will set you free.' What do you think that verse is talking about, Chris?"

"Well, it's obviously talking about the truth of salvation through Jesus," Chris responds, sounding bored, "but I think we can get more from it."

"Go on, my dude."

Someone snorts at Arnold.

"What I mean is, there's a reason Jesus speaks so much about truth. We can take something away from that saying, 'The truth will set you free.'"

"And what's that?" Arnold prompts.

"Let's say, you're keeping something a secret," Chris continues, staring right at me. "That secret can hurt you over time. Twist the way you see things, even drive you crazy. But just like the verse says, the truth can set you free. It takes that burden away, so you don't have to deal with it alone."

"What a great point," Arnold agrees. "We all carry secrets, right? And here's one of mine. Yes, even I carry secrets. What Jesus is saying here is that—"

I've heard enough of this. I roll over the side of the bean bag, climbing to my feet. No way I'm going to sit here and have Chris beat me up for something he has absolutely no say in.

"Where are you going?" Arnold asks as I leave the group.

"Moved by the spirit," I say, patting my stomach.

Arnold chuckles. "'Nuff said."

I push open the doors to the hallway and duck into one of the empty classrooms.

Where the hell does this guy get off, thinking he can guilt me into coming out? He of all people should know this is *my* decision. I will do it on my terms.

Whatever those are.

Let's be honest here, Big Guy, I'm not even sure I want to come out. As You can imagine, there are more than a few conflicting emotions rolling around inside my head at the moment. Seriously, what am I supposed to do right now?

I wait around for an answer that isn't coming, fretting until I hear the sounds of people walking down the hall. Taking a steadying breath, I escape my hiding place and run headfirst into Tanner.

"Hey!" He grabs my arms to keep from knocking me down. "Jesus, you scared the sh— the crap out of me."

"Sorry." I replant my feet, so he can let go of me.

"No worries." Tanner laughs. "Hey, what's up with Jackie this morning? Is this about that thing we can't talk about?"

"I think so," I tell him. "As long as you're talking about the thing I think you're talking about."

"I'm talking about that thing you told me. Oh, for

fuck's sake." He slaps his hand across his mouth. "Just come on. We're ditching service."

That's more than fine with me, so I follow him up the stairs and out into the parking lot. We climb into his car, and he cranks it up to get the air going.

"All right." He shifts toward me in his seat, pushing his glasses up the bridge of his nose. "Tell me everything."

I fill him in on my evening at Clark's Cup with Jackie and Chris. I leave out the parts where I purposely didn't say something, and the awkward drive home.

"So, I guess Tabby cat was right...." Tanner muses.

"Ew." I groan. "Please don't call her that."

"Sorry." He waves me off. "Jesus, what a mess."

"You're not going to say anything, are you?"

"No way." Tanner looks offended I'd even ask. "I only deal in petty, minor gossip. I never spread the earth-shattering, life-ruining stuff. I just bear that in silence."

"Good."

"You all right, Mike?" he asks me. "Seems like this topic has you a bit on edge. He didn't hit on you or something, did he?"

"What? No, of course not! Shut up!"

"Dude—" Tanner raises his hands. "Chill. I was only joking."

"R-Right." I fake a pained laugh.

"You sure you're—"

"Totally. I'm good."

"Okay then." Tanner turns on the radio. "I think you need to unwind a little. You and Jackie coming over after church?"

"Can't speak for her, but I'll be there."

Maybe things will make more sense when I'm high.

THIRTY

"**WHERE'S YOUR LITTLE BOYFRIEND?**" **TANNER ASKS JACKIE AS SHE CLIMBS** out of her car. We've been waiting on the stoop for at least twenty minutes for her to show up.

"Who?" She almost sounds believable.

"Oh, never mind." He bounds up two stairs and heads inside.

Jackie looks at me, wrinkling her nose as if it's a Tuesday by the dumpsters.

"What?"

"Oh, nothing." She sniffs, passing me.

I'm not going to deal with this. Not from my best friend. Chris can take a lot of things from me, but not her.

"Bullshit." I follow her into the house. "If you have a problem with me, why don't you just come out and say it."

"I really don't think this is the best place to discuss this, Michael."

"Michael?" I laugh. "Okay, *Jacquelyn.* Two can play at that game."

"What's going on in there?" Tanner calls.

"Nothing!" Jackie shouts then turns to me. "Don't say anything."

"About Chris?" I can't believe she's this defensive over him. "Too late! He already knows. In fact, he knew before you did, Jackie."

"What?" She looks hurt.

Tanner walks in with an armful of snacks. "What do I know?"

Jackie turns on him now. "You knew about Chris being gay?"

"Well… I… You see… I wasn't sure until I heard it from Mike."

"What? How could you do that, Mike?" Jackie reels back to me.

"Do what? All I did was confirm a rumor Tanner had already told me. It's not like I outed him."

"That's exactly what you did!" she shouts. "How do you not see that?"

Why is she getting so upset over this? I'm the one who should be upset. I'm the one who's actually gay.

"What does it matter, Jackie?"

"What does it matter? Jesus, Mike! Chris trusted us enough to share that part of himself, and all you did was sit there like a fucking corpse. Would it have killed you to show an inkling of support?"

"Okay." Tanner tries to step between us.

Jackie smacks his shoulder. "Stay out of this!"

I've had it. Something snaps inside me, releasing a torrent that spews from my mouth.

"What do you want from me, Jackie?" I shout over her. "Do you want me to call Chris over here? Do you want me to hold his hand and tell him everything's going to be okay? To tell him his parents are going to accept him for who he is? Because news flash, they won't!"

Jackie blinks.

"Do you want me to tell him the congregation of people he shares a religion with are going to welcome him with open arms? Because that's a fucking lie too! How can you expect me to say everything's going to be okay when it's not! It's not okay! He's not okay! And I don't have to stand here and explain myself to you."

Her lips trembles, but I don't let up. The words just keep pouring out.

"And who are you to say otherwise? Who are you to say it gets better? Who are you to say anything will change? You, a silly little straight white girl who thinks she knows something? The sooner he realizes these things are lies, the better off he's going to be."

"Mike…"

Tanner takes a step toward me, but Jackie is faster.

Her fist slams into my nose with a crunch.

"Fuck!" I shout, hand cupping under the blood dripping from my nose.

Jackie's chest heaves as she shakes her hand. "I really hope that hurt." She grabs the collar of my shirt with her uninjured hand. "You homophobic little shit."

With a shove, I'm on my ass, and Jackie storms out the front door.

I touch my nose, wincing as pain shoots through me.

"Hey, Mike?" Tanner looms over me. "Can you try not to bleed on Mom's rug? She's going to crucify me."

Fuck.

THIRTY ONE

I CONVINCE MY PARENTS TANNER AND I WERE THROWING A FOOTBALL, AND I took one to the face. My lack of hand-eye coordination must really sell it because they buy it hook, line, and sinker.

Dad drops me and Rosy off outside school on Monday. "Tell Coach you need to stay out of the water until that heals up," he tells me.

I stop myself from walking toward the dumpsters. No way am I going to give Jackie the satisfaction of seeing my bloodied and bruised nose. Chris will probably be over there with her. Sharing some sob story, I'm sure.

I have to do something. It's one thing for him to manipulate me, but stealing my closest friend? I won't take that lying down.

Walking the halls, I'm in desperate search mode. Though, I'm not exactly sure what I'm going to say to him when I do find him. Finally, I resort to waiting by Dr. Redford's door, ready to catch him before he scoots through just in time.

Sure enough, at three past nine, he comes jogging down the hall. He freezes in his tracks when he sees me.

"Whoa," he breathes. "What happened to your face?"

"Why don't you ask your new bestie?" I scoff.

"Huh?"

"We need to talk," I say, grabbing him by the arm. He struggles against me, but I drag him into the nearest men's room.

"What are you doing?" he asks, looking nervous, the door shutting behind us.

"Do you care to explain yourself?" I demand.

"You're going to have to be more specific."

"Tell me why you've poisoned Jackie against me."

"Poisoned?" Chris chuckles. "Aren't we being a bit dramatic?"

"Well, she punched me in the fucking face yesterday, so you tell me."

"Oh, God. Jackie did that?"

"Don't sound so impressed!" I wince as pain radiates from my nose. "Now talk."

"Honestly, Mike. I have no idea. I haven't said a single thing about you to her."

"Yeah right." I sneer. "Then it's just a coincidence my best friend of ten years suddenly hates my guts and calls me a 'homophobic little shit' before socking me in the face. Sounds to me like you told her about what happened between you and me."

"Why would I do that?" Chris rebuts, throwing his hands in the air. "What would I possibly have to gain by doing that?"

"I-I don't know!" I shout, forgetting where we are.

"All I know is my life was just fine before you fucked it all up!"

"And how exactly did I fuck up your life, Mike?" He steps closer to me. "Did I make you gay? No. That was all Him." He points a finger skyward. "All I did was hold on to your sketchbook and say I had a crush on you. You're the one who filled in the blanks. And, say what you want, but maybe Jackie responded the way she did because of *your* behavior, not mine."

"Fuck you."

"Ha!" Chris laughs. "Very mature, Mike. Once again, you refuse to face the truth. Look, if you want to blame me, fine. I get it. But don't for a second think throwing your little tantrum is going to change anything."

"I am not throwing a tantrum."

"Well, whatever this is, are you about done?"

I don't answer, just cross my arms.

"Good. Now then, if you'd be so kind as to let me out, I just might make it to New Testament before Redford locks the door."

Deflated, I step to the side, allowing him to pass.

He places a hand on my shoulder. "And, just for the record, I wasn't trying to guilt you into doing anything yesterday. I was simply saying the truth is a heavy burden to carry alone." He rolls his shoulders. "It's so much easier if you share."

Chris pulls the door open, and I'm left alone looking like an asshole.

Or so I think.

Before I can move, the sound of feet hitting the floor echoes against the aged tile. Hushed voices follow.

"I knew that Myers kid was a queer!" a female voice whispers. "And sounds like Hernandez is his little boy toy."

You got to be shitting me. Ice fills my veins, holding me frozen.

"Yeah, whatever," a male voice says. "Are you going to finish me off, or do I have to do it myself?"

"Yeah, yeah," the girl says a little louder. "Keep your pants off."

Holy shit, that's Tabby.

No. Nope. This isn't happening.

I pull open the door as quietly as I can. My body locks up, panic seeping into my bones and joints until I look like the Tin Man limping down the hall. I keep going, instinctively trying to put distance between myself and my impending doom. A hand catches me at the elbow before I can run into a locker door.

"I hope you're happy," Chris's voice hisses in my ear. "You got me locked out."

I blink. There's a disconnect between my brain and my body. I can't process who's talking to me.

"Jesus, Mike. You're white as a sheet."

"We're fucked," I whisper, my knees suddenly giving way. I sink to the floor before Chris can catch me.

"Dude!" He kneels to help me up, but I can't seem to get my legs to cooperate, so he sits next to me, backs pressed against the lockers. "What's going on?"

"Tabby Freeman."

"Who?"

"Tabby Freeman," I repeat. "She was just in the bathroom. She heard the whole thing."

"Oh." He doesn't seem surprised. He doesn't seem to realize this is the worst thing that's ever happened in the history of things happening. That our lives are about to shatter into a million pieces, never to be put together—

Chris's hand wraps around mine, a steady vibration causing my arm to jostle. I look over to see the color draining from his face, the other hand shaking violently and his lips forming soundless words as he stares straight ahead.

Maybe he does see the gravity of our situation. I give his hand a squeeze to try to calm the shaking.

"What was she even doing in there?" he whispers.

"From the sounds of it, giving some guy a blow job."

"Ugh." Chris clutches his stomach. "That poor bastard. Doesn't he know where that mouth has been?"

On a normal day that would have been hilarious.

"What are we going to do?"

"Well, there's not much we *can* do about it." He sighs. "If she says something, then the worst case is we get reported. That involves a meeting with the counselor, and the school calling our parents."

"Oh, God. We're fucking toast."

"Tell me about it." Chris takes a deep breath. "This is not how I saw my Monday going."

A noise escapes my chest, halfway between laughter and a sob.

This kind of stuff shouldn't happen. Not to a sixteen-year-old. My biggest issue should be deciding what to do on the weekend, not being outed by the school slut with an oral hygiene problem. It's not fair.

"This could change everything," Chris says, his voice small.

That's putting it lightly.

"I-I'm sorry." I manage to coax out. "This is all my

fault."

"Yeah, it kinda is."

God, I'm such a piece of shit.

"Well," Chris says as he heaves himself off the ground, still latched onto my hand. "Since we're already fucked, I say we play hooky for the day."

I raise an eyebrow. "You're kidding."

"What?" Chris actually manages a smirk. "We're about to be kicked out, anyway."

And he's right. There's nothing left for me to lose here. I nod, and he hoists me to my feet.

"What did you have in mind?"

Despite the somber moment, a twinkle of mischief sparks in his eyes. "I don't know about you, but I could use a drink."

THIRTY TWO

He hands me the bottle of whiskey, climbing into the driver's seat. I eye it suspiciously. "You keep this stuff on hand?"

"Not usually," he says, pulling out of the school parking lot. "But after my last little bender, I had to pick up a refill bottle, and it's been rolling around my trunk ever since."

"That explains why it's so hot."

"Just set it in front of the air vents. It'll cool in no time." He plugs his phone into the auxiliary cord, selecting a song.

"Would you laugh at me if I said I've never been drunk before?" I ask over the synth-pop beat.

"Seriously?" Chris raises a brow. "Here I was thinking *I* was sheltered…."

"My parents don't drink." I swirl the brown liquid around the bottle, watching the bubbles spin. "I did get to steal a swig of my Abuela's sangria last Christmas, but it was disgusting."

"All of it is," he says. "But thankfully, you don't have to like the taste to get the benefits."

A flash of lightning streaks through the sky to our left and the resounding thunderclap shakes the car. Rain hits the windshield, as if on cue, quickly distorting the outside world.

You know what they say about Georgia. If you don't like the weather, stick around. It'll change.

"Where are we going?" I ask, no longer able to make out the road signs.

"You'll see."

That's not a creepy answer at all.

Big Guy, we both know I've watched way too many seasons of Criminal Minds. Sometimes on repeat. Please don't let this turn out like season three, episode seventeen. I really don't want to end up strangled in public.

I pull out my phone, ignoring the thirty-seven emails begging me to delete them. Maybe I should text Jackie, to let her know I won't be at lunch. That way someone can account for my last known location before I end up murdered. Then again, I don't think she's speaking to me right now. And that's mostly Chris's fault.

"Why did you do it?" I can't stop the question.

"Once again," he replies, turning off the main road, "your vagueness doesn't help anyone."

Anger flickers in my gut. "Did you have to come out to *her*?"

His grip tightens on the wheel. "Seriously? You're asking me that?"

"Whatever." I scoff, turning from him. "I don't care anymore."

"Why does this upset you?" The rain intensifies, so he raises his voice. "I mean, I know she's your friend."

"Best friend," I correct him.

"Okay, *best friend*. Now, tell me why it matters?"

Actually…I'm not sure why it does. I haven't really been able to pinpoint a specific reason.

"It just does."

"Uh-huh." He nods, unconvinced. We turn into a driveway, and I glance out the window to see a front yard with a 'For Sale' sign.

The car shudders as he kills the engine, rain keeping a steady pace on the roof.

"Want to know what I think?"

His eyes are on me, and a shiver spreads up my spine.

It's just the rain, Mike.

"I think you're upset because *you* didn't tell Jackie that night."

"And why would you think that?"

"Because I could see it written all over your face." He lets out a sigh, leaning back against the door. "And I get it. Look, I didn't think about how it would affect your relationship. All I know is Jackie is the first person in my life I've encountered who wasn't afraid to talk about what I'm feeling right now. She's helped me more than you know over the last few weeks, and I felt like I could trust her with that part of myself."

Chris breaks away, his eyes drifting to watch the rain stream down the windshield. Another flash of lightning transfigures them to honey for a fraction of a second. The image burns in my mind.

A boom of thunder covers my second shiver.

"I'm sorry," he says, still gazing through the glass. "I didn't intend for you to get hurt."

"No, you're right," I whisper, the realization galvanizing inside me. "About me," I say louder. "I guess I didn't want to admit it to myself."

"How bad is it?" Chris asks. "You and Jackie, I mean."

"The last time she spoke to me, this happened." I motion to my face.

"Yikes," he says, and his voice is saturated with a satisfying amount of guilt. "I'll try to talk to her about it, if it helps."

"No." I run fingers through my hair. "I'm going to have to sort this one out on my own. I said some pretty messed up things."

"That mouth gets you in trouble a lot, doesn't it?" Chris grins at me.

"Shut up," I retort, but can't help the smile tugging at the ends of my lips.

"Okay, okay." He reaches his arm out in front of me, and I stiffen. He grabs the bottle of whiskey and unlocks his door. "We're going to have to make a run for it."

"Run to where?"

"Just follow me." He smiles again. He opens the door, causing a spray of precipitation to spatter his clothes as he climbs out.

Once I unfasten my seat belt, I join him in the downpour. He dashes behind the vacant house, splashing through the soggy yard. I pursue him, nearly slipping in the mud. It's raining too hard for me to see where we're going, so I focus on keeping up.

Chris makes it to the line of trees along the back of the yard but only pauses for a moment to make sure I'm still there. He continues through the cluster of pines and maples, the branches offering a slight reprieve from the incessant rain.

Before long, I'm able to make out our destination—a

rope ladder hanging down from a treehouse.

He grabs the ladder, hauling himself up into the opening. I hesitate, wiping the stream of water from my face.

"Come on!" Chris calls from above me.

I figure if he *does* intend to murder me, then at least they won't be able to kick me out of school. Silver lining, right?

I climb the unstable ladder, only making a fool of myself once as my foot slips off a rung and I end up straddling it. Once I recover, it's smooth sailing.

"Well, I'm soaked." Chris laughs, pulling the bottle of whiskey from his blazer. He sheds the jacket, throwing it onto a wooden bench that rests along the far wall.

"We're not going to get arrested, are we?" I ask, still catching my breath. The treehouse is impressive. Definitely not something built by a father and son in an afternoon. A small table and two chairs rest on one side of the room, and another bench on the opposite with an old school desk/chair combo overlooking a cutout window. The storm continues outside.

"Not likely," he replies, twisting the cap off the plastic bottle. He takes a swig, making a face as he swallows. "This was my friend Russell's treehouse," he explains. "I've been sneaking up here for the past year since his parents moved." He traces his hand along a portion of wooden planks covered in doodles.

Russell. That was his best friend when he was younger. That much I remember.

"It's nice to remember him."

His voice is quiet, so I move closer.

"To know there was a time when we were both

happy."

That doesn't sound good.

Chris takes another drink from the bottle, then he hands it over.

I take it, raising the rim to my lips. The whiskey burns its way down to my chest. *Jesus*, that's gross. But I like the warmth spreading across my torso.

"Where did they move to?"

"His folks moved across town," he replies, still facing the wall of memories.

"He didn't go with them?"

"No." Chris shakes his head. "He died last summer."

"Oh." Last summer?

I take another drink. It's better than shoving a foot in my mouth.

"I didn't even know about his funeral." Chris continues his path along the wall. "His parents asked my dad to perform the service, and he never even told me about it. How fucked up is that? I found out a month later Russell had died. I didn't speak to my father for months."

"Why didn't he tell you?"

"Because of the way Russell died." He reaches the window, propping an elbow on it. "Guess he didn't want me to freak out. Remember how I told you we were close as kids?"

I nod.

"Well, apparently there was a reason for that."

The rain drowns out his words, so I have to move closer.

"Russell came out to his parents when he was thirteen. Didn't go too well. His parents flipped out, mostly his dad. You know all those nightmares you hear about these nut jobs putting kids through? Well, Russell went through the list. I had no idea it was even happening."

His eyes are hazy like he's lost in time. "We hadn't seen or heard from each other in years. I only found out because his boyfriend sent me a link to a Tumblr page Russell used as a journal. It almost killed me, reading through it all.

"After they'd exhausted all legal options, his parents sent him to a conversion camp the summer he died. They called it a last-ditch effort to save him. Joke's on them, I guess, seeing as he hung himself a week after he got home."

Christ on a cracker. What do I say to that?

A rumble of thunder shakes the treehouse, and Chris dabs his face. "Can you imagine what that must have been like?"

His words twist my stomach into knots. I mean, *Jesus Christ,* that could have been me! Would my family have reacted the same way?

"Even though he was gone," Chris continues, "Russell gave me a gift the day I found out. His death pushed me to finally accept the fact I *couldn't* keep believing in a god that would let that happen."

What is he saying?

"Anyway." He shoves off the window, grabbing the bottle from my hand and taking a long draw. He coughs. "His parents finally put the house up for sale. So, I've only got a little while longer to enjoy this place."

"Chris," I say, but no other words form on my tongue. I can't think of anything that will make him feel better.

Big Guy…how could You let that happen?

"Sorry," he apologizes, handing over the bottle. "I don't know why I brought you here. I guess…it's comforting. Knowing, no matter what happens, you can remember the happy times too."

"It's okay." I want to comfort him, but I don't know how.

"I guess we should talk about this Tabby thing."

Shit. I'd almost forgotten about that. Russell and I may soon share a few more things in common.

"Do you think we should go talk to her?" I ask.

"It's worth a shot," he answers, pulling off his soggy tie. "The worst she can do is say no."

"Or breathe on you."

That makes him crack a smile.

"That's just a risk I'm going to have to take."

He laughs, and I join in.

I take another sip of whiskey. My head feels light and my neck loose. My nose hurts less too.

Oh, shit. Am I getting drunk?

I offer the bottle back to Chris.

"You did eat breakfast this morning, right?" he asks.

Uh oh. I shake my head.

"Oh boy." He pulls the bottle away from me. "Oops. I probably should have asked that first."

"What's tha have to do wif anything?" My words slur together. I blink, pressing fingers against my lips. *Why aren't they working right?*

"Let's sit you down." Chris grabs hold of my arm, guiding me to the table across the room. A layer of dust is caked on the surface, but underneath is a series of painted squares. It takes me a second to realize it's a checkerboard.

"Oh my God!" My volume control apparently has gone along with my articulation. "Checkers!"

"That's right, Mike." Chris chuckles.

"Can we play?"

He gives me an amused look. "You want to play checkers?"

I nod vigorously.

"With everything that's going on... All right, fuck it. Let's see if they kept the pieces." Chris pulls a small drawer from the side of the table, producing a velvet bag. He shakes it, smiling with the sound of rattling. He drags his sleeve over the table, leaving a wet sheen on the stained wood. "Do you want to be red or black?"

"Red," I say. My thoughts are getting really fuzzy. Chris is cute wet.

"Alrighty then." He dumps the pieces out onto the table, separating them.

"I have an idea," I say. Chris is really cute wet.

"I'm not playing strip checkers with you, Mike."

"No!" I say but can't help the giggle that comes after. "No, I mean I think we should play loser takes a shot."

"That won't be fair," Chris argues. "You're already drunk."

"Nuh-uh."

"Fine, fine," he concedes, placing black checkers alongside his half of the board. "But I feel it's only fair to warn you I'm a checker champion. Undefeated six years running."

"Really?" I ask, in momentary awe.

Chris only laughs. "Are you that drunk?"

My cheeks flare as I realize he was joking. Jesus, I'm a lightweight, apparently.

"Loser takes a shot," I repeat, aligning my pieces.

"Deal?"

"It's your liver," Chris replies, sliding a checker forward.

"Game on."

THIRTY THREE

The world spins as Chris helps lower me into the front seat of his car. He fastens my seat belt, and I giggle as he brushes up against my leg.

"Don't throw up in my car," he tells me.

"You're silly. Why would I do tha—?" My stomach lurches, and I have to focus on breathing for a moment. I close my eyes, and that seems to help with the spinning.

"Just lay back," Chris says.

I hear my door close, the other opening as he climbs into the driver's seat.

"Take me home," I say, fighting the urge to purge.

"Are you sure you want to go home right now?" he asks, the car engine sputtering to life.

If I open my mouth, I know I'm going to toss my cookies, so I simply nod.

"Okay, just remember it's your decision."

The car moves, and a sudden panic sets in.

"Should you be driving right now?" I sit up in my seat a little too fast, and my head feels like it's going to float away.

"Mike, it's almost seven," Chris answers. "I sobered up about four hours ago, after the fifth checkers game."

"Fifth?" I repeat. "I thought we stopped after four?"

"I tried to make you stop," he explains. "You called me a pussy and insulted my mother."

"Oh, God…" I rub my temples. "Did I?"

"Yup." Chris laughs. "Then you pissed out of the treehouse window and passed out for a couple hours. I caught up on some homework. Not that it's going to matter soon."

A vibration shoots up my leg, and I have to fish for my phone.

"Your mom called a few times," he tells me. "I was going to answer it, but I decided that might not be the best idea if you drunkenly blathered in the background."

Perfect. I'm sure Mom is freaking out by now. Surprisingly, when I check my phone, I only discover three missed calls and one text that says:

Call me. 4:45pm

"I also may have texted Jackie to cover for you." Chris smiles sheepishly.

I scroll through my texts. Jackie's came in about an hour ago.

You owe me, shithead. 5:34pm

"I suppose I should thank you," I say, leaning my head against the cool window.

"Don't mention it."

"Wasn't actually planning on it."

Silence falls between us. The weather's cleared, and the last few rays of sun are peeking over the horizon, shading everything in brilliant hues of gold. I watch the light wash over Chris. How it pronounces the freckles running along his cheekbones and the warmth it lends to his eyes, framed by those long lashes.

My chest tightens with familiarity, and I really hope it's just the alcohol.

"What?"

I blink, Chris glancing over at me. "Huh?"

"You're staring at me," he says, eyes trained back on the road.

Shit. I totally am. "I was not."

"O-kay," he drawls out.

"I wasn't."

"Whatever you say, Mike."

Help me out here, Big Guy. Now is not the time to get caught up with how cute this boy is. Did I just say cute? Damn it! Sorry, I mean...

I don't know what I mean. I really need to sleep this off.

"Your new stuff is good," Chris says, motioning to my messenger bag on the floor. "I hope you don't mind, but I looked while you were incapacitated."

A new heat rises to my cheeks.

"You went through my sketchbook?"

He nods, not looking the slightest bit guilty.

"What the fuck?" My voice shoots up an octave.

Chris laughs. "Couldn't help myself," he says. "It was too good an opportunity to pass— Ow!"

I smack his shoulder a second time.

"Cut it out!"

"No." After a third hit, he grabs my wrist, eyes not leaving the road. "Don't fucking kill us!"

"Then stop hitting me!" He's still smiling despite the serious tone.

"Fine." I pull free of his grip, sinking back into my seat as I simmer down. So, he saw my sketchbook, big whoop. I haven't added anything noteworthy since he had it.

Except...

"That one of me was really good." Chris smirks. "You really captured me."

You could fry an egg on my face.

"I— You— I can't— Shut up!"

He howls with laughter. I contemplate crashing the car. At least we wouldn't have to deal with Tabby and this whole ugly situation if we're wrapped around a tree.

I seethe as he pulls the car into my driveway. The sun has finally set, so it's dark when he shuts the headlights off. I can just make out the outline of his frame in the glow of the dashboard lights.

"I'm flattered, by the way." He angles toward me. "I wish I had that kind of talent."

"Yeah, whatever." I clutch my bag to my chest, cursing the day I ever picked up a pencil.

"I really do mean what I said," he continues. "Your drawings are incredible."

I don't say anything, but my eyes are drawn to search for his in the darkness. They reflect the points of light, like a swarm of fireflies.

My chest gets tight again. I shake my head to try to clear the fog. I don't like being drunk. It's dangerous.

"I'm going to talk to Tabby tomorrow," Chris says,

shifting forward as he stretches, letting out a yawn. "You know, since I kinda started this whole mess."

"Yes, you did," I agree.

"I *am* sorry, Mike."

"Me too. There's enough blame to share."

I know I should open the door, but I can't get my arms to cooperate. So, I just sit here.

"Mike, can I tell you a secret?"

"What is it?" I ask, leaning closer to him instinctively. What else could I not know about him?

"I..." He stops, taking a beat. "I really want to kiss you right now."

It's like a hand is squeezing my heart. I need to get out of this car right now, but my body refuses to move.

"W-What?"

"Can I kiss you?" He moves closer, and his hot breath blows against my cheek.

"Uh, I... That is... Um..."

"I figure since we're both going to hell," he whispers, sending waves of goosebumps across my skin, "why not have a little fun on our way?"

I swallow loudly.

"Okay."

"Okay?" he echoes. His hand cups the side of my face, and I shudder as his thumb slides along my cheekbone.

I nod against his touch.

And his lips are on mine, hesitant and soft. That foreign constriction in my chest eases up, releasing a pulse of warmth through my limbs. Chris breaks away after a second, exhaling. His dark eyes hold me, and I don't have to think about what to do next. I ignore my throbbing nose.

Wrapping my fingers around his shirt, I pull him into me, lips finding each other in the dark. He's still hesitant, but I can't contain myself any longer. My touch is urgent as I claw at him. I have to do this.

A groan comes from Chris's chest as he pushes me away.

"What's wrong?" I ask, breathless.

"Nothing." He pants. "I just need a second."

A shadow moves outside the car, a silhouette against the house's lit windows.

"Oh, shit." I press myself against the window, peering through.

The front door opens, and Rosy shuts it behind her. "Shit!"

"What is it?" Chris asks, still leaning into me.

"My sister," I scramble to open the door. "I think she saw us!"

"Wait, Mike—"

"See you tomorrow!" I tell him, already sprinting to the door. I quickly realize I'm still very drunk as I stumble up the stairs. Vomit threatens its way out, but I swallow it as I fling the door open.

"Michael?" my mother calls from the other room.

I don't have time for her as I dash to the stairs. "Rosy?"

She saw me. She saw me kissing a boy. If she tells Mom and Dad, my life is over.

"No, no, no…" My legs feel like noodles as I sink onto the third stair—unable to go any farther. I bury my head in my arms to keep the room from spinning.

"Michael?"

My mother's hand clamps onto my shoulder, but I don't look up. I can't let her see me like this. That would require an explanation.

"What's going— *Sweet Lord,* Michael. Why do you smell like you've been swimming in bourbon?"

I can't respond, even if I wanted to.

"*Michael Hernandez.*" Mom pulls my arm, jerking me upward.

My stomach lurches, and I can't hold it back this time. I heave, my mother shrieking as I bathe her in regret and whiskey.

After the waterfall of bodily fluids eases up, I try to speak, but she stops me with her hand.

"Shower." She shakes some vomit from her leggings. "Now."

THIRTY FOUR

After a couple rounds of vomiting and a shower, I'm feeling worlds better. The ceiling fan spins lazily above me. Mom and Dad will be in any minute to deliver a punishment for my crimes. I wonder if Rosy has spilled the beans yet. I mean, underage drinking is one thing, but making out with the pastor's son? Pretty sure that's grounds for immediate execution around here.

Mom already confiscated my phone. I can only pray Chris is smart enough not to text me anything that will speed up my timely demise.

A knock on my door sounds like the gavel at my sentencing.

"Michael?"

I sit up slowly, stomach still uneasy. Dad opens the door, his tie hanging loose around his neck. He probably just got home even though it's almost nine thirty.

"Your mother tells me you've had quite the evening." He walks over to my desk, lowering himself into the spinning chair.

I nod. I'm too smart to give verbal confirmation.

"She also said you seemed pretty upset about something," he continues, shuffling through my sketches on the desk. "I think we should talk about that first."

"There's nothing to talk about," I lie, averting my gaze.

"Mike, how many times do we have to go over this?" Dad chuckles. "You're a terrible liar, just like your old man."

Apparently not, seeing as I've been lying to you for years now.

"Was Jackie drinking with you?"

"No!" I half shout. "She... She gave me a ride home, that's all." That's the story Jackie agreed to, keeping Chris out of the picture. Don't need them snooping around him.

"Does this have something to do with your little accident yesterday?"

Accident?

"Did someone hit you, Mike?"

Oh. My nose. I shake my head.

"No, it's not that."

"Then what on earth has gotten into you, *hojito?*"

"Nothing." I sigh. I don't want to talk anymore.

"Not a good enough answer."

"Really, it's nothing."

"Michael, you just ralphed enough booze to stock a bar on your mother. Are you really telling me you just decided to get wasted on a whim?"

"Yup."

"Michael," he grunts as he rises from his seat, "you have to meet me halfway here."

270

"There's nothing going on!" I yell, temper flaring. "I wanted to drink, so I did! End of story."

The look in my father's eyes is enough to make me cry, but I bite my bottom lip to stop the trembling. If I show weakness now, if I break, there's nothing I won't tell him.

"All right," he says, exasperated. "If you don't want to tell me, I can't make you. But, now, you're grounded for two weeks." He digs in his pocket for my phone, tossing it on the bed beside me. "I disabled all your data. So, that's only to be used as a way for your mother and me to reach you. Is that clear?"

"Yes, sir."

"Good." Letting out a deep breath, he leans forward, kissing me on top of my head. "I love you, son. I'm glad you're all right."

And that's enough to make the tears spill over, so I quickly turn away from him.

My door shuts a moment later, and the first sob tears through my chest like an animal.

A SPLITTING HEADACHE AND MOUTH DRIER THAN THE Sahara Desert greet me with my alarm. I silence the electronic squawking, trying to toggle open my Tumblr app before remembering my parents have rendered my phone useless.

No way my parents will let a hangover be an excuse to stay home from school, so I have to will myself out of bed. Details from yesterday filter in as I search for a clean towel.

I recall a checkerboard, a rope ladder, flashes of lightning, and headlights passing in the dark on our way home. The feeling of Chris's lips against mine.

I hold the towel strategically as I stumble down the hall toward the shower.

Rosy stands in front of the mirror, brandishing a mascara wand.

"Hey," I say, keeping my distance from her. The shower head sputters to life with the turn of a knob.

"I'm almost done," she says without looking away from her work.

How do I bring this up? I mean, there's a chance she didn't even see anything last night. I could be freaking out for absolutely no reason. Then again, she could also have already told Mom and Dad and is planning on being the only teenager left standing in the house.

Would she do that?

She closes the tube of makeup with a snap, tossing it into her bag. Without a word, she exits the bathroom, closing the door behind her.

I exhale.

This is going to be a very long day.

"—DON'T MENTION IT," JACKIE SAYS AS I ROUND THE BRICK WALL INTO our trash sanctum. She glares at me, cigarette flaring to match her anger.

Chris turns, grinning like an idiot when he sees me. Then he catches himself and tries to dial back the elation. It's cute.

Shit. No, it's not!

"Hey." I give a small wave. The smell of rancid milk isn't helping my nausea. They must have dumped the spoiled cartons early today.

"You gotta lot of nerve." Jackie huffs.

For once, I'm thankful for the smell of tobacco. It overpowers everything else.

"Jackie—" Chris starts.

She doesn't let him finish. "How's your nose?" she asks without even a hint of remorse.

"Hurts like hell," I answer.

"I'll bet." She smiles. "It's some of my best work. What did you tell your parents?"

"Tanner hit me with a football."

Her laughter is explosive. "You got to be shitting me. The only thing more ridiculous than you trying to catch a football is Tan-Tan being able to throw one."

"I'm glad to see you're getting some enjoyment out of this."

Chris stands behind her, and I have to keep myself from looking at him. No matter how much I want to.

"So, what do you want?" Jackie snaps me back into focus.

"To say I'm sorry, I guess."

"Sorry?"

"For what I said the other day," I elaborate. "I was out of line."

"Yes, you were." Jackie drags her cigarette across the wall. "And I suppose I should probably apologize for breaking your nose."

"It's not broken," I tell her.

"Well, it sounded like popcorn." She laughs. "But I'm no doctor."

"Can you stop being mad at me now?"

She hesitates, pursing her lips. "I suppose that can be arranged."

I hold out my arms, and after a moment of hesitation, she hugs me.

"You two are going to make me cry," Chris interjects.

"It's been a real Hallmark moment." Jackie slings her backpack over her shoulder. "But I gotta go grovel for an extension on my Theology paper."

She tries to flick my nose as she passes, but I duck out of the way. And now Chris and I are alone with only the comforting scent of rotting dairy to keep us company.

"Hey," he says, stepping beside me. My nerves are on edge like an electric current is passing between us. The closer he gets, the stronger the sensation becomes.

This certainly didn't happen before last night.

"*Hola.*" I shuffle my feet.

"Did you talk to your sister last night?"

"No," I answer. "I was too busy yakking all over my mom and getting grounded for the rest of the month. Have you seen Tabby?"

"Not yet," he replies, shrugging on his uniform jacket. "But I have second period with her, so I'll corner her then. I haven't really thought about what I'm going to say when I do find her…."

"You'll come up with something." I try to sound encouraging despite the fact our lives practically hang in the balance.

Okay, Big Guy. I know we've had our differences in the past, but I could really use Your help at the moment. But here's a question. Is it wrong of me to ask You to strike Tabby down with some kind of minor plague? I'm not talking leprosy or anything like that, but maybe laryngitis?

Or herpes of the mouth? Anything that will keep her from talking would be awesome.

"Mike?"

"Huh?"

Chris has an eyebrow raised. "I lost you for a second."

"Right." I shake my head, dispelling thoughts of Tabby's tongue covered in boils. "What were you saying?"

"I said we should probably get to class before we're locked out two days in a row."

"That's probably for the best." I turn to escape the smelly brick fortress, but he catches me by the elbow.

"Just one sec."

Chris plants his lips firmly on mine, and my body goes rigid.

He breaks away from me, cheeks tinted pink and letting out a shuddered breath.

"Sorry," he says, grinning. "I've just been thinking about that all night."

"R-Right," I stammer, my face feeling white-hot. "We should get going."

I almost break into a run as we cross the grassy patch and enter the school.

THIRTY FIVE

LUNCH ROLLS AROUND AND I HAVEN'T PARTICIPATED IN A SINGLE MOMENT OF education today. How could I when every molecule of my brain has been preoccupied with Chris? It was one thing for us to share a moment of drunken passion, but for him to just kiss me like that so close to school was a reckless and childish decision.

And I hate myself for how much I enjoyed it.

I *should* be fretting over when the other shoe will fall and when Tabby will expose Chris and me.

I'm practically a vibrating pile of nerves by the time I make it to my seat at our usual table.

"Have you seen this?" Tanner holds his phone out to me, a video playing on the screen. I laugh along with Katie, who's beside me, but I can't even focus enough to comprehend what's happening.

"That's crazy!" Katie gushes, leaning into my shoulder to get a better view.

I've already stopped pretending to watch, eyes scanning the cafeteria in search of a certain dark-haired boy. But he's not here. Which I hope means he found Tabby and is currently disposing of her body in the dumpsters along with last week's milk.

"Are you seriously still watching that?" Jackie berates, plopping down on my right. "Give it a rest already, Tanner."

"I can't!" he replies, pulling the phone back.

"Hey!" Katie pouts. "It was still playing."

"Get over it," Jackie mutters, stirring her peas around.

She's in a sour mood.

"Who spit in your grits?" Katie questions.

"Wow." Jackie scoffs. "That was the most idiotically southern thing I've heard all morning."

Tanner laughs, and Jackie cracks a smile, but Katie shuts down, her gaze dropping to the table.

"Aww, Katie, you know I'm just yanking your chain, right?"

"Whatever." Katie rises from her seat, sliding her tray down to the other end of the table.

"Someone's extra fragile this morning," Jackie says through a mouthful of creamed corn.

"Hey." Tanner's opened his laptop, fingers dancing along the keys. "Has anyone seen Tabby? She's usually humping my leg by this time of day."

I freeze, ears perking up at the mention of my new nemesis.

"She's sick," Larry calls from the other side of the table. "Monica said she got strep."

"Yeah right." Taylor laughs beside him. "She's probably contracted some terrible STD of the throat."

Holy shit. You work fast, Big Guy.

My hands are shaking as I dig my phone out of my pocket, typing a message to Chris.

"That **blows**," Tanner says, moping, "in more ways than one I **suppose**. She said she had something super juicy to tell me."

Oh shit.

"Why **doesn't** she just text **you**?" Jackie asks.

"She **said** it would be better in person," he replies.

That bitch. She wants to milk this thing for all it's worth. I can only hope Chris gets to her before she gets to Tanner. What would he do if he found out? I would like to think he'd have my back and tell Tabby to go fuck herself. Then again, could he really keep her from spreading it?

Would he do that for me?

"There you are, Myers."

My head shoots up so fast I *definitely* have whiplash.

"Sorry I'm late," Chris says, sinking into the seat beside Tanner, across from me. "Had something I was trying to take care of."

"That's not vague at all," says Tanner, eyeing Chris suspiciously.

"Leave him alone," Jackie intervenes.

I want to hug her. My nose throbs as if to warn me against such a gesture.

"I'm only joshing you, Myers." Tanner wraps an arm around Chris's neck, jostling him playfully.

"Careful you two," Jackie warns, "you don't want someone to report you for 'inappropriate behavior.'"

Tanner releases Chris with a laugh, his attention falling back to his laptop.

Chris makes eye contact with me, and I can't help

278

the grin spreading my lips.

The table falls back into its usual cliques, leaving me to risk glances across to the boy I really want to kiss again.

THIRTY SIX

"WHAT ARE YOU DOING TONIGHT?" CHRIS ASKS IN A HUSHED TONE AS I stack my books back into my locker.

"I'm under house arrest, remember?" I shut the door with a *clang*. Chris hovers so close, making it tough to focus on anything.

"Damn," he mumbles. "Even if you have a good friend who's in desperate need of help with his Theology homework?"

"You have an A in theology."

"You're missing the point."

"Oh."

"Come on." Chris smiles. "It's worth a shot."

"My parents would never go for it."

"Not even if it's to help the P.K.?" He raises an eyebrow.

I let out a sigh. "Fine, I'll ask."

"Awesome!" His smile becomes even wider if that's possible.

"I'll let you know what she says." I sling my bag over my shoulder. "Do I dare ask what we'll actually be doing tonight?"

"It's a surprise," Chris responds. "But I'll pick you up around seven!"

"Okay, that sounds go—"

"Mike!"

I turn to see Rosy tapping her foot at the end of the hall.

"Gotta go," I tell him. "Might see you tonight?"

"Fingers crossed." He gives me an awkward, over-the-shoulder-no-we're-not-gay hug.

I linger for just a second too long.

"Come on, Mike!"

We break apart, and I turn to walk toward my impatient sister. She's still tapping her foot when I reach her.

"What? You're speaking with me now?"

She doesn't respond, just huffs and lugs her violin case toward the door. I wave a final time to Chris, then follow her through the heavy metal doors into the inferno of the parking lot.

For someone who's five-foot-two, Rosy can really move. She's already to Mom's Escalade before I can even clear the sidewalk.

I open the passenger door, relishing the air-conditioned interior. Mom pulls out of her parking spot, a frown dragging her features down.

"Buckle," she orders.

I gladly comply as she accelerates onto the road, tires screeching. I suppose she's still upset about her shower of shame last night. Her driving pattern varies heavily based on her emotional state.

"Mom, are you okay?" I ask, holding onto the sissy bar as if it's my lifeline.

"I don't know Michael," she replies, blinking a few times like she's trying to keep from crying. "Would you be all right if you had to spend an hour of your night cleaning vomit out of your hair, worrying yourself into a tizzy over your child making an asinine decision that could have gotten him killed, and all the while thinking to yourself, 'where did I go wrong?'"

I sit in stunned silence.

"You scared the 'you know what' out of me last night, Michael."

"I'm sorry," I offer, a sinking sense of guilt settling in my stomach. "I really am, Mom."

A tear rolls down her cheek, and I want to cry too. "Just promise me you won't ever do that to me again."

"I promise."

"Good." She wipes the side of her face, checking her mascara in the mirror. After she's satisfied, she flips the radio on, humming off tune to the painful Christian music.

I figure now is as good a time as ever to ask.

"Hey, Mom?"

"Yes?"

"I know I'm rightfully grounded and all." I try to sound nonchalant. "But Chris Myers asked me if I could help him with his Geometry homework tonight."

"Oh."

She bites her bottom lip, which I know means she's thinking about it.

"I suppose he could come over to the house."

"No!" I respond before quickly reigning myself in.

Think fast, Mike. Why can't he come over?

"I-I mean, he's, um…"

"Mom," Rosy interrupts, "you and Dad are supposed to take me shopping for new strings tonight. Remember? He told you about it on Saturday."

"Oh darn," Mom mutters. "I'm sorry, Rosy. I don't remember that at all."

"You never remember anything." Rosy sighs, folding her arms.

Wait, a second. Is she lying?

"I know, sweetie, I'm the worst," Mom apologizes.

"Guess they'll just have to study at Chris's place," Rosy offers.

"Is that all right, Michael?" Mom asks.

"O-Oh, yeah it's totally cool," I reply. "I'll just double check with Chris, but I'm sure it's fine. He can probably even give me a ride home."

"That's so considerate," Mom says. "He's just such a nice young man."

"Y-Yeah." I throw a glance over my shoulder to Rosy, but she's looking at her phone. "He sure is."

Mom turns the volume back up on the music, joining into a chorus of "Amazing Grace" that has us all wishing for The Rapture.

THIRTY SEVEN

IT'S A QUARTER TO SEVEN, AND I'M DOODLING BETWEEN NERVOUS GLANCES AT my phone. Chris was ecstatic when I told him we were all set, and I've been obsessing over figuring out just what he has brewing for tonight.

A sharp rap on my door makes me jump.

"Who is it?" I call, setting aside my sketchbook.

"The freaking pope," Rosy sasses, sticking her head in.

"Wow, you look great for your age."

"Thank you." She steps into my room, shutting the door behind her. "It's from all the babies I kiss. I'm actually stealing their souls in exchange for eternal youth." She looks around, finally settling into my desk chair.

"What do you want?" I ask.

"Just wanted to come see my big brother," she replies, spinning slowly in the chair. "See what you're wearing on your date tonight."

"Excuse me?"

"You heard me." Rosy ceases her spinning. "I want

to know what you're wearing on your date with Chris."

"M-My what?"

"Jesus, you're slow." She rolls her eyes. "I saw the two of you last night when I was walking over from Abby's. You seemed pretty chummy…"

So, she *did* see us.

"What exactly did you see?"

"Fine. I'll spell it out for you, lughead. I saw you and Chris playing tonsil hockey in his car. There, are you happy?"

"I-I can explain—"

"Dude, calm down." Rosy stands up, crossing the room to sit next to me. "I mean, seriously, you look like a Chihuahua. You're shaking so bad."

She's right. My teeth are chattering out of my skull.

"Here." She takes my hands in hers. "Just breathe, Mike. In and out. In and out. That's better."

I exhale a third time, and surprisingly, I do feel better.

"T-Thanks," I say, at a loss. "I'm sorry. I just…"

"Look." Rosy still holds onto me. "So, you like to kiss boys. Well, so do I! Who knew we had so much in common?"

A broken sound comes from my chest that I think was supposed to be a laugh.

"And, although I think you could do sooo much better than Myers," she continues, "I wanted you to know I got your back."

"You're not going to tell Mom and Dad?"

"Hell no. It's not my business to tell." She shrugs, releasing my hands. "Besides, no way am I taking that bullet for you. If you want them to know, you're going to have to tell them yourself."

I nod, wiping away the moisture that's been building in the corner of my eyes.

"Gross. Don't get all weepy on me," Rosy chides.

I try to give her a smile. "Thank you, Rosy."

"Eh, don't mention it." She shoves me off the bed. "Now if you'll excuse me, I have parents to distract, and you need to get ready."

"I am ready."

"Oh *Jesus*, Mike." Rosy scowls. "You poor thing."

"What's that supposed to mean?"

"Never mind." She crosses to the door. "Just have fun."

"Rosy?"

She turns. "Yeah?"

"Is this...?" The words get caught, and I have to swallow the lump in my throat. "Am I *wrong* for wanting this?"

She pauses, looking down at the floor. "Everyone wants to be loved, Mike. As far as right or wrong, I...I can't answer that. That's one you're going to have to figure out for yourself."

With that, she closes the door.

TRAFFIC IS HELL AS CHRIS AND I RIDE UP ROSWELL ROAD. I'VE BEEN QUIET this far into our drive, replaying my conversation with Rosy over and over again in my head. The relief of her knowing my secret was short-lived, but it has lightened my burden. Marginally.

She told me to figure it out, but do I really have to do

it by myself? What I wouldn't give for someone with a little insight. Someone going through the same thing.

Like a pastor's son. Who also happens to be gay and sitting right next to me.

Jesus, I'm an idiot.

"Chris?" I raise my voice over the music.

He reaches for the dial. "What's up?"

"What if we're wrong?"

He glances over at me. "I'm not following."

"What if we're *wrong*?" I say again. "About everything. I can't get it out of my head. What if all those things your father said about us is right? That we're some affront to God's plan? What if we're just weak and giving into temptation? Like drug addicts or something."

Chris remains silent, so I keep going.

"Maybe something is wrong with my brain. Maybe it's broken or something. Like, maybe, my mother dropped me. 'Oops! Sorry, son. I guess you like boys now!'"

"Do you honestly believe that?" Chris asks.

On an exhale, I continue, "I...I don't know *what* I believe right now."

"Look, Mike, I can't give you what you're looking for. So, don't think I can." His frown deepens like he's thinking hard about something. "Listen, if there's anything I've learned in my short time on this Earth, it's that there are no definitive answers."

"That's not very helpful."

"Fine. Here," he says as he reaches out his hand, palm side up. "Give me your hand."

"Why?"

"Just do it."

I place mine in his and he wraps his fingers around it.

"Now put your other hand here," he says, tapping the side of his neck.

I do as I'm told, pressing slightly against his skin. I can feel his pulse, throbbing in a quick and steady rhythm.

"Do you feel that?" he asks me. "My heart is racing because I'm holding your hand. It doesn't do that for anyone else. And that fact tells me what I need to know. My body was *made* to do this. Every cell within me reacts to your touch.

"I know it's not much to go on." He shrugs. "But it's enough for me."

I pull my hand away from his neck. My own pulse echoes in my ears. I've never thought of it like that.

"The world is so much bigger than you've been told, Mike." Chris gives my hand a squeeze. "It's only one perspective, one side of the story you've heard. And I know it's difficult, but trust me on this. There's so much more to experience."

I nod, turning my gaze to the window.

Chris has been so honest with me. More honesty in one day than I've received in a lifetime.

"My sister knows," I say. "She told me right before you picked me up."

"And?"

"And that's it. She thinks I can do better than you."

Chris laughs, melting some of the tension in my gut. "I'd have to agree with her."

"Shut up," I say, a grin spreading across my lips.

"So, does this mean we're dating?"

"Oh my God!" I pull my hand out of his. "You're

ridiculous."

"That wasn't a no."

"Just drive!"

Chris smirks. "Maybe *I* could do better...."

"Yeah, right."

THIRTY EIGHT

CLARK'S CUP TEEMS WITH LIFE AS WE STEP INSIDE, BODIES HUDDLING around tables and draping over furniture.

"What are we doing here?" I ask Chris as he moves toward the counter.

"You'll see," he replies. "Just keep your pants on. Or, on second thought…"

"Shut up!"

He laughs, stepping up to the register. "Can I get an Iced Mocha, please?"

"Sure thing, Chris," says the barista.

My cheeks go red when I realize it's Davy.

"Hey, Mike!" he calls, waving at me.

"H-Hey, Davy." I move alongside Chris. "How's it going?"

"Oh, you know. It's poetry night, so naturally coffee grounds are everywhere. I think some might be in my shoe right now…" He makes a face, then hands Chris his receipt.

Chris nods his thanks and moves toward the end of the bar.

"Are you going to do a latte again?"

"Yeah," I answer, pulling out my wallet.

Poetry night, huh? Is this what Chris had planned? I need to think of an excuse to get out of this.

"Don't worry about it." Davy grins, a curl of blond hair sticking out from under his hat. "It's on me."

"T-Thanks."

"My pleasure." After another wink, he moves down the line to start on our beverages. I'm thinking those may be intentional.

Chris has an amused look on his face as I join him at the end of the bar.

"What?" I ask him.

"Should I be jealous?"

I raise a brow. "What are you talking about?"

"Jesus, Mike. You *are* oblivious, aren't you?"

"Huh?"

"Never mind." He laughs.

"Here you go, guys." Davy slides two cups over the counter. "Enjoy!"

I balance my saucer as we walk, taking the only available table left in the joint.

"Good evening, everyone," a voice says over the speakers as we settle in. A balding man slouches on the makeshift stage across the room. "Welcome to Clark's Cup and our open poetry night."

A round of applause ripples through the crowd.

"Thank you, thank you. I would ask you to please remember this is a safe space tonight. We're coming together to share the different experiences we've been given. Please respect others. We're going to get the ball rolling here with our first artist this evening, coming from the east village, so please give it up for Victoria!"

Another round of applause as a woman with blood-red hair and a collection of piercings steps up to the microphone. It takes me a moment to realize I've seen her before.

"Chris!" I whisper. "That's the chick from the piercing shop!"

"No shit," Chris breathes, leaning forward in anticipation.

The woman—Victoria we can only assume—clears her throat as she locks her gaze on a spot in the back of the room. "Thank you." She adjusts the microphone slightly as the crowd goes quiet. "I will be reading a selection from my poem entitled, *Bitch.*

"I broke my Granny's antique candy dish when I was ten.
It shattered against the floor into thousands of fragmented bits.
Maybe that's why it sounded so familiar,
when I heard the same noise inside the day she left.

"But, now, she's back, this crazy bitch.
She says she's sorry, she repeats herself again and again.
But I've heard this song before, on an endless loop,
my dad mouthed it each time he'd come back.

"Except that last time, when he didn't bother.
I expect this will end the same way.
No word. No explanation. Just a sudden absence,
both terrifying and liberating.

"She holds me tight and makes me feel safe.
Embraces and embraces. Soft kiss and stare.
How can I keep myself from feeling
those things that make me wish for more?

"The Bitch is back, and it looks like it's to stay.
Another day, another day, another day.
Every time she makes me smile
I wish and pray she feels the same way."

I shiver as Victoria's words fade, and applause takes over the silence left behind from her voice. I look at Chris, and he has gone pale. He fidgets in his chair, hair hiding his eyes.

"Chris?"

"Thank you, Victoria." The announcer shuffles back onstage. "Another powerful testament to your talent. And thank you for leaving out a certain four-letter word."

Victoria blows the man a kiss before flipping him the bird.

Charming.

"Our next artist is one of the youngest entries we've had in a while." The host carries on, unfazed. "So, please give a warm welcome to Chris!"

Oh. That explains the nerves. I look at him, but he's already risen from his chair and is moving toward the stage. He steps in front of the microphone, having to angle it downward since he's a good foot shorter than Victoria.

I'm drawn to the edge of my chair. This is the first time I'll get to hear Chris's work. It's slightly embarrassing how excited I am.

"Hello," he starts, voice cracking with nerves. He clears his throat and continues. "This is called *There Goes Sunday School.*

"Sunday morning, dark skies overhead,
I sit along the wall, pen drawn but thoughts gone.
There's a struggle to find words,
to match what bounces round my head.

"I feel so out of place here,
things once comforting, now alienating.
Familiarity replaced with the dread
of those I know finding what bounces round my head.

"I've kept it bottled up so long, this thing
I hide, fermenting and wasting away.
Too ugly to show the light of day.
Too lonely to know the words to say.

"An urgent sound centers my thoughts,
driving me out with the rest of our herd.
We huddle close, threats of danger blaring
through sirens and words.

"The God I no longer seek has found me, I think.
His wrath released on the boy who turned his back.
Punishment dealt for the sin no one wants to acknowledge,
For the life I never chose to live.

"It's cruel that my sentence seeks to claim us all,

wind tearing and lightning crashing.
I slip through the door, unnoticed.
Maybe my absence will bring them relief.

"The world outside bends to His wrath,
but inside His house, His voice is quiet.
I wish to return to my seat, paper, and pen.
To carve my final words before He claims me.

"But, once again, words fail to capture what's real,
and I weave aimlessly through the skeletons of
absence.
Reflection of days long past, staring me in the face
in constant conflict with what bounces round my
head."

Chris's voice grows stronger as he reads, a steady
rhythm building in his words.

"Another clap of thunder, and I'm tumbling,
skidding backwards on paper and falling on
cement.
When I rise from the ashes of klutz, there's
something new
nestled in the crook of my arm. A book, cover
open.

"The first page is magic—light filtering through a
forest of leaves,
each gray stroke subtle perfection.
Blended beautifully.
Something moves, stirring in my depths.

"Water flows from the second page,
pouring out around me until I'm swimming.
Tossed back and forth from rock to rock
along the monochrome river's bumpy edges.

"Page three is stark white.
Its emptiness echoes inside me,
reverberations making their way up
to silence what's bouncing around in my head."

The audience sticks like glue, not uttering a word while he speaks. I follow suit, but there is a difference between me and them. I know exactly what he's talking about.

"Fingers follow fingers,
turning and turning and turning
till I near the end of the line.
At last admitting the journey is over.

"Yet another path is open, hidden in plain sight.
Pages releasing their hold on one another
to reveal the treasure,
and lead me to what I had no idea I was seeking.

"Bodies, folded into one under silken skin.
Lips and hands, and my heartbeat hammering in
my chest.
Fire burning in my cheeks, along with something
more.
Something new, terrifying, and strong.

"With one, final turn, a name burns itself

into my brain, letters forever engraved.
Who would have thought? Someone already
knows what bounces round my head.

"In sudden haste, the flock returns to its pasture,
grazing on gossip and sugary-smothered
breakfast as I quietly fade into the background,
a wolf desperate to be a sheep.

"My discovery hides out of sight,
waiting to serve as a catalyst.
There's more than one of us here.
In the words of my father, 'there goes Sunday
school.'"

Chris folds the paper, stowing it back into his pocket as the audience applauds. I clap along with them, the weight of his words still carving their way into my brain.

There goes Sunday school.

I can't help laughing. It's a play on his father's favorite phrase to describe anything he doesn't agree with. "There goes the neighborhood."

Who knew my artwork could mean so much to someone? Especially someone like Chris. Then again, I guess I really don't know him that well. Perhaps he's *exactly* the person my work would touch.

He finds his way back to the table, cheeks flushed with the energy of being exposed.

"Excellent work, Chris." The announcer speaks into the microphone. "A lot of potential from a very talented young man. Our next artist is one of our favorite locals."

"What did you think?" Chris asks, breathless. He sips from his sweaty iced mocha.

"I got chills," I say, rubbing my arms for emphasis. I want to say more, but I'm not really sure how to.

"Is that a good thing?"

I nod, clutching onto the warm mug to steady my hands.

"I know I already apologized," Chris starts, "but I want to say again how sorry I am about taking your book."

"Don't worry about it," I tell him. "Ancient history."

"If it helps my case," he says, still flushed with nerves, "you should know those sketches helped pull me through a really tough time."

"Really?" My stomach twists like a pretzel. I hate talking about my art. I just want it to speak for itself. But I can't help asking, "How?"

"It's hard to explain," Chris replies, resting an elbow on the edge of the table. "But I guess you could boil it down to hope."

"Hope?" What does that have to do with anything?

"Yeah." He nods in agreement. "They gave me hope there was someone out there like me. That somebody had it all figured out. That I had a chance to feel something again."

"I don't have anything figured out," I admit, my back hitting the chair. "I was actually hoping you did."

"That's the thing," he says with a snap of his fingers. "I don't think anyone has it figured out. We're all kinda making it up as we go along."

Another person has taken the mantel of the stage, standing at the microphone, but I'm too distracted to comprehend the words flowing from him.

"But we're not alone anymore," Chris continues, leaning forward with intensity in his eyes. "We can—"

"Well, well." A new voice derails my train of thought. Victoria looms over us, all smiles. "If it isn't my favorite little couple. I swear, I just want to put you two in my pocket and carry you around. Unfortunately, the misogynistic bastards that designed this dress neglected to give me any, so I don't have a place for you."

"How unfortunate," I say. Chris chuckles.

"I'm Victoria." The tall woman extends her hand. "You can call me Tori if you want."

"Mike," I respond, taking her hand. She has a very firm grip.

"And, obviously, you're Chris." She turns her pierced head on him next. "Your rhythm sucks, but the material's not half bad."

"Thanks," he replies. "I really enjoyed yours too."

"Ugh. I had to edit a lot of it out, seeing as they won't let me drop the f-bomb," Tori bemoans. "At least not in the microphone. I guess I can say it all I want now. Fuck. Fuck, fuck, fuck. That's really refreshing." She sighs deeply, then blinks a few times as if she'd forgotten we're sitting here. "I'm sorry, was I interrupting something?"

"Actually," Chris starts, "we were—"

"Not at all," I interject. Things are getting a little too real. I need a distraction. And what more of a distraction can you ask for than an obscenity-spewing-six-foot-three-red-headed lesbian?

"Well, I can't stay long," she says, pulling up a chair. "It's drag-karaoke night, and I've still got to go home and change."

299

"Drag-karaoke?" I repeat, flashes of sequins and big hair coming to mind.

"Oh yeah." Tori laughs. "It's a blast. I'd invite you guys along, but sadly, they don't let kids in."

"We're not kids," Chris corrects.

"Oh *please.*" Tori strokes a finger along Chris's cheek. "Not a speck of stubble. I'm fairly certain I have shoes that are older than you."

"That doesn't mean—"

"Tori," I say as I place a hand on her arm, breaking up the developing spat. "I've always wanted to know what you call that piercing." I point to my upper lip.

She turns away from Chris. "What, this?" She flicks the two balls in front of her teeth with her tongue. "It's a frenulum, or Smiley piercing. Hurts like a sommabitch."

I wince. "I don't doubt that."

"Were you thinking of getting one?" she asks, flashing a smile as if to accentuate the ring.

"Not exactly," I sheepishly admit.

"That's a shame." She sighs, rising from her chair. "Well, kiddos, it's been real. It's been fun. Can't say it's been real fun. I have a date with a man that looks prettier in makeup than I ever will."

She gives an impressive curtsy, then heads for the door.

"What a strange person..." I muse, watching the woman until she disappears through the door.

"That's an understatement."

Another round of applause smothers the conversation, and I drain the rest of my latte.

"Hey, Mike?"

I set the cup down with a *clink.* "Hm?"

300

"Do you wanna get out of here?" Chris asks, looking down at his phone.

"Sure." I shrug, just glad he isn't looking at me like he was just a moment ago. I'm not sure exactly where we stand at the moment, but I know I want to keep this as uncomplicated as possible. "What did you have in mind?"

"I was thinking about grabbing a bite. You hungry?"

"Starved," I admit.

"Awesome." With a jingle, he waves his car keys. "I'll go get the car."

"Yeah." I stand up and the sudden urge hits me. "I'm going to make a pit stop."

"Okay." Chris nods. "I'll be outside."

The trip to the bathroom is uneventful, and the hand soap smells like coffee somehow, which is kind of awesome. But it gives me a chance to think. Here I am, on a pseudo-date with a cute guy who loves my artwork and is totally into me. Not exactly what I had planned, but I can't be mad.

After my hands are dry, I push open the bathroom door and someone catches it halfway.

"Whoa!" a voice exclaims from the other side.

"Sorry!" I apologize, sticking my head through the opening.

Davy holds his hat to keep it from falling, his other hand wrapped around the edge of the door. "It's okay." He laughs, pulling the door the rest of the way. "No harm done."

"R-Right." I shuffle awkwardly into the hall, running a hand through my hair. Heat rises to my cheeks from just being this close to Davy.

He's just so damn cute in his uniform….

I'm thinking Chris is right, Big Guy. I mean, this is obviously an involuntary reaction here. It's not like I want to find this boy adorable... It just is the way it is. So, is that still wrong?

"How's the date going?"

"Excuse me?"

Davy blinks at me. "Sorry." He smiles. "I just assumed that's what was going on between the two of you."

"Oh! N-No," I stammer, taking a step back. I bump into a decorative table, quickly grabbing the vase of flowers before they tumble from their perch. "I-I mean, that's hilarious! You... You're so funny, Davy."

"Whatever you say, Mike." He raises an eyebrow but doesn't press the subject.

"See you at school!" I don't give him a chance to respond, just turn around and head for the door.

Davy might be a problem. I'll have to deal with him sooner or later. But then again, tomorrow might be the day Tabby decides she's going to ruin our lives, so maybe I won't have to. I have to remember I'm living on borrowed time. Better enjoy it while I can.

"Everything all right?" Chris asks as I climb into the passenger seat.

I adjust the air vent, so it blows directly on to my face. "Everything's peachy."

"Okie dokie then." He flips the radio on, pulling out of the parking lot.

I prop myself against the window, watching the lights of the city twinkle from afar.

THIRTY NINE

"OH, MY GOD." MY FORK CLANKS AGAINST THE EMPTY PLATE. "I'M SO FULL."

Chris watches with wide eyes across the table.

"What?" I graze my fingers across my lips. "Is there something on my face?"

"No." He shakes the look from his face. "I've just never seen pasta disappear so quickly."

"I told you I was starving," I say, cheeks burning.

He laughs, then sips on his cherry Coke.

My phone goes off, and I have a small panic attack. It's my mother. "Shit! Keep quiet," I tell Chris, swiping to answer the call. "Hey, Mom. What's up?"

"Where are you?" She comes out swinging.

"Uh... We got hungry, so we're on our way to a drive-thru."

"Got it." She seems convinced. "How's the plotting and graphing going, sweetie?"

"Graphing?"

"They still graph in geometry, right?"

Shit. I totally forgot that's what I told her this afternoon. "Right! The graphing is going great! I think we're about to move onto scatter plots."

Mom coos with excitement. "I love statistics! Give me a call if you two get stuck, I can help out!"

"Y-Yeah, I'll do that."

"Good," she says.

I hear Rosy in the background calling for her.

"Got to go, sweetie. Try not to have too much fun, you're still grounded."

"Yes, ma'am."

"Love you."

"Love-you-bye."

Chris snickers as I hang up the phone.

"What?" I ask.

"Graphing? What exactly did you tell her we were doing tonight?"

"Geometry homework," I say, and that really gets him going. "Why is that funny?"

"Because," he replies, grinning. "I'm in Calculus."

"Oops. Guess I should have asked."

"I think we'll be okay. I'm more interested in how you managed to convince your parents to let you out."

"Rosy totally saved my ass, actually," I admit. "I was bombing, hardcore, but she swooped in and took out both parents at once. She's scary sometimes."

"Sounds like it." Chris laughs. "It must be nice, having someone who has your back."

"Honestly, it's still a new feeling. It wasn't long ago, we just got on each other's nerves. You're so lucky you don't have any siblings to torture you."

"I've actually always wanted an older brother or sister," Chris says, pushing his ravioli in a figure eight on his plate. "Someone to look up to, ya know? Who would come to bat for me if I needed them?"

"Sounds nice." I laugh. "I want a sibling like that too."

"Yikes." Chris makes a face. "Is Tommy that bad?"

"It's not just the tormenting. That's normal for most siblings. I dunno, I guess it's different with Tommy and me. We never really bonded. I mean, the only thing we have in common is swimming. So, all our conversations revolve around that. I can only say so much about the butterfly stroke.

"We weren't into the same stuff. He liked football, and Star Trek, and girls. I like graphic novels, and Harry Potter, and...not girls."

"So, you don't miss him?"

"I don't know yet, I guess. He's only been gone for a few weeks, though. It may change."

Honestly, there's been so much going on the past month, I haven't had time to settle down and think about Tommy. I wonder how he's doing out there. Maybe I'll text him tomorrow, just to check in.

"Are we ready for dessert, guys?"

Our server just so happens to be ridiculously attractive. Imagine that.

"What do you think?" Chris looks to me.

"Oh, hell yeah. Can I get tiramisu?"

"Same," echoes Chris.

"You got it," hot-server-guy says, taking our entrée plates.

"What happened to 'I'm so full?'"

"There's always room for dessert, duh."

"Ooh, I see."

He grins, and I do too. We probably look like a couple on their first date. Which is exactly what's happening, and that fact is sinking in. How'd we get here again?

"Um…" I start, but hot-server-guy returns with an apologetic smile.

"Sorry guys, we're down to our last slice. Did you want to share it?"

"Totally," Chris says with a smirk.

"Awesome." He sets the plate down in the center of the table, placing a spoon on either side. "Let me know if you need anything else."

The plate's edge is covered in little hearts drawn with chocolate sauce. The back of my neck itches. I slash through a few with my spoon, feeling very self-conscious.

"Everything okay?" Chris looks at me. I want to say yes, but I'm also trying not to freak out, so I just nod.

Halfway through dessert, I ask a question.

"Where are we?"

"Um…Sandy Springs? I think it's called Little Italy, but I can check the menu."

I can't stop myself from rolling my eyes. "That's *not* what I meant. Where are *we*? What are we doing right now?"

"Ah." Chris sets his spoon down, arms folding across his chest. "Well, Mike. Where do you want us to be?"

"I'm not really sure I know."

"Look," he says, unfurling his arms, "if this is about last night, don't worry about it. I'd never hold you to anything you did while blackout drunk."

"But what if…" I pause, trying to swallow the frog in my throat. "What if I liked it?"

"Did you?"

My face burns as I nod.

"Then I guess that's different," he replies, fingers

306

fiddling with the edge of the tablecloth. "To be honest, Mike, I have no idea where we stand."

He looks up, dark eyes trained on mine like he's trying to read my thoughts. I wish I could just tell him what I'm thinking, but it's way too jumbled to come up with anything coherent. Thoughts aren't doing me any good at the moment, so I focus on what I'm feeling. A familiar gnawing fills my stomach, twisting its way through my intestines. My heart has adopted a strange fluttery rhythm for the last minute or so. It keeps fluctuating every time Chris makes eye contact with me.

His hand slides across the table, closer to me, and these squirmy, weird feelings intensify. He pauses, licks his lips, teeth scraping against the bottom one.

Holy shit, I really want to kiss him right now.

In unison, we wave over to hot-server-guy.

"Check?" I mouth, and I think he gets the idea.

Chris grins like an idiot, and I'm sure I'm blushing more than I care to admit.

It seems like an eternity for us to settle the check, and by the time I get my change, Chris and I are running out the front door.

We jump in his car, the engine purring to life. We take a minute to find a secluded spot, but that just helps the anticipation build. It's difficult to keep my hands to myself as he parks, shutting the lights off.

He looks at me, dark eyes catching the smallest specks of light. I swallow hard.

The distance between us disappears as we collide, and I dip my head slightly to align our lips. We exhale in sync, and Chris grabs hold of both shoulders, pulling me into him as our kiss deepens. My fingers wrap around the edges of his shirt, clawing for more.

We're panting like animals as we break apart, his hands still clinging to my shoulders. We take a second, each catching our breath.

"Was that okay?" he asks.

"Um, yes. Very okay. Super amazingly okay. The okayest. The most—"

"I get it." He smiles, pleased with himself. "Follow me."

With a bit of difficulty, he climbs over the center console and into the back seat. I've never moved so quickly in my life.

We face each other, my breath still heavy with excitement. The next collision is just as passionate— lips, tongue, teeth, and sweat. When I break away to trail my mouth down his neck, Chris lets out a groan that melts my insides into a puddle.

"Oh *God...*" Chris mutters as I scrape my teeth against his skin.

His reaction just eggs me on, and I nibble my way down to his collarbone.

"S-Stop. Stop for a second."

I pull away from his chest, but I can't stop myself at this point. I kiss him, and he kisses me back, my hands running up his thighs. He shivers against my touch. As I graze the front of his crotch, he lets out a whimper.

It's the hottest noise I've ever heard.

It's all the encouragement I need. His lips part and I feel his tongue hit mine as I drag my palm against the front of his jeans. He bucks in response, grinding himself against me.

Chris straddles my leg, and my head tilts upward

as we continue to make out. He moves back and forth, the bulge of his jeans rubbing on my thigh. It strikes me, while his tongue is down my throat, that Chris isn't really experienced in this capacity.

And yet, for someone new to the game, he sure can hold his own.

"Mike," he whispers, pausing his motion.

I brush against him, and he squirms.

"No, no, no… Shit!" He flops backward on the seat, and a dark stain spreads along the front of his jeans. His face, already flushed, turns three shades deeper.

"Whoa." I laugh. "I guess someone's having a good time."

"I-I…I'm sorry." He attempts to cover it with his shirt.

"Dude, relax." I assure him, "It happens all the time."

"Really?"

"Oh yeah." I laugh. "Especially with me. I guess I'm just that good."

"Pfft," Chris huffs.

He smiles again, and it makes me want to kiss him over and over, but I restrain myself.

We both take a ragged breath, just watching each other for God only knows how long.

"Are we going to talk about what just happened?"

"Only if you want to," he replies.

"I think we should," I say. Or we could just keep making out. I'm rock hard over here.

He nods but doesn't speak.

"I think I might like you, Chris."

"W-hat did you say?" His voice cracks.

"I said I like you."

"You said you *think* you *might* like me."

"See? You heard me just fine."

He latches onto my arm, no hint of joking in his eyes. "Please don't say that just for my sake." His fingers dig into me.

"I'm not," I tell him, peeling his hand off me. "Look, even through all this bullshit, I can't help what I'm feeling right now. Being with you, *kissing* you, it just feels right. And I don't know why, it just does."

He lets go, jaw tight, leaning back against the car door.

"Is something wrong?" I ask, reaching for him. He shies away from my touch.

"I-I just need a minute," Chris says, sitting up. He takes deep, calculated breaths.

"Did I say something?"

He doesn't answer, just stares blankly ahead. I'm freaking. Did I fuck this up? Or is he coming to his senses now that he's jizzed? "Chris, I'm sorry if I did something—"

He holds his hand up to silence me. I wait as he takes another ragged breath.

"I'm sorry, Michael. This isn't you, okay? I just… I have to process this."

I nod. "Take all the time you need."

"I never thought this would happen," Chris finally says. "Or at least, not like this. I mean, honestly, the first time I said I had a crush on you, I was enamored with an idea. This beautiful lie we could somehow be together, and maybe you could help chase these doubts I had away.

"But then you found the book, and I realized you weren't this fantasy I'd imagined, you were a real person, scared out of his mind. Who was I to try to fit you inside this delusion I wanted for myself? So, I had to let go of those plans and hope I'd be able to find new ones. I'd let go of that infatuation, in search of something real.

"And once again, here you are Mike, fucking up my plans. The more time I spend with you, the more infatuation becomes something else entirely."

The moisture in his eyes catch twinkles of light.

"And last night, you could have blown me over with a fucking feather after you kissed me. I knew I'd royally screwed things up between us from the start, but for a second, I knew what it felt like to have you want me, and it scared me shitless.

"I'm still scared Mike, for so many reasons, but most importantly because I don't want to screw this up again." He stops to let out a sigh. "I know I'm kinda dumping this on you but—"

Burying my fingers in his shirt, I pull him into me, our lips meeting for the thousandth time tonight. He folds into me as if his body were made to compliment mine.

We separate, and he looks to me for answers I can't give him.

"Stop," I tell him. "Just stop thinking for one night. We have enough going on right now. Let's just enjoy tonight and leave tomorrow in tomorrow."

He nods, wiping at the sides of his face. "God, look at me." He laughs. "I gotta get my shit together."

"You never have your shit together," I tease. "That's one of your more endearing qualities."

He smacks my chest but smiles.

"Do I need to get you home?"

"Fuck 'em, I'm already grounded."

He falls on top of me again, and that's all I can fit in my head.

FORTY

At just before eleven, we pull into the driveway, and Chris flips the lights off to avoid drawing any extra attention.

"Here we are," he announces, fingers laced in mine. They've been that way the entire ride home, and I'm in no hurry to change that.

"Yup." I nod. "We certainly are. Here."

A stretch of time passes, and I don't move.

"Mike?" Chris squeezes my hand.

I ignore him, soaking up every last moment of tonight. Tomorrow starts another day. Another day of constant anxiety that it might be the last normal day I have. Everything will change when word gets out. If it hasn't already. And I don't know if I'm ready for it.

"You okay?" Chris asks, and this time, I look at him. He must see what I'm thinking because he nods. "I know how you feel. But you can't just stay in my car all night."

"Why not?" I laugh.

"I'd imagine your parents might freak out if you don't make an appearance."

"But I'm with Chris Myers, I can do no wrong!"

"There's plenty of *wrong* we can get into," Chris says, "but tonight's not the night."

I know he's right, but it doesn't make this any easier.

"When I open this door." I rest a hand on the handle. "Then time starts again, and I have to worry about what's going to happen when we walk into school tomorrow. And how I'm going to go one more day pretending to be the person my parents think I am. And how I'm going to lie to my friends, and to my family, and to myself." I let out a staggered breath. "I don't think I can do this anymore, Chris."

"Okay," he replies, tugging on my arm so I turn back to him. "Then let's think this through. What would happen if we waltzed into Stronghold tomorrow as a couple?"

"We'd be kicked out of school," I tell him. "Plus, your father would probably disown you. My parents would probably blame themselves and then have me go to conversion therapy, or worse, one of those camps."

The words come out before I can stop them.

Chris stiffens in his seat.

"I'm so sorry," I start. "Chris, I didn't mean to bring—"

"It's fine," he tells me, though I'm certain it isn't. "Okay, so that all happens. Let's say we're expelled, tossed out of our homes, and left to fend for ourselves. Would it be worth not having to hide anymore?"

It's another one of his impossible questions.

"I want to say yes," I admit, "it would be worth it in the end, and I could finally look myself in the eye and not hate the coward staring back at me. But I can't,

Chris. I honestly don't know if I could do it—give up everything."

"So, you forfeit who you are."

"That's not fair."

"None of this is," he replies. "But that doesn't change anything."

"Are you telling me you're ready?" I question, anger flaring. "You'd give it all up tomorrow, throw your life away just to tell the world you're gay?"

"What life?"

I jump as Chris slams a fist on the steering wheel.

"This isn't living, Mike. This hiding and shame and self-torment, I'm sick of it! I'm so tired of hating myself for something I didn't have any say in and pretending to worship a god who doesn't care. For once in my stupid existence, I want to *like* myself!"

He crosses his arms, exhaling.

"And you think coming out will let you do that?"

"Not entirely," he answers, gaze focused forward through the windshield. "But it would be a start. A step in the right direction. And if I have to forfeit my comfort to do that, then I say yes. It's worth it."

Would he really do it? Would he risk everything he has ever known for this? I'm not naïve enough to believe this is about me. He's wanted this longer than he's wanted me.

"Open the door, Mike," Chris says, looking over. "Or don't. But know one thing. If it never opens, you'll always be stuck."

A pop of the handle, and my door swings wide, letting in the humid night air. A shiver makes its way up my spine as I climb out of the car. The resounding thud echoes against the house as I shut it.

"Mike?" The window retracts as Chris leans over the center console.

I hesitate, his voice keeping me anchored.

"I'm sorry if I sounded harsh." His eyes sparkle in the darkness, hoarding every glimmer of light they can find. "This isn't easy for either of us. But I'm glad I have someone to share it with. The weight would be too much to carry alone."

A nod is the only response I can deem appropriate.

"See you in the morning." He flashes a devilish grin. "Sleep tight."

Leaving me blushing and speechless, Chris puts the car in reverse, my pulse racing as he narrowly misses the mailbox on his way out.

Crickets and cicadas are the only noise now, a choir of voices in the dark. They sing their song as I trudge toward the door, muddling through the events of the night.

FORTY ONE

ANXIETY HAS BECOME MY CLOSEST FRIEND, SECOND ONLY TO GUILT. MOM has a rare day off from work today, so she's prepared a spread of breakfast I politely decline. Food at this point would just make the nausea worse.

Stronghold stands intact when Dad drops Rosy and me off, and students mill around the lawn like any other day. They're careless, my fellow teens. None of them privy to the warfare raging in my head.

Jackie isn't much help this morning either, she just exhales pungent clouds of nicotine and ash, texting away as my sanity slips slowly out of my ears.

It's almost time for first period, and I haven't seen Chris anywhere.

"Why do you look like you've committed a crime?" she asks, flicking the end of her vice.

"What are you talking about?" I run my hands along the strap of my bag.

"You." She tosses her butt to the ground, stomping on it. "You just seem a little off. Oh God, did I scramble that measly brain of yours when I laid you out the other day?" She snaps her fingers. "That has to be it. I've unlocked the psychopath inside you, and now, it's only a matter of time before you kill everyone you love!"

She strikes a pose, one hand over her heart, the other pressed to her forehead.

"Are you sure you don't want to audition for theater this semester?"

"As if." She snorts, breaking character. "You're as bad as my mom."

The bell rings in the distance, fueling the gnawing anxiety in my stomach.

Jackie brushes a patch of ash from her skirt. "All right, American Psycho, let's get to class before people get suspicious, or you butcher me and toss me in the dumpster."

I grunt a response to her ridiculousness, and we head for the side door.

Jackie waves as our paths branch off, and a cold layer of sweat breaks out across my palms.

Thoughts of Chris and our night together are the only thing keeping me going. Without those, I would have curled up in a dark corner somewhere, paralyzed with fear.

Dr. Redford seems especially bored as I make it to my seat, Chris's empty desk doing nothing to help my nerves. Without him here, I feel like I'm drowning. Then again, it's like that when he *is* here, but I get a burst of air every now and again.

In true Chris Myers fashion, he skirts in just as Redford goes to lock the door. Flushed and breathing hard, he rounds the desk and plops down. He leans over to speak to me, but Redford interrupts him.

"I have the results of yesterday's test," Redford announces. "And, for those of you who assumed prayer was enough to get you through it, I'm afraid to say faith without work gets you nowhere."

An audible groan swells through the room as he condemns the class to their subpar grades. Chris writes something on a slip of paper.

He hands it over and I hide it in my lap, waiting for the moment Redford is busy destroying someone's GPA.

I quietly unfold it, scanning the tiny handwriting.

My fingers shake as I fold it back, stowing it in my pocket. Three words bore into my mind and seep into my lungs until they fill them, forcing out all the air.

I'm so sorry.

The apology says everything.

We're fucked.

"Mr. Hernandez," Redford says, standing over me, glasses pulled down and magnifying his eyes into dinner plates. "Excellent work, as always." His voice comes from a distance, muffled and reverberating.

Shallow breaths come quick, and the edges of my vision go dark.

"Michael?" Redford sounds miles away.

Big Guy, can I just go ahead and get beamed up? I'm pretty sure my heart's about to explode and I'd really prefer not to be here for that moment. Is there an express lane option or something?

"—the nurse," he says, crouching down to my level. "Michael, Laura's going to help you to the nurse, all right?"

Laura Platt helps me to my feet, my knees so wobbly I have to lean on her. Thankfully, she's the captain of the volleyball team, so she's sturdy. But I can't will my feet into motion and everything's getting so dark.

The sensation of falling overtakes me, and I blackout before I hit the ground.

FORTY TWO

My forehead is freezing. Heaven must be super cold. That, or maybe, they got things mixed up and Hell is just a frozen wasteland where Satan makes you shovel snow for the rest of eternity. Which, in retrospect, I guess isn't so bad.

But I'm not dead, and a towel full of ice rests on my forehead. I pull it away, opening my eyes to blinding fluorescents and a pounding headache.

The nurse's office smells of cleaning chemicals. Ms. Harden, the school nurse comes to my side, placing a wrinkled, fluffy hand on my cheek. "You had me worried for a minute," she coos in her soothing, grandmother tone.

My mouth is drier than Mom's cornbread. "What happened?"

"From the looks of it, you had an episode of acute hysteria brought on by stress." She holds my wrist with two fingers, monitoring her wristwatch. "In other words, you freaked out, kiddo."

"Oh." Well, that certainly explains the sudden loss

of my whereabouts. Here, I was thinking Heaven was really just a nurse's office and God, a gray-haired woman with a tattoo of a bird on her neck.

"Your mother should be here in a few minutes." Ms. Harden releases my arm. "So, I'll leave you to rest until she gets here." She gives me one last comforting smile before crossing the room. A voice comes through the door as soon as she opens it.

"—he all right?"

"Calm down, Christian." Ms. Harden's hushed voice carries. "He's fine, but you really need to get back to the office."

"Can I see him?" Chris pleads.

"I'll tell you once more, it's against school policy. Now, I really have to ask you to please go back—"

The door shuts, reducing the voices to murmurs as I stare at the paneled ceiling. My pocket vibrates, and I fish out my phone.

> Are you okay? 10:01am

I've been out for almost an hour?

> I'm not dead, if that's what you mean. 10:02am

Chris starts typing an answer, but those three dots just keep disappearing and reappearing, doing nothing to settle my nerves.

Mom will show up soon, and no doubt make a scene gushing over me. She'll want me to go to the emergency room and have them run fifteen different tests. At least I'll be away from here when the shit hits the fan. I can only guess at what Chris's message meant, but I have a pretty good idea. Tabby's talking again.

An excruciating half hour passes before my mother arrives in a tizzy. She bursts through the door like a woman possessed and jumps into twenty questions.

"What happened? Did you experience any facial paralysis? Did you smell burning toast? Did you soil yourself? Was there any—"

"Mom! Jesus!" I push her off me.

"Mrs. Hernandez," the nurse tries to interject but gets swept aside.

"I told you not to skip breakfast this morning." Her hands are on the sides of my face, manipulating me to look her in the eye. "Maybe this is a blood sugar issue? Did you check his glucose levels?"

"Ma'am, if he's not a diabetic, there's no reason to—"

"Well, obviously, there's some *reason*. Come on, Michael. I'm taking you in to see Dr. Bradford."

"Mom, please stop," I plead. "I'm just fine."

"You are not fine, Michael. People who are fine don't just pass out in the middle of first period. Now, grab your things, and I'll pull the car around."

"Mrs. Hernandez?"

A new voice catches my attention, coming from the tall man standing in the entranceway. He has salt and pepper hair and a charcoal suit that's been tailored to perfection.

"Principal Peters." Mom's voice shoots up an octave. This may be the first time she's seen the Principal outside of PTO meetings.

Peters, the Double P, leans over to catch my eye.

"How are you feeling, Michael?"

"Much better, sir," I answer, straightening my tie out of habit.

"Mrs. Hernandez, may I speak with you in private for just a moment?"

Mom stiffens like she's speaking to the president instead of the man who's about to ruin her life. I can't help her now. I can't prepare her for what's about to happen any more than I can prepare myself.

"Of course." She steps forward. "Mike, I'll be right back, sweetie."

I nod, the words caught in my throat.

The two of them leave the room, and Nurse Harden motions for me to join her by the door. "The Principal asked me to escort you back to the front office," she tells me. "Just to make sure you'll be all right."

Or to make sure I don't run away. That's a lot more likely.

We exit her office, walking along the quiet halls. It's almost lunch time now.

Nurse Harden delivers me to the office where Double P's secretary asks me to take a seat. The window looking into his office is closed, blinds covering the view. They're in there, most likely discussing what to do about my…*situation.*

I wonder if Chris will get dragged in here too, made to suffer the same fate. Will they call his dad? I can only imagine the shit show that's about to begin.

My leg bounces uncontrollably as the minutes tick by, every second another personal hell pulling me closer to the realization of exposure.

I nearly jump out of my skin when the receptionist's phone rings. She picks up the receiver. "Yes?"

All is silent while she listens, nodding.

"Absolutely. You're very welcome."

Why's she looking at me?

"Michael," she says, rising from her seat. "Ms. Owens will come and collect you in just a moment. Would you mind waiting here?"

Ms. Owens? What's the councilor have to do with this?

"Um, sure." My head still hurts, so I dig a finger into my temple, attempting to calm it. "It's not like I'm going anywhere."

The door to the office opens, and two dark-haired people, in the midst of a heated discussion, step inside.

"—it obviously isn't helping. I mean his grades have improved, but that doesn't mean—"

"Honestly, Roger, just give him the benefit of the doubt. I'm sure this is nothing serious."

Chris's parents step up to the receptionist, and I become one with my chair.

"Can I help you?"

"Yes," the man says, a phony smile spreading across his lips. "I'm Pastor Myers, and this is my lovely wife, Vanessa. Principal Peters says it is an urgent matter."

"One moment." She dials something on the phone, then speaks quietly into it. With a nod, she hangs up. "Please, go on in."

Well, there goes the slim chance this has all been some misunderstanding.

It's inevitable, I guess. My life is about to get turned upside down, and nothing I can do will change that fact. But there is one thing I still control. And that's how I come out to Jackie.

I won't let them take that away from me.

I unlock my phone, selecting Jackie number. My hands shake as I type.

> Jackie, I'm gay. 10:47am

The sound of the sent text echoes in my ears, and I blink to keep from tearing up. Jackie's bound to have a million questions, so I shut my phone off before they can come. I'll deal with it later. That is, *if* I survive the next few hours.

"Michael?"

A woman stands outside the door to the left of Double-P's office, a kind smile curling the side of her lips. It takes me a minute to recognize her. "Yes, Ms. Owens?" I pretend I don't know what this is all about. Only one reason comes to mind why the school councilor would talk to me and plausible deniability is my only option.

"Do you mind if we chat for just a few minutes?" she asks, tucking a strand of long blonde hair behind her ear.

"Sure." I rise from my chair, legs unsteady.

"Chris," she says into her office, "if you would please wait outside the principal's office a little longer."

Stone-faced, Chris exits Ms. Owen's office, the two of us crossing paths. He tries to give me a smile, but a grimace is the best he can do. He takes the seat I just left, and I enter the councilor's office, settling on the cushioned couch. I half expect her to pull out one of those, 'where did they touch you?' dolls.

"I'm glad to see you're feeling better," says Ms. Owens, shutting the door behind her. "I heard you had an episode earlier this morning."

I nod, not wanting to say a word.

"You must be wondering why you're here right now." She sits across from me, unfolding a pair of brightly colored reading glasses and sliding them on. "But something tells me you might already know."

I'm here because I'm gay and some bitch with a serious disregard for personal space turned me in.

But I remain silent.

"This must be a very confusing time for you, Michael. I want to help you work through these thoughts you're having and help you see there are alternative options to the lifestyle you must feel is unavoidable."

"And what lifestyle is that?" I ask, my voice as small as a mouse.

"I think you know."

"Do I?" I scoff. "I think you should just mind your own goddam business."

Ms. Owens doesn't recoil from my words but simply crosses her legs. "You're angry, Michael. Is that because, deep down, you know what you're doing is wrong?"

"What am I doing that's so wrong, Ms. Owens?"

"Michael, there's no need to lash out. We're both aware of the behavior you've been—"

"You can't even say it!" I explode. "Jesus, it's not that hard! You called me in here because I'm a *fag*, and I need help. Is that it?"

"Those are your words, Michael." The councilor writes something down. "Do you believe them to be true?"

I lean back into the cushion, crossing my arms. "Whatever."

"Let's talk about yesterday, Michael."

"What about it?"

"What were you doing yesterday morning before first period?"

Yesterday? What *was* I doing yesterday? All I can think about is last night and the weight of Chris on top of me.

"I was outside the school," I tell her, straining to remember. Where is she going with this?

"And what were you doing?" she asks again.

"Nothing, just talking with my friend Jackie."

"Anything else happen?"

I think back through the conversation. Other than Jackie smoking, nothing happened that they'd consider— Oh!

Chris kissed me.

I'm suddenly very itchy, heat rising to my cheeks as I squirm on the sofa.

"Michael?"

But who would have seen that? Who could have known about the kiss? Jackie and I have been hanging out back there since freshman year, and no one's ever busted her for smoking.

"I want to show you something, Michael." Ms. Owens picks up a tablet from the table between us, swiping a password to illuminate the screen. She finds what she's looking for and then turns it to me.

My heart sinks when I see a grainy photo of Chris kissing me beside the dumpsters.

"This was sent to Principal Peters early this morning from an anonymous source."

Anonymous my ass. I know exactly who sent that picture in... Except, I don't. Tabby wasn't at school yesterday, so it couldn't have been her.

Who else would have taken it?

"You're aware it's against school policy for this inappropriate behavior to take place between same sex parties, Michael?"

I nod.

"But more importantly," Ms. Owens says as she sets the tablet down, "I wanted to talk about what brought you to act out this way in the first place."

I ignore her ignorance, wracking my brain, trying to come up with a name. Someone with the motive to do this. Did I make an enemy without even knowing it?

"Same sex attraction isn't innately wrong, Michael." The councilor continues, "In fact many young men your age struggle with it. But it's in understanding God's plan for us that we can overcome these temptations and focus on devoting ourselves completely to Him. I know that's what you truly want, deep down."

An opportunity arises. "And what proof do you have?"

"Excuse me?" Ms. Owens lowers her glasses. "I'm not sure I understand your question."

"What proof do you have that homosexuality is wrong?"

"Michael, I'm sure you're well aware the Bible makes it very clear God's intention is for a man to be with a woman."

"Oh, I'm clear about a lot of things they mention in the Bible," I inform her. "But my question is, why is this one thing different?"

"Once again, I'm not sure what you mean."

"Do you eat shellfish, Ms. Owens?"

"What?"

"Shellfish," I repeat. "Crab, mollusk, lobster?"

"If you're referring to—"

"I'm referring to the very same book that condemns homosexuality in the Bible. They say a whole lot of things are 'abominations' including, eating shellfish, wearing jewelry, cutting your hair, getting a tattoo, and harvesting honey."

"You're taking these things out of context, Michael."

"Am I?" I laugh, shaking my head. "I've lived for sixteen years listening to these stories, Ms. Owens. *Sixteen years.* I've endured countless hours of sleepless nights, wallowing in guilt over the things that come naturally to me. Do you know what that's like? To wake up every single day and think to yourself, I wonder if I'll ever be happy?

"*I* know what it's like. It's been like that my entire life. But, now, I found someone who makes me feel like I'm not a mistake. Who makes me feel things I've never thought I would be able to. Who silences the questions in my head with just a touch of his hand. That feeling led me to act out.

"So, to answer your previous question, yes. Yes, I am aware the school policy dictates that any inappropriate behavior between members of the same sex is forbidden. And, no, I will not apologize or repent for what we did because I don't think it was inappropriate behavior at all."

Ms. Owens removes her glasses, mouth moving as if she's chewing her words.

God, I feel free. Like every word I said erased a part of the heaviness I've been carrying. I have to keep this momentum going.

"And if you don't agree," I say, rising from my seat, "I respect your opinion, but we have nothing further to discuss." Not looking back, I turn the door handle and march out of her office.

"Michael!" I hear her call.

Chris jumps to his feet when he sees me. The muffled sound of shouting is coming from the Principal's office.

"What's going on in there?" I ask.

"No idea." He grabs hold of my hand, our fingers interlacing. "Your dad just showed up and it started."

"Uh-oh." I can't decipher any words, just frustration in their tone. I don't want to listen anymore, so I give Chris a smile. "Want to get out of here?"

He mirrors my grin. "Thought you'd never ask."

FORTY THREE

SUNLIGHT POURS THROUGH THE WINDOWS AS WE PULL OFF THE HIGHWAY. You'd think the warmth would have done something about the teeth chattering thing I'm currently going through, but it doesn't. At least the traffic is lighter this time of day. Chris's hand hasn't left mine since we fled, and it's the only thing keeping me tethered to the earth. Without it, I'll float away, lost in the new feeling of weightlessness.

We opt for silence, neither of us feeling up to music. In fact, I don't think we've said a single word to each other the entire ride. That being the case, I know exactly where we're headed. He doesn't have to say it.

After a few miles, we park along the side of the street. It's lunchtime, which means a decent flow of foot traffic. Chris releases his hold on me, and for a second, I think I'm going to drift off. But then we're out of the car and his fingers wrap around mine again as we walk. It's nice. Like, *really* nice.

It feels like a different world than a few weeks ago when I first walked this street. Things between Chris and me certainly are different.

Before long, we've reached the familiar rust-colored door. Chris ushers me inside, and I smile as I walk under the folded paper cranes.

The teal-haired goddess greets us as we move to the counter. They've just opened, so there are only two other people in the café.

"Hey, guys." The woman smiles. "What can I get for you?"

"Just a pot of dandelion, please."

"And a latte," I add.

Chris swipes a card on the terminal, and I try to distract myself with the colorful displays.

Our parents are probably freaking the fuck out by this point, but I'm trying not to think about that. Honestly, I'm trying not to think about anything. Other than Chris.

We move in silence to our table by the window. The paintings above the old piano are just as colorful as I remember. I take a moment to re-attune myself to them.

"Mike?"

It's the first thing he's said to me in over an hour.

"Yeah?" I keep staring at the canvases.

"I'm really sorry."

The ship rests on top of the blue wave.

"It's not your fault."

"I know, but where does this leave us?"

The flowers are in bright contrast to the dark background.

"I don't know."

"Can you at least look at me?"

I move from one work of art to another. His eyes

catch the sunlight and the colors meld into honey and amber. Freckles stand out against his pale skin and the slight bend in his nose throws off the symmetry. His imperfections make him perfect in my eyes, and it hurts to think about not having him by my side.

"Here you go, guys." The teal-haired woman sets the pot between us, followed by my coffee and two cups on saucers. She gives me a smile then flutters away.

Chris stares at the teapot, watching the steam rise from the spout.

"What did you say when they asked you about yesterday?"

The silence stretches between us.

"I didn't really say much of anything," Chris says, grabbing the pot and filling his cup. "I just shut down. She talked for a good twenty minutes before finally letting me go. It was the usual bullshit." Chris pauses, taking a sip. "What about you?"

"Well...I kinda went off on her." I tell him about our conversation and the look on her face when I walked out of the office.

"That's the best thing I've ever heard." Chris grins. "What I would have given to see her face."

A buzzing noise cuts off the conversation, and Chris reaches into his pocket. "About time..." he mutters, silencing the phone call.

"Is it your dad?"

He nods, setting the phone down next to him. "I just want a little more time." He takes my hand from across the table. "Is that selfish of me?"

"Not at all," I tell him. "It's all I want too."

Just one more afternoon, Big Guy. I just want to be happy

for one more afternoon.

"I told Jackie," I say, thinking about turning my phone back on to check her reaction. But that would mean letting everyone else in, and that's not something I want to deal with right now.

"Really?" Chris breathes. "That's incredible, Mike!"

"Not really." I laugh. "I mean the entire school is about to find out, so it can't be."

"But that's different. You can't help that. You told your best friend, and you did it on your terms. I'm so proud of you!"

My cheeks burn. "Shut up."

Chris raises his cup into the air. "A toast," he says, "to your first coming out."

"You nerd," I say, clinking my mug against his.

"Call me whatever you want," Chris says. "That doesn't mean I'm gonna like you any less. Hey, who are you going to tell next?"

"Can we not talk about this anymore?" I swirl the foam around in my cup. "I just want to enjoy one more date with my boyfriend before I'm homeless."

Chris gives a weak smile, but soon it turns into his signature smirk.

I would give anything for him to keep it.

FORTY FOUR

"Are you sure you want to do this?"

The warm sun and Atlanta sidewalks seem worlds away as I sit in my driveway. Chris and I spent the entire day together, and I don't want it to end. Once again, Chris's car has become this awesome time capsule that keeps me safe from the outside world. I don't want to leave.

"I have to face the music sooner or later." I try to sound brave, but I'm scared shitless.

"Call me when it's over? I can come get you if I have to."

"You have your own problems to sort out." My hand rests on the handle. "Don't worry about mine."

He catches my elbow. "Your problems *are* my problems, Mike. And it's going to stay that way, as long as you want."

And, as if gravity is pulling me, I'm drawn into him, lips finding his with ease. For a moment, I forget everything that isn't Chris. He fills my mind, pressing everything else out. This may be our last moment together, so I soak it in.

Too soon, he pulls away, leaving me breathless and disoriented.

"I-I... Goodnight, Chris."

"Goodnight, Mike."

I open the door, climbing out of his car.

There are no more words, so I watch him pull out of the driveway, lingering until his headlights have long vanished around the curve.

Hey Big Guy, I just wanted to say thank you. For today, I mean. It could have been so much worse, and I got to have just a little more time with Chris. I couldn't have expected more. It was really cool of You. Thank You for that.

I've stalled long enough. There's nothing left to do but walk inside and face my parents. I just hope they don't kick me out right away. Maybe I'll have a week to formulate a plan before they toss me on the street.

Climbing the stairs to the door, I raise my keys and turn the lock with a click. Taking one last deep breath, I step inside.

The foyer is quiet. No television noises coming from the living room, no music from Dad's office, no annoying video playing on Rosy's phone. Nothing.

The door closes behind me, and I toss my messenger bag at the foot of the stairs.

"Michael?" Dad's voice comes from the kitchen.

Making my way down the hall, I push open the swinging door to the kitchen. "Yeah?"

"Oh, thank God!" My mother grabs me by the collar and drags me into the room. She hugs me so tight I can't take a breath. "Where have you been? Why aren't you answering our calls?"

"Mom...can't...breathe."

"Sorry." She releases me, mopping up tears with a paper towel she clutches. She looks like she's been crying for a while.

And that certainly doesn't make me feel like shit.

Dad grabs my shoulder, giving it a squeeze. "We were worried sick about you, Michael. What made you think it was okay to drop off the radar like that?"

I can't help laughing. "You're joking, right?"

My parents share a look. "Why would we be joking?"

"Well, after that cluster fuck this morning, I would think it would be understandable."

"*Michael,*" my mother scolds, "language!"

"Get the fuck over it, Mom. I think my language is the furthest thing from the topic at hand here."

My mother falls into her seat at the table, a stunned look on her face. I should feel guilty, but I don't. Not today.

"You both know where I was." It's an accusation. How dare they try to act naïve? I don't have the patience for it. Today happened, and we all need to deal with it. "So, let's just stop beating around the bush and get this over with." I waltz around the table, pull out a chair, and have a seat.

I don't know when I grew these balls, but I'm not backing down now. If they're going to kick me out, then I won't give them the satisfaction of seeing me cry.

"Well, alrighty then." Dad runs a hand through his hair before joining us at the table. "I guess we're just going to jump right in. Michael, first of all, I want to say we're glad you're home safe."

I nod. "I'm sorry I didn't answer your calls, but as you can imagine, I had a lot going on."

"Fair enough," Dad replies, resting his elbows on the table. "So, it's safe to assume you were with Chris?"

"Yes."

"Where did you go?"

"Does it matter?"

"Michael, please don't take that tone."

"Dad! Jesus, we went into the city to get away from the bullshit! It's not like we joined a gang. Why does it matter?"

"It matters," Dad repeats, "because you've apparently been lying to us for God only knows how long! It's hard to know when to believe you. And you cut school!"

"That's not fair."

"None of this is fair." He sighs, lowering his voice. "Fine. You don't have to tell us. As long as you're safe now, that's all that matters."

"I'm perfectly fine."

"Good. Now, is there anything else we need to talk about?"

"You tell me, Dad."

"Michael, have I done something to deserve this treatment?" He leans back in his chair. "Because, if I have, I apologize for it. I just want you to be honest with us."

Maybe I am being a jerk. But I have to keep my defenses up. They'll be the only thing keeping me from falling apart when the shit hits the fan.

"No, you haven't," I admit. "Not directly, at least."

"Then please, drop the attitude and talk to us. We're here for you. We want to know what's going on with you."

My frustration has reached a boiling point, and it

overflows.

"What's there to talk about, Dad?" I bang my fist on the table, and my mother flinches. "We could talk about the fact I've been lying to everyone I love for the past six years? Or maybe the part where I've been dragged to a horrible place where, twice a week, they tell me I'm an abomination that deserves to be tossed into the fiery pits of Hell? Or maybe we could chit-chat about the fact I'm getting kicked out of school for kissing the only person who's ever made me feel like I was *normal*."

They're both silent, and I let out a shuddered breath.

Blinking away tears, I continue. "Look, I'm sorry you two had to find out that way. If I'd had my way, I would have never said anything. We all could have lived our lives, ignoring the elephant in the room. But I can't change what's happened, no matter how much I wish I could."

A small whimper forces me to look up, my mother raising a hand to cover her mouth.

All the time spent imagining this moment didn't prepare me for the horrible sinking feeling her reaction causes. I can't even look at her.

"You never would have told us?" she asks, pulling her hand away.

I shake my head, the lump in my throat too thick to speak around.

"Michael," she says, grabbing my hand across the table, "we *love* you. There is nothing in this world you can't tell us. If we haven't made that clear, that's our fault. Not yours."

"That's right, *hojito*." Dad leans forward again. "We understand why you kept this from us but know you don't have to anymore. We love you. Unconditionally. And that's not going to change, no matter what."

More tears stream down my face. I don't blot them. I just let them fall.

"Talk to us, Michael."

"Please, Mike."

"I'm gay," I whisper.

My dad actually chuckles. "I think we got that part, Mike."

"Bert," Mom cuts him off.

"I…" I swallow hard, so I can speak. "I think I might love him. Chris, I mean. It's too soon to tell, and it's kind of a first for me."

"And how does he feel?" Dad asks.

"He feels the same." I wring my hands together under the table. "At least, that's what he tells me. I don't know! I haven't felt this before."

"Does he treat you well?"

"Yes." I nod. "Of course."

"Are you two being safe?"

"Dad!" I cringe, squirming in my seat.

"Bert!" Mom gapes at him.

"It's an important question, Nancy! Just because they can't get pregnant doesn't mean—"

"I'm not listening!"

I laugh, and the tears keep falling, but that sinking feeling gets lighter with each breath I take.

My parents continue a hushed discussion as I marvel at them. No one yells. No one screams or threatens to evict me. This isn't exactly what I prepared for.

You're just full of surprises, aren't You, Big Guy?

"What did Double— I mean, Principal Peters say?" I ask.

My father's expression darkens. "Well, after Roger stopped screaming long enough for him to speak, he gave us an ultimatum. Either you would drop all your extracurricular activities and attend mandatory counseling three times a week, or they would ask you to leave Stronghold."

"I kinda figured that would happen."

"But don't worry, son." Dad has fire in his eyes. "When I'm through with that man, he's going to wish he—"

"Bert," Mom says, cutting him off, "we can't do anything about that right now. It's their rules. How can we expect them to make an exception for one person?"

"You heard those ridiculous conditions." Dad's on a roll. "They won't even let him interact with his friends. He'll be a pariah!"

"I'm not saying he should stay there," Mom says, "but we have to think of something quick or—Michael, I'm sorry. I know this has been a lot for you in one day. Honestly, it's been a lot for everyone."

"Surprisingly, I'm okay," I tell her.

"How's Chris doing?"

"I'm not really sure," I admit. "He seemed all right when he dropped me off, but he's doing the same thing I am by now. I can imagine it's not going to go well. I wouldn't be surprised if his dad kicks him out."

Mom and Dad share another look.

"I mean, can you picture Pastor Myers being this cool about it?"

"Well, what about Tommy's room, Nance?"

"Yeah." Mom nods. "I was just thinking that. We could throw in another bed for when he comes down during breaks, but I don't think he'll mind."

"Let me call Tammy over at the office, I think she was trying to get rid of a bed frame last week."

"Wait." I raise a hand. "What are you talking about?"

They look at me with confusion.

"Chris, dummy." Dad laughs. "Tell him, if he needs a place to stay, he's always welcome here. In separate bedrooms, of course."

"Are you serious?"

"I mean, we'd have to draw some guidelines," says Mom, "but of course we are. We aren't going to leave him out on the street."

Okay. Now, I *am* feeling like a jerk. Maybe I had this all wrong. Maybe I've been making a bigger deal out of it then I needed to.

"Just to be clear here." I gesture to catch their attention. "You guys are totally okay with me being gay?"

They share a concerned look that has me worried for a moment.

"I'm not going to lie and say I'm thrilled," Mom says as she folds her hands, "or that I completely understand it because I don't. This means your life will be rife with difficulties. But it's your life, sweetheart. How can we not be okay with it?"

"We're assuming you've given this idea a considerable amount of thought?" Dad adds.

"I have."

"Then what's there to discuss?" He shrugs. "You know yourself better than anyone else. Who are we to tell you who you're supposed to love?"

You could blow me over with a whisper.

"I wish Rosemary were home," Mom mutters. "I

want to make sure she's not blindsided."

"Oh, she already knows," I confess. "She caught me and Chris in the car last week."

Mom slaps her hands over her ears. "That's enough! I don't wanna hear about it."

Dad and I laugh as she hums under her breath.

Once the giggles have subsided, he looks at me with that soul-piercing-dad-stare. "You okay?"

"Better than okay." I smile. "Honestly, I was planning my escape route before coming in here."

"Well, put it away," he says with a touch of hurt in his eyes. "You're safe here, and you always will be."

"Thanks, Dad."

"Think we should stop her?" He points at Mom who's still humming a tuneless rendition of *Amazing Grace.*

"Why ruin her fun?"

FORTY FIVE

I LEAVE MOM AND DAD TO TALK ABOUT SCHOOL PLANS, RETREATING TO THE sanctity of my room. I pull out my phone, realizing I never turned it back on. Once it's powered up, I ignore the slew of text messages, and dial Jackie's number by heart.

She picks up on the second ring. "You'd better be lying dead in a ditch."

"Hey..."

"Anything else you wanna say?"

"Would you mind coming to get me? I think you, Tanner, and I need to have a little talk."

I count ten seconds of silence on her end before she sighs. "I'll be there in ten."

"I'M SORRY," I START, LOOKING AT JACKIE AND TANNER AS THEY SIT ON HIS bed. "You don't know how many times I wanted to tell you guys. It's just...complicated."

345

I gauge their reactions. Tanner's vacant eyes and blank expression point toward shock, while Jackie's curled lips and furrowed brow make her the human embodiment of an angry hornet's nest.

"Did you think we wouldn't be okay with it?" she asks.

"I'm sorry I didn't tell you guys before." I have to keep talking or I'll puke. "But I really wasn't even planning on telling *anyone*. Chris found my sketchbook when it went missing, and everything just spiraled out of control. Then Rosemary saw us kissing in the driveway. I thought my parents would find out. So, I covered my tracks even more. Then we—"

"Dude!" Tanner interrupts. "Just hold on a second." He pulls his frames off, pinching the bridge his nose.

"Sorry," I say, wringing my hands together. "I know this is kinda out of the blue, but I— Ow!"

Jackie recoils her fist. "That was for being an idiot." She rears back and slugs my shoulder a second time. "And that was for keeping us in the fucking dark." A third punch, and I can feel a bruise forming.

"Ow! What was that one for?"

"That one was because I'm fucking pissed at you."

"Fair enough…" I rub out the sting.

Jackie sinks beside Tanner, anger fading. She brushes a strand of dark hair from her face, bottom lip quivering. "God, I feel like such an idiot."

Holy shit. I haven't seen her crack like this since her dog died when we were ten.

"What are you talking about?" I ask.

She swipes the back of her hand across her cheeks. "I should have known, Michael. I mean, not that you're like super obvious or anything, it's just… *Jesus*, Mike.

And then that night with Chris, you let me punch you. Why didn't you tell me?"

Because it was easier to get punched in the face than come out to you. I don't say that, though. I just shrug.

"Not good enough," Jackie chides. "What, did you think I wouldn't support you?"

"That's not it." My fists are clenched, fingers turning white. "I was scared, I guess. Of anyone knowing, not just you two."

"So, what about school?" Tanner replaces his glasses. "What did Double-P say?"

"We kind of bailed before we met with him," I admit, "but I'll most likely be transferring to another school."

Jackie and Tanner share a look.

"When?" Jackie asks.

"ASAP."

"That's such bullshit," Jackie snaps. "They overlook all the fucking and drug abuse and go for the gays. It's such a double standard! You know they can't actually kick you out, right?"

"No, but they can encourage you to leave of your volition," Tanner answers her. "And I'm pretty sure that's going to be worse. Remember Kat Kelly a couple years back? She was a senior, two months away from graduation when they found out she was a carpet muncher. Two days later, she left and was never heard from again."

"What do you mean, 'never heard from again?'" Jackie sneers. "She plays lacrosse for Georgia Tech now. Didn't you see her face plastered all over their billboards when they won the championship?"

"Oh." Tanner chuckles. "My bad. I get caught up in the drama of it all."

Jackie cracks a smile, and I can't help smiling back. Even through the anxiety of telling them, it feels nice that they know. They know and they're not condemning me. Both my families know now. It's a pretty fucking awesome feeling.

"Oh, shit." Jackie ends her laughter abruptly. "How's Chris?"

"I don't know," I tell her. "I haven't heard from him yet."

"Good God, I can just imagine what Myers is doing to him." Jackie frowns. "I mean the man is practically gay Hitler."

"That reference is highly offensive," Tanner interjects, "and ignorant because he persecuted the gays too, so you could have just left it at regular Hitler."

Tanner is not only the best source for gossip but history as well. You don't want to get him started on Hamilton. He'll go for days.

"Let me know as soon as you hear anything," Jackie says. "I'm worried about him."

"Me too," I agree.

"Well," Tanner says as he heaves himself off the bed, "I guess it's time for the movie then?"

"That sounds perfect." I move out of his way, desperate for something to distract me.

"And I got just the movie." Tanner smiles, grabbing the remote.

"We're not watching *The Matrix*." Jackie groans.

"Actually," Tanner says, throwing a curt smile over his shoulder, "I was thinking *Brokeback Mountain*."

"Not funny," Jackie hisses, smacking his shoulder.

"Ow!" Tanner jumps away from her. "I was just

kidding!"

Laughter swells in my chest, bubbling over until I can't contain it anymore. I'm laughing so hard, there are more tears. I'm laughing because my friends are still my friends. I'm laughing because I don't want to think about tomorrow. I'm laughing because, for the first time in a very long time, I don't feel like I'm living a lie.

Jackie's got Tanner pinned under her, pummeling him with playful punches.

My cheeks are hurting as I slide onto the floor beside the bed, hugging my knees to my chest.

Jackie finally crawls off Tanner, slumping next to me, huffing and puffing. "So," she says, trying to catch her breath, "what movie do *you* want to watch?"

"It doesn't matter," I mutter, leaning my head against her shoulder. And for once, she doesn't shy away from my touch. She simply rests her own head against mine. If feels nice to be so close to her even though I can smell the stale cigarette smoke in her hair.

"Let's just check out Netflix," Tanner suggests, scrolling through our options. "Oh! How about Bill Nye?"

"Sounds perfect," I tell him.

"Awesome," he says, selecting the show. "It's buffering. I'm gonna go grab some popcorn and soda."

"Diet please," Jackie chimes.

"Gross." Tanner leaves the room, and Jackie and I watch as the gray bar fills along the bottom of the TV.

"I really am sorry I didn't tell you sooner."

"I know you are," she says, patting my knee. "And I'm sorry this was the way you told us. Wish it had been under better circumstances."

"Me too."

Jackie wraps her hand around mine, interlacing our fingers. The awkward feeling between us dissipates.

It feels so nice.

FORTY SIX

JACKIE AND I ARGUE ALL THE WAY HOME OVER BOYS. APPARENTLY, WE HAVE very different taste, but that's perfectly fine by me. My parents are still talking to each other in hushed tones when I open the door, but they smile and wish me goodnight. Once I'm nestled in bed, I flip through my sketchbook, fingers tracing the lines as I go. Reaching the sketch of Chris, I carefully remove it from the binding. Balancing, I tack it up on the wall next to my other portraits. No need to hide it anymore. I'd pin up some of the others, but this is the only one that won't give my mother a heart attack.

I check my phone again, hoping I have a text from Chris. Still nothing, but, I told him not to worry about me.

A creative itch spreads down my arm, making my fingers twitch. I'm way too wired to try to sleep, so it's as good a time as any to draw.

Grabbing a pencil from my bag, I flip to a fresh page in the book and set to work on an outline. I know exactly what this sketch will become, and I work feverishly to bring it to life.

Hours pass, and I set aside the pencil to give my hand a rest. He looks up at me from the page, those dark eyes smudged just right to mimic light reflecting in them. The line of freckles is the hardest part to get right. I have to keep erasing them until I've matched their perfect imperfection.

The doorbell rings from downstairs, pulling me away from my work. I glance at the clock and see it's past midnight. Who would be at the door? I grab my phone, but the screen is blank. It must have died while I was working.

I hear my dad descend the stairs, then pause before he answers the door.

"Jackie? What are you doing here?"

"Is Mike here?" A frantic tone clings to her voice.

I leave my room, jogging down the stairs to meet her. "What's going on, Jackie?"

"You didn't pick up your phone." She huffs. "But you need to come with me."

"What's going on?" Dad asks.

"Don't freak out," she says in a tone that makes me really want to freak out. "But Chris has been in an accident."

"What? Where?"

"He and his dad were in the car," Jackie continues. "That's all I know. His mom just called my mom. Apparently, they're on their way to the hospital now."

"Holy shit." I'm pacing the floor. "Is he okay? Please, tell me he's okay."

"I don't know, Mike. Listen, Mom's already there with Vanessa. She's in shock and couldn't drive. You and I can head over there."

"Okay, okay, that sounds good. Jesus, just when I thought this day was over." I stop at the foot of the stairs. "Dad, are you okay with me going?"

"I don't think you'll have to worry about missing school in the morning." He chuckles.

I don't laugh.

So, he just adds, "Of course."

I bolt up the stairs to my bedroom, grabbing the pair of sneakers from under my bed.

The sketch of Chris stares at me from the bed. Suddenly, it feels like a memorial. Turning it over, I shove my sneakers under my arm and sprint out of the room.

FORTY SEVEN

THE EMERGENCY ROOM IS IN CHAOS WHEN WE ARRIVE. GURNEYS AND NURSES move in tandem, transporting patients and filling out notes on clipboards. With the beeping and alerts, it's almost as if they're dancing to the rhythm.

Jackie's mom, Melissa, waves us over to the row of chairs where Vanessa sits. She looks horrible, puffy faced and pale. Never mind frail. She looks fractured.

"Hey Mike." Melissa gives me a hug. She smells like lavender, which normally I would find calming. Not today. "Crazy day, huh? How you holding up?"

"I'm fine." I brush her off. "Where's Chris?"

"They're both stable," she tells me. "It looks like Chris took the brunt of it. He's pretty banged up, but not nearly as bad as it could have been."

I allow myself to exhale. Chris is alive. He's okay.

You're really putting me through the ringer today, aren't You, Big Guy?

"What happened?" Jackie asks.

"That's what we're waiting to find out," Melissa replies in a hushed tone. She looks back at Vanessa.

"It's not a good situation."

"Michael?" Vanessa looks up from her daze, spotting me. "Would you come over here?"

Shit. What am I supposed to say to her? I'm the reason her son is getting kicked out of school. And the reason her family is falling apart. And, now, I'm supposed to go talk to her? That's a lot to ask of a sixteen-year-old.

"Hey, Mrs. Myers," I say, shuffling awkwardly over to her. "Are you okay?"

"I'm fine," she half whispers, "just a little overwhelmed at the moment."

"Can't imagine why," I joke.

She cracks a slight smile. It's just like Chris's, which only makes my heart hurt.

"I'm sorry, Michael." Pain overwhelms her expression. "I know this must be so hard on you, with everything that's happened."

Oh. That's not what I was expecting.

"Don't worry about me," I tell her. "I'm just glad Chris is all right."

"Me too." Her voice cracks, and I really want to walk away. But I stay because I know it would mean a lot to Chris.

"What happened?" I ask.

"Roger wanted to speak with Chris when he got home," she whispers, eyes distant. "He seemed so calm, like maybe he'd accepted the fact Chris..." She stops herself, taking a deep breath before continuing. "Chris didn't want to hear it, but Roger convinced him to take a ride, like they used to do when he was little. Then, I got a call from the ambulance..."

She trails off, sniffling.

I've got no clue what else to say, so I just stay put. Jackie and her mom are whispering to each other. I wonder how much Jackie's filled her in on.

But I don't have the chance to ask them before a nurse walks over to us.

"Mrs. Myers?"

"Me." Vanessa raises her hand.

"Can you come with me for just a moment, ma'am?"

"Of course." She moves toward the woman in scrubs. "Is everything okay?"

"It's better if we speak in private, ma'am."

The two women walk behind a swinging door, leaving the rest of us behind.

"I'm going to go grab a cup of coffee," Melissa announces. "You two need anything?"

"No, thank you," I reply.

Jackie rubs her stomach. "I'm good. Dinner's not really sitting well already."

"That's what you get for eating nothing but mac 'n' cheese," Melissa teases.

"Not the time, Mom."

Melissa is still laughing as she leaves.

"You okay?" I ask her.

"Yeah, just haven't been feeling too hot all day. I think you gave me an ulcer from all this drama."

"You?" I laugh. "Think about me? I wouldn't be surprised if this whole ordeal causes my hair to turn gray. I'll be the only silver-haired senior in the whole school!" I have to laugh or else I'm going to cry.

"Oh yeah." Jackie doesn't join in my merriment. "Have you decided what you're going to do about school?"

"Not yet." I fold my arms. "So, I guess I'm stuck

there until they kick me out. Maybe Chris and I should just make out in the hallways. That'll speed up the process, I'm sure."

"Maybe they'll let you stay." She wraps an arm around my elbow. "It would be nice to have my best friend close by."

I give her arm a squeeze. "I wouldn't count on it, Jackie."

There are so many uncertainties now.

Jackie makes a pitiful noise beside me, clutching her stomach. "Blegh... I'll be right back." She hurries off toward the bathroom.

And I'm alone, watching the coming and going of healthcare workers and patients. I pull out my phone, but it's still dead and only offers a comforting weight in my palm. Chris is okay. I repeat that over and over again, but it doesn't help my nerves.

Shouting from down the hall shakes me from the doldrums. I can't understand what they're saying, but whoever it is, they are making quite a ruckus.

A couple security officers move toward the commotion, and I fight the urge to go investigate the source. It's probably some druggy strung out on enough meth to fund my college education.

"—if you ever come near him again! I mean it, Roger!"

The name snaps me into focus. I rise from the chair, peering around the corner of the hall.

"Vanessa, calm down. You're making a scene." Pastor Myers has a long cut along his forehead and some blood on his shirt. "This is all just a—"

"Keep him away from my son," Vanessa tells the security officer. "He's insane! Roger, if I see you in this hallway, I'm calling the police!"

"Ma'am," one officer says, "I need you to calm down. They're going to want you to answer some questions."

I quickly turn my face as the other security guard hauls Pastor Myers in the opposite direction. When I look back, Vanessa is being ushered away.

What the hell is going on here?

A nurse hurries past, and I catch her elbow.

"Sorry, but do you know where Christian Myers is? I'm his brother. I just got here."

"Sure, sweetie." The nurse huffs, grabbing a chart off the counter beside her. "Three doors down on the left." Then she heads down the hallway.

I try to look inconspicuous, but no one cares as I open his door and sneak in.

The room is dark with only a small light above his bed illuminating the space. Chris sits propped up, arm in a sling across his chest. Lines of red streak across his face, no doubt from windshield glass. The bruise around his eye looks worse too.

He doesn't notice me at first, just continues to stare out the window on the opposite side of the room. I make it to the edge of the bed before he looks at me. The faintest of smiles plays across his lips, and my heart breaks a little.

"Hey." His voice is hoarse.

"Hey."

I move to the side of the bed, pulling a chair closer to him.

"I didn't think you'd be here," he mutters. They must have given him something for the pain because he's glassy-eyed.

"Why wouldn't I be?"

"Figured you'd be wandering the streets of Atlanta by now, looking for the perfect underpass for us to live under." He chuckles, and it's a pitiful sound.

"In a shocking turn of events, my parents are actually way cooler than I thought they were. My dad even asked if we were having safe sex, at which point my mother almost fainted."

Chris laughs harder, but it's cut short with a wince. "Well, at least one of us has decent human beings as parents."

"I saw them out in the hallway," I tell him. "What exactly is going on?"

Chris closes his eyes. "My father is a piece of shit. That's what is going on."

"Well, we already kinda knew that. Has something added to his shitty factor?"

"How about the fact he tried to kill me?"

I wait for him to laugh and say he's joking.

He doesn't.

"What the *fuck*?"

Chris lets out a sigh, eyes opening just enough so he can see me through his long lashes. "When I got home," he says, "he was waiting for me. Said he wanted to take a ride, like old times. I should have known he was lying, but he sounded so sincere. I thought maybe he wanted to try to work things out. Maybe he wasn't actually scum of the fucking earth. So, I said yes.

"We got in his car. I went to buckle in, but the seatbelt stuck, and I couldn't get it down. I asked him about it, but he just brushed it off by saying he's been meaning to get that fixed. Being the idiot I am, I didn't think twice about it. We started down the road, and he wasn't saying anything, just gripping the steering wheel really tight.

"He'd been drinking, I could smell it on him when we got in the car. But I still went with him. I think there's something wrong with me, Mike. I mean, who's dumb enough to keep looking for acceptance from a man who's completely turned his back on you?"

"You're not dumb." I reach out, taking his uninjured hand. "You may be a bit naïve but never dumb."

He wraps his fingers around mine, and I want to cry.

"We got out on the freeway, and he still wasn't really talking. So, I decided to get the ball rolling. I asked him why he wanted to talk to me, and he just balked and said he wanted one last car ride with his son. I should have known then. Thirty seconds later, we were careening off the road. I still would have thought it was an accident if he hadn't jumped out of the driver's door before the car hit that tree.

"I went into the windshield, but thankfully not through it. Then the stupid airbag went off too late and broke my fucking arm. I thought I was dead until Dad pried open the door and got me out. I was losing consciousness, but I swear I heard him crying and saying he was sorry over and over…"

Shock silences anything I might say.

"Then I woke up here, with him beside my bed, and I wished to myself I *had* died. Then I wouldn't have to accept the fact my own father tried to kill me."

Suddenly, Vanessa's behavior in the hallway makes total sense.

"Is it wrong that I still don't hate him?" Chris's eyes leave me and drift to the ceiling. "I keep trying to, but

I just can't."

"You're a far better person than he is," I tell him. "And he deserves to rot for what he tried to do."

"Mom thinks so too." His eyes shut again, and he sounds so defeated. "She snapped when I told her what happened. I thought she was going to kill him, she was so upset."

"She almost did." I tell him about her explosion in the hallway. "The security guard had to step in."

Another ghost of a smile tugs at Chris's lips. "Go, Mom."

He falls silent, and after a few minutes, his hand goes limp in mine as a soft snore escapes his nose. I carefully detach myself from him, standing just as his mother enters the room. Once again, her face is splotchy, but a fire that wasn't there before burns behind her eyes.

"How is he?" she asks in a hushed tone.

"Surprisingly okay, all things considered."

"He told you what happened?"

I nod.

"I just finished speaking with someone from the sheriff's department. They're going to be doing a full investigation of the crash."

"How could he do it?" I can't help asking. "What kind of man can even think about hurting his own son?"

Vanessa recoils like I've slapped her. "What kind of mother allows it to happen?" she says so quietly I think she's speaking to herself.

"You couldn't have known." I place a hand on her shoulder with a reassuring squeeze. "Don't blame yourself."

"That's what you do as a parent." She laughs, wiping a tear from her cheek. "You blame yourself for everything and wish you could have done it differently."

"He's alive." I pull her into an embrace. "That's what matters. And he needs you."

Vanessa clings to me for a moment, then pushes me away gently. "He's lucky to have you, Michael."

But I don't feel the same. In some way, I know this is my fault. I'm the reason Chris is lying in this bed right now.

She presses a hand to my cheek with a smile. "You should get home, it's late. I'll let you know how he's doing in the morning."

"Thank you." I toss one more look back to Chris sleeping peacefully, then head out.

FORTY EIGHT

THE NEXT DAY, I GO BACK TO STRONGHOLD. MY PARENTS TRY TO TALK ME OUT of it, but I want to show them I'm not so easy to get rid of. Double-P said I had a week to decide if I would agree to their terms, so here I am.

I make it to lunch with nothing serious happening, and the gang is all here, minus Chris. Vanessa texted me this morning, letting me know that as soon as the hospital clears Chris and gets his arm in a cast, they'd be going to stay with her parents for a few days while the whole situation gets sorted out.

That means I don't know when I'm going to see Chris again, and it's killing me.

Jackie elbows me in the side and I look up. Tabby's standing at the table, holding her tray and glaring at me.

"Can I help you with something?" I ask, trying to control my temper.

"What are you doing here?"

"What does it look like I'm doing here." I motion to my tray of food.

"You're not allowed here anymore," she says, clenching her teeth. "They were supposed to expel you."

"Well, they tried." I stand so I'm on her level. "But you get one last week of me, so enjoy it while you can."

"Good riddance." She sniffs, turning her nose up at me.

"Hey, Tabby." I stop her from walking away. "Who did you get to take that photo, by the way?"

She furrows her brow. "What photo?"

"The one that got sent into the principal," I say. "The one of me and Chris kissing."

The table goes quiet, and everyone's eyes are on me.

"I don't know what you're talking about, fairy-boy."

"Then how'd you know what's going on with Double-P?" Jackie asks.

"Because my parents are on the board," Tabby answers. "They said you and that other fag are out of here."

"If it wasn't you." I look to Tanner, but he only shrugs. "Then who was it?"

From the end of the table, Katie gets up from her seat. She clutches her backpack to her chest, then bolts out the side doors.

No way.

"Hey, Tanner." Tabby taps him on the shoulder. "I'm sitting over here if you'd like to join me. I just heard the funniest story about Dr. Bernhard."

"No thanks, Tabby." Tanner brushes her off. "You're about the last person I want to sit with."

She huffs, giving me one final stink eye before skulking off.

"I'm going to go find Katie," I tell Jackie and Tanner.

They nod, turning to catch the questions exploding from the other side of the table.

"All right, settle down, you Neanderthals!"

The hallway is quiet, but a soft crying comes from the door to the stairwell. I push it open, finding Katie sitting on the bottom stair. She raises her head, and the crying gets louder.

"I'm so sorry, Mike," she says, wiping her face. "I-I didn't mean for it to happen."

"So, it was you." I take a seat beside her, the cogs in my head turning a million times a minute as I try to process. "Can I ask why?"

She tucks a strand of hair behind her ear. "I-It's not what you think."

"Well, I honestly don't know what to think. So, why don't you explain it."

"I wasn't trying to get you two in trouble." She lets out a breath, calming the tears. "I saw Chris and Jackie go behind the dumpster wall, and I couldn't help myself. I felt so jealous…"

So, Jackie was right. Katie has a crush on Chris.

"You like him."

Katie looks at me, fresh tears in her eyes as she shakes her head. "That's not it. It's just…"

If it's not Chris, then what could she possibly be jealous about?

Then something clicks. "Oh, Katie. It's Jackie, isn't it?"

She whimpers, nodding.

Holy shit. That's why she kept staring at the party. Jackie didn't realize it was her, not Chris. On the bright side, I guess she's right. Everyone falls in love with her.

"Then why did you take the photo?"

"I-I don't know." She's a little hysterical. "I-I guess it was j-just a way for me to remind myself I'm not alone."

"Were you the one who sent it into the principal?"

"N-No!" She wipes more tears away. "It was my parents. They've been going through my photos, and they recognized your uniforms. They sent it in as an anonymous tip."

What a mess. I wouldn't believe it if it didn't make so much sense.

"I'm so sorry, Mike," Katie apologizes. "This is all my fault. You have to know I never meant to cause you two trouble. I looked up to you, and now, I've ruined everything. God, I'm just a worthless piece of trash."

"Hey." I take her tear-moistened hand. "Don't say that. You don't have anything to apologize for."

"B-But it's my fault." She's heave-crying now. "I-It's my fault."

I wrap an arm around her, pulling her into my chest. She folds into me, body shaking as she cries. And I let her, just holding on as she gets it all out.

I know exactly how she feels.

After her tears have dried, she disentangles herself from me, eyes puffy and bloodshot.

FORTY NINE

IT'S BEEN THREE DAYS SINCE CHRIS'S ACCIDENT, AND MY ALARM GOES OFF AT the normal time on Sunday morning.

Mom's hairdryer is blasting, which signals the normal routine. But it isn't a normal Sunday morning because Thomas got in late last night to visit and we haven't had the chance to talk yet.

So much has happened since he left. Honestly, I'm not sure where to start.

Dad hasn't knocked on my door yet, which means he doesn't expect me to want to go to church. Seeing as the Pastor just tried to murder my boyfriend, I'm not exactly going to argue. I sort of can't believe they're going, but I guess they have commitments.

Maybe I'll just turn over and sleep the rest of the morning away. I don't remember the last time I slept in on a Sunday. It was probably in the womb.

I try to go back to sleep, but I'm wired. Instead, I dig for my sketchbook and flip it open to a new page. Another drawing of Chris I finished last night sits on my bedside table, under a couple other doodles. I'll figure out where I want to put it at some point, but for now, it's nice enough just knowing it's not hidden away.

After a few minutes of mindless strokes of my pencil, a knock raps against the door.

"Come in," I call.

Thomas sticks his curly-haired head through the cracked door. "Hey, man." He smiles. "Can I come in?"

"Yeah, of course."

And in he walks. It's been over a month since I've really seen Thomas, but he looks the same. Except for the ridiculous soul patch he's grown.

"I think you missed a spot shaving," I tease him, touching my chin.

He only laughs, stepping over to my drafting table. He shuffles the papers around, grabbing a sketch of the capitol building in Atlanta I did a few weeks ago. "This is great." He lifts the drawing.

"Thanks." I set the sketchbook aside as he takes a seat on the edge of the bed.

I'm weird and jittery around him right now. I don't like it.

"Mom and Dad say we have some catching up to do," he says, folding his arms across his chest. "How about me and you play hooky and go grab some breakfast?"

My stomach rumbles in response. "That sounds great."

"Awesome." Thomas shoves off the bed, heading back for the door. "Get ready, I'll be waiting downstairs."

He shuts the door behind him, and I untangle myself

from my sheets. I grab a towel and throw it over my shoulder, heading to the shower.

"Mornin'." I yawn at Rosy.

"Hey." She's in front of the mirror, blinking into her mascara. "How you doing?"

"I got to talk to Chris last night," I tell her, turning the shower on. "He says they should come back next week at some point."

"That's great." She caps the tube, blinking a few more times. "I can tell you I'm not looking forward to sitting through service today. Arnold's taking over preaching duties while Myers deals with the DUI."

That's what everyone thinks happened. A simple accident. I guess it's better that way, but I can't believe Vanessa isn't pressing further charges against him.

"I don't envy you." I laugh, sticking a hand in the stream of water to feel if it's warm yet. "Me and Thomas are going to grab breakfast and catch up."

"You gonna tell him?" She lines her lips with a pencil.

"Yeah."

"Need me to come with you?"

"I'll be okay," I reply. "Thanks, though."

"No prob." She rolls a layer of red lipstick on, then zips up her bag and opens the door. "Love you, nerd."

I smile as she shuts the door.

WE GRAB THE LAST AVAILABLE TABLE, SUCCESSFULLY BEATING THE HANGOVER crowds. Our server takes our order then drops off my coffee and Thomas's coke.

"So, what's been going on, bro?"

I try to keep my hand steady as I add sugar into my mug. Why is this so hard? He's the last in my family to find out. I thought it would be easier at this point, but I guess not. This is just going to be part of my life from now on. I'll have to come out countless times. But it's far better than the alternative.

"There's way too much," I say. "So, let's start with you first. How's school?"

"It's so awesome." Thomas leans his elbows on the table. "I mean, my schedule is hell, but I love it. I've been training to do the butterfly, so I can compete in two different styles, and it's kicking my fucking ass."

Thomas taught me how to cuss, and it's one thing I love about him.

"How's your time looking this year?"

"Not great," I admit. Of course, we're talking about swimming. "There's been a lot going on."

"That sucks, man. Just keep practicing, and you'll beat my record one day."

"We'll see." I laugh.

"That's all I got man," he says. "So, it's your turn to spill it. Bring me up to speed."

"Well…" I hesitate. "School's going pretty good. A's and B's. Jackie and Tanner are good. Jackie's got a secret boyfriend, and Tanner's been coding this game for more than a month. I think he's almost finished."

"He's either going to be filthy rich," Thomas says with a chuckle, "or get arrested for hacking a government server."

"The possibilities are endless…" I take a sip of my coffee to calm my nerves. It doesn't work. I should have ordered decaf.

"That can't be all," Thomas presses. "Mom and Dad made it seem like it was something major. You didn't knock someone up, did you?"

"Uh, no. That's definitely not it."

"Good." Thomas laughs. "I'm too young to be an uncle."

"I am seeing someone though," I add. Maybe I can just slide into this.

"Oh yeah?" Thomas raises an eyebrow. "Well, spill it, little brother."

"We've been seeing each other for a short while," I tell him. "It's been a little dramatic so far, but it's nice. I haven't really felt this way before."

"I'm sorry to say it, little buddy, but it sounds like love."

"I think it might be." My cheeks are burning. "Time will tell, I guess."

"So, who's the lucky lady?"

"Well," I say, letting out a breath. "Actually, his name is Chris. Chris Myers."

"Oh." Thomas's mouth hangs open for half a second. "Wait, *Chris Myers?* As in the Pastor's son?"

"Y-Yeah." I nod. "That's him."

"Well, fuck me." He leans back in the booth, scratching his head. "I mean… *Holy shit.* Sorry, I don't mean that in a bad way."

"It's okay. It's weird, right?"

Thomas remains quiet for a good minute, eyes darting back and forth as he rubs that ridiculous soul patch.

I'm sweating like a whore in church. Then, he blurts, "Well, okay then!" He smiles at me. "I guess that was kind of a big deal. You doing all right?"

"Yeah." I nod again. "I think I am. It's been easier than I thought it would be. Definitely easier than it's been for Chris."

"What's his dad think about all this?"

"Umm…"

"Here we go, guys."

Our server returns and fills the table with plates.

"Let me know if I can get anything else for you."

"Look, we have plenty of time." Thomas smiles, grabbing his fork. "Let's eat."

He doesn't ask about Chris's dad again, but our conversation floats back to its usual topics of sports and family and college stories.

By the time we're finished eating, everything feels like it's back to normal.

Does that mean gay is normal?

FIFTY

"WHAT ABOUT THIS ONE?"

Mom hands me yet another pamphlet, a happy student smiling up at me from the glossy pages. It looks a little suspicious, like I might have my brain sucked out and replaced by an alien or something.

"They have one of the best-rated art programs in the state."

We've been rifling through school options all morning, and my head is about to explode.

"Can I just close my eyes and pick?" I whine, burying my face in my arms. My options have overtaken the kitchen table, and Mom keeps scrolling through more of them on her laptop.

"I know it's a lot." She pats my arm. "But we have to get you enrolled before you fall behind, Michael. Oooh! This one looks fun! And, look. They have a rainbow flag on the cover!"

I groan, fleeing the table. She means well, but Mom is kinda driving me crazy with the support. First, it was a rainbow coffee mug she makes a point to drink from every morning, then it was the matching t-shirts and rainbow scrubs for work, and most recently an "I love my gay son" bumper sticker I flat out told her to peel off the car.

My phone buzzes in my pocket, and I jump at the excuse to step out on to the back porch.

"Hey," I answer.

"Hey," Chris replies. I've been waiting impatiently for our phone call all morning. This has become our routine while he's away at his grandparents. They're supposed to come back sometime this week.

"How's North Carolina?"

"Just as boring as yesterday when you asked."

"Oh, right." I lean against the railing of the porch. "I guess I ask that a lot."

"It's okay." He laughs. "We're coming back today."

"Really?" It comes out far more enthusiastic than I was shooting for.

"Yeah, we have to…settle some things. But I should be free this afternoon. Can I come pick you up?"

"Totally." Just the thought of seeing him again has me grinning like an idiot.

"Perfect. Well, hey, I have to go help Mom load up the car. I'll call you when we get home?"

"Yeah." I let out a sigh.

"I miss you, Mike."

His words rob the air from my lungs.

"I-I miss you too."

"See you soon."

"Bye."

I hang up the phone, cheeks flushed. Back in the house, Mom waves her hands over her head like she's just won the lottery.

"I found it!" She calls me over. "This is the one!"

"That's great," I tell her. "Mom, Chris is coming back home today. Is it all right if we go catch a movie or something?"

She pauses, her jubilance wavering. "Will you two be alone?"

"Uh, n-no!" I backtrack. "I think we're going to get Jackie to go with us."

"Uh-huh." Mom nods slowly. "Well, I guess that will be all right. Just be on your best behavior, young man."

"Yes, ma'am."

"Was that Chris on the phone?"

"How'd you know?"

"Your rosy cheeks."

She pinches one, and I push her hand away, laughing.

"It's nice to see you like this, Michael."

"Like what?"

"Happy." She grins. "You seem happy."

And maybe, she's right.

CHRIS PULLS UP TO THE HOUSE, AND I SAY GOODBYE TO MOM AS I RUSH DOWN the stairs. She stands in the front door, watching as I climb into the passenger seat. Chris gives a wave with his good arm and she returns it, smiling as he puts the car in reverse.

Once we're around the corner, he stops the car and leans over the console to kiss me. We get lost for a moment, picking up right where we left off. Fingers twist hair, breaths come in gasps, and warmth radiates from my body.

"Ow." Chris rubs his shoulder as he pulls away. "Sorry, I'm still a little sore."

"That's okay," I tell him, panting. His face still has the red lines from the partially healed cuts. There's a cast on his left arm, held in place by a sling across his chest. He's battered and broken, but I've never found him more attractive. I think that's just the teenage hormones talking.

"I packed us a cooler," he says, shifting the car into drive again. "How about a little picnic at Piedmont?"

"That sounds perfect," I muse, fastening my belt.

He nods, pulling out of the neighborhood.

We talk as he drives. I fill him in on the school search and tell him all about the one Mom and I decided on earlier today. I secretly hope he'll get the hints I'm dropping and try to get enrolled there too. He tells me about his grandparents' house and the time he's spent with them. They sound like really kind people.

We're all caught up by the time we reach the park, sun sinking toward the horizon. I drive the cooler, allowing Chris to lead the way. We pick a hill, and I set to work, laying down the blanket and unpacking.

"Wow." Chris leans against the trunk of an oak tree. "I could get used to this."

"Well, don't," I tease, tossing him my phone. "You're in charge of the music. And I don't expect you to be in a cast the rest of our lives."

"Huh."

"What?" I ask, grabbing the baggie full of sandwiches.

"You said the rest of our lives," he says. "That

sounds…really nice."

Music lingers in the background as I finish unpacking, Chris trying to help where he can. Mostly, he just distracts me, and I have to pull him in for a kiss. Golden light washes everything in these beautiful tones, and I never want it to stop.

I'm smiling. More than I can ever remember. One thought brings me this joy. The two of us, together, in a space that's just ours. I can picture it, the scene flashing like those last few moments of a dream—a kitchen with granite counters, an open window above the sink, and curtains blowing with the breeze, Chris standing over the stove with an apron and laugh lines and salt and pepper hair.

I shiver with the wind. It's all I want.

Chris pours us two cups of soda as we settle on the blanket, watching the sun set behind the Atlanta skyline. It's absolutely perfect.

"These are delicious," I say, sinking my teeth into a sandwich.

"Why, thank you," he says, adjusting his sling. "My mother made them. Isn't that romantic?"

We laugh, and I close my eyes, enjoying the last few moments of sun.

When I open them, Chris is staring at me, smile absent from his face.

"What is it?"

"Nothing. It's just…" He looks down, scratching the end of his nose. "I'm really going to miss this. You and me."

"Huh?" He must be talking about school. "I mean, I know it will be hard at first, but we can see each other in the afternoons and at the weekend—"

"Stop, Mike." Chris holds his hand up to silence me. "I have to tell you something."

My heart pounds like a drum. "Okay. What's up?"

"My mom and I are leaving." He plays with the edge of the blanket, pulling out thread one piece at a time. "We're going to stay with my grandparents."

"For how long?" I ask. He's already been gone for a week, what's another few? I can wait.

"You don't understand." He sighs. "We're moving. Like, to live with them. Mom's going to work in Gramp's store."

"W-Wait, but, why?"

"Dad lost his salary," Chris continues. "And mom wants to put some distance between them. Thinks a fresh start might be just what I need, too."

"And us?"

He doesn't answer, just pulls another thread, holding it in his open palm until the wind carries it away.

"Chris?"

"I love you."

The words echo off grass, bouncing along the blades like skipping rocks.

Did he just say that?

Chris grabs my hand in his. "Or, at least, I think I do. And, if that's what this is, then I finally understand what all the fuss is about."

"Chris, I-I…"

"I know I'm not being fair," he says in a fevered pitch, "but I wanted you to know before I go."

"Just, just slow down for a second okay?" I shake his hand off, staggering to my feet. The earth gives way as I pace back and forth. I might work a path into the grass. "When are you leaving?"

"Tomorrow." He sulks, head drooping. "I start my new school on Monday."

And just like that, my daydreams vanish with the sinking sun. I shiver as it falls beneath the horizon. Lights come on along the walking paths, but they do nothing to lift my spirits.

"What the fuck am I supposed to do, Chris?" I ask when I can't stand staying silent any longer. "What are *we* supposed to do?"

"What can we do, Mike?" he pleads. "I'm open to suggestions!"

"You could stay here," I offer. "Mom and Dad were ready to let you stay with us when we thought you were getting kicked out."

"I can't leave Mom," he replies, hugging his knees with his good arm.

"Then we can just keep doing what we've been doing all week." I drop to the ground beside him. "We'll talk and text and see each other when we can. I'll get my license next month, and I can drive up to see you."

"It's a six-hour drive, Mike."

"You're worth it."

"I don't want to make you do that."

"You aren't! I'm choosing to!"

"Look." Chris presses his hand to my chest. "I don't want to talk about it anymore. I don't want to waste the rest of the time I have with you arguing."

Tears, hot and plenty, fall down my face. "This fucking sucks."

"I know it does." He pulls me closer, our foreheads coming together. "But it's not forever. Maybe one day, when we're older, we can be together again."

My chest deflates with an exhale. "You sound like a Hallmark movie."

He snickers, and we stay like this for a short while—locked in a moment of intimacy.

"What am I going to do without you?" I ask him.

He pulls away just enough so his eyes find mine. "You'll be fine." He smiles. "You'll draw and watch bad movies with Tanner and Jackie. You'll crush your junior year at your new school and win some art contests, I'm sure. And, most importantly, you're going to be yourself. No lies, and no hiding. Got that?"

I nod, wiping my face with a sniffle.

"Good." Chris leans forward and plants the softest kiss against my cheek. "Now, let's leave tomorrow in tomorrow, and enjoy the rest of the time we have."

And that's exactly what we do.

EPILOGUE

"HOW ARE YOU WEARING THAT?" I ASK JACKIE AS SHE TOSSES THE END OF HER wool scarf over her shoulder. "It's like ninety degrees outside."

"It's October, Mike," she says as if that answers all my questions. "Fall. As in the official start of scarf season. Come on, are you really sure you're gay?"

I roll my eyes, opening the door to Clark's Cup.

Tanner waves over his laptop from the table in the corner, and Jackie and I join the line for coffee.

"Still liking the new school?" she asks, slithering an arm through mine.

"Yeah, actually I am. You wouldn't believe the supplies they have at this place. I think they even still have lead paint. How cool is that?"

"Only a true artist goes blind for their passion, Mike."

We laugh, stepping up to the counter.

"Well, look here," Davy greets us from behind the counter. "I was wondering when I'd see you again, Mike."

"What about me?" Jackie feigns offense.

"I see you every day," he claps back, "and it's more than enough."

I laugh. "It's good to see you, Davy."

"What'll it be today? Latte and a hot chocolate?"

"Extra whip," Jackie chimes.

"Done and done." Davy punches the register, and I hand him my card.

"I'll grab the drinks," I tell Jackie, moving to the end of the counter. She goes to join Tanner, shutting his laptop as she sits down. The two start a slap fight, making me giggle from across the room.

"Here you go, Mike." Davy smiles as he slides the mugs over the counter. He brushes a blond curl out of his eye, then pulls his apron over his head. "And it's officially quitting time for me."

I feel a twinge in my chest, and I pause.

"Something wrong?" Davy asks me, looking down at the drinks. "Look, that's as much whipped cream as I can fit on her drink, if she wants more than—"

"Do you want to sit with us?" I interrupt.

He blinks, a smile creeping across his face. "Actually, I'd love to. Give me a second to hang up my stuff?"

"Cool." I motion toward the table. "We'll be over here."

"Yeah." Davy smiles wider, and I turn toward my friends.

"Are you blushing?" Jackie asks as I set the mugs down.

"What? No, of course not."

"You totally are!" She slaps my shoulder. "Isn't he, Tan?"

"He's a regular Bashful Betty," Tanner adds, opening

his laptop again.

"Scoot over," I tell Jackie, pulling another chair over to the table.

"What for?" She swipes a finger through her pile of cream.

"I invited Davy to come hang out," I tell her, avoiding eye contact like the plague.

"Aha!" She points a finger at me. "I *knew* it! You totally were blushing."

"Whatever." I sit down, rubbing my cheeks as if that will help disperse the blood.

"I totally approve," Tanner says from behind the screen. "If I swung that way, I'd be all over that."

"Gross," I moan.

"Have you heard from Chris lately?" Jackie sips the side of her hot chocolate.

"Yeah." I pull out my phone. "He sent me a picture earlier today from his hike. He's loving the mountains." I turn the screen around so she can see.

"Who's with him?"

"Oh, that's Ryan. They met at his new school."

"Oh reeeally?" Jackie wiggles her eyebrows.

"Knock it off," I chide. "I'm happy he has someone to connect with up there. After all that time alone, he needs friends."

"And a boyfriend."

"*And* a boyfriend," I add.

"Whose boyfriend?" Davy sinks into the open chair, his hair untamed without his cap.

"Nobody," says Jackie, tapping Tanner on the shoulder. "Hey Sasquatch, come buy me a cookie."

"But I'm in the middle of taking over a tower, I can't just—"

Jackie smacks him on the arm, and he gets the message.

The two of them leave the table, taking their time to meander over to the counter.

"How was your shift?" I ask Davy, hoping to break the awkward tension.

"It was all right," he says, brushing through curls with his fingers.

"At least you get free coffee," I offer. "That would be worth it to me."

"To tell you the truth, I don't even like coffee," Davy admits, looking down at his paper cup. "But I'd cut a bitch if they touch my hot tea."

"Tea?" I grin, leaning my elbows on the table. "I know a place that's got the best tea around."

"Really?" Davy perks up, his baby blues sparkling. "You don't say."

"Oh, yeah," I tell him, "I'll have to take you there some time. They have more choices than you can even imagine."

"Sounds dreamy," he muses.

"Oh my God." Jackie's back, munching on the end of a giant cookie. "These are so good, Davy. Do you guys make them?"

He laughs. "No. They come in a box and I microwave them."

"Eh, still delicious."

"And expensive." Tanner retakes his place, typing resuming.

"Oh, shut up, Tan. There's no price on my love."

"If there was, I might sell it."

"What?"

Davy laughs as Jackie launches into another tirade

against Tanner. My phone lights up and I swipe it open, pulling up the picture of Chris. I zoom in, seeing the smile stretching over his teeth.

He looks happy.

I lock the screen, catching my reflection in the glass. We both do.

MORE FROM ALEXANDER C. EBERHART

WWW.ALEXANDERCEBERHART.COM/LOCKANDWEST

Dear Reader,

Thank you so much for reading *There Goes Sunday School*! I hope you laughed, cried, swore off carbs after eating an entire sleeve of Oreos, promised to vote in your next eligible election, and at last learned to love. If you failed to do any or all those things, I hope at least you enjoyed the book.

If you'd like to keep up with my latest projects and shenanigans, pop on over and sign up for my newsletter at my official website: **www.alexanderceberhart.com**. You'll get exclusive updates on my Works In Progress, friendly reminders when a new book drops, the occasional cat video, and absolutely no spam (unless you're into that kind of thing, no judgement.)

Want to help me personify the illusion I have friends? Follow me on social media! You can find all the links to my various and redundant SM Accounts on my aforementioned website.

Lastly, if you enjoyed reading this book (or using it as a doorstop, coaster, flyswatter, etc), please consider leaving a review or suggesting it to your local library!

Jokes aside, thank you for taking the time to humor me. You are the reason why I get to do this crazy thing I love. I hope you'll continue to enjoy my work for years to come.

All the best,

-Alex

ACKNOWLEDGEMENTS

THERE GOES SUNDAY SCHOOL (henceforth referred to as TGSS) has been such a delight to bring to life. From its first moments of infancy to the final round of edits, this book has taken me from heartbreak to triumphant joy. So many people touched this story, helping me breathe life into it.

My first thanks go out to my parents, whom have been pillars of support for me and have always pushed me to strive for excellence. My dad even took on the impossible task of trying to edit and piece together my writing back in high school—a herculean task for sure—so extra kudos to him. Don't worry, Dad, I've improved by leaps and bounds and you don't have to weep over sentence fragments any longer.

My next thanks goes to my amazing best friend and favorite person in the world, Amy Bailey. She's been so incredibly supportive of this project from the first time I messaged her with the idea more than two years ago. Since then, she's suffered through so many endless questions and beta reads that I almost put her name on the cover right next to mine!

I must also thank all of the literary agents that offered their time and advice for my manuscript, especially Patricia Nelson from Marsal Lyon Literary Agency. Patricia, your kindness and support is the reason this story exists.

A humungous THANK YOU to my fantastically supportive team at 7 Sisters Publishing. There's Molly Phipps who worked tirelessly to ensure TGSS looks its best and the incomparable Amber Garcia who spearheaded the marketing campaign. Also, Cassandra McGilvray, whom I keep making cry (sorry about that…). I couldn't have done this without all of you, and you have my eternal gratitude.

Speaking of my publisher, I have to take a moment to personally thank 7 Sister's Martina McAtee, without whom TGSS would not have been possible. Martina has championed this story since the moment she finished the last page. She's offered sage advice, answered every dumb question I've thrown at her, and been the driving force behind getting this book into the hands of people that really needed it. You're amazing, Martina.

There are so many other amazing people in my life who I want to acknowledge—Zach, Josh, Anna, Chloe, Preston, Sara, Cecil, Melissa, Elise, Brandon—the list could go on forever. You are the friends who make the difficult days bearable and the good days so sweet.

And last, but certainly not least, I want to thank you, Reader. I can only hope this story touches your life like it's touched mine. It's been an honor and privilege to meet so many incredible readers. I can't wait to share more.

With love,

-Alex

ABOUT THE AUTHOR

ALEXANDER grew up in the Metro Atlanta Area, moving from suburb to suburb, just on the outskirts of the city. He's always had a passion for writing, even from a young age. He still lives on the cusp of Atlanta, inching his way ever closer to finally becoming the City Dweller he's always wanted to be.

In the meantime, he spends his days writing stories with queer characters and drinking an unfathomable amount of coffee. When he isn't crafting quality queer fiction, you can find Alexander most likely curled up alongside his boyfriend, watching a movie or some other equally lazy task.

Find him online at:
WWW.ALEXANDERCEBERHART.COM

Made in the USA
Monee, IL
06 January 2020